MOUNTAIN MANHUNT

The Utes saw Nate the moment he broke from cover. Shouts, then arrows flew all around him. He ran a zigzag course to make it harder for the Utes to hit him. A glance showed all five Utes had darted from concealment and were in hot pursuit.

A speeding shaft caught Nate high on the right shoulder and spun him completely around. Somehow he retained his balance and his momentum carried him forward into the trees. He collided with a trunk, bounced off, and stood still, fighting off the shock that threatened to numb his mind and seal his doom.

Nate sprinted for all he was worth, racing deeper and deeper into the forest. The harder his legs pumped, the faster he bled, and he worried about weakening from the loss of blood. It was a risk he had to take. He dared not slow down until he lost the warriors. If he lost them . . . .

TENDERFOOT

"Where is it, Pa?" Zach whispered. He tried to keep his voice steady so his father wouldn't suspect how scared he felt.

"It could be anywhere. Keep your eyes peeled."

Nate's horse had raised his head to sniff the breeze. Nate could guess why. "Get set," he said softly. "If it's going to attack, it won't wait long."

Zach, struck dumb by terror, made no reply, and he saw his father glance at him. At the very same instant he saw something else: the panther, its claws extended, vaulting from concealment strai

D1516957

WILDERNESS

DOUBLE EDITION:

MOUNTAIN MANHUNT/ TENDERFOOT

David Thompson

LEISURE BOOKS NEW YORK CITY

A LEISURE BOOK®

August 1998

Published by

Dorchester Publishing Co., Inc.
276 Fifth Avenue
New York, NY 10001

ISBN 0-8439-4423-4

MOUNTAIN
MANHUNT

To Lisa and Vail Marie Kendall—
the apples of Scott's eye.

Chapter
One

Nathaniel King was warily descending a gradual slope when he heard a low, wavering moan from somewhere below him. All around him branches were being rustled and bent by strong northwesterly gusts, so he assumed the sound he heard was nothing more than the wind howling among the pines that covered the lower half of the mountain. When the sound was repeated, though, he reined up and cocked his head, listening intently. There had been an odd quality about the noise, and a free trapper abroad in hostile Indian territory could ill afford to ignore any strange sounds. When the moan was repeated for the third time, he became certain it was a human voice and not the wind.

Squaring his broad shoulders, Nate hefted his Hawken rifle and guided his Palouse in the direction the moan came from. The wind whipped the fringe on his buckskins and stirred his shoulder-length black hair and beard. If he read the signs right, a storm was brewing. By nightfall it would strike.

Since he was in the heart of Ute country and the Utes had long been after his hair, he checked his many weapons as he advanced. Wedged under his wide brown leather belt, one on either side of the large buckle, were two flintlocks. On his left hip hung a butcher knife, on his right a tomahawk. Crisscrossing his broad chest was a powder horn and an ammo pouch. He was ready for trouble should it come, but he preferred to avoid fighting the Utes if he could.

Near the bottom he spied a clearing, and at its center the smoldering remains of a campfire. Halting, he surveyed the valley beyond, then focused once more on the clearing. There was no sign of anyone. If the Utes had been there, they must be gone. But who, then, had moaned?

Yet another pitiable wail drew his attention to a tall fir bordering the east side of the clearing. For a few seconds he saw nothing except deep shadows. Then, with a start, he realized there was a naked man hanging upside down from a rope. This man, who was facing the other way, dangled a good 15 feet above the ground.

Nate looked around again for others but saw no one. Half-convinced the man was alone, he touched his thumb to the hammer of his rifle and slowly advanced until he reached the edge of the clearing. Fresh tracks told him part of the story. There had been Indians here, seven or eight of them, and not long ago. After stringing up their victim they had ridden off to the southwest.

Turning to the right, Nate rode around the clearing until he could see the man's face. Then he stopped. It was a white man, 40 or so, lean of build but muscular, his eyes closed, his arms dangling limply, blood dripping from a nasty gash on his forehead. Otherwise he appeared unhurt. "Hello," Nate ventured softly.

The man's eyes snapped open and he looked right and left until he spotted Nate. He blinked, licked his thin lips, and said, "You ain't no damn Ute."

"Luckily for you. I'm surprised they left you alive. Usually they're not so charitable." Nate moved closer while constantly scouring the vegetation, not relaxing his guard for an instant.

"They wanted this coon to hang here for a spell while they went off to tend to some business. They're fixin' to come back and finish the job shortly."

"They told you this?"

"I overhead 'em jawin'. Couldn't make out every word but I know a little of their tongue." The man gingerly touched his brow. "After one of the bastards walloped me I played possum. I was hopin' they'd get careless and give me a chance to escape, but they stripped me down and strung me up here with my own rope." He sadly shook his head. "Hell of a note."

"I'll climb that tree and cut you down."

"No need, friend. Just toss me your pigsticker and I'll take care of it."

Nate rode directly under the limb from which the man hung, then introduced himself as he drew his knife.

"I'm Solomon Cain," the man revealed, and added with a lopsided grin. "My folks were real Biblical when it came to namin' their young'uns."

"Here," Nate said, tossing his knife, hilt first, straight up. With a jab of his heels he moved the Palouse to one side in case Cain should miss and the knife should fall back down, but Cain deftly caught it by the dull side of the blade.

"I admire a man who knows how to keep his knives sharp," Cain commented after lightly pressing his thumb to the keen edge. "Scalped many Injuns with this?"

"A few," Nate admitted, displeased by the question. Scalping was not a practice he believed in or practiced

7

regularly, even if he was an adopted Shoshone.

"I never have," Cain said, and began to slowly ease his torso upward. "Too savage for my tastes."

Nate's estimation of the man rose a notch. He kept one eye on Cain and the other on the valley on the chance the Utes might return ahead of schedule.

Cain gritted his teeth and raised his hands level with his knees. His face turned beet red, his stomach muscles quivered violently, and suddenly, with a gasp, he sank back down again. "Damned noggin'," he muttered. "Poundin' worse than a cannon."

"Sure you don't need my help?"

"No, thanks. I got myself into this fix, I'll get myself out," Cain replied. Again clamping his teeth together, he tilted his head to gaze at his bound ankles, then surged upward with all the strength he could muster. This time his left hand touched his left ankle before the tremendous strain and the irresistible pull of gravity caused him to fall back. "Damn. Damn. Damn," he mumbled. "If I ever get my hands on Flying Hawk, I'm goin' to skin him alive."

"You *know* the Ute who did this to you?"

"Sort of."

"How do you 'sort of' know someone?"

"He's sort of my brother-in-law since I sort of stole his sister for my wife," Cain said. "Ever since then he's had it in for me."

"I can't imagine why," Nate said dryly, amazed by the disclosure. So far as he knew, no other white man had ever taken a Ute woman for his wife simply because the Utes either drove off or killed any whites they found in their territory. While not as bloodthirsty as the widely feared Blackfeet, the Utes were a proud, independent tribe who fiercely prevented any attempts by outsiders to penetrate their domain, and they had been doing this for more years than anyone could remember. During

8

the last century, when the Spanish were spreading their dominion over the southwest and often venturing into the rugged Rockies, the Utes had repeatedly raided Spanish settlements, driving off large numbers of horses in the process. There were some old-timers who claimed the Utes had been among the very first Indians to own the animals that wound up totally changing the Indian way of life, at least for those tribes dependent on the buffalo for their existence.

Cain had ignored the sarcasm. Tensing his body, he abruptly surged upward and succeeded in grabbing hold of his left ankle. Then, holding fast, he sawed at the knots, parting strand after strand.

"You'd better . . ." Nate began, about to warn Cain to grab onto the length of rope secured to the tree limb, but before he could complete his sentence the loops around Cain's ankles parted and the man plummeted earthward.

Cain tried to flip in midair so he would land on his feet, but he was only halfway around when he struck, hitting hard on his buttocks and rolling end over end until he slammed into the base of a tree.

Quickly sliding off his gelding, Nate ran over. "Solomon? How badly are you hurt?"

"I'm fine," Cain said, grunting as he uncoiled and stood. There was a dark circle on his left shoulder and pine needles were caked to his skin. "Just bruised, is all." He leaned against the tree and frowned. "It hasn't been a good day."

"So I gather," Nate responded, gauging the other's size. "I have a spare pair of leggins you're welcome to use if you want. They'll be a little big on you but we can tie them up with some rope." He spotted his knife on the ground and retrieved it.

"I don't want to be a bother."

"You'd rather go around naked?"

"I reckon I wouldn't," Cain conceded. He stared out over the verdant valley. "And you'd best hurry. I know my brain's been addled by the fall, but I swear that's a dust cloud I see yonder."

A glance confirmed there was a party of riders descending a barren hill to the southwest. They were better than half a mile off, yet there was no mistaking the way some of them were energetically using quirts on their mounts and the fact that a few of the riders weren't wearing shirts.

"The Utes," Nate said, and dashed to his horse. It took but a moment to open the proper parfleche and remove his extra leggins, which he immediately carried to his new companion.

"The devils are comin' back sooner than I figured," Cain commented as he stuck first his right leg, then his left into the buckskin britches. "I knew they would! Nothin' is going the way it should lately." Swiftly he pulled the leggins all the way up and bunched the waistband in his right fist. "Flying Hawk probably couldn't wait to roast me alive."

"Can you ride?" Nate asked.

"If I can't I'll sprout wings."

"Climb on behind me," Nate directed as he stepped to the Palouse and swung up. "Pegasus can bear both of us for quite a spell. With luck, we'll lose those Utes."

"Pegasus?" Cain repeated. "You gave your horse a name?"

"Why shouldn't I?"

"No reason. But I make it a practice never to give a name to something I might have to eat one day."

Nate gave the Palouse a pat, then lowered his right arm. "I'd never eat this horse. It was a gift from the Nez Percé, and I've never known a finer animal anywhere."

"A man who is hungry enough will eat anything," Cain asserted, taking hold of Nate's hand. "I should know. I got myself lost once, ran out of food, couldn't find so much as a chipmunk to shoot, and I wound up eating some bugs I found under a log."

The mere thought of swallowing a mouthful of crunchy insects made Nate's stomach churn. He hauled Cain up behind him, then clucked Pegasus into a trot, bearing to the northeast, out across the valley. There were plenty of trees and thickets to afford cover, enabling him to cross to a stark mountain on the other side without being seen by the Utes. Angling upward, he climbed high enough to clearly view their back trail, and beheld a sight that made his blood race. A quarter of a mile off were the seven Utes, coming on fast. "One of them must be a good tracker," he commented.

"Flying Hawk is. His sister claims he can track an ant over solid rock."

"Let's hope she's mistaken," Nate said. "Hang on!"

They were galloping to beat the wind when they reached the bottom and cut sharply to the right. Nate wisely hugged the mountain until a curve hid most of the valley from sight. Then he veered to the right to scale a ridge. In a stand of aspens at the top he drew rein and twisted in the saddle. "Sit tight while I'll discourage them."

Cain glanced at the Hawken. "I'd rather keep ridin' if it's all the same to you."

"If I kill one or two the rest might give up."

"You said your horse can outrun them."

"For a while. But why run Pegasus into the ground when a few shots might end this right here and now?" Nate said.

"You might hit Flying Hawk."

"So?"

"So his sister would never forgive me."

Annoyed and baffled, Nate reluctantly resumed their flight. He didn't know what to make of Cain. One minute the man wanted to kill Flying Hawk. The next he wanted to spare the Ute from harm. Any sane man would want Flying Hawk dead, particularly if the Ute was after Cain's scalp as Cain contended. Then there was this business of the sister. Why was Cain so concerned about the feelings of a woman who must despise him terribly for spiriting her away from her people? None of it made any sense to him, and he speculated on whether or not Solomon Cain might be touched in the head.

It wasn't a common condition, but it wasn't all that rare either. Quite a few trappers had been overwhelmed by the devastating hardships of life in the Rockies and succumbed to the secret terrors that fester in men's souls. He remembered one trapper in particular who had sunk to the depths of depravity, going so far as to become a cannibal when during the middle of an especially severe winter the man and his Flathead wife ran out of food and they were unable to hunt because of snow over ten feet deep outside their isolated cabin. The trapper had done the only thing he could to survive, and forever after he had borne the mental scars. Crazy George, they'd all called him. Not until much later did the other members of the trapping fraternity learn why he had gone over the edge.

Such gruesome thoughts disturbed Nate greatly. He didn't like the notion of riding with someone who might see fit to yank out his own knife and slit his throat at any moment. Then he reminded himself that he had no proof that Cain was crazy. And there might well be a perfectly logical explanation for Cain's behavior. Still, he rode with his elbows tucked close to his body so that Cain couldn't grab for his knife or tomahawk without him being aware of it.

For half an hour he pushed Pegasus as hard as he dared, deliberately sticking to the roughest terrain and the hardest ground. When he saw rocky tracts, he crossed them. When he came to a narrow stream he entered it and rode downstream for a mile before riding out onto the bank. Always he stayed shy of the skyline. During his time with the Shoshones he had learned to ride as they did, and he now employed every trick they had taught him.

Presently he climbed a ridge for a bird's-eye panoramic view of the countryside. He was elated to discover there was no sign of the Utes. Yet, anyway. "Maybe we've lost them," he mentioned hopefully.

"I wouldn't count on it," Cain said. "They want Smoky Woman back in the worst way. But I'll never let 'em get her." He paused. "I love her, King, with all my heart."

Nate was tempted to ask if the Ute woman felt the same about Cain, but he decided not to. One of the first lessons a trapper learned was to never, ever meddle in the personal affairs of others. Then too, he knew how he would feel if anyone had the audacity to question his love for his own wife, Winona, a lovely Shoshone.

"We should keep goin'," Cain advised. "Once I know for sure we've given 'em the slip, I'll guide you to where Smoky Woman and I are livin'. It's not all that far. She'll be worried sick if I don't make it back soon."

"You mean to say you haven't moved as far from her people as you can?"

"We figure on stayin' right where we're at come hell or high water. Why?"

"Oh, no reason," Nate said, heading down the opposite side of the ridge. "I just thought it might be a little dangerous staying around here with the Utes after your hide and all. Why not move somewhere else, somewhere safer? Thirty miles to the north is about the limit of their territory. Go there and the Utes might never find you."

Cain appeared shocked by the suggestion. "I couldn't do that to Smoky Woman. She was born in this area. She loves it here."

"Is staying worth you life?"

"I'd sacrifice anything to make her happy," Cain said. "I don't suppose you can understand this, but my life without her would have no meanin'. So everything I do, I do for her."

Nate did understand the man's tender sentiments, but he labeled the sacrifice Cain was making as extremely foolish. If Smoky Woman cared a lick for Cain, she'd agree to go off somewhere, go off *anywhere,* just so the two of them were out of harm's way.

"Do you have a wife, King?"

"Yes," Nate answered, and told Cain about Winona.

"And I bet there isn't a blamed thing under the sun you wouldn't do for her," Cain said. "True love always works that way."

Pondering those words, Nate rode at a canter across a grassy meadow, pausing momentarily once to check the ridge they had just traversed. Then he plunged into dense woods, and winced when the tip of a branch nicked his cheek. More vigilant now, he weaved among the countless trunks until they came to a series of rolling hills. The Utes had still not appeared, and he was becoming increasingly confident he'd given them the slip.

A game trail frequently used by elk and black-tailed deer enabled him to pick up the pace. Once among the hills they stumbled on a spring, and Nate promptly reined up. He let Cain get down, then dismounted and held the reins while Pegasus greedily drank.

"What matters most in life to you, King?" Cain unexpectedly inquired.

"Call me Nate. And I'd have to say it's my family."

"Are you doin' a good job of providin' for them?"

"The best I can. We get by."

"Have you ever thought about doin' more than just gettin' by? Ever thought of being able to give them everything they could possibly want?"

Nate was puzzled by the line of questioning. Sinking to one knee, he splashed a handful of cool water on his cheeks and neck, then said, "There isn't a husband and father alive who doesn't have such dreams. But we have to be realistic. The fur companies aren't paying as much for prime beaver pelts as they once were. I'm happy if I can just put some money away for the future every now and then."

"You'd like to do better, though, wouldn't you?"

"Who wouldn't?" Nate retorted. "What are you getting at?"

"I was curious where you stood, is all."

Nothing else was said until after they had been riding again for over ten minutes. Cain tapped Nate on the shoulder and commented, "I owe you for pullin' my fat out of the fire back there. If you hadn't come along when you did, those devils would be torturin' me right about now."

"I did what any man would do."

"Maybe so. But the fact is you did it for me. Makes me beholden to you and I always make good on my debts." Cain placed his left hand on his hip and smugly surveyed the verdant hills. "One of these days I'm goin' to be the richest son of a gun who ever lived and I'll be able to pay you back with interest. Mark my words."

"Do you aim to do like Jed Smith did and bring in almost seven hundred pelts in a single year?"

Cain snorted. "When I talk about gettin' rich I'm not thinkin' of beaver. The only ones who make a lot of money off the trappin' trade are the owners of the fur companies. No, I have something else in mind."

Suddenly Nate detected movement in spruce trees off to the left perhaps 40 yards. Tensing, he slowed and held the Hawken in both hands while probing among the lower boughs. A vague shape materialized, a large black shape that moments later lumbered into the open. It was a bear, but not the most dreaded of all Rocky Mountain animals, not a savage grizzly. This was a full-grown black bear making its daily rounds. One look at them was enough to compel it to flee, and Nate listened to the crashing of its heavy bulk through the underbrush until the sounds became faint and faded.

Further on he saw a solitary brazen buck watching them from a nearby hilltop. Had the Utes not been on their trail he would have shot the buck for supper. As it was, his stomach growled and his mouth watered when he imagined biting into a thick slab of roast venison.

"Another mile or so should do 'er," Cain mentioned. "I guess I was wrong. You did give those Utes the shake."

"We were lucky," Nate said.

"No, you're good," Cain countered. "You're a handy man to have around in a pinch. I bet you've tangled with Injuns before."

"Once or twice."

"You even dress a lot like they do. If a man didn't know better, he might mistake *you* for an Injun."

"In a sense I am."

"How's that?"

Nate explained about being adopted by the Shoshones after his marriage to Winona, and how he was rearing his son to appreciate the customs and cultures of whites and Shoshones alike. He concluded with; "They both have a lot of good to them, but most folks, Indians and whites, are so busy criticizing what they don't understand in one another that they never see the good parts. They can't see the forest for the trees."

"Never thought of it quite that way before," Cain said. "You must exercise your brain muscles a lot."

"My wife would disagree."

Cain laughed and clapped Nate on the back. "Smoky Woman is the same way sometimes. I swear, women must be the most contrary critters in all of creation. I doubt I'd ever understand them if I lived to be a hundred."

"How's your head holding up?" Nate asked.

Before Cain could answer the rarefied mountain air was rent by the pounding rhythm of driving hoofs, and around the base of a hill up ahead swept the band of Utes, who broke into frenzied whoops of raging anticipation the instant they laid eyes on their quarry.

Chapter
Two

Uttering an oath, Nate wheeled Pegasus and fled. All his efforts to lose the warriors had been in vain, merely so much wasted time. There must, he reasoned, be a shortcut through the hills known only to the Utes, or else the band had ridden like mad and circled around to get out in front of them. Now the warriors were less than two hundred yards distant, and once the gap was narrowed to half that distance the Utes would use their bows.

"Damn their bones!" Cain cried.

Nate was doing some fast thinking. He couldn't hope to outrun the band, not with Pegasus so tired. His only recourse was to find a convenient spot to make a stand and to do it quickly. But where? There was plenty of forest to hide in, but he wanted a spot where the Utes would have a hard time getting at the two of them. Moments later he saw a bunch of boulders halfway up a hill on his right, and without hesitation he took the slope on the fly, shouting, "Hang on tight!"

Cain's arms encircled his waist.

The whoops reached a crescendo when the Utes realized his intent.

Pegasus was almost to the boulders when the first arrow streaked out of the blue and smacked into the earth within a yard of the gelding's neck. A second shaft missed by even less. A third struck a boulder to one side of them. Then they were behind another boulder the size of a Shoshoni lodge, one of five of similar size forming a crude natural fortification, and they could hear more arrows cracking against the impenetrable stone surfaces.

Nate was off the Palouse and at a crack between two of the boulders before Solomon Cain began to lift his leg to climb down. The seven Utes were charging up the slope, spreading out as they did, all with bows in their hands and firing as rapidly as they could nock shafts to their bowstrings. Clearly they were counting on overwhelming Nate and Cain by sheer force of numbers.

Nate had other ideas. He pressed the Hawken to his right shoulder, cocked the hammer, and took a quick bead on the foremost Ute. Barely had the sight settled on the warrior's brawny upper chest than Nate squeezed off the shot. The ball flew true and the Ute toppled in a whirl of arms and legs.

Darting to the left, to the end of the boulders, Nate drew a flintlock and had it cocked and leveled by the time he stopped to aim at a second Ute. A buzzing shaft smacked into the earth at his feet. Another nipped on his sleeve. Concentrating on the Ute, he fired, then jumped to safety as the warrior crashed to the ground.

The charge was broken. Breaking to the right and the left, the surviving warriors made for the nearest cover, some vaulting from their mounts before the animals stopped moving. In seconds there was no sign of a single Ute, they were so well hidden.

Nate wedged the spent pistol under his belt and began reloading the Hawken, first putting the butt between his feet, then pouring the proper amount of black powder into his palm, measuring by sight. Next he hastily fed the powder from his palm down the muzzle. Swiftly wrapping a ball in a patch, he pushed both into the muzzle with his thumb, then used the ramrod to shove them down on top of the powder. All the while the slope below was eerily quiet. As he replaced the ramrod in its housing he glanced at Pegasus, and was shocked to see Solomon Cain still on the horse, bent forward over the saddle. "Were you hit?" he asked.

"No. It's my head," Cain answered. "I can barely think straight. That wallop must have rattled me worse than I figured."

"Get off and lie down," Nate directed, stepping forward. He drew the pistol he hadn't fired yet. "Here. Hold onto this. They might try to rush us again."

"Thank you," Cain said, taking hold of the flintlock by the barrel instead of the butt end. "And I want to also thank you for the loan of your horse."

Nate, already starting to turn away, stopped and glanced up. "My horse?" he said, and too late saw an object sweeping at his head. Instinctively he tried to duck but the blow connected, slamming him backwards, stunning him. His vision swam and he fell to his knees. He heard Pegasus heading up the slope and bellowed, *"No!"* Solomon Cain paid no heed. It took only five or six seconds for Nate's vision to return to normal, yet by then the gelding was a dozen yards off and gaining ground with each stride.

From scattered points below came yells of surprise, and several arrows chased the Palouse but lost the race.

Without thinking Nate whipped the Hawken up and sighted on Cain's back midway between the shoulder blades. All he had to do was pull back the hammer, then squeeze off the shot. Yet he hesitated. Shooting a man in the back went against his grain. In his estimation it was the same as cold-blooded murder, and while he had killed many times to save his life or the lives of those dear to him, he took consolation in the fact he wasn't a wanton murderer.

His hesitation didn't last, however. Cain was stealing his horse, leaving him afoot, stranding him in the middle of nowhere with a band of bloodthirsty Utes about to close in. Now was not the time for scruples, he reflected, and his trigger finger tightened.

Cain cut into a stand of trees and disappeared.

Furious, Nate relaxed his finger and moved closer to the boulders. He was hoping to see Pegasus emerge from the evergreens, riderless, and trot back to him. The gelding had a passionate dislike for being ridden by anyone else. If a stranger tried to climb up, the Palouse would shy away, kick or buck. Not this time, though. Apparently, since Cain had already been on Pegasus, had in fact ridden double a considerable distance with Nate, Pegasus had grown accustomed to Cain's presence and didn't mind Cain being in the saddle.

A shrill whistle alerted Nate to a more urgent problem.

He crouched and peered through a crack. Some of the Utes were stealthily working their way toward the boulders. He glimpsed two of them, fleeting shadows impossible to shoot. Soon they would be on him.

Nate scowled in anger at the turn of events, girded his legs, and sprinted to the left, going from boulder to boulder until he was in the clear and racing madly for fir trees a score of yards off. The Utes saw him the moment he broke from cover. Shouts broke out, arrows flew all around him. He ran a zigzag course to make it harder for the Utes to hit him. A glance showed all five Utes had darted from concealment and were in hot pursuit. Two of the three abruptly realized they would fare better on horseback and ran for their horses, which had strayed toward the bottom of the slope. He had to reach the trees before they mounted and came after him or his life was forfeit.

His feet fairly flew over the ground. He tried not to think of what would happen should he trip. The Utes were howling, certain they would soon have him in their clutches. The tree line drew closer. And closer. Now he could see the individual leaves and the knots on the trunks. Just a few more feet and he would be there!

A speeding shaft caught him high on the right shoulder and spun him completely around. Somehow he retained his balance and his momentum carried him forward into the trees. He collided with a trunk, bounced off, and stood still, fighting off the shock that threatened to numb his mind and seal his doom.

Waves of agony washed over him, eclipsing the shock, restoring his senses. The bloody point of the slender arrow jutted several inches out from his throbbing shoulder and he could see red drops spattering onto his shirt. His hand still held the Hawken, but his fingers were beginning to feel numb so he reached across and took the rifle in his left hand. Then he ran.

The fleetest Utes were within 15 yards of the tree line.

He sprinted for all he was worth, racing deeper and deeper into the forest. The harder his legs pumped, the faster he bled, and he worried about weakening from the loss of blood. It was a risk he had to take. He dared not slow down until he lost the warriors. If he lost them.

At length his legs began to tire. A look back showed that he had temporarily outdistanced the Utes, who must have lost sight of him and would now be tracking him down. He slowed, then slanted to the right, heading up the slope where he might find a spot where he could try and hold the Utes off. If a fight came he wanted the advantage of the high ground.

Eventually the trees gave way to a rocky stretch of slope. There he exercised extreme care, jumping from stone to stone wherever possible to leave as few tracks as possible. He came to a place where erosion had worn out a shallow gully and into this he sank, lying on his left side with the Hawken in front of him.

Now he could catch his breath and take stock. The wound had stopped bleeding but hurt abominably. He knew the arrow must come out, and the sooner the better. Gripping the shaft below the point, he clamped his front teeth together, bunched his muscles, and exerted all the pressure he could. The shaft trembled, aggravating the torment. He could feel sweat covering his forehead. The veins on his neck were standing out. And suddenly the arrow broke with a loud snap.

Nate tossed the bloody tip from him in disgust, then twisted and tried to get a grip on the part of the shaft protruding from his back. His slick palm slipped twice, so he wiped it clean on his leggins and tried again. This time he succeeded in taking hold, but strain as he might he did no more than move the shaft a fraction of an inch. How was he ever going to get it out?

Letting go, he sank down, his brow in the dirt, and took deep breaths. He was in the fix of his life. Sooner or later the Utes would track him to the gully. Should he stay and fight or keep running?

Shouts broke out below. Propping himself on his elbow, he saw a pair of Utes on horseback near the cluster of boulders where he had made his stand. They were yelling and pointing at the crest of the hill. Shifting, he discovered the reason. Solomon Cain had reached the top and stopped to gaze down. The Utes took off after him.

So now there were three to contend with, Nate reflected. Sinking back, he accidentally bumped the arrow against the side of the gully and grimaced at the fresh pain that engulfed him. His right arm tingled and nausea gnawed at him.

He had to keep climbing. Grabbing the Hawken, he rose awkwardly and scanned the slope. Cain had vanished and the two Utes were halfway to the crest. Nothing moved in the forest, which meant little. The three remaining Utes might already know where he was hiding and be waiting for him to show himself.

Nate stepped out of the gully, hunched over, and continued climbing. He felt sluggish and had extreme difficulty concentrating. Fearful he might collapse and pass out, he hurried as best he was able. Constantly he checked the forest below, and also noted the progress of the two Utes going after Cain, both of whom soon went over the top. He saw them go with mixed feelings. On the one hand he wanted them to overtake Cain and give the bastard a dose of his own medicine, but on the other he was worried about them taking Pegasus.

He went 30 yards before his legs gave out. One second he was plodding steadily upward in grim determination. The next his face was in the dirt and he was inhaling dust. Angered by the betrayal of his own body, he rolled onto his back, then managed to sit up. Nearby was a waist-high boulder, the only cover available.

Using the stock of the Hawken as a crutch, Nate got himself behind the boulder. Sitting with his back to it, he closed his eyes and struggled with the tide of exhaustion on the verge of overwhelming him.

When would he learn? he asked himself. How long would it be before he realized he couldn't blindly trust every stranger he came across in his travels? Several times, now, his unthinking trust had jeopardized his life. He had to do as his best friend and mentor Shakespeare

McNair advised, "Be neighborly but keep your hand on your gun."

The sunlight warmed his face, making him drowsy. His eyelids fluttered as he valiantly strived to stay awake. But the ordeal proved too much for him. A black cloud seemed to consume his consciousness and he faded into oblivion.

He awoke to the sensation of small drops of moisture striking his face. Disoriented, he sat with his eyes closed, trying to recall where he was and what had happened. In a rush of memories he recalled everything just as thunder boomed in the distance.

Nate blinked and looked all around him. He was amazed to see twilight shrouded the Rocky Mountains because it meant he'd slept for hours. Miraculously, the Utes hadn't found him. More drops struck his cheeks and he stared up at the roiling clouds sweeping past overhead. The storm he had expected was almost upon him.

Lightning lanced the sky to the west, emphasizing how exposed he was to the elements. The last place he wanted to be was out in the open when the storm unleashed its full fury. Wounded and weak as he was, a thorough soaking might be all that was needed to render him helplessly ill.

Bracing his left hand on the boulder, he shoved to his feet. The Utes, evidently, were long gone since their horses were no longer to be seen. He headed for an isolated stand of trees to the east, and just reached them when the rain changed from tiny drops into great big ones and the heavens rumbled mightily.

Finding a patch of undergrowth, he dropped to his hands and knees and crawled into the brush, parting branches with his rifle so they wouldn't catch on the arrow. There, partially sheltered, he lay flat and listened to the howling wind.

He would be going nowhere for a while. Resting his chin on his left forearm, he contemplated the folly that had led him into the fix he was in. His never-ending search for beaver had taken him far from his usual haunts, where the beaver were harder to find with each passing trapping season. He needed somewhere new to trap, somewhere where the animals hadn't been depleted. And since few whites had ever ventured into Ute country, he'd figured he should be able to find an ideal locale there.

If he'd had any brains he would have listened to Winona and gone into the remote country to the northwest of their cabin, not to the southwest into Ute land. Now the harm was done, in more ways than one.

The rain was pouring down, the wind curling the saplings and shaking the branches of the taller trees. Some of the drops got through to him, but not enough to make him uncomfortable. A dank scent filled his nostrils. Drowsiness returned but he resisted an urge to sleep.

Since he was stuck there, he might as well make the best of it, he decided. Drawing his knees up under him, he lowered his forehead to the ground, then reached back with both hands and grasped the arrow. His right shoulder pulsed with exquisite anguish, which he shut from his mind. The arrow had to come out. To leave it in much longer invited infection.

Grunting, he pulled on the shaft with all of his strength. The arrow stubbornly budged a fraction of an inch but no more. Again he tried, working the shaft from side to side to loosen it, and felt fresh blood trickle down his chest. He broke out in perspiration from head to toe.

Repeatedly he pulled on the arrow, and gradually it began to slide out. After each strenuous exertion he had to rest for a few minutes. Then he had another go at it. His buckskin shirt around the entry and exit wounds was soaked with blood when, to his joy, the shaft slid free.

Exhausted again, he slumped down and stared at the bloody arrow. He hadn't thought to examine the barbed point earlier to see if it had been coated with poison, which could prove a fatal oversight. Sometimes Indians dipped the heads of their shafts in rattlesnake venom or dead animals. Contact with warm blood released the poison into the system and death was a slow, agonizing affair.

Nate put the arrow down and sat up. Beyond the thicket the storm was in full swing. Lightning lit the sky again and again. More rain was reaching him, yet so far he had avoided being drenched. He quickly collected a handful of small, dry twigs and dry weeds. Forming them into a compact pile with a depression in the middle, he leaned over the pile to further protect it from the rain, then opened his bullet pouch and took out his oval fire steel, his flint, and punk. Placing the punk in the depression, he set about producing sparks by striking the flint with slicing blows of the fire steel. Soon he had the punk burning. The tiny flames spread to the grass. By adding larger branches he got a small fire going in no time.

Now came the hard part. Replacing the steel and flint in his pouch, he removed his shirt. Then he pulled the Hawken's ramrod out and held the ramrod over the flames until the heated end practically glowed red hot. He was ready. Aligning the hot end with the exit wound in his shoulder, he bit down on a thick piece of branch, held his breath, and shoved the ramrod into the hole. Searing pain shot through him. He could smell his own burning flesh. His courage faltered and he almost released the ramrod, but didn't. The wound had to be cauterized. If the point of the arrow had been poisoned this was the only way of saving himself.

The ramrod went halfway and became stuck. Yanking it out, he once more applied the end to the fire. A job half-finished was no job at all. Shortly, the ramrod was hot enough and he stuck it into the hole. This time the task was easier and he poked the ramrod all the way through, unable to resist a shudder at the uncomfortable sensation.

Once he had the ramrod out, he sank down onto his left side, limp and weak, drained of all energy. He lay still, hearing the crackling fire and the intermittent crash of thunder. If he survived until morning, he would be out of danger. His next priority would be to regain his strength. Then what?

There could be only one answer. He was going after Solomon Cain. He would get Pegasus back. And he would insure that Cain never stole another horse from anyone else.

A cold breeze gave him gooseflesh and revived him. His fire had died. Sluggishly, he sat up, realizing the rain had stopped. The sky was silent. Craning his head, he peered through the branches and spotted twinkling stars.

He'd slept again! Yet he was far from being refreshed. Donning his shirt, he curled up into a ball, his hands between his legs for warmth, and permitted sleep to claim him once more.

When next Nate opened his eyes the sun ruled the heavens. He rose to his knees to gingerly inspect his shoulder. There was no trace of bleeding, no evidence of swelling or discoloration. Apparently the cauterization had been successful.

He checked the Hawken because he couldn't remember if he'd reloaded it or not, and found he had. The pistol, though, needed loading, so he did so before he turned and crawled from his hiding place. Squinting in the bright light, he slowly rose and adjusted his knife and his tomahawk so they hung properly.

Although he could hardly wait to pursue Cain, he knew he needed nourishment first. His jerked venison, pemmican, and the other food Winona had packed for him were all in a parfleche on Pegasus. To eat he had to find game.

Cocking the Hawken and touching the stock to his left shoulder, he hiked toward the bottom of the hill, deliberately making as much noise as he could as he went from brush patch to brush patch. When, minutes later, a rabbit bolted to the west, he was ready. Or thought he was. For he found that holding the Hawken in exactly the opposite way as he normally did and sighting along the barrel with his left eye instead of his right was an ungainly experience. He couldn't seem to get a bead on his breakfast, and was about to lower the rifle when the rabbit helped him out by stopping to stare at him. A second later a ball ripped through its brain.

Nate dashed over to the twitching animal, then scoured the hill and the surrounding countryside. If the Utes were still in the area they might have heard the shot. It would be wise to head elsewhere to cook his meal. Accordingly, he reloaded the rifle as fast as he could with his right arm being so stiff and sore, then picked up the rabbit and made for the crest.

At the top he halted in dismay on finding the barren earth a blank slate. The storm had washed out every last hoofprint. Now he had no way of tracking Cain, of reclaiming Pegasus.

Simmering with frustration, Nate hiked down into dense woodland. For over a mile he pressed on until he came to a clearing flanked by a gurgling stream. There he slaked his parched throat, then built a small fire directly under overspreading tree limbs so the branches would disperse what little smoke the fire gave off.

Gutting and skinning the rabbit was easily accomplished. He sharpened a stick, jabbed the pointed end through several pieces of raw meat, and held the make-shift spit over the low flames. The tantalizing aroma the rabbit soon gave off made his mouth water in antici-pation.

Presently the meat was cooked enough to suit him and he took a bite, savoring the delicious taste. Closing his eyes, he chewed slowly, knowing he might become sick if he bolted his food. While he had often enjoyed rabbit in the past, it had never ranked as one of his favorites. He much preferred deer and panther meat, especially the latter, which was the most flavorful meat in all creation according to those privileged to eat some. But this rabbit, he mused, had to be about the best meat he'd ever had.

Suddenly Nate froze. He thought he'd heard the soft pad of stealthy footfall. Gulping down his mouthful of meat, he opened his eyes and swiveled around to find a lone Ute stalking toward him with an arrow already trained on his back.

Chapter
Three

Nate King was certain he was going to die, certain he would momentarily feel the warrior's shaft tear through his torso. He'd left the Hawken propped against the nearby tree, perhaps five feet away, so near, yet not near enough to grab before the Ute let the arrow fly. But he still had a flintlock. He started to rise, his left hand falling to the pistol, when the Ute barked a single word. The warrior now had the arrow aimed at his face and was advancing swiftly. There was no way the man could miss at such close range, even if Nate tried to leap aside.

The Ute spoke a string of words and motioned with the bow, indicating Nate should lift his hand away from the pistol.

Nate hesitated. Evidently the Ute intended to take him alive, which might buy him time to turn the tables. One thing was for sure; he'd rather chance being able to catch the warrior unawares later than die right then and there.

Reluctantly he raised his hands to shoulder height.

The Ute halted eight feet off and again addressed him.

"I don't savvy," Nate said in English. Then, in Shoshone, "I do not understand."

By the warrior's expression it was obvious he had no idea what Nate had said. The Ute gestured with the bow and bobbed it up and down.

At first Nate failed to comprehend. Then the man made a jabbing motion at his waist, and the meaning became all too clear. He was being instructed to dispose of the flintlock and his other weapons. Using two fingers and exaggerated, slow movements so the Ute could see he was not about to do anything rash, Nate pulled the pistol out and gently placed it on the ground. He did likewise with his butcher knife and the tomahawk, then stepped back when the Ute indicated he should do so, and kept on stepping until the Ute signified he should stop.

The warrior appeared to relax slightly.

Nate held himself perfectly still and waited for the Ute to make the next move. He expected the warrior to either give a yell to attract the rest of the band or else force him to turn and kneel so the Ute could bind him, although what the man would use he had no idea since the only other article the warrior had was a knife. To his amazement, the man abruptly lowered the bow to the ground and straightened with his palms held outward to show he had peaceful intention.

"Where is he?" the Ute then inquired, using sign language. "If you can talk with your hands, tell me."

So surprised was Nate that he simply stood there until the warrior repeated the question. Collecting his wits, Nate finally signed in response, "Who do you mean?"

"The white devil whose tongue knows no truth," the Ute elaborated.

"Solomon Cain," Nate muttered in English. His hands flowed in flawless sign. "If I knew where he was I would cut out his tongue and feed it to coyotes."

Now it was the warrior's turn to seem dumbfounded. "He is not your friend?"

"No."

"But you cut him down and rode off with him."

"That was my mistake. If I had known he would try to split my skull and steal my horse I never would have helped the dog," Nate signed, and was mystified when the Ute's features hardened.

"He does it to his own people too. Truly he is a man without honor."

"Would you care to explain?"

The Ute's hands moved. "I am Flying Hawk," he began.

"You are the brother of the woman the dog took as his wife," Nate interrupted, and tensed when the Ute suddenly rushed toward him. He thought the man was about to attack, but the warrior halted a yard away.

"You saw her? You saw Smoky Woman?"

"No. He told me about her."

"What did he tell you?"

"That he stole her and made her his wife, and that you have been after him ever since."

Flying Hawk had the look of a man who wanted to kill something. Or someone. "False Tongue has told the truth for once. My sister was out with other women gathering berries when he took her against her will. All the men in our village went after them but he was too clever for us. That was when I took a vow to find him and save Smoky Woman no matter how long it takes. Some of my friends agreed to go with me. We have been hunting him for a long time."

"And you finally found him," Nate signed when the warrior stopped and bowed his head.

"Yes. We took him by surprise and hung him from a tree while we decided what to do with him. Some of my friends wanted to cut off his fingers and gouge out his eyes unless he told us where Smoky Woman was. I was afraid he would die before he told us and then we would never find her. He heard us talking. He claimed she was at his camp, over the next hill. So we rode off to see, leaving him there since we expected to quickly return."

Nate didn't need to hear the rest. That was when he had happened along and set Cain free, ruining any hope Flying Hawk had of rescuing his sister. "I am sorry," he signed. "Had I known I never would have helped him."

Flying Hawk studied Nate for a moment. "I do not blame you, white man. False Tongue is as clever as a fox."

"False Tongue? Is that the name your people have given him?"

"It is the name *I* gave him after he lied to me."

"How long has he had your sister?"

"Four moons."

Four months! Nate could well imagine the emotional misery the warrior must have gone through since the abduction. "How old is your sister?"

There was a haunted aspect to the Ute's dark eyes when he answered. "She has lived sixteen winters."

Nate's initial reaction was to think, "She's so young." Then he reminded himself that Indian maidens often married at that age or even younger. Sometimes the marriages were forced on them by parents eager to have their daughters marry prominent warriors or chiefs for the prestige involved. Frequently the young brides found themselves marrying men who already had one or two wives, which was a perfectly acceptable practice in many tribes since there was a chronic shortage of men. And now and then a maiden would be captured by enemy warriors in a raid, taken back to their village, and made a bride whether she liked the idea or not.

"I hoped you could tell me where she is," Flying Hawk signed forlornly. "That is why I spared you when I should have killed you for shooting two of my friends. I should still kill you, but you impress me as being an upright man. So you may go in peace. But should we ever meet again, know that I will slay you on the spot."

The man's acute desperation was almost contagious. Nate pondered for several seconds, then signed, "Where are your friends? What will you do now?"

"My friends took the bodies of those you killed back to our village. I refuse to go back until I find Smoky Woman." Flying Hawk paused. "While I was searching for sign of False Tongue I came on your tracks and followed them. Now I will continue my hunt."

"All by yourself?"

"My friends will be back in nine or ten sleeps."

"How would you like some help until they return?"

"You?"

"Me."

"Why would you help me, white man? My people and yours have long been enemies."

Nate glanced past the Ute, into the trees, where the warrior's horse was tied. If he was to convince Flying Hawk, he must be completely honest. "I have two reasons. First, False Tongue stole my horse and I want to get it back. On foot I would stand little chance. Riding double with you means we can cover much more ground faster."

"And your other reason?"

"I am a white man, true. But I am also an adopted Shoshone. My wife is Shoshone. I have great respect for the Indian ways." Nate paused to arrange in his head how he would phrase the next sequence of signs. "I do not like to see any man—white or Indian—do evil. What

False Tongue did to your sister was very wrong. He deserves to pay for his wickedness and she must be freed."

In the protracted silence that ensued Nate heard sparrows chirping gaily and the chattering of a squirrel. He couldn't tell by the Ute's impassive features whether his argument had prevailed.

"Your words show you to be a good man," Flying Hawk signed after a bit. "But I do not know if it would be wise for us to join forces."

"Do you happen to know a Ute named Two Owls?"

Flying Hawk blinked. "Yes. He is chief in another village and an important man among my people. Why?"

"He and I joined forces once some moons ago against the Blackfeet. I did not betray his trust. I would not betray yours."

"You are Grizzly Killer?"

"I am."

The warrior came a stride nearer and examined Nate closely. "Two Owls told us about you at a gathering of all our people. He said you are the only white he has ever known whose tongue always speaks the truth. He said you have the body of a white man but the spirit of an Indian."

Nate made no comment. He was recalling how Two Owls had helped him save Shakespeare McNair and another man from a war party of Blackfeet that had penetrated deep into Ute territory.

"Very well," Flying Hawk suddenly declared, thrusting out his arm and resting his hand on Nate's shoulder. Then he signed, "Until we find my sister and your horse we will be as brothers. And perhaps, when this is done, I will go back to my people and tell them the same thing Two Owls did, that not all whites have bad hearts."

Smiling in gratitude, Nate touched the Ute's arm. "You will not regret your decision. Between us we will catch False Tongue and make him pay." He nodded at the fire. "Perhaps you would like some food before we start? I would be happy to share my rabbit."

"Thank you. I accept," Flying Hawk replied. He walked off and picked up his bow and arrow, sliding the latter into the quiver on his back. The bow went over his left shoulder. As he came back he pointed at Nate's wounded shoulder. "I an glad my arrow did not kill you."

In the act of stepping to his weapons, Nate stopped. "*You* were the one who shot me?"

"Yes. I tried to get you through the heart but you ran like an antelope."

"The next time I will try to run slower," Nate joked. He slid the pistol under his belt, recovered the toma-hawk and knife, and squatted by the fire, across from the Ute.

"You took the arrow out all by yourself?" the warrior asked, staring at the wound.

"Yes."

Flying Hawk folded his arms on top of his knees. "You have much courage. It is a pity most white men are not like you."

Soon Nate had more chunks of meat roasting over the fire. He picked up the stick he had dropped when the Ute appeared and brushed bits of grass off the pieces of rabbit, then heated them again. Not a word was spoken during the meal. Nate was self-consciously aware that the warrior stared at him the whole time. He, in turn, made it a point to act as natural as he could. Eventually the Ute asked him an unexpected question.

"Will more of your people come to these mountains?"

"Many more, I am afraid. Once the whites who live east of the Great River learn how beautiful and won-derful this land is, they will flock here by the thou-sands."

Flying Hawk wiped his greasy fingers on his leggins. "I have been told this would happen but I hope you are wrong. My people, as well as the Cheyennes, the Kiowas, the Sioux, and many other tribes will not let your people drive us off. We will fight to keep our land."

"I know."

"On which side will you fight when that happens?"

"I have not given the matter much thought."

"You should."

The man had a point, Nate reflected as he doused the fire. What *would* he do if it came to pass? The mere notion of hordes of settlers spreading out over the plains and the mountains, staking claim to every available square foot of land, was enough to give him the jitters. Part of the appeal the wilderness made to men like him was the virtue of soothing solitude. The vast expanses of shimmering grasslands and towering peaks stirred a man's soul like no towns or cities ever could. Out here a man could live as he pleased, accountable to no one but himself and his Maker. There weren't countless laws to obey, countless rules to follow. Freedom—pure, unadulterated freedom—was there for the taking. All that would change once civilization arrived. A man would be at the mercy of politicians, and to Nate's way of thinking that was a fate worse than death.

With the Hawken tucked under his left arm, he followed the Ute to where the sturdy roan waited. He waited for Flying Hawk to reach down, then swung up behind the warrior.

They rode to the northwest, over hills, through valleys, and around mountains, always on the lookout for tracks. Toward noon they scaled a steep slope, crossed a low saddle, and came out on a splendid high country park lush with spring growth. There Flying Hawk reined up and twisted so Nate could see his hands.

"There is a spring here. We will stop and rest my horse, then go on."

At the bottom of a cliff on the north side of the park was a crystal-clear pool of ice-cold water. Nate dropped to the ground, walked to the water's edge, and sank onto all fours to drink. As he lowered his face he happened to glance to his left. His thirst was immediately forgotten. For clearly imbedded in the soft soil were large hoofprints not over a day old. Rising, he signed, "You are closer to your sister than you think. Look at these."

Flying Hawk's face lit up like the full moon. He ran his fingers lightly over the tracks, then stood and slowly walked in a half-circle, reading the sign. "Do you think these were made by your horse?"

"I would say so, yes. I know the tracks of my animal as well as I do my own." Pivoting, Nate gazed the entire length of the park. At the north end reared a seemingly impassable barrier of bleak, barren mountains. Either there was another way out of the park further on, or else Solomon Cain was hiding somewhere near those mountains.

The Ute came to the same conclusion. "We have him, Grizzly Killer. You have brought me luck. After searching for so long I find him this easily."

"Do not get your hopes too high. As you say, False Tongue is exceedingly clever. Who knows where this trail will lead?"

"We shall see."

Flying Hawk pulled the roan away from the spring and climbed up. He impatiently gestured for Nate to join him, and at a gallop they rode northward, the roan's hoofs drumming dully on the thick carpet of grass. Occasionally they saw clear tracks, but for the most part the prints were smudged or partials. Cain, after leaving the spring, had cut catty-corner across the park toward a foreboding mountain crowned by three separate pinnacles of rock that resembled the three prongs of a pitchfork.

They lost the trail at the base of the mountain where the grass gave way to loose rock and hard-packed earth.

The Ute stopped and peered upward. "He must be somewhere up there."

So it seemed, but Nate couldn't see why Cain would have picked such a godforsaken spot to hide out. True, plenty of water and grass was readily available in the park. But the oddly sinister mountain, on which not so much as a single weed or blade of grass grew, was fit neither for man nor beast alike. He looked at Flying Hawk, expecting the warrior to begin climbing at any moment, and was startled when he saw the Ute give a barely perceptible shudder.

"I know this place," Flying Hawk signed. "My people call it the Mountain of Death. No one has ever gone up it and returned."

Nate straightened and smiled. So that was it! The wily Cain had picked a spot taboo to the Utes, using their primitive superstition to his advantage. "Are there eaves on this mountain?" he asked.

"Let us find out."

The lower portion of the facing slope proved easy for the roan. Above it the going was too steep, compelling them to dismount and walk. Small stones clattered out from under their feet. So did small puffs of dust. Their moccasins were caked by the time they came to the mouth of a ravine. In the earth at the entrance were fresh tracks.

"We have him!" Flying Hawk signed excitedly.

Nate hoped so. Once he had Pegasus back he would head for home, tell his wife what had transpired, then resume his search for choice areas to trap beaver far to the northwest. He'd learned his lesson the hard way. Venturing into Ute country was tempting Fate, a notoriously harsh mistress. From now on out, he decided, he would stay shy of Ute territory unless he had a damn good reason for doing otherwise.

In the confined space between the high ravine walls the clopping of the roan was unusually loud. Nate scanned the rims above, bothered at being a potential target should Cain be perched up there with a rifle. He grinned when he spotted the end of the defile and hefted the Hawken.

Flying Hawk had pulled a shaft from his quiver and notched it on the bow string.

A strong breeze struck them, growing in intensity the closer they drew to whatever lay beyond the ravine. Nate tugged his hat down and narrowed his eyes to reduce the bright glare off the ravine walls. Then they were there, and he stopped in midstride on seeing the landscape that unfolded before their astounded eyes.

An arid wasteland of gorges, plateaus, and bluffs formed a virtual maze of inhospitable terrain stretching for miles in all directions. Scattered bushes and scrub trees comprised the only plant life. A solitary golden eagle soared on high on the air currents. Otherwise, nothing moved. The breeze, a hot blast of wind, hit them full force.

"There!" Flying Hawk signed with the bow in his left hand, and pointed using his right.

Nate screened his eyes from the sun, using his palm, and saw the reason the warrior was so excited. Far out in the wasteland rose a thin tendril of white smoke, so faint as to be almost indistinguishable.

"False Tongue!" the Ute said. "Now I know why I could not find him. He is even more clever than I believed." He replaced the arrow, slung the bow, and swiftly mounted. "Hurry, Grizzly Killer. My sister is close. I can feel she is."

Nate mounted also, and the roan broke into a gallop, raising a cloud of dust in their wake. Nate tapped Flying Hawk on the shoulder and bobbed his head at the dust.

Scowling in displeasure, Flying Hawk slowed.

Keeping the smoke in sight proved difficult. Unless the angle of the sun was just right they would lose track of it. Often they had to skirt bluffs, and then had to look hard to find the smoke again when they were in the open. Several times they passed through gorges and were denied sight of the wispy column for minutes on end.

Nate feared the fire would be put out before they got close enough to pinpoint its location. Mile after mile fell behind them. The roan began to tire, its head drooping. Nate himself felt as if he was roasting alive. Often he mopped his brow and ran a hand over his neck. He was sorry now that they hadn't taken the time to drink their full back at the spring in the park.

After two hours of grueling travel Nate was about to advise Flying Hawk to stop and rest when the wind brought to his sensitive nose the acrid aroma of burning wood. The Ute smelled it too, because he stiffened. They rode for another hundred yards, to a point where the dry wash they had been following made a sharp turn to the right around a rise. The smoke appeared to be wafting skyward on the other side.

Flying Hawk drew rein and slid down. He left the roan standing there and beckoned for Nate to make haste.

And Nate did, although he didn't like rushing in when common sense dictated they should go slowly and warily. The element of surprise was essential if they were to take Cain without a fight. That is, if the Ute wanted to avoid bloodshed, which he doubted. He caught up with the warrior as they neared the turn, and they both dropped onto their hands and knees and crawled to where they could see past the rise.

The fire was 50 yards off, outside of the dark mouth to a large cave situated in a rock wall over a hundred feet high. Pegasus and two other horses were tethered outside the cave, in the shade, close to a small pool.

Nate saw a shadowy figure move in the cave mouth, and seconds later a beautiful Indian woman in a beaded buckskin dress, her raven hair flowing down to her hips, emerged carrying a tin pot and walked to the fire.

Flying Hawk could barely contain himself. "That is my sister!" he signed, beaming broadly. "But where is False Tongue?"

Shrugging, Nate scoured the area but saw no trace of the man they sought. Suddenly a shadow fell across them, and glancing up he felt his breath catch in his throat.

Looming tall on the brim of the wash, a cocked flintlock held steady in each tanned hand, wearing buckskins and moccasins and smirking in triumph, was Solomon Cain.

Chapter
Four

"Payin' a visit, are you?" Solomon Cain asked merrily.

Flying Hawk spun and went to lift his bow, a futile act since all Cain had to do was twitch a forefinger and the Ute would receive a ball in the chest or head. Nate, out of the corner of his eye, saw the warrior spin, and flicked out his hand to stop the bow from rising. Flying Hawk glared at him and tried to tear the bow loose, then froze when Cain spoke sternly in the Ute tongue. Hissing like an enraged viper, the Ute removed his fingers from the bow and held his hands aloft.

"Sensible cuss, ain't he?" Cain addressed Nate in English. "Now why don't you do the same with your guns and such or I'll be obliged to put some lead into your system."

With the twin barrels of those pistols fixed on his person, there was nothing else Nate could do but ease his weapons to the ground.

"Now stand and step out of temptation's reach," Cain ordered, and issued a similar statement in the Ute language.

Side by side, Nate and Flying Hawk backed off.

"I must admit I am surprised," Cain said, giving each of them a firm scrutiny. "I never expected you two dunderheads to ever find me." He jumped from the top of the wash and landed lightly on the balls of his feet, his pistols swiveling to cover them as he dropped.

"You stole my horse, you son of a bitch," Nate growled, more so because he was mad at himself for blundering into Cain's grasp than anything else.

"And a nice horse it is," Cain responded blithely. "Didn't give me a lick of trouble until I came through the ravine. Then it acted up considerably. I guess it wanted to go back to you, but I got it here anyway."

"Too bad Pegasus didn't throw you off and bust your head wide open."

"My, you are in a feisty mood today," Cain quipped, then transferred his attention to Flying Hawk and spoke in Ute. The warrior, flushing crimson, clenched his fists.

"For a fierce Ute he sure has a soft hide," Cain said, and laughed. "All I did was tell him how pretty I think his sister is."

Nate debated whether to try and reach Cain before the man could fire and had to face the truth. He'd be shot down before he took three steps. A distraction was called for. But what? "You may have us," he mentioned when an idea occurred to him, "but the others will get you. There are ten more Utes about a mile behind us. You won't stand a prayer."

"Is that the best you can do?" Cain retorted. "I happened to be up on the rise when I spotted the two of you. And do you know what? I watched and watched and never saw anyone else. How naughty of you to lie like that, King."

Thwarted, Nate struggled to remain calm, to not let his anger at being captured gain the upper hand. Only by doing so would he be ready to make his move if an opportunity presented itself. For the time being there was no denying they were completely at Cain's mercy, which meant they might not have long to live. For lack of anything better to do, he elected to try a risky bluff. Putting a grin on his face, he said, "Do you really think the Utes would give themselves away? I thought you knew more about Indians than that."

A hint of uncertainty crept into Cain's eyes.

"Go ahead and shoot," Nate blustered. "They'll hear the shot and come on the run."

"You're lyin' through your teeth."

"Am I? Are you absolutely sure?"

No, Cain wasn't, and his expression conveyed as much. Turning slightly, he shot a glance over his shoulder, then regarded Nate in annoyance. "I ain't goin' to buy your story, King. Not even a little bit." He wagged his pistols. "But I'm not one to play the odds when the stakes are so high. We'll wait and see if more Utes show. If they don't, you and I are goin' to do some chawin' about what happens to them who lie to me."

"Talk about the pot calling the kettle black," Nate taunted.

Solomon Cain motioned with the flintlocks. "I want the two of you to start walkin' to my cave. Walk slow and keep your arms where I can see 'em. If you don't, I can guarantee you'll be sorry." He looked at Flying Hawk and repeated his instructions in the Ute's tongue.

If ever two men were the picture of depression, it had to be Nate and the warrior as they hiked along the wash until it ended, and then climbed out and made for Cain's hideaway. Nate wished he could plant a foot on his own backside for being so careless. He'd acted like a greenhorn and paid the price for his folly. But all was not lost. He'd bought them some time by instilling doubt in Cain about the possible presence of more Utes. Until Cain became convinced the two of them were indeed alone, they were safe unless they gave him cause to shoot.

They had hardly cleared the top of the wash when Smoky Woman spotted them and squealed in delight. Like a doe she bounded toward them and hurled herself into her brother's arms.

Nate halted when Flying Hawk did. He watched the two warmly embrace and heard them exchange a few urgent words. Smoky Woman then glanced at Cain and spoke some more. Cain replied curtly. At that moment Nate would have given anything to be fluent in the Ute tongue. He knew a few words from the time he hooked up with Two Owls, but nowhere near enough to conduct a conversation. For lack of anything else to do, he studied the woman indirectly responsible for their dilemma.

The beauty of youth animated her finely chiseled features. Her eyes were a soft brown, her complexion as smooth as a baby's with nary a wrinkle marring her skin. Her full lips were a tantalizing cherry color, while her full bosom swelled with each breath she took. She was a living work of art, and Nate had no difficulty understanding what Cain saw in her and why Cain had abducted her. If nothing else, the bastard had excellent taste in women. She appeared to be quite upset at her brother being held at gunpoint, but all her arguments were apparently wasted on Cain.

Nate stared at the cave as they neared it. The heady odor of simmering venison filled the air, and he saw that Smoky Woman had stew going. Pegasus, spying Nate, tried to come over, only to be stopped short by the rope. Just inside the cave, piled against the wall, were saddles, parfleches, blankets, and other provisions. "Looks like you plan to be here a spell," he commented.

"Another month or two should do me," Cain responded.

"What then?"

"I go back to St. Louis and buy the biggest mansion there is. The rest of my born days are goin' to be lived in the lap of luxury. Fine food. Fancy clothes. Expensive carriages. You name it, I'll own it."

"It costs a lot of money to do all that," Nate observed.

"I'll have something better than money."

"Such as?"

Cain cackled, or started to, his laugh abruptly changing to a strangled grunt. He stopped for a second, astonishment plain on his face, then he cackled again, only louder. "Why didn't I think of this before?" he declared.

"Think of what?" Nate asked as he came to the fire and turned.

"You'll see soon enough. You and this poor excuse for an Injun," Cain said.

The undisguised contempt in the man's tone troubled Nate, and he looked at Smoky Woman. Arm in arm with her brother, she was speaking so softly the words were nearly inaudible.

"I want both of you to get on your knees and put your hands behind your backs," Cain commanded, then repeated, yet again, the same instruction in the Ute language.

Sighing in reservation, Nate obeyed, but as he swung his hands around he dragged his left hand along the ground and scooped up a small handful of loose dirt. Then he set himself and waited. Once Cain stepped close enough, he was going to hurl the dirt in the polecat's face and tackle him, come what may.

Flying Hawk refused to kneel. Folding his arms, he stood immobile, his chin jutting proudly, and glared at

Cain as if daring Cain to do something.

Cain did. Addressing Smoky Woman in Ute, he took a couple of paces toward her, then abruptly shifted, took a single long bound, and slammed his right flintlock against Flying Hawk's temple. The warrior crumpled. In a burst of sheer savagery, Cain struck the Ute two more times, and would have gone on doing so had not Smoky Woman leaped to her brother's defense and seized hold of Cain's arm.

Nate began to rise, thinking he could pounce before Cain knew what hit him, but the wily Cain spun and extended his free arm, pointing the other pistol straight at Nate's face. Although Nate was boiling like a teapot about to bubble over, he had no choice but to sink back down.

Cain suddenly shook Smoky Woman off and raised his hand as if to cuff her. He was fury incarnate, yet at the last instant he caught himself and slowly lowered his arm to his side. Then he said something to her, something that caused her to bow her head in apparent guilt. Pivoting, she entered the cave, going to the wall where their supplies were piled.

What hold, Nate wondered, did Solomon Cain have over the young woman? Why did she meekly submit when the life of her own brother was in jeopardy? Intuition told him there was more going on here than met the eye.

When Smoky Woman returned she was carrying a coiled rope and a hunting knife. Walking up to Nate, she unwound a length of rope and cut it off. Then she moved behind him.

This was not what Nate had expected. He'd counted on Cain doing the tying. Throwing the dirt in Smoky Woman's face would accomplish nothing, and Cain wasn't quite close enough. Maybe he could remedy that. "Do you always let a woman do all your work for you?" he asked sarcastically.

Cain made a clucking noise. "You must figure I'm a greenhorn, King. I ain't about to get near enough for you to jump me, so forget any hare-brained notions you have. Just go along with what I want and you might live to see that wife and kid you were tellin' me about."

Nate felt his wrists being encircled by loops of rope. "This is so senseless," he remarked. "All I want is my horse, and all Flying Hawk wants is his sister. If you leave her here and ride off, right now, we'll let you go in peace."

"You never stop tryin', do you?" Cain said. "As for your offer, I know better. Flying Hawk ain't the forgivin' kind. Neither, I suspect, are you when it comes to havin' your horse stolen. If I was to ride off, one or both of you would be on my trail before the dust settled. No, thanks." Grinning, he wagged both flintlocks. "We'll keep things the way they are."

Nate shrugged. "I gave you a chance. It's up to you whether you live or die." He gazed at the rise. "I just hope those Utes show up soon."

The reminder had the desired effect. Cain stiffened and half turned to survey the area.

Smoky Woman finished tying Nate's wrists, then bound his ankles. Rising, she took two steps toward her brother. Cain snapped at her and jabbed a flintlock at Nate.

This time it was easy to guess what had been said. Nate saw Smoky Woman flush crimson, then she moved back around him and knelt. He could feel her working at the rope, loosening the knots, but only so she could bind him much tighter than before, so tight the rope bit into his skin. Cain, Nate deduced, had been afraid she wouldn't do a proper job. Perhaps Cain reasoned she might deliberately leave enough slack for them to eventually slip free. Now they wouldn't be able to. The man, evidently, always thought of everything.

Dejected, Nate watched the woman tie her brother. Flying Hawk groaned when she gently touched him. A tear formed in the corner of her eye, yet she made no move to brush it away until the deed was done. Rising, she took the knife and the remainder of the rope into the cave.

"I'm goin' to leave you in her capable hands while I go have a look-see for these Utes you keep talkin' about," Cain said. "But don't do anything stupid 'cause I'm pickin' up your weapons on the way. That includes your fine Hawken. If you move from that spot, I'll shoot you with your own gun. And believe me when I say I'm a tolerable shot with a rifle."

Nate believed him. Frontiersmen, by virtue of necessity, had to become adept. Those who couldn't shoot straight seldom survived run-ins with hostiles and were hard-pressed to fill their bellies. So Cain's threat was no idle boast, especially since a Hawken was one of the most accurate guns ever made. Some trappers liked to joke that a Hawken was so good it aimed itself.

Cain wedged his pistols under his belt and commented, "Don't look so glum, King. You're still alive, which ought to count for something."

Watching the man hasten off, Nate speculated on Cain's purpose in holding them as prisoners. There was no rhyme or reason to it that he could see. Cain would have to keep his eyes on them the whole time, knowing full well if one of them broke loose he was a dead man. Not that Nate was complaining. So long as he lived he would continually try to escape.

Shortly Flying Hawk revived with a start and sat up. He looked around, spotted Cain, then rotated on his backside and spoke harshly to his sister, going on at some length. Smoky Woman listened with her chin lowered. Twice she gave one-word replies. When, after a while, Flying Hawk gestured with his bound arms for her to cut him loose, she mumbled a few words, rose and hurried inside, leaving her brother to gape in disbelief.

Nate sadly shook his head. How strange Fate could be! he reflected. What cruel jokes it played! Here he was, held prisoner by a white man he had befriended, in the company of an Indian who hated all whites and had put an arrow into him, while the Indian's sister, who they had come to rescue and who could free them then and there if she wanted, refused to help. He would have laughed if he wasn't feeling so miserable.

The Ute, sliding his legs under him, began to rise.

Nate looked and realized Cain had disappeared into the wash. Flying Hawk probably thought it was safe for him to stand. But Cain might reappear at any instant, and if the warrior was on his feet Cain would undoubtedly shoot him. Nate shook his head and started to warn Flying Hawk about Cain's threat. The next second, though, Smoky Woman practically flew from the cave and pushed her brother down again.

Irate, Flying Hawk barked at her and she responded in kind. Again the warrior attempted to rise. Again she shoved him back.

So engrossed did Nate become in their bickering that he failed to see Cain emerge from the wash. When next he glanced in that direction he was surprised to find Cain a third of the way up the rise. "Hey!" Nate said to get the attention of the Utes. When he had it, he bobbed his head at Cain, certain once Flying Hawk saw Cain with a rifle he would know not to stand up.

The warrior appeared on the verge of throwing a fit. Instead, he verbally lashed his sister, bringing moisture to both of her eyes. Wheeling, she walked off, over to the horses, and stood with her back to her brother.

Nate knew Flying Hawk blamed Smoky Woman for foiling his escape, when in reality she had saved his life.

The last thing they needed was to antagonize her. But he was helpless to change the situation since he had no way of communicating with his hands tied.

So he sat and brooded. He saw Cain reach the top of the rise and hunker down at a vantage point that afforded a bird's-eye view of the cave and them. The man then had the brazen gall to smile and give a cheery wave.

It was hot there, under the blistering sun, and Nate sweated freely. He looked longingly at the pool and licked his lips. As the minutes dragged by it occurred to him that Cain might stay up there for a long time to be absolutely certain there were no other Utes around. He glanced at Smoky Woman and said, "Pardon me, but could you fetch me a some water to drink?"

She stood like a statue, unhearing, too upset over her clash with her brother to care about anything else.

Nate had to think a bit before he recollected the Ute word for hello. He now tried that, but she still didn't budge. Again he said it, louder this time, almost shouting.

At last Smoky Woman glanced around to regard him quizzically.

Smiling his friendliest smile, Nate indicated the pool and made a show of swallowing in great gulps. She understood right away. Going into the cave, she returned bearing a large tin cup which she filled and brought over. But not to Nate. First she stopped beside her brother and held the cup close to his mouth.

Flying Hawk deliberately turned his face away.

Her slender shoulders sagging, Smoky Woman stepped to Nate's side and touched the cool tin to his lips.

Nate drank gratefully, draining the entire cup. Some of the water spilled over the brim, across his chin, and down his neck, providing additional relief. When he was done, he beamed and absently said in English, "Thank you."

"You welcome," Smoky Woman replied softly.

Surprise made Nate gape. Then he realized she had been with Cain for four months. It was inevitable she would have picked up some of the language in that time. "You are very kind," he said quickly as she turned to go. "This all must be very hard on you."

"Yes," she said, staring morosely into the empty cup.

Nate didn't want her to leave. If he could get her talking, if he could befriend her, she might become an ally in his campaign to free himself. And too, he might be able to learn what Cain was up to, which she must know. So when she took a step, he blurted out, "Wait! Please!"

Smoky Woman paused, then faced him.

"I am sorry your brother is so mad at you. He doesn't know that you were saving his life. But I do. And I admire you for it. If I spoke enough of your tongue I'd tell him, but I know very little."

"I know little English," Smoky Woman said, pronouncing the last word "Ainlish."

"You do right fine," Nate complemented her. "My tongue isn't easy to learn." His racing mind hit on a way to solicit her sympathy. "My wife speaks it fluently, but then she's got more brains in her little finger than I do in my whole body."

"You have wife?" Smoky Woman asked as if deeply disturbed by the news.

"A wife and a fine young son," Nate disclosed. "I love them both with all my heart, and I surely do hope I get to see them again."

Her sadness intensified. "What your name?"

"Nate King. Or you can call me Grizzly Killer."

"Why you here?"

"I came to help your brother save you. Flying Hawk must love you as much as I do my wife because he has never stopped hunting for you. He's never given up hope. The whole time you've been with Cain, your brother and his friends have been scouring the countryside."

She pursed her lips and surreptitiously looked at the warrior. "We close. He good man."

Here was an opening Nate thought he could exploit. "And Solomon Cain? Is he a good man?"

Smoky Woman's face darkened ominously. "Not talk about him."

"I'm sorry. Don't be upset. I didn't know you cared for him. Flying Hawk led me to believe Cain took you against your will, and I just naturally figured you wouldn't like him much."

"Not talk about Cain!"

Nate was shocked at how upset she was. He'd inadvertently angered her, and the fragile bridge of friendship he was trying to build threatened to collapse around his ears. "Again, I'm truly sorry," he said quickly, frantically seeking another subject to talk about. The mouthwatering aroma from the stew gave him inspiration. "Please forgive me," he said, and grinned. "I need to stay in your good graces so you'll give me some of that stew of yours. It smells delicious."

She stared into the cup again.

"Your cooking reminds me of my wife's," Nate went on. "She can turn a pot of water and meat into the tastiest concoction this side of Heaven. Some women have the knack, I guess. Me, I'm happy if I cook a meal where half the food isn't burned."

His humor was wasted on her. Frowning, she lowered the cup and glanced at the cave.

"How far back does that go?" Nate inquired before she could leave.

"Far."

"It must be a bit dank and dreary in there," Nate mentioned. "Caves are fit for bats and vermin, not people. I bet it's nothing at all like living in a lodge, is it?"

"It all right. Keep us dry when rain, warm when night."

"Well, bears seem to put great store by caves, so I suppose living in one does have its advantages," Nate commented.

"People live here. Many winters ago."

"What's that?" Nate responded, unsure whether he comprehended. "Do you mean other people have lived in this same cave?"

"Yes. They paint walls. Paint buffalo. Paint other things."

"I'd like to see for myself," Nate said, genuinely interested. He'd heard rumors of trappers occasionally finding evidence of an unknown people who had lived in the land long, long ago, but he had yet to see any evidence for himself. Adding to the mystery, some Indian tribes claimed their ancestors had encountered strange people back in the dawn of antiquity, back in the earliest days of remembered Indian history, which was passed down from generation to generation by word of mouth. These mysterious ancient ones had resented the inroads of the Indians and been exterminated in ruthless warfare. Or so the tales went. He was going to ask about the cave paintings when he heard the crunch of footsteps and he looked over his shoulder to see a grim Solomon Cain approaching.

Chapter Five

Nate had no idea why Cain wore the look of a man who wanted to kill someone, but it was not at all hard to guess *who* Cain wanted to slay. The man's flinty eyes bored into him like twin knives, and he had the impression Cain was going to attack him as soon as he came close enough. Since in his helpless state he would be unable to ward off an attack, he managed a smile and said innocently, "Back so soon?"

"What have the two of you been jawin' about?" Cain demanded, with a sharp glance at Smoky Woman.

"Nothing much," Nate said.

Cain halted in front of him and fingered the Hawken, as if contemplating whether to pound the stock down on Nate's head. "I want a straight answer," he snapped.

"We talked about her brother being mad at her," Nate said, keeping up his air of innocence. "And she told me about the paintings in the cave."

"That was all?" Cain inquired suspiciously.

"Pretty much. Why?"

"I don't want you talkin' to her when I'm not around."

"How was I to know? You never told me."

Cain's brow knit for a moment. Then, apparently appeased, he slowly lowered the Hawken to his side. "No, I didn't. But I'm tellin' you now. Don't do it again." He rested the butt end of the rifle on the ground and idly wrapped his fingers around the barrel. "If I was you, King, I'd do everything I could to get free. Which is why I wouldn't put it past you to try and fill her head with unflatterin' notions about me."

Nate, gazing past Cain, saw Flying Hawk tense his entire body, the warrior's muscles standing out like iron cords. What was the Ute up to? he wondered.

"You're stuck here until I decide otherwise," Cain was saying. "So you might as well—"

In an explosive burst of speed, Flying Hawk threw himself onto the ground and rolled, his body a blur as he barreled into Cain's legs and upended their captor.

Nate, seated in front of Cain, was unable to move aside in time to avoid being flattened when Cain toppled on top of him. As they fell, the Hawken's barrel struck him a jarring blow on the jaw, causing pinpoints of light to flare before his eyes. He felt Cain's weight on top of him and heard the man's furious curses. Twisting and squirming, he tried to disentangle himself. A fist to the chin stopped him.

Stunned, he barely heard the sounds of a strenuous commotion. Dimly he realized Cain and Flying Hawk were struggling beside him. A flying elbow accidentally jarred his side. A lashing foot caught him on the shin. Then his vision returned to normal and he rolled onto his side, planning to aid the Ute. He was too late.

Solomon Cain, his features flushed crimson with rage, was astride Flying Hawk's chest and flailing away like a madman, raining punch after punch on the warrior's unprotected face. Flying Hawk's lips were split and blood poured from his nose, but Cain still wasn't letting up. He whipped his arm on high for another savage swing.

Suddenly Smoky Woman was there, seizing Cain's arm and holding fast to prevent him from striking her brother again. She cried out, "No! Please! No more!"

For a second Nate thought the enraged Cain was going to hit her, but a peculiar expression, almost one of shock, came over Cain and his fists gradually unclenched. His body lost its tension as he gulped in air. She reached out to stroke his cheek, whispering, "Thank you."

"Damn him," Cain said hoarsely. "He made me do it. If he'd behave himself, this wouldn't happen."

"I know."

Nate was appalled by Smoky Woman's attitude. She should be incensed at the pounding Flying Hawk had suffered, but she was more concerned about Cain's feelings. What kind of person was she that she could so callously disregard her own flesh and blood?

Cain turned and stared accusingly at him. "You were party to this, weren't you? It was your job to distract me while he knocked me down."

"I had no idea he was going to do what he did," Nate said.

"Liar! Do you take me for a simpleton? You were fixin' to knock me out, take my knife, and cut yourselves free."

"I'm telling you the truth."

"And horses can fly!" Cain declared. "If I didn't need you, King, I'd shoot you right here and now. As it is, you stay healthy so long as you don't pull a dumb stunt like this again. If you do, you'll be sorry."

Recognizing the futility of disputing the accusation, Nate sat quietly and waited for Cain's wrath to spend itself.

"This is what I get for going easy on you. I should have beaten you some to show you what would happen if you acted up. If only I had a pair of shackles or leg irons, I'd fix your hash! But I guess I'll have to make do."

Smoky Woman interrupted, pointing at her bloody brother. "May I help him?"

"No!" Cain barked, snapping upright. He picked up the Hawken, then grabbed her by the wrist and stormed off into the cave, vanishing around a bend.

Nate promptly sidled over to Flying Hawk. The warrior was conscious but badly battered; his lips had been smashed, his nose was bleeding profusely, and his left eyebrow had been split open. "Are you all right?" Nate asked, knowing Flying Hawk couldn't understand the words but hoping his tone would suffice to convey his worry.

The Ute pushed off the ground and shook his head a few times as if to clear it, his mane of black hair flying. Then he looked at Nate and the corners of his bleeding mouth tugged slightly upward.

Smiling at the warrior's indomitable spirit, Nate sat up. He was sweating profusely again and his mouth was dry. Lying in the dust nearby was the tin cup, but it might as well be lying on the moon. He glanced at the inviting spring, and longed to be able to go over and enjoy a refreshing drink. Rather than torment himself with the impossible, he turned away and gazed forlornly at the slate-blue sky.

Flying Hawk's stunt was bound to make escape harder, he reflected. Cain would be more cautious from then on out, seldom if ever giving them the chance they needed. It was wiser to play along for the time being, to put Cain off guard. Yet how could he convince the Ute of that when he couldn't even employ sign language until his hands were loose? There was no way.

Dejected, Nate listened to the gusty wind coming from the northwest and waited for Cain to reappear. He had a long wait. The broiling sun climbed steadily higher and higher. By his estimation an hour went by, then two. His thirst progressively worsened. Now and again he debated whether to sit back to back with Flying Hawk so he could try to untie the warrior, but he never carried through with the thought. The risk was too great. At any moment Cain might emerge.

The afternoon was half over when their captor finally strolled into the sunlight. He wore two pistols and his knife and had his thumbs hooked under his belt. "Gets hot here, don't it?" he remarked, strolling over. "Hot as an oven."

"I don't mind," Nate lied, straightening and composing himself. He refused to give Cain the satisfaction of seeing him in misery.

"Sort of reminds me of the desert," Cain said. "The heat there can roast a man alive in a day or so if he ain't careful. You ever been to the desert, King?"

"Not yet."

"I have. It's no place for greenhorns. There are scorpions that can kill a man with stingers no longer than your little fingernail. There are rattlers that move all funny-like, from side to side instead of goin' along in a straight line. There are toads as big as rabbits. And there are ugly lizards that bite down on a man so hard he can't ever get 'em off. All sorts of strange critters live there."

"How interesting."

Cain sighed. "Here I am tryin' to be civil and you act like you hate the sight of me."

"I do."

"Would you feel different if I said that I'm sorry I blew up earlier? Hell, you've got to admit I had good reason. Now I want us to be on speakin' terms again.

61

Is there anything wrong with that?"

Nate motioned with his arms. "Not at all. And since you're in such a kind mood, cut me free and I promise to behave myself."

"I can't do that."

"Figured as much."

"You just don't understand."

"Enlighten me then," Nate prompted, utterly perplexed by Cain's erratic behavior. Two hours ago the man had been primed to blow his brains out. Now Cain was acting as if they should be the best of friends. Perhaps his previous hunch was correct; Cain wasn't right in the head.

"I suppose it is time at that," Cain remarked. Drawing his knife, he leaned over to slash the rope binding Nate's ankles. He did the same with Flying Hawk. Then, before either of them could stand, he glided to one side and drew a pistol. The knife went back in its sheath and the other pistol took its place.

Nate heard the distinctive metallic clicks as both hammers were cocked simultaneously, and he looked up into the menacing barrel pointed at his forehead. "I hope you don't sneeze," he said.

A cold smile was Cain's reply. "On your feet, both of you," he directed. "Slowly, please."

As Nate complied the same order was given to Flying Hawk, who jumped up and stood with his eyes fixed in hatred on Cain. Nate feared the warrior would commit another rash act, but Flying Hawk made no aggressive moves.

"Here's what we're goin' to do," Cain said. "I want you to walk ahead of me into the cave. When I tell you to stop, stop. Don't try any tricks or you won't see daylight again." As usual, he translated his statement for the Ute's benefit.

Nate turned and took the lead. He saw Smoky Woman standing contritely near the entrance. For some reason she refused to meet his gaze when he went by her.

The interior of the cave was spacious, 15 feet from wall to wall and ten feet from the ground to the ceiling. Someone had dug out regularly spaced niches in the walls for candles, only a few of which were currently lit. Past the supplies the passageway turned to the right.

Nate rounded the corner and stopped short in surprise. The passage widened, forming a large chamber lit by a bright lantern. To the right lay thick buffalo robes for sleeping purposes. To the left, propped against the wall, were picks, shovels, chisels, and other tools. Directly ahead, where the chamber narrowed again, was a huge pile of pale rocks and dirt. Near the pile were a half-dozen closed packs.

"Figure it out yet?" Cain asked.

"No," Nate admitted.

"You will soon," Cain said, and snickered. He spoke in Ute.

Smoky Woman walked across the chamber, knelt by a pack, and opened the flap. Taking out a rock, she returned and held it out in the palm of her hand for Nate to see.

In the glow of the lantern the brilliant yellow hue was unmistakable. With a start Nate realized he was gazing on a treasure few men had ever beheld, a solid gold nugget the size of a hen's egg. He glanced at the bulging packs, the full implications hitting him with the force of a physical blow. Behind him Cain laughed.

"I reckon you understand now."

"*All* those packs?" Nate blurted.

"Yep." Cain stepped in front of them and gazed at the nugget, caressing it with his eyes. "It's taken me months to dig out that much. About broke my back doin' it too." He waved a pistol at the tunnel beyond the pile. "And there's more where that came from, tons of gold in a vein of quartz, the richest find ever."

"How did you find it?"

"Over a year ago I was out lookin' for beaver with my partner, Simon. We found that park and were scoutin' around for a way out the other side when we came on the ravine. I wanted to go back but Simon voted to go on. Am I glad he did." Cain chuckled. "Well, we started across this hellhole toward the mountains to the west. The way we saw it, no one had ever been in this part of the country and the beaver in those mountains would be ripe for the takin'. Then, about the time we laid eyes on this cave, a thunderstorm came along and drove us to cover."

Nate was trying to calculate the wealth those packs must contain, the total soaring into the millions. If Cain was to head for St. Louis at that very minute, he'd still be one of the wealthiest men on the continent, perhaps wealthier than John Jacob Astor, the king of the fur trade, widely acknowledged as the richest man in America.

"We found some old brush in here and got a fire goin'. Simon took to pokin' around, carryin' a firebrand with him so he could see. The next I knew, he was screamin' like the Devil himself was after his soul and I ran on back to see why." Cain paused, his face aglow with the memory. "My eyes about bugged out when I saw all the gold. We knew we were rich. Anything we wanted would be ours. You have no notion of how that felt. Why, we whooped and hollered so loud we about lost our voices."

"What then?" Nate asked. Despite his dislike for Cain he was fascinated by the tale.

"We chipped off a few nuggets and went on out for the supplies we'd need," Cain answered. "Got back here about five months ago and set right to work."

"Where's your partner now?"

The joy on Cain's face drained away, leaving his skin ashen, his lips compressed. "I don't rightly know."

Nate's first reaction was to suspect Cain of lying. Since the dawn of time men had fought and died to possess the precious metal. Wealthy Egyptians, it was said, had been the first to go gold crazy. They had adorned themselves in gold collars, gold bracelets, gold necklaces, gold rings, and other gold jewelry as a symbol of their status. In the Middle Ages alchemists had tried to make gold from lead and mercury. The Spanish had scoured the world for the mythical El Dorado, a land where gold was supposedly as common as sand. Gold was the treasure of treasures. Because of the value placed on it, men would do anything to obtain some. Greed and gold went hand in hand. Lying, stealing, even killing were justified in the eyes of those who craved the metal. How natural, then, that Cain had let greed overwhelm him. He abruptly realized the man was speaking.

"You don't believe me."

"I didn't say that."

"You don't have to say a word. Your face gives you away." Cain made a low hissing noise and began pacing back and forth. "What you think shouldn't matter to me one way or the other, but it does. I didn't kill Simon, King, if that's what you're thinkin'. He up and vanished without a trace."

"Leaving all this gold behind?"

Cain whirled on Nate and leveled both flintlocks. "Damn your bones! Simon was like a brother to me. We'd trapped together for pretty near six years. He saved my hide plenty of times and I did the same for him." He gestured angrily at the packs. "Take a good look. There's enough gold there for ten men. Why would I mind sharin' with him? Tarnation, man! I needed him to help get the gold out."

The sincerity in Cain's voice was real. And Cain was right about needing a partner, Nate conceded. It wouldn't be smart for a lone man to try and pack that much gold safely out of the mountains and all the way to St. Louis or wherever. The going would be slow, taking weeks longer than usual. Traversing some of the steep, narrow trails would be downright hazardous. And once on the prairie, out in the open where roving war parties could easily spot him, a lone rider would be easy pickings.

Cain's indignation had subsided and he had lowered the pistols. "A little over four months ago it happened," he said softly. "We were doin' real fine 'til then, minin' more ore than we figured we would. At the rate we were goin', we aimed to mine for another two months and then head for civilization." He gave a shudder as if cold. "There hadn't been any trouble at all. The Utes, near as we could tell, never came anywhere near this place. We had it all to ourselves. Or so we thought until Simon found the footprints."

"What footprints?"

"Down by the wash. Clear as day, right there in the dirt, was a line of tracks. Whoever made 'em had been barefoot. He'd come out of the wash and stood there starin' at the cave for a spell, then went back into the wash and ran off. We backtracked him a mile or so, but lost the tracks on rocky ground."

"It must have been a Ute," Nate speculated.

"You ever see an Ute go around barefoot?" Cain responded. "The young'uns do, but the adults all wear moccasins." He paused. "Anyway, the feet weren't right for an Ute."

"How so?"

"Indian feet ain't much different than ours. These tracks were made by somebody with short, wide feet, shorter and wider than I ever seen."

"Did the tracks show up again?"

Cain swallowed hard. "The day Simon vanished. We'd worked late the night before and I was tuckered out, so I slept in later than usual. Simon got up first, afore daylight, and went out to make coffee. I remember catchin' a whiff of it and thinkin' of how good it would taste."

Nate listened closely.

"I dozed off again, and when next I woke up I knew something was wrong. Don't ask me how. I just knew. So I jumped out of bed and went outside to find Simon. The first thing I saw was the sun, two hours high if it was a minute. Simon would never have let me sleep in that long." Cain licked his lips. "Then I saw the pack animals were gone, all three of 'em, and our saddle horses were loose. I started yellin' for Simon but he never answered."

If a piece of rock had fallen from the ceiling Nate would have jumped a foot.

"I couldn't figure it out. Right away I went after the horses and brought 'em back. As I was leadin' 'em to the spring I came on the tracks, more of the barefoot kind, only this time there had been six or seven of 'em, and they'd come off the rise instead of out of the wash."

"And your partner?"

Cain spoke so low he could barely be heard. "I found his tracks by the fire where he'd squatted while he got the coffee goin'. He'd had his back to the rise, and I expect he never saw the ones who grabbed him. 'Cause that's what they did. Snuck up on him and took him off, and him a big, strappin' son of a gun who could lick his weight in wildcats."

Nate no longer believed Cain had killed Simon. He was sure Cain was telling the truth for once. The hint of fear in the man's eyes was proof of that.

"I got my rifle and ran on up to the top of the rise, but there was no sign of anyone. Whoever they were, they'd taken our pack animals and Simon and done it all so quiet I never heard a thing." Cain slowly shook his head in evident disbelief. "I don't know why they didn't take our horses too, unless maybe the horses broke loose and they couldn't bother to round 'em up 'cause they wanted to get out of here quick-like."

"Did you backtrack them?"

"I tried. But it was the same old story. The trail led to rocky ground and I lost the sign again."

"And you stayed on after that? Didn't you think they might come back for you?"

"I'm no fool, King. It was all I thought about for the next few days. I didn't hardly know what to do. Leavin' didn't seem right. I kept hopin' Simon would show, and the notion of cuttin' out made me feel guilty, like I was yellow or something. But after a while I got to thinkin' and knew he was never goin' to come back. Whoever took him had killed him. And since I wasn't partial to sharin' his fate, I decided to pack up all the gold we'd mined so far and head out of these infernal mountains."

"What stopped you?"

"Two things. First off, I only had the two saddle horses and they ain't used to carryin' heavy packs. Second, if I loaded both of 'em with the gold I'd have to walk and it's a far piece to Missouri." Cain was calm again, his voice rising. "I knew there was Utes in this region, so I figured on stealin' some of their horses to use as pack animals. The first village I came on was Smoky Woman's. I saw her and some other women off a ways from the lodges, and I started to swing on around 'em when I got a good look at her." He smiled. "I tell you, I never saw any woman so pretty in all my life. I knew I had to have her, and hang the horses till another time."

Nate glanced at the lovely Ute, who was staring at her brother. "So you brought her here? As dangerous as it is?"

"Where else could I take her?" Cain countered. "Besides, with her here the cave felt more like a home than a hole in the ground. And you know what? I wasn't so worried about those barefoot fellas anymore. Havin' her for company made me remember I'm a man." He puffed up his chest. "I'd only leave her for short spells to go out and hunt down a deer or whatever. This last time Flying Hawk and his band found me. And now you know the whole story."

"Have your visitors returned?"

"Not that I know of. Every mornin' I take a look all around but I've not seen a single track. The way I figure it, they were happy with Simon and the pack animals and they won't be back this way again for a long while."

"What if you're wrong?"

Cain grinned wickedly and tapped Nate's chest with a pistol. "That's why you're here."

Chapter
Six

Nate didn't like the sound of that one bit. "What do you mean?" he asked.

"I refuse to be run off by a pack of murderin' savages who don't even have enough sense to wear something on their feet when they're walkin' on hot rock. I don't know what tribe they belong to, but it doesn't matter. I aim to mine a few more packs of gold before I leave here, and you're goin' to help me."

"Don't count on it."

"Oh?" Cain said, and stepping up to Flying Hawk he touched the end of the flintlock barrel to the Ute's forehead. "You'll either help me or I'll put a hole in your Injun friend."

The warrior, Nate noticed, had not batted an eye. Nate glanced at Smoky Woman, thinking she would protest, but she stood docilely, her features downcast.

"I've got it all worked out," Cain bragged, lowering the pistol. "If the ones who took Simon come back, we can hold 'em off easy. And with the two of us workin', we can dig out all the ore I need in half the time it would take me by my lonesome. So I get out of here that much sooner."

"And when the time comes, what about us?"

"I'm takin' Smoky Woman with me. Flying Hawk and you can go wherever you want."

"Just like that?" Nate said skeptically.

"Sort of. I'm not dumb enough to give your weapons back when I know full well what you'd do to me. No, I'll likely tie you up before I ride out, but not so tight you can't get free after a while, which will give me the head start I need. And I'll leave your Hawken and such in the ravine that leads into the park for you to find once you get there. How's that sound?"

You expect me to believe you? Nate wanted to say, but he didn't. Cain had already shown his true colors once, and Nate wasn't about to trust the man a second time. "Seems to me it doesn't matter what I think. You've given me no choice but to do as you want."

"Keep that in mind and we'll get along dandy," Cain said. He took several steps backward, then glanced at Smoky Woman. "Untie him. He has some work to do."

Covered by the two flintlocks, Nate stood still while the young woman removed the rope. Bringing his hands in front of him, he rubbed his sore wrists and awaited Cain's pleasure.

"I want you to go fetch the horse you rode in on and put it with the others. And don't dawdle. There's a lot to do."

"You'll let me walk on out of here all by myself?" Nate remarked.

"Why shouldn't I? I know your type, King. You're an honorable man. You're not about to ride off when you know I'll shoot Flying Hawk if you don't come back. So off with you. And be quick about it."

Nate was a prisoner of his own principles. Cain had him pegged perfectly. He wouldn't do anything to endanger the Ute, even though the two of them could hardly be called friends, and so long as Cain had the upper hand there was nothing he could do. Turning, he walked out of the cave, squinting in the brilliant sunshine, and across to the wash. A glance back showed Smoky Woman at the cave entrance, watching him, perhaps at Cain's request.

Going to the bottom of the wash, he hurried along until he came to where Cain had surprised them. A pair of objects lying to one side caused him to halt in surprise, then he darted forward and scooped up Flying Hawk's bow and full quiver. For a man who seldom made mistakes, Solomon Cain had made a big one. Perhaps, Nate reasoned, Cain hadn't wanted to be burdened with the bow and quiver after taking the Hawken and cramming all their other weapons under his belt. Now he could turn the tables on the bastard.

Or could he? Nate hefted the bow and pondered. It wasn't as if he could conceal the bow on his person and get close enough to Cain to use it. And since he didn't have much experience as an archer, he might miss anyway. Viewed realistically, the bow did him little good. Either he hid it somewhere to use later if the opportunity presented itself, or he took it back with him. He didn't want to just leave it lying in the wash, at the mercy of the elements. Warriors had to work many hours to produce quality bows, and this was as fine a one as he'd ever seen.

Slinging the bow over his right shoulder and the quiver over his left, he resumed hiking. The horse was where it should be, sweaty and impatient to get out of the sun. Leading it by the rope rein, he headed back. Riding would have been faster, but he wanted time to think. There had to be a way to trick Cain, to disarm the man or kill him if necessary. He could throw dirt in Cain's eyes, or maybe jump on Cain when the man wasn't looking, or simply rush him and hope Cain missed. All involved an aspect of risk that couldn't be avoided. Whichever way he picked, he must be sure when he struck, absolutely sure he stood an even chance of prevailing.

As he walked, he gazed out over the wasteland at the jumble of boulders, gorges, and ridges to the west. The distance to the next range of mountains, he judged, was no more than five miles, twice as far as the distance between the mountains to the east and the cave. He wondered if any white men had ever visited that mysterious range, and imagined the streams and rivers overflowing with beaver. Perhaps, he reflected, after this was all over he would pay those peaks a visit.

He came to the turn and made for the cave. Suddenly he stopped, his eyes narrowing, puzzled by a man-like shape silhouetted on a ridge half a mile away. He couldn't determine if it was the trunk of a tree or a slender column of rock. Then the shape moved and he knew it was neither.

Nate instinctively lowered his hands to his belt, his fingers closing on thin air. He watched breathlessly as the figure moved to the right. It was a man, a man watching him! A tingle of apprehension rippled through him as he realized it must be one of the savages who had taken Cain's partner.

The figure abruptly disappeared.

Nate blinked and questioned whether he had really seen what he thought he saw. It was easy for the eyes to play tricks on a man in the wilderness; heat, elevation, shadows, distance, they all conspired to fool even the most sharp-eyed trappers and warriors. This time, however, he felt he had not been deceived.

Had the strange Indians returned for Cain and the remaining horses? Or was there just the one? Should they anticipate an attack? These and other worries occupied him until he reached the spring and permitted Flying Hawk's horse to drink. Then he stepped over to Pegasus, and was rewarded with a muzzle in the face.

"I've missed you too," Nate whispered, stroking the Palouse's neck and scratching lightly behind its ears.

"My, my. Ain't this a touchin' sight!"

Nate didn't bother to turn. He kept on rubbing Pegasus and commented, "Your visitors are back."

"What?"

"I saw someone on a ridge to the west of us. He was too far off to make out clearly, but I figure it was one of the same band that took your partner."

"You're lyin'. You didn't see anyone."

Turning, Nate met Cain's defiant stare calmly. "Not everybody is like you. Some of us make it a habit to always tell the truth."

The insult was effective. Bristling, Cain advanced a few strides, then caught himself. He'd tucked the pistols under his belt again, but now he drew one and gestured angrily. "Why'd you bring back the bow?"

Nate, wondering why Cain had changed the subject, started toward the entrance. "Flying Hawk might want to use it later to kill you," he replied.

"Drop it, and the quiver."

"What about the man I saw?" Nate asked, pausing long enough to deposit both items at his feet.

"I'm not convinced you did see someone. And even if you did, it could have been an Ute or an Arapaho or a Cheyenne or even a Navajo."

"The Navajo never come this far north," Nate said. "And the Arapahos and Cheyennes never come this far west."

"They might every so often," Cain stated with a total lack of conviction. Gazing westward, he gnawed on his lower lip. "It doesn't matter one way or the other who or what you saw. We're not leavin' until we have enough gold to suit me, and that's final. I know there's a risk involved, but I'd put my own ma at risk if it meant the difference between livin' out my days like old King Midas or windin' up poor and miserable."

At that juncture Smoky Woman emerged and went to Cain's side. She studiously avoided looking at Nate.

"What are we going to do at night? Take turns standing guard?" Nate inquired. "We'll be inviting trouble if we don't. I suggest we each keep watch for three or four hours at a stretch. That way all of us will get some sleep."

"You'd like that!" Cain declared. "If I fell asleep while you were on watch, I'd wake up with my head split open if I woke up at all. No, we won't bother to keep watch. Whoever these Injuns are, they haven't gone into the cave yet. I figure they're scared to enter. We're safe inside."

"You hope. But what if you're wrong?"

Cain shrugged. "You'd better pray I'm not." Motioning for Nate to precede him into the passage, he said, "Right now I've got something I want to show you. Walk slow and keep your hands where I can see 'em at all times."

In the main chamber Nate found Flying Hawk trussed up on the floor, his ankles bound as before. "Was this necessary?"

"It was if I don't want to be lookin' over my shoulders every minute of every day," Cain answered. "He'll kill me first chance he gets and I ain't about to give him that chance." Cain smirked. "Don't worry, though. He'll be untied to eat twice a day. I wouldn't want to upset you by starvin' him to death."

"You're quite the Good Samaritan."

"Just keep walkin'."

Nate went past the huge pile of quartz and dirt and into a narrow tunnel only seven feet high. A lantern suspended from a rock chisel that had been pounded into one wall afforded ample illumination. In moments he came on the vein, situated on the left-hand side at chest height, and saw where Cain and Simon had removed the ore. The wide vein of sparkling white quartz, streaked as it was with liberal clusters and pockets of gleaming gold, dazzled him. There was so much gold in the vein that it imbued the quartz with a yellowish tint. He couldn't help himself. He gaped in awe.

"That's about how I looked the first time I laid eyes on it," Cain mentioned. "I thought I must be dreamin'."

Like all free trappers who had spent many an hour yarning around crackling campfires with boon companions, Nate had heard the many fantastic stories about the tremendous wealth just waiting to be found in the far-flung Rockies. It was common knowledge that the Spanish had operated many fabulous gold and silver mines in the mountains, and most of those mines had still been producing when the Spanish had been forced to retreat southward by hostile tribes and other factors. Thinking they would be back to continue their mining operations, the Spanish had cleverly concealed their mines, but left tantalizing clues carved into rocks and trees to help them relocate the sites when they returned. But they never did return.

In recent years quite a few trappers had discovered such markings, but as yet no one had found one of the lost mines. Because legend had it that there had been so many, several dozen at least, the trappers logically concluded there must be other gold and silver deposits still waiting to be found by anyone lucky enough to stumble across them.

And here was one, right in front of Nate. He reached out, tentatively, and touched a streak of smooth gold.

"Beautiful, ain't it?" Cain said.

"Yes."

"And it's all mine."

The spell was broken. Nate glanced sharply at his captor and said, "You're a fool, Solomon."

"Oh?"

"Yes. There's enough gold here to make ten people rich. You didn't have to force anyone to work for you at the point of a pistol. You could have offered me a small share and I would have been happy to help out. Hell, any trapper would be happy to lend you a hand mining this vein if you gave him enough to make it worthwhile. But no. You're too greedy. With your partner dead you want it all to yourself."

Cain took the reproach in stony silence, then said, "Who are you to lecture me, King? You trailed me all the way here just to get your horse back, to reclaim your own, and then you have the gall to blame me for wantin' to protect my own? I couldn't just go out and invite the first man I met to join me. I wouldn't know a thing about him. How could I tell if he was honest or not? Once a stranger saw the vein, once he saw how much gold there was, he just might put a knife in my back so he could have it all to himself." Cain shook his head. "Your way is for fools, or for those who are too trustin' for their own good."

Nate didn't bother debating the issue. He folded his arms and awaited further orders, but Cain wasn't done justifying himself.

"I feel bad about this, King. I truly do. After all, you did save me from Flying Hawk. And like I said before, I can see that you're an honorable . . ." Cain stopped and blinked, as if astonished by a thought. Then he glanced at the vein. "Hmmmm."

"What?"

"Maybe I'm goin' about this the wrong way. I know you'll jump me the first chance that comes along if you figure you can do it before I put a ball into Flying Hawk.

I'll have to be on my guard every minute. Unless . . ." Cain said, and let his voice trail off.

Nate was becoming impatient. He stared at the pistol fixed on his midsection and gauged whether he could batter it aside before Cain fired. Unfortunately, he wasn't quite close enough.

"The more I think about it, the more I like your idea," Cain suddenly declared. "I know you're a man of your word. If it means I won't have to watch my back all the time, it's worth it."

"What is?"

"Givin' you a share. You had two parfleches on your horse, as I recollect. I put 'em with the rest of my supplies. What say I let you fill 'em both with all the gold you can stuff into 'em in exchange for you agreein' to help me mine until I'm ready to cut out?"

The totally unexpected offer flabbergasted Nate. A parfleche would be able to hold 30 or 40 pounds of ore. Maybe 50. Two parfleches filled with gold wouldn't put him in the same class as John Jacob Astor by any means, but he'd have enough to tide his family over for quite a few years to come.

But was the offer sincere? Given Cain's past performance, Nate doubted it, even though the gold he'd receive was a small fraction of the total in the vein. Cain didn't just want a lion's share of the wealth; Cain wanted it all. Yet Cain was smart enough to wait until the mining was done before showing his true colors, and by then Nate would have worked out a way to put Solomon Cain in his proper place.

"What's your answer? Do you agree?" Cain prompted.

"I'm tempted," Nate confessed. "But what about Flying Hawk?"

"What about him?"

"If I agree, will you allow him to go back to his people?"

78

"And have him come back with a war party to take my scalp? Are you out of your mind?"

"What if I get him to give his word that he'll leave you alone?"

"I wouldn't care if he swore on his mother's grave. I still wouldn't trust him. He stays here until I'm done minin'."

"Then I can't accept your offer."

Cain made a curt gesture toward the chamber. "You'd pass up thousands in gold for some Injun? What the hell for? What's so special about him?"

"No man, white or otherwise, deserves to be treated like an animal."

Muttering under his breath, Cain began tapping his right foot. "Damn me if you ain't the most righteous son of a bitch I've ever met! You missed your callin'. You should have been a minister." He shook the flintlock as if he wanted to pound something. "I'm bein' as generous as I can and you throw it back in my face."

"Let me talk to Flying Hawk."

"No."

"Hear me out. How about if I talk him into promising not to harm you, and get his word he'll stay right here where you can keep your eyes on him until we're done mining?"

"No."

"He might listen to reason."

"No, damn it."

"Put the idea to Smoky Woman. I bet she'll agree to help us persuade him."

"You just don't understand," Cain said bitterly. "Nothin' I say or do is goin' to stop Flying Hawk from killin' me once he learns about his sister. And he will, sooner or later. She can't hide a thing like that for long."

"I don't follow you."

"She's carryin' my child."

Nate was so shocked he took a step backwards and nearly tripped over a chunk of quartz lying on the tunnel floor behind him. Straightening, he glanced down the passage and glimpsed Smoky Woman as she moved about in the chamber. Her condition explained a lot. No wonder she had refused to take sides when Cain and her brother clashed. And no wonder she had been so defensive about Cain.

"I want to tell you something," the father-to-be said. "It's none of your affair, but I want you to know so you won't think I'm worse than I am." He paused. "I didn't force her, King. As God is my witness, I've treated her decently since I took her. I've never beat her. Never so much as hit her."

Now Nate fully understood why Smoky Woman acted so ashamed when she was around Flying Hawk. In the eyes of her tribe she had shamed herself and her people by what she had done. Her brother, she must fear, would hate her once he learned the truth.

"Do you see the fix I'm in?" Cain asked. "I can't shoot Flying Hawk 'cause he's kin to the woman I've grown to love. And I can't let him go neither, if I want to keep on breathin'." He gestured angrily with the pistol. "You tell me. What am I supposed to do?"

"It's not for me to say," Nate replied.

"She can't go back to her people now. They'd treat her as an outcast. And they'd sure as blazes never accept me as her husband. So I have to take her away with me even though this land is her home." Cain leaned his shoulder on the wall. "I know you'll think I'm lyin', but she's the reason I hit you on the noggin when Flying Hawk and his bunch were closin' in on us. All I could think of was her, here alone with no one to depend on but me. I got scared, King. Not for me. For her. I knew the two of us on horseback would never get away from Flying Hawk, but I figured I could alone. So I did what I did and I'm mighty sorry."

"I see," Nate said thoughtfully. Although he still didn't condone Cain's treachery, he felt some small sympathy for Cain's plight. There were many other trappers, himself included, who had fallen in love with Indian women, but in those instances the tribes involved were all friendly to whites. Cain had the misfortune of loving a woman whose people despised the mountain men and who might slay him for the outrage he had committed on her.

"I figure this gold will buy us the happiness we need," Cain commented, gazing fondly at the glittering vein. "We'll live in a mansion surrounded by high walls, with servants to wait on us hand and foot. I know there will be gossip, and a lot of the wealthy folks will look down their noses at us. But I don't care. We'll keep to ourselves and be perfectly happy."

"True happiness, someone once said, must come from within."

"Don't start preachin' at me again. I'm miserable enough as it is." Cain squared his shoulders and raised the flintlock. "Enough palaver. I've jawed more in the past five minutes than I have in the past five years. Give me your answer and give it to me now. Will you help me out for two parfleches of gold?"

"Yes."

"Good. You won't regret it," Cain said, wedging the pistol under his belt.

Nate touched the gold again, vaguely troubled by his decision. There was still the issue of Flying Hawk to settle. Somehow he must come up with a way of having the warrior freed. And there was one more thing. "I'll need my rifle and my flintlocks and all the rest back."

Cain visibly hesitated.

"If you don't trust me enough to hand them over, I won't help you," Nate said, facing around. This was the supreme test of Cain's sincerity. If Cain refused, Nate would know for certain the man had no intention whatsoever of ever sticking to the letter of their agreement.

"I reckon I should."

"And from here on out no one rides my horse but me."

"Anything else?" Cain asked, grinning.

"Just this," Nate said, and punched Cain flush on the jaw, his knuckles cracking hard against bone, the blow tottering Cain backwards to fall onto his back.

"What the hell!" Cain roared, scrambling up on his elbows and grabbing at a pistol.

Nate hadn't moved. "That was for the knock on the head," he explained harshly, and tensed to pounce should Cain draw the weapon.

But Cain froze, his mouth dropping open. "Well, I'll be damned!" he exclaimed, and erupted in hearty laughter, laughter that muffled the sound of approaching footsteps. Neither of them noticed Smoky Woman until she was right there, beckoning urgently.

"Come quick!" she cried. "Horses upset. Something outside!"

Chapter
Seven

Filled with fear that Pegasus would be stolen—again—
Nate raced along the tunnel and into the main chamber,
heedless of a shout from Cain urging him to stop. In
his haste and anxiety he momentarily forgot he was
unarmed. Past Flying Hawk he sprinted, then around the
bend, past the piled provisions, and out into the bright
sunshine, where he halted and glanced to his right.

Flying Hawk's horse was gone! The rest were indeed
agitated, whinnying and straining at the ropes that secured
them to nearby boulders.

Nate was afraid Pegasus would break loose. He ran
over, seized the rope in his left hand, and said, "Whoa
there! Calm down!" while patting the gelding on the
neck. Pegasus and the two other mounts, he noticed,
had their heads tilted upward and were peering intently
at the top of the rock wall. Turning, he craned his neck
and sought the cause of their fright. Barren rock was all
he saw.

"What the hell is the matter?" Cain demanded, arriving on the scene. "Where's Flying Hawk's animal?"

"I don't know," Nate said, continuing to stroke the Palouse and to scan the heights above. "Something is up there."

Cain stared at the lofty rim. "A panther, I reckon. This is the only spring for miles and critters are comin' around all the time." He pointed at hoof tracks leading to the southwest. "Its scent spooked the horses and Flying Hawk's done run off."

"Maybe," Nate acknowledged, although he had grave misgivings. Wild animals wouldn't be the only creatures drawn to the water. He saw Smoky Woman appear at the entrance and called to her. "Tell me. Do the Utes know of any tribe that lives in this barren region?"

She walked toward them, her hands clasped at her waist. "Old men say so. But no one see many, many winters. Think all dead."

"Does this tribe have a name?"

Smoky Woman spoke in Ute, caught herself, and translated slowly, choosing her words with care. "The Rock People."

What an odd name, Nate thought, although it was highly appropriate if there actually was a tribe frequenting the wasteland, which he was inclined to doubt. No one in their right mind would want to live in such a stark, lifeless domain. The way he saw it, the barefoot Indians were simply passing through the arid region on their way between the mountain range to the west and the range to the east. Naturally they would stop at the spring. He shifted to survey their general vicinity, but saw no one.

Cain addressed Smoky Woman. "Why didn't you tell me about these here Rock People?"

"You not ask."

Nate gazed westward at the setting sun, a third of which had disappeared below the far horizon. "It'll be dark soon," he commented. "There's no time to go after Flying Hawk's animal now. With a panther on the prowl, we'd be smart to move our horses closer to the cave so we can keep an eye on them."

"Suit yourself," Cain said, "but you're wastin' your time. No panther is goin' to come anywhere near the spring with all the man-scent hereabouts."

Untying Pegasus, Nate led the Palouse to the entrance. A roving panther, in his opinion, was the least of their worries. More dangerous would be a return of the band that had taken Simon, and he couldn't understand why Cain wasn't more concerned over the possibility. Maybe, he mused, the sparkling allure of the gold had blinded the man to reality. Cain wanted that gold more than anything so he discounted everything that would cause a more rational man to give second thoughts to staying.

A convenient projection of rock to the right of the opening gave Nate an anchor to which he tied the gelding. One after the other he brought over the other two animals and did the same with them. While he was thus engaged, Smoky Woman took a large pan to the spring and filled it. Cain kept close to her. As they were coming back, Nate remarked, "There's not enough forage around here to feed a gopher, let alone three horses. What have you been doing?"

"Smoky Woman and me been sort of takin' turns goin' to the park every other day so they can eat their fill. She goes most of the time 'cause I'm too busy diggin' out ore. It's the best we can do under the circumstances."

After conducting a last check of the high rock wall, Nate followed the pair into the chamber. Flying Hawk had made no effort to escape in their absence; he lay on his side, slumped in dejection. Nate glanced at three rifles, one his Hawken, propped near the buffalo hide bed, and said, "I want my guns and things back now."

In short order Cain turned over the Hawken, both pistols, Nate's butcher knife and tomahawk, and showed Nate where his parfleches and other possessions had been placed. "There," Cain said. "That's all of your stuff. See? I'm holdin' up my end of the bargain."

Nate checked the flintlocks to be certain they were properly loaded. He couldn't help but wonder if Cain would still hold up his end of their pact when the time came to ride off with the gold. That was when the crucial test would come.

Smoky Woman, meanwhile, had busily gathered the items she needed to fix their supper. Now she headed back outside.

Seeing her go, Nate started to join her to serve as her protector when a hail from Cain made him turn.

"I have something to show you," Cain said. Picking up the lantern, he walked to the wall opposite from the bed. "Come over here a second," he beckoned. "What do you make of these."

Revealed in the rosy glow were numerous crude paintings depicting men and animals, but they were unlike any men or wild beasts Nate had ever beheld. The men had block-like bodies and long hair down to their waists. A few held short spears. Others held odd weapons not much bigger than their hands. Almost always the men were portrayed in the act of hunting game. In one scene a half-dozen figures had surrounded an enormous beast resembling an elephant only it had a great shaggy coat, small ears, a pair of curved tusks, and a bulge on top of its head. In another scene several men were battling a large panther-like animal sporting two top teeth exaggerated out of all proportion.

"Who could have drawn all this?" Cain wanted to know.

"Indians, maybe," Nate guessed. "Indians who lived in this cave ages ago." He based this assumption on the fact that the paint which had been used, a pigment derived from berries or perhaps from mixing water with clay as some tribes currently did, showed signs of having faded considerably.

"That's what I figured too," Cain said. "Until I saw this down here." Stepping to one side, he squatted and nodded at another painting.

In one respect the scene Cain indicated was much like the rest. It showed a group of men chasing a herd of elk. But in another respect this particular depiction was extremely unusual; the yellowish-brown streaks of paint had been applied much more recently than the rest. They almost glistened. The color was so much brighter the difference was like that between night and day.

"I'd say this was done not more than two years ago at the most," Cain mentioned. "Wouldn't you?"

"Yes," Nate agreed, feeling unduly disturbed. It was just another painting, he reasoned, yet it gave him the same sort of uneasy sensation he experienced when he encountered a grizzly and didn't know if the bear would charge or flee.

"Whoever painted it might still be around," Cain said.

"True," Nate responded, thinking of the mysterious footprints and Simon's disappearance.

Cain stepped toward the middle of the chamber. "Some of the bones don't look too old either."

"What bones?"

"That's right. I ain't taken you there yet." Cain headed into the tunnel. "Follow me and I'll show you what else we found."

They went past the exposed vein, around a curve, and along a straight passage extending for over 60 feet. Abruptly, the walls widened and they were in a second large chamber. Here fine particles of dust hung in the air. Dust caked the walls, coated the floor. And covered a mound of bones rearing over six feet high in the middle of the chamber.

Astounded, Nate stepped forward to examine them. He saw one bone he recognized immediately, the leg bone of a buffalo. A bear skull jutted from the bottom portion of the mound. On one side was the partial skeleton of a panther. None of these remains had the same effect on him as did the many human skulls that dotted the pile from top to bottom.

Human skulls! He couldn't quite accept the testimony of his own eyes. There had to be 20 or 30 he could see, and probably more buried underneath. Why, he mused, hadn't the people who lived in the cave buried their dead or else suspended them in trees or on platforms as did many Indian tribes? How uncaring to just dump the dead into this chamber with the remains of wild beasts.

Then he spied a human arm bone and he bent over for a closer look. There were odd scratches and grooves on the bone that perplexed him until he glanced at the bones of the animals and saw similar marks. Insight hit him like a bolt out of the blue. *Those were teeth marks!*

Nate snapped erect and clenched his Hawken so hard his knuckles turned white. "It can't be!" he blurted.

"It can't be, but it is," Cain said. "Took me a while to mull it over, but I figure the folks who lived here ate people as well as animals." He laughed. "Don't that beat all?"

Revolted by the images conjured up, Nate backed away from the mound. He was close to the tunnel when faintly into the chamber wafted the spine-tingling sound of a scream of mortal terror.

"Smoky Woman!" Cain bellowed.

Whirling, Nate took the lead, his legs pumping as he fairly flew along the tunnel. The scream died suddenly, filling him with gnawing dread. One of them should have gone with her. If something happened to her he was partly to blame for being so careless. Had it been Winona he would never have let her go out alone.

In the main chamber Flying Hawk was in the act of rolling frantically toward the entrance. Nate vaulted over him without breaking stride, went around the bend, and out into the murky gray of twilight.

Smoky Woman was gone.

He looked to the left and saw the horses were still there. Her scream, he figured, had forced her captors to flee before taking any of the mounts. Then he saw the pans and food scattered near the fire, showing she had put up quite a struggle.

Something made him glance at the rise. He was just in time to see several hurrying forms vanish over the crest. Wheeling, he dashed to get his saddle and nearly collided with Cain.

"Where is she? Where the hell is she?"

"They've got her."

"Oh, God!" Cain cried, advancing into the open and searching right and left. "Which way did they go? I'm goin' after 'em."

"No, I am," Nate said as he grabbed his epishimore, a square piece of blanket he used under his saddle.

"She's my woman, not yours."

"And Pegasus is my horse, not yours. He's the only chance we have of overtaking them. You've ridden him. You know how fast he is."

"I'll take him, then. You stay here in case there are more of the bastards skulkin' around."

Nate brushed past Cain and began saddling up. "You said yourself that he began giving you trouble before. He doesn't like being ridden by anyone but me."

"She's my woman, damn it!" Cain reiterated, putting his hand on Nate's shoulder. "I'm the one should go."

With a quick jerk Nate pulled loose and turned. "We don't have time to waste, Solomon. Which is more important, your pride or her life?"

Cain opened his mouth to reply, froze for a second, then changed his mind and stood aside. "You go."

In less than a minute Nate was in the saddle. "Keep the fire going so I have a beacon to guide me back here. If all goes well I won't be long."

"God go with you, King."

A gust of wind whipped by Nate as he swung the Palouse and made for the rise. His wounded shoulder ached from the exertion of throwing on the saddle, but not enough to impair his thinking, which was good because he'd need his wits about him when he caught up with the ones who'd abducted Smoky Woman.

Pegasus seemed eager for some exercise. The gelding went up the slope at a gallop, head low, mane flying.

Just over the top Nate reined up to scour the land in front of him. He didn't stop on the crest itself because he would have been silhouetted against the ever-darkening sky. Ahead lay a barren maze. Which direction should he go? He doubted the Indians had gone to the south where the land was more open since they would be more readily detected. Nor would they have gone to the north where a butte barred their path. Due east, he believed, was the right way to go.

He was sure he couldn't be more than three hundred yards behind them, if that, and consequently he pushed Pegasus at a reckless speed. Smoky Woman's abductors were bound to hear him coming, which couldn't be helped. He cocked the Hawken, set the trigger, and held the Hawken across his thighs, ready for action.

Behind him a rifle cracked.

Nate almost stopped. It was Cain who must have fired, at what he couldn't guess. Twisting, Nate listened for more shots, a sure sign the cave was under attack. But there were no more. Counting on Cain being able to hold his own, Nate galloped on into the night.

Suddenly, off to the left, a bird called. Another bird, off to the right, answered.

In all the years Nate had spent in the Rockies he had never heard birds like these. Suspicious, he looked both ways but saw only dark, bleak terrain. What if he had miscalculated? What if there were more Indians than he thought? Or were they even worthy of being called Indians? If they were related to the occupants of the cave, to the vile people who had eaten their own kind or their captives, then they didn't deserve to be dignified by the word. Savages would be more like it.

He recalled reading about the Aztecs in school. Rulers of ancient Mexico, they had built stupendous cities and been as civilized as any society that ever existed, except in one important respect. The Aztecs had indulged in ritual sacrifice and often engaged in cannibalism. Their priests would cut out and eat the hearts of those being sacrificed, while the bodies of the unfortunates would be given to the common people to be devoured at public feasts. When he'd first read the account, he'd shuddered in revulsion. Now, here he was about to tangle with a band that might be just as bad.

From out of nowhere materialized a short, stocky figure not 20 feet off. Nate glimpsed a muscular, naked body, and a wild mane of black hair. Then he glimpsed a slender object flashing toward him and realized the savage had hurled a spear. So superb were his reflexes that the instant he perceived the danger he ducked low and angled Pegasus to the right.

The spear missed them by inches.

Straightening, Nate raised the Hawken to fire but the figure was already gone. He reined up and swiveled, scanning in a circle. Now the night was quiet except for the rush of the wind, giving him the illusion he was the only soul alive in the midst of a vast alien landscape. Yet he knew better.

He also knew not to stay in one spot too long. Jabbing his heels into Pegasus, he trotted eastward once more. He touched each flintlock, insuring they were in place. So were his knife and tomahawk.

For a hundred yards the night was deceptively tranquil. He began to suspect he was going in the wrong direction and considered changing direction to the northeast or the southeast. But which should it be? Unexpected aid came in the guise of a stifled shriek to the northeast.

Hunching low over the saddle, Nate galloped across a rocky flat, the gelding's hoofs cracking like gunshots. Just when he thought he had misjudged where the shriek came from he spotted a cluster of figures straight ahead.

There were five of them, four husky, naked savages and Smoky Woman. Two of them had her in their grasp and she was striving mightily to break free. A third had his hand clamped over her mouth from behind. The fourth, trailing his companions by a few feet, heard Pegasus first and whirled.

Nate saw the man's right arm sweep back, then streak forward. But there was no spear in the man's hand, so Nate didn't slow up or turn aside. And had the savage not rushed the throw, Nate would have died then and there.

He heard a buzzing noise, as if a dozen hornets were winging past, and felt rather than saw something strike his saddle with a distinct smack. Glancing down, he was amazed to find a slender object imbedded close to his left thigh. There was no time to pull it out and inspect it, though, because seconds later he was among the savages.

Barking in a strange tongue, they scattered, one of them hauling Smoky Woman by the wrist.

Ignoring the rest, Nate snapped the Hawken to his left shoulder instead of his right, which had started acting up again after he'd slugged Cain, and sighted carefully. The

Hawken spat lead and smoke and the savage keeled over as if felled by an axe.

The moment Smoky Woman was free, she turned and ran to meet him, holding her arms up to make his next task easier.

As it was, her weight was almost too much for him with his weakened shoulder. Gripping the Hawken and the reins in his left hand, he swung low in the saddle and looped his right arm around her slim waist while at a full gallop. The shock of her body hitting his arm almost wrenched him from his perch. Had she not leaped at that precise instant, adding her momentum to the backward swing he had started, he would certainly have fallen.

As lithely as a lynx she slid up behind him and grabbed him about the waist.

There were angry shouts from several directions. Another buzzing projectile almost struck Nate's face.

Then they were out of range, riding hard, bearing to the southeast in a wide loop that would eventually take them back to the cave. Nate could feel her warm body pressed to his, reminding him of the lovely wife waiting for him in their comfortable cabin many miles away. If he had any brains, that was where he'd be instead of fleeing for his life from primitive Indians who'd enjoy having him for their evening meal. Literally.

Once he believed they had left the savages far behind, he slowed to a walk to reduce the amount of noise Pegasus was making. For all he knew, other bands might be abroad and he wanted to avoid them if at all possible.

"Thank you," Smoky Woman whispered at length.

"You're welcome," Nate whispered in reply.

"Cain?"

"He's fine. Mad as a bee in a bonnet, but fine. He wanted to come after you himself but I talked him out of it."

"Why?"

Nate explained about Pegasus's finicky nature.

"My brother?"

"He's fine too," Nate assured her, mentally noting that she'd asked after Cain first. He added, "I sure do hope the two of you will be back on friendly terms soon. Brothers and sisters have a special blood bond between them. They should always try to love each other."

"My brother not love me again."

"He'll come around. Men can be stubborn cusses, but we see the light sooner or later."

"See light?"

"Yes. We learn not to be so stubborn."

"My brother never see light."

"Don't be so hard on him. He might surprise you."

"I know him."

"Have you told him about the baby yet?" Nate inquired, and felt her arms briefly constrict on his midsection.

"How you know?"

"Cain told me."

Smoky Woman fell silent. Nate assumed she was upset he knew. Perhaps she viewed her pregnancy as highly personal and no business of anyone else except Cain and her.

The wind had died. Stygian gloom shrouded the wasteland, relieved only by a quarter moon and the myriad of shining stars. From the southwest came the lonesome yip of a solitary coyote.

Nate reloaded the Hawken as he rode. He had to measure the amount of black powder by the feel of the grains in the palm of his hand, which was always a tricky proposition. If he put in too little his next shot would lack the usual wallop and might fail to down an attacker at a critical instant. If he put in too much he risked bursting the percussion tube of his rifle. But he had reloaded by feel so many times he was confident he put in just the right amount.

His nerves on edge, the stock of the Hawken resting on his left thigh, he searched for some sign of the blazing fire. It should be easy to spot, yet over the course of the next 40 minutes the blanket of darkness lay unbroken on the land. Had Cain neglected to keep the fire going? he wondered. Or was there a more sinister reason for its absence?

He grew certain they were near the high rock wall. Stopping, he listened and looked. To his right was the familiar rise. A black patch was all that could be seen of the cave. He couldn't even tell if the other horses were still there.

Goading Pegasus forward, Nate leveled the Hawken in case the savages lurked nearby. He was within 20 yards of the entrance when a rifle boomed and the ball whizzed past his ear.

Chapter
Eight

Since, in Nate's estimation, none of the savages possessed guns and they wouldn't know how to use a pistol or a rifle if they had it, only one person could have fired at him. "Cain! You idiot! It's King! Don't shoot!"

A yelp of joy greeted his shout. "Sorry! I thought you were one of those devils! Come on in!"

Smoky Woman's grip slackened as they neared the entrance, and Pegasus had barely stopped when she jumped off and ran into the outstretched arms of Solomon Cain.

Nate was dismounting when another figure strode from the cave. "Flying Hawk!" he declared in surprise, for not only was the warrior free but Cain had even given back the Ute's bow, arrows, and hunting knife.

"Let's get under cover and I'll fill you in," Cain said, motioning for Nate to go first. "We took the other horses inside so the bastards can't steal 'em."

The animals were between the entrance and the bend. Nate tied Pegasus in the feeble light from a single candle placed so as not to be visible beyond the opening. As he did his gaze fell on the slender object imbedded in his saddle. He had to wrench hard to pluck it out.

It was unlike any weapon Nate had ever heard of. The only thing he could compare it to were the darts used in popular games played in taverns back in the States. This dart was made of stone and had two slim raven feathers tied to a groove at the back end to add stability in flight. Simple, but extremely deadly.

"What have you got there?" Cain asked, walking over. He whistled softly. "So that's what some of the sons of bitches were throwin'! I heard a couple go by me and one nicked my sleeve."

"And I heard your shot. What happened?"

"You weren't gone very long when I spotted a pack of savages sneakin' up on me from the west. I let 'em get close, and when one jumped up and went to toss a spear I shot him smack between the eyes. Some of the others tried to nail me but I made it in here. Had to kick out the fire on my way, which made me a good target. But they didn't want to get too close. Guess they were afraid of the rifle." Cain paused to smile at Smoky Woman. "While I reloaded I could see 'em movin' around out there. That set me to thinkin'. If they rushed me all at once, I wouldn't stand a prayer. So I did the only thing I could. I ran on back and told Flying Hawk I'd free him if he'd help us. He agreed, but only till his sister is out of danger."

And then what? Nate reflected. Once Smoky Woman was safe, what would Flying Hawk do? Kill Cain? The warrior was at the entrance, keeping watch.

"He was the one thought of bringin' in the horses," Cain commented. "Smart move too."

"Have the savages attacked yet?"

"Nope. They were flittin' around like butterflies until a few minutes ago. I figure they heard you comin' and lit out."

"They won't give up so easily," Nate said, tucking the dart under his belt next to a pistol. Hurrying to the Ute, he signed, "See anything?"

Flying Hawk grunted and pointed.

At the limits of human vision ghostly forms were gliding about like wolves around trapped prey, moving from one place of concealment to another. Sometimes two or three would meet, confer, and separate.

"Are they still there?" Cain asked.

"Yes. They must have let Smoky Woman and me through their lines so they'd have us all boxed in together."

"Damn their hides."

Nate heartily concurred. Primitive they might be, but the savages weren't stupid. He must not make the mistake of underestimating them.

"I say we make a break for it," Cain declared. "Load up the gold on the three horses and head out before the bastards charge us. We'll be on foot, but it's so dark they might miss."

"Might," Nate said, conjuring up a vision of what a hail of darts and spears would do to them and the horses. "But there are so many out there now that the odds are we'd never get fifty feet."

"I'm willin' to chance it if you are."

"The only way we'd make it is if we left the gold behind," Nate mentioned. "On foot, leading the horses, we wouldn't stand a prayer." He looked at Solomon. "Even if we leave the gold, one of us will have to ride double with Smoky Woman. The horse would take longer crossing the flat to the wash, and we both know what that would mean. Do you still want to chance it?"

"No," Cain answered, gazing affectionately at the woman. "No, I reckon I don't. And I sure ain't leavin' the gold."

"Then I suggest we make a barricade using the supplies and the packs of gold."

"The gold!" Cain exclaimed. "Not on your life. I want it in the chamber where it's safe and sound!"

"Those packs are the heaviest things in the whole cave. We can put them on the bottom as the foundation for our barricade," Nate said. "We have nothing else to use in their place."

Clearly Cain hated the idea. His face scrunched up as if he'd just swallowed a mouthful of bitterroot. "All right," he spat. "You've convinced me."

Flying Hawk stood guard while Nate, Cain, and Smoky Woman worked swiftly. Fifteen minutes of industrious labor produced a makeshift wall three feet high and extending two-thirds of the way across the cave opening. Standing back to inspect their handiwork, Nate shook his head in disappointment. The barricade was too flimsy and incomplete to hold out a concerted rush for very long. But it was the best they could do.

Cain must have entertained the same thoughts because he said, "We can use my shovels to scoop out a wall of dirt to finish it off."

And that's what they did, or started to, when Flying Hawk spoke a word of warning and jabbed a finger to the south.

The ghostly forms were converging on the cave.

No words were necessary. Nate retrieved his Hawken and crouched near the gap between their barricade and the east wall, the most vulnerable spot. "Make every shot count," he said softly.

Cain ran to the flickering candle and extinguished the flame with his thumb and forefinger. Then he took up a post close to Nate. To Cain's right was Flying Hawk. Behind them, clutching a pair of flintlocks Cain had taught her to use, squatted Smoky Woman.

Smiling grimly, Flying Hawk notched an arrow to his bow string.

"Wait until I give the signal," Nate said, and heard Cain repeat it in the Ute tongue. Their breathing was the only sound after that. Oddly, the savages weren't making any noise as they charged, unlike typical Indians, who invariably whooped when engaged in a battle.

"King?" Cain whispered.

"What?"

"If something should happen to me, don't let these bastards get their hands on Smoky Woman. We both know what they'll do to her. Promise me you'll take care of it."

"I promise," Nate said, hoping he wouldn't have to. But if the worst did occur, he wasn't going to let them take him alive either.

By now the savages were 30 feet off. Strung out in an uneven line, they bounded forward like a pack of hungry wolves, their manes of black hair blowing in the breeze. Some were armed with spears, some with war clubs, some with their unusual darts.

Taking a steady bead on one of the foremost runners, Nate held his breath, cried, "Now!" and fired. Cain's rifle also cracked, followed a second later by the twang of Flying Hawk's powerful bow.

There was no time to reload the Hawken. Nate set it down, drew both pistols, and extended his arms. The initial volley had caused some of the savages to slow, but the undaunted majority were still closing. He aimed at one and squeezed off his shot, aimed at another and emptied the second flintlock. Cain was also shooting. Four or five of the savages were down, several thrashing in agony.

Nate discarded the pistol and yanked out both his knife and his tomahawk. This was the moment of truth. Fully a half-dozen savages would reach the barricade in the next few seconds.

The bowstring twanged, reducing the number to five.

A burly Indian bearing an upraised club hurled himself at the gap and Nate moved to meet him. Nate blocked the downward sweep of the savage's club with the tomahawk, then speared his butcher knife into his foe's chest.

The man roared and jerked backwards, tearing the knife out. Heedless of the hole and his spurting blood, the Indian snapped the club up and sprang.

Nate deftly blocked the blow with the tomahawk, then lashed his knife in a tight arc, going for the savage's throat this time. Nimble as a bighorn, the Indian swerved, shifted, and slammed his club into Nate's side. Incredible pain sheared through Nate's chest. For a desperate moment he thought his ribs had caved in. Doubled over in torment, he glanced up to see the savage raising the club for the death stroke, and with a sinking feeling in his gut he knew he lacked the strength to dodge.

An arrow abruptly skewered the burly Indian's throat, sinking in almost to the eagle feather fletching. Driven rearward by the impact, the savage grasped the shaft and snapped it off as easily as Nate might snap a mere twig. Furious, seemingly unfazed, the man took a step and prepared to bash Nate's skull in. A second arrow, however, transfixed the Indian's chest, and he toppled where he stood.

Nate finally straightened, intending to thank Flying Hawk, but another savage had already taken the place of the first. This one carried a spear that he slashed at Nate's face. Nate pivoted, the spear fanned his nose, and with a mighty surge of all the muscles in his left shoulder he sank his tomahawk into his enemy's forehead. Like an overripe melon the brow split right down the middle, the keen blade cleaving the brain. Instantly the savage went into violent convulsions, nearly tearing the tomahawk from Nate's grasp before he could rip it loose.

Nate turned, expecting more adversaries, finding none. Five bodies lay sprawled over or near the partially crumbled barricade, while the rest of the primitive Indians were retreating into the impenetrable cover of the night. Elated, he leaned on a parfleche in front of him, but only for a heartbeat. The savages, he realized, might regroup and mount another attack. Sliding the tomahawk under his belt and the knife into its sheath, he gathered up his guns to reload them. A groan made him look to his right.

Cain was braced against the back wall, a slain savage at his feet, a bloody knife in his right hand. His left shoulder sagged as if under a tremendous weight, and he swayed when he took a step away from the wall. In a flash Smoky Woman was at his side, supporting him.

"What happened?" Nate asked as he pulled the Hawken's ramrod out. "How bad is it?"

"Took a damn club in the shoulder," Cain answered, his lips drawn back in a grimace. "I think the bone is busted."

"Sit down and rest. I'll be with you in a bit," Nate said. With Cain temporarily indisposed, his first priority was to reload all their guns, not just his own, or they'd never survive another onslaught. Flying Hawk, he observed, was staring intently at Smoky Woman.

"I can manage," Cain said, stepping to the barricade. He leaned over to pick up his rifle, then groaned louder than before and slowly sank to his knees. "Hurts like hell!" he declared. "Almost blacked out there."

"Hold on," Nate urged, his fingers moving quickly. They needed Cain badly. Smoky Woman could shoot, but she was nowhere near the marksman Cain was.

Without him they would drop fewer savages when the next rush came, meaning more would reach the barricade and possibly overwhelm them by sheer force of numbers.

An unnerving silence now claimed the countryside. Nothing moved. The erratic wind had subsided to a whisper.

Relying on Flying Hawk to warn him if the savages reappeared, Nate concentrated exclusively on feeding black powder and balls into gun after gun. Soon he had all the rifles and pistols reloaded. His flintlocks once again under his belt, he dropped to one knee beside Solomon Cain, who sat slumped against the barricade. "Is the pain still bad?"

"I feel like a grizzly clamped its jaws down on my shoulder and won't let go."

"Let me take a look," Nate said, gingerly touching the wounded shoulder.

Cain flinched, then hissed as if angry at himself and sat up straight. "I'm gettin' right puny of late. Must be all this soft livin'." He mustered a wan grin.

"I'll try not to hurt you," Nate said, but it was unavoidable. Twice he made Cain gasp as he probed carefully to measure the extent of the damage. One gasp came when he touched a bone that moved when it shouldn't. "You were right," he said after he was done. "Your clavicle is broken."

"My what?"

"Your shoulder bone."

"Of all the stinkin' luck," Cain muttered.

"I can try to set the bone and bandage you up. It won't be as good as a sawbones would do, but it'll hold you together if you don't go out and wrestle any wolverines."

Cain gazed at Smoky Woman. "Forget me. Those bastards may try again. You need to keep watch so they don't catch us by surprise."

"Your skin is split open. The longer we wait, the more chance of infection setting in," Nate said. He nodded at the barricade. "We might wind up being penned in here for a long time. If you get sick, we won't be able to give you the doctoring you'll need. So don't be mule-headed. Allow me to do what I can now and save us a lot of trouble later."

"If you put it that way," Cain said.

"I do." Nate slipped an arm around Cain's waist and helped him to rise. "Have Smoky Woman take you back into the main chamber. See if she can somehow get a fire going. I'll need hot water if I'm to do this right."

"All right." Cain chuckled. "You sure have a knack for givin' orders. Forget bein' a minister. Join the army and you'll be a general in no time."

Nate leaned his forearms on the top of the barricade and scanned the land fronting the entrance. The savages had yet to show themselves. Could it be that they had departed? They'd suffered heavy losses, undoubtedly more than they had expected. Would they risk as many lives in another attack? Or would they do as the Apaches often did when the Apaches met stiffer resistance than they anticipated, cut their losses and go in search of easier pickings? Suddenly a finger touched his shoulder.

Flying Hawk moved his hands in exaggerated movements so the signs he made would be conspicuous in the dark. "You are a fine fighter, Grizzly Killer. I no longer doubt you are worthy of your name."

"Thank you," Nate signed in the same exaggerated manner.

"Do you know the secret my sister is keeping from me?"

The blunt query caught Nate flat-footed and he paused before responding, uncertain whether he should reveal the truth or deny he knew anything. He loathed lying, but by the same token he didn't have the right to meddle in Smoky Woman's personal affairs. She must have an excellent reason for not informing her brother.

"Do not try to deny she is hiding something," Flying Hawk signed. "I know her well, Grizzly Killer, as well as I do myself. She can hide nothing from me for very long."

"If she does have a secret," Nate signed tactfully, "it is for her to tell you. I would be out of place were I to give it away."

The warrior did not respond immediately. His features obscured by shadow, he stood as still as if carved from stone. Finally his hands moved. "Very well. I will respect your wishes." Shifting, he glanced toward the bend. "But I already think I know what her secret is, and if I am right I must take steps to prevent her from staining our family and our people."

Nate straightened. "You cannot mean that. She is your own flesh and blood."

"If what I suspect is true, she should have killed herself rather than lie with him."

"Maybe she loves him. Have you thought of that?"

"Love is no excuse for lying with an enemy."

"You disappoint me, Flying Hawk. I thought you had come to see that not all whites are as bad as some of your people might claim."

"I have. By knowing you I have learned there are white men who are brave and truthful, but this does not change anything. It does not change what has happened and what will happen. Already have your kind killed most of the beaver. One day your people will want these mountains for their own. You said so yourself. Do friends take that which does not belong to them? No. This is an act of an enemy. So whether you like it or not, your people and mine are enemies."

Nate knew there was nothing he could say to change the warrior's mind. Flying Hawk's logic was irrefutable, and were he in the Ute's place he'd feel the same way.

"If my people were to find out my sister has slept with a white man, they would shun her. The child would be treated even worse. Do not look at me like that. I have heard that your people do not think highly of mixed unions either."

"Some do not," Nate admitted, and would have gone on to appeal to the warrior's sense of fairness if not for the untimely arrival of Smoky Woman.

"Have fire. Need water." She held out a pot. "I fetch."

"Not on your life," Nate said, snatching it from her hand and moving quickly to the end of the barricade to forestall any protest. Hunching down and staying close to the cliff, he trotted toward the spring. Not until he had covered over ten feet did the gravity of the risk he was taking sink home. And all for a man he didn't like all that much.

No, he told himself. That wasn't quite true. He wasn't doing this for Cain so much as he was for Smoky Woman. For her he felt acute sympathy, and he wished there was something he could do to lessen her misery. There wasn't, though. She had made the difficult choice and she must now live with the inevitable consequence.

The smooth surface of the pool reflected the stars overhead, a glimmering mirror afloat in a dull sea of rock and packed earth, easy for him to distinguish. He halted a dozen feet off and crouched. Slowly, his mind cautioned. To rush now would prove fatal. There had to be savages nearby, and perhaps one or two were keeping an eye on the spring.

Of a sudden the wind picked up again, cooling his cheeks and brow. He ran his eyes over every boulder, every shadow. Any savages in hiding were invisible.

Easing onto his stomach, the Hawken in his left hand, the pot in his right, he snaked toward the pool, advancing an inch at a time, moving first one limb, then another, much like an oversized turtle moving in slow motion. He had to be extra careful not to scrape the rifle or the pot on the ground. Once he slipped up and the pot made a scratching noise. Freezing, he waited to see if there would be a reaction. The night mocked his anxiety with its tranquility.

At the water's edge he inhaled the dank scent and touched his fingers to the cool surface. Cupping his right hand, he ladled water to his mouth and drank quietly. Then he slowly lowered the pot in. Water flowed over the sides, filling it rapidly, making it heavier and harder to hold.

Somewhere to the west arose a faint clattering.

Nate lifted the pot out and set it down to free both hands for using the Hawken. The clattering stopped before he could identify it. Staying motionless, he fixed his eyes blankly on the entire scene before him rather than on any one specific spot. It was an old trick used to detect the slightest movement anywhere within one's view.

Over a minute must have gone by when a light-colored apparition materialized to the southwest. Assuming it must be a savage, he tucked the Hawken to his shoulder and leveled the rifle across the pool, the barrel so close to the surface it was nearly touching. Gradually the apparition solidified, transforming into a small doe, not much over a year old. Demonstrating the age-old vigilance of her species, she would take several steps, then pause to test the wind.

Nate knew the animal was coming to drink. In order to avoid giving her a scare and having her bound off, making all kinds of noise as she fled, he backed away from the pool, taking the pot in his right hand. He had gone a yard or so when he saw the most remarkable sight.

From four directions at once sprang four husky savages, swooping down on the startled doe in a blur of lightning speed. She bounded to the left, saw a savage bearing down on her, and reversed direction, bounding to the right. Another savage blocked her escape route. Spinning, she sought to flee the way she had come but another savage was there. They had her completely hemmed in. Game to the last, she darted between two of them, or tried to, but they were amazingly fast. One got her by the neck, the other dived and grabbed her front legs, and she bleated in terror as she went down.

Nate distinctly heard a loud snap.

The four savages huddled around their kill, tearing at her with their hands. One of them, exhibiting superhuman strength, tore off her hind leg and commenced greedily devouring her raw flesh. Another leaned down to rip into her slender neck with his teeth.

Nate had seen enough. Now, while they were distracted, was the perfect time to head for the cave. Turning, he crawled but three or four inches when he saw another savage, this one standing at the base of the cliff wall between the pool and the cave. And the man was coming toward him!

Chapter Nine

Nate had the Hawken up and aimed in the blink of an eye, and he was all set to cock the hammer when he realized the savage was *backing* toward him. The man hadn't seen him yet. He surmised the Indian had snuck close to the cave entrance, perhaps to see or overhear what was going on inside, and now was sneaking off to make a report to the rest of the band. Lowering the Hawken, he drew his tomahawk. Stealth and silence were in order. Should those eating the deer hear a commotion, they would be on him before he could reach safety.

He marveled at how quiet the savage was. Strain his ears as he might, he heard nary a whisper of sound. Nate held the tomahawk flat in front of him and smelled the odor of drying blood. There had been no time to wipe the tomahawk clean after the battle, and he certainly couldn't do so now.

Suddenly the savage turned away from the cliff, bent at the waist, and sprinted off to the south, his gaze on the cave the whole time. Soon the night swallowed him up.

Nate felt some of the tension drain from his body. That had been too close for his liking! How lucky the man had been more intent on not being spotted by someone within the cave than on his surroundings! Tucking the tomahawk back under his belt, Nate gripped the rifle and the pot and resumed crawling.

From the look of things, the savages intended to stay there for a while. They were more persistent than Nate had imagined. And when he regarded the situation from their perspective, he realized they had everything to gain and little to lose by waiting around. Eventually he and the others would run out of food, and they would run out of water too if the savages thought to keep a closer watch on the spring.

Nearing the barricade, Nate whispered, "It's me!" so Flying Hawk wouldn't put an arrow into him. Then, rising, he ran the remaining distance and sank low behind the barricade with water sloshing over the rim of the pot.

The Ute and his sister were also hunched low, glaring at one another. Evidently they'd had another argument. Neither moved for fully half a minute, until Smoky Woman turned, took the pot without speaking, and hurried off, carefully holding the pot so she wouldn't spill it.

Nate leaned the Hawken against the barricade and rose high enough to peer over the top. Someone had to keep watch, and Flying Hawk was too preoccupied. Nothing moved out there. Craning his neck, Nate tried to catch a glimpse of the four savages consuming the doe, but they were too far off. A hand touched his right shoulder.

The warrior had moved closer and now employed sign, holding his hands close to Nate's face so Nate would have no problem reading the gestures.

Nate concentrated so he wouldn't miss a one. From long practice he mentally filled in the articles and other words that were lacking in sign language but which were needed to flesh out the statements into their English equivalent. In this instance Flying Hawk signed, "Sister want go white country with False Tongue. Question. Whites make her heart bad."

Sign language, incorporating as it did hundreds of hand gestures and motions, could convey a nearly endless variety of meanings and sentiments through the proper combination of symbols. But there were deficiencies, one being that in sign there were no gestures for "what," "where," "when," and "why." The sign for "question" was used instead. So when someone wanted to ask, "What are you called?" they would sign, "Question you called."

There were others areas in which sign language was lacking, from an English language standpoint, and some trappers had difficulty in reading and using sign because of this. They were accustomed to structuring their talk in a certain way and they couldn't get the hang of doing it differently. Others, like Shakespeare McNair, were as adept as the Indians themselves.

Nate raised his arms and replied. "Your sister will be treated kindly by some, not so kindly by others."

"She should stay with her own people. I do not like this."

"It might be for the best," Nate said, although he wasn't entirely convinced that it would be. Half-breeds were not highly regarded in either culture. Whites tended to treat breeds with contempt, while the attitude of the Indians varied from tribe to tribe. The Shoshones and Apaches accepted them; the Utes and Blackfeet did not.

"I will not let her go."

"She is a grown woman. She can do as she pleases."

"That is the white way, not ours."

"Should you stand in her way if her love for False Tongue brings her happiness?"

"She must not be permitted to shame our family and dishonor our people."

Sighing, Nate let the subject drop. It was a hopeless case, he reflected. The warrior's prejudices were too ingrained. He suddenly recalled he had promised to tend Cain's wound. "Keep watch," he signed. "If they attack again give a shout."

Tendrils of acrid smoke performed aerial dances in the main chamber. Although Smoky Woman had intentionally kept her fire small, the lack of ventilation was causing the smoke to accumulate swiftly. Steam rose off the water in the pot, giving the air a muggy feel.

Solomon Cain was on his back on a thick buffalo robe. He looked up at Nate and asked, "Are the sons of bitches still out there?"

Nate nodded. "And I suspect they have no intention of leaving any time soon. They might try to starve us out."

"I'm not about to sit in here until I'm too weak from hunger to lift my guns. We'll make a break for it come first light."

"I thought you'd decided against that notion."

Cain shifted to make himself more comfortable. "A man can change his mind, can't he? I've been lyin' here thinkin', and I have me a plan."

"Let's hear it."

"You let Smoky Woman ride double with you. Your horse is the best of the bunch, and even with her on board it'll do right fine. Until we hit cover I'll ride on one side of you and Flying Hawk will ride on the other. Between us we'll keep those pesky devils off your back."

"That's your plan?"

"Do you have a better one?" Cain said gruffly. "We sure as hell can't stay in here and rot. Sure, we might be able to hold out for a spell, but think of the horses. They can't go for long without food and water. We have to cut out, if only for their sake." Cain paused. "Unless you want to try and reach the mountains on foot."

No, Nate most definitely didn't. Kneeling, he placed the Hawken at his side and did some calculations. On foot, during the daylight hours, it would take them six hours or better to get to the eastern range, six hours of grueling travel over hot terrain with the savages dogging then every step of the way. If they went at night the journey would take even longer, but the blistering heat wouldn't be a factor.

"What do you say?" Cain prompted.

"Let's wait and see how things go," Nate hedged, bending over. "Right now we have to get your shirt off."

"Use your knife. I ain't about to try liftin' my arm."

The blade sliced into the buckskin garment easily enough. Nate started at the elbow and sliced upward, using exquisite care so as not to cut Cain. Once he had a slit from Cain's elbow to Cain's neck, he peeled back the buckskin for a closer examination. In the flickering light of the candles he saw a nasty gash, over an inch deep, above the clavicle. Blood still trickled out.

"Ain't a pretty sight, is it?" Cain asked.

"I've seen worse."

"In a way Providence was lookin' out for my hide. The vermin who did this was tryin' to bash in my head. Nearly caught me by surprise." Cain grunted when Nate touched the gash. "Go easy there, hoss. This coon ain't been in such pain since the time I tangled with a grizzly near the Green River. He came chargin' out of the brush and took a swat at me. Just one, mind you. That was enough to send me flyin' over twenty feet. About stove in all my ribs, he did."

Nate glanced at Smoky Woman. "Is the water boiling yet?"

"No."

"Let me know when it is," Nate said, and cast about for something to make bandages from. Everything except the buffalo hide and Cain's possibles bag had been taken out to use in building the barricade. "What do you have in there?" he asked, nodding at the big leather bag.

"The usual. My pipe and kinnikinnick, some sewing needles, a spool of thread, pemmican and whatnot. Why?"

Nate told him.

"I got me a white Hudson's bay blanket in my supplies. A three-pointer. Best blanket I ever owned, but it won't do me no good if I'm gone beaver. Look for a parfleche with a bunch of blue beads on the front in the shape of a raven's head. It's stuffed in there."

"I'll be right back," Nate said, and went to the barricade. Flying Hawk was now standing, leaning against the wall at the point where the barricade began. The Ute offered no comment as Nate searched until he found Cain's parfleche. Pulling out the heavy blanket, he hurried back.

By then the water was boiling vigorously. Nate cut off a towel-sized piece of blanket, partially filled a tin cup with scalding water, and squatted next to Solomon Cain. "I don't need to tell you this will hurt like the dickens."

"At least it ain't an arrow in the hump-ribs."

Cutting another, smaller, square off the Hudson's bay blanket, Nate gave it to Cain. "Something to clamp down on," he advised.

"You're right considerate."

First Nate had to wash the wound thoroughly. He did this by dipping the improvised towel in the tin cup, then applying the blanket to the gash. Cain's eyes bulged and

114

he uttered intermittent gurgling noises. The water in the cup became red with blood and Nate refilled it. Presently he had the wound clean, so he put the cup down. "I going to try and set the bone," he announced.

Cain merely grunted.

The task wasn't for the squeamish. Nate had to slide two of his fingers into the gash until he touched the sagging broken bone, which he then tugged upward until he felt it make contact with the other half. His skin crawled when he felt the two sections grate together.

Beads of perspiration dotted Cain's forehead and his hair hung limp and damp. Twice he arched his spine and turned the color of a setting sun. When the sections of bone touched he let out a strangled cry, his eyelids quivering, then slumped back, barely conscious.

Nate extracted his fingers and wiped them on his leggins. Next he cut four long, wide strips off the blanket. As he began to apply one to Cain's shoulder, Smoky Woman came over.

"Let me."

The eloquent appeal in her eyes convinced Nate to relinquish the strips. Cradling the Hawken in the crook of his elbow, he walked around the bend. Pegasus nudged him, trying to get his attention, but he walked on to the barricade. "False Tongue will be fine before a moon has passed," he signed.

Flying Hawk scowled. "It would have been better had he been killed. My sister would not abandon her people then."

"And what about her baby? Do you want her to raise the child by herself?"

"There will be no baby."

The vehemence with which the warrior gestured alarmed Nate. "You would not harm an infant?"

"There will be no baby," Flying Hawk reiterated, and turned away to stare out into the night.

Deeply disturbed, Nate walked to the horses and pretended to be interested in the Palouse while his mind whirled with the dreadful implication of the Ute's statement. Should he warn Cain and Smoky Woman or keep his mouth shut? The squabble was none of his affair but he couldn't stand by and do nothing, not with the life of an innocent at stake.

During the next hour nothing of note transpired. Nate checked on Cain and found him slumbering peacefully, Smoky Woman sitting at his side. Flying Hawk appeared to be in a foul mood so Nate left him alone.

As more time elapsed and the savages failed to attack, Nate knew his guess about their strategy had been accurate. The Indians were going to starve then out. He made a check of the food and figured there was enough to last then for a week if they ate sparingly. But, as Cain had pointed out, there was no feed for the horses.

The harrowing events of the day and night took their toll. Nate's eyelids became leaden. He made bold to approach Flying Hawk and suggested they take turns keeping watch in order for each of then to catch some sleep. The Ute agreed and volunteered to stand guard first.

Spreading his blanket near the horses, Nate reclined on his back, his head propped in his hands, and stared at the inky ceiling. Sometimes he had to wonder what could have possessed him to venture into the brutal heart of the untamed wilderness when back in New York City he could have lived in perfect safety and comfort! His Uncle Zeke had been the one who enticed his by implying he would acquire the greatest treasure a man could own. And off he'd gone, mistakenly believing Zeke was referring to gold, when all the time Zeke had been talking about an entirely different and greater treasure, the priceless gift of untrammeled freedom.

Was true freedom worth all he went through simply to stay alive? The question itself was ridiculous. He remembered life in New York City, with countless thousands scurrying to and from work each day, toiling ceaselessly to make ends meet, to put food on the table and keep a roof over their heads. Yes, they lived in safety and relative comfort, but at what price? They were slaves to the money they earned, caught in a vicious circle from which there was no escape unless by some miracle they should become rich, in which case they would hoard their wealth like squirrels hoarded pine cones and nuts, as miserly with their riches as they had been in their poverty.

He started to yawn, and suppressed it lest he make a sound. Closing his eyes, he envisioned his wife's beautiful face floating in the air above him, and he wondered if he would ever see that face again.

Sleep abruptly claimed him.

The light touch of something on his shoulder brought Nate up with a start. His hand closed on the Hawken as he blinked and looked around to see Flying Hawk beside him.

"Your time," the Ute signed.

"Oh," Nate mumbled in English. He shook his head to clear lingering cobwebs, then stood and motioned for Flying Hawk to use his blanket. After a moment's hesitation the warrior accepted the offer.

By the position of the few stars Nate could see from behind the barricade, he estimated the time to be close to four in the morning. Flying Hawk had stood guard for more than half the night. Settling down where he commanded a clear view of the area outside, Nate leaned the Hawken within easy reach.

Soon dawn would break. The temperature would climb steadily until by noon they would be sweltering even in the cave. Without water they would be parched by sundown.

Idly glancing to his left, he was surprised to see the dead savages had been piled in the gap between the barricade and the far wall, effectively blocking off the opening. Flying Hawk had been busy during the night.

As he stared at the corpses his memory was jogged. Somewhere, sometime, he'd heard something about Indians who were just like or very similar to these. But where? Then he recollected the Rendezvous of '27. Or was it '28? In any event, he'd been seated around a campfire with nine or ten other men listening to Jim Bridger relate various adventures.

At one point Bridger told one of his favorite stories, about the time back in '24 when he and a group of friends took to arguing over how far Bear River went. Bets were wagered. Bridger was picked to go find out. He shot a buffalo and stretched the skin hide over a framework of willow branches to make a bullboat. Then off he went.

Mile after mile Bridger followed the river until he came to a huge body of water no white man had ever laid eyes on before. When he dipped his hand in he was astonished to find the water was salty. Bridger had just discovered Big Salt Lake, as the trappers usually referred to it.

During the course of this story Bridger had talked about various Indian tribes inhabiting the region, and then repeated a story told to him by a Snake warrior. West of the Salt Lake, the Snake had claimed, lived a tribe known as the Root Eaters, or Digger Indians, who went around stark naked and lived on roots, seeds, fish, frogs, and whatever else they could find. Some of them were supposed to be as hairy as bears. The Snake had spoken of then with contempt, comparing them to animals.

Were these the same tribe? Or another just like the Diggers? Bridger had not mentioned anything about the Root Eaters having a taste for human flesh, as the bones in the back chamber indicated these did. Perhaps, Nate reasoned, his imagination was getting the better of him. Perhaps these Indians didn't eat captives. Nonetheless, they were extremely dangerous.

Shortly the sky grew progressively lighter. The stars faded by gradual degrees. A pink and orange tinge painted the eastern horizon and transformed the snowcaps on the regal peaks into crowns of radiant glory.

Nate stretched and rubbed his eyes. He could use ten or twelve hours of undisturbed sleep, a luxury he was unlikely to enjoy for quite some time. Since he had taken over the watch there had been no sign of the savages, but as sure as he was breathing he knew they were lurking out there, hidden, just waiting their chance.

The soft patter of feet made him turn.

"Good morning," Smoky Woman said softly.

"How's Cain doing?" Nate inquired.

"Very weak. Very hot. Skin burn."

"Do you still have some of the water left?"

"Yes," Smoky Woman answered, and held up her hand, her thumb and forefinger extended and several inches apart. "This much."

Which wasn't much at all, Nate reflected dourly. Before noon they must decide whether to make a dash for the spring or to suffer through the whole day and try after dark. Given Cain's condition, they could ill afford to wait that long.

"I forget thank you what you do last night," Smoky Woman said."

"I did what I had to."

"You not like him?"

Rather than hurt her feelings by being frank, Nate said, "I've met more trustworthy folks in my time."

"Cain good man."

Only a fool disputed with a woman in love over the object of her affections, and Nate was no fool. "I hope you're right, for your sake," was all he said.

An uncomfortable silence descended. Nate, aware he was wasting his time, occupied himself by scanning their vicinity for concealed savages.

"You like pemmican or jerky for breakfast?" Smoky Woman inquired.

"Jerky will do me fine," Nate said, his gaze on her until she rounded the turn. He saw Flying Hawk's eyes snap open and suspected the warrior had been awake for some time. "Morning," he said with a smile.

Flying Hawk gave a curt nod and slowly stood. The quiver went across his back. The powerful bow was held in his brawny left hand as he stepped to the barricade and peered out.

"All has been quiet," Nate signed.

As if to prove Nate wrong, a lone savage 40 yards out darted from one boulder to another, his body a blur. One moment he was there, the next he wasn't. If not for a tiny swirl of dust the man made, Nate would have doubted his eyes.

Flying Hawk had whipped up the bow, but the savage was under cover before he could nock a shaft.

"I wonder how many more are out there," Nate mused aloud. He'd seen five last night, but there might be many times that number. When the time came to try for the spring he'd probably find out exactly how many there were.

That time came sooner than anticipated. An hour and a half later, with the heat rising steadily, Smoky Woman came to Nate and said urgently, "Come see. Cain very bad."

One look at the sweat glistening on Cain's feverish brow, listening to Cain mutter incoherently as he tossed and turned on the buffalo hide, was enough to persuade Nate they must obtain fresh water immediately since the pot was almost empty. Smoky Woman had been draping wet cloths on Cain's brow and neck to keep his temperature down. Since they couldn't exactly stroll out to the spring and back, they'd need a better container than the pot to hold the water or risk spilling most of it along the way. "Does Cain own a water bag?" he inquired.

"I think yes," Smoky Woman responded. "I see." Spinning, she scurried off.

Nate stayed with Cain, sopping sweat off the man's face, until she came back bearing an old, empty water bag made from a buffalo bladder. It had not seen use in quite a spell. He would have to remember not to fill it to the top or it might burst. "We'll need your help," he told Smoky Woman.

"Anything."

He led her to the barricade and gave her Cain's rifle and pistol. "You stay with your brother. No matter what happens, don't let those savages get in here."

"You go alone?"

"One of us has to," Nate responded, and set down the Hawken. He wanted his hands free to carry the water bag and to bring his pistols into play when the savages tried to stop him, as they surely would. Giving her a reassuring smile while butterflies swarmed in his stomach, Nate placed a hand on top of the barricade and tensed to vault over it.

Chapter
Ten

Flying Hawk suddenly stepped forward and grasped Nate's arm, then he addressed his sister, speaking swiftly.

"What does he want?" Nate asked when the warrior finished.

"Want both you go," Smoky Woman translated.

"No. Tell him he must defend the cave. If we both went, and if we both should be taken captive or worse, you'd be on your own. I can't allow that," Nate said. He waited impatiently as his words were relayed. Then, before the warrior could lodge another objection, he vaulted over the barricade and instantly broke into a run, going at his top speed toward the spring. Once again he hugged the wall, but little good it did him.

Nate had not covered ten feet when a chorus of shrill whoops signified the savages had spotted him. A grimy brute popped up as if spewed from the earth itself and bore down on him with an uplifted club. Nate's right hand flashed for a pistol. The next moment a streaking shaft struck the savage on the side of the neck and went completely through, the bloody point protruding six inches. Staggered, the savage stumbled, clutched at the shaft, then whirled and made for another boulder.

Nate never broke stride. A lance glittered as it arced on high, swooped down at him, and thudded into the earth a yard to his rear. Darts rained down, a few at first, then more and more. He began weaving and ducking to make it harder for them to hit him. When he drew within 20 feet of the pool he nearly died.

A chunk of rock the size of his thigh came hurtling down from above, missing his by less than six inches, and slammed with terrific force into the ground. Unable to stop, he tripped over the rock and sprawled onto his hands and knees. Twisting, he shot a glance at the rim and saw several heads outlined against the sky just as one of the savages shoved a large boulder over the edge.

Nate flung himself away from the wall and rolled. He heard a tremendous crash, and swore the earth shook when the boulder smashed down on the exact spot where he had tripped. Pushing erect, he raced madly for the spring.

A dart nearly took off his nose.

Then he was there, dropping to his knees and shoving the open water bag under the surface. Bubbles rose in a flurry. One hand holding the bag, he shifted to check behind him.

Two savages, one armed with a lance, the other a club, were rapidly closing.

His pistol blossomed in his hand and spat smoke and lead. The savage with the lance, shot in the shoulder, jerked at the impact and fell. Fearlessly the second savage came on, his club waving in the air above his head.

Nate dared not let go of the water bag. It was becoming heavier and heavier as it filled, and if he let go it might sink to the bottom. He was forced to tuck the spent flintlock under his belt and draw his other one with his left hand alone, which slowed him down so much that the savage was almost upon him before he got the other pistol out. The club whizzed at his head. Dropping low, Nate hastily pointed the pistol at the man and fired. He meant to send the ball into the savage's chest but in his haste he shot too low.

The ball bored into the Indian's groin, sheering off part of his organ. Howling like a banshee, the savage dropped his club and clutched his shattered manhood. He looked at Nate, his lips flecked with spittle, his eyes aflame with hatred.

Nate hit him, a short swipe of the flintlock that clipped the Indian on the temple and brought the man to his knees, stunned. As Nate raised the pistol for another blow the savage abruptly surged straight at him, head lowered, a human battering ram. Nate tried to get his arm down to block the rush but failed. In dismay he felt the man's head slam into his chest, propelling his rearward, into the pool.

A cool, wet blanket enveloped his body. He sank under to his chin. Somehow he retained his grip on the water bag and the pistol. His legs thrashing to keep him afloat, he saw the savage also in the pool, treading water and reaching for him with thick fingers formed into crushing claws.

Nate evaded the Indian's clutches, pedaling backwards. He had to get out of the pool and get out fast. Should another savage appear he'd be killed in an instant. Angling to the left, he swam for the edge, hauling the almost full water bag in his wake. The savage pursued him, swimming awkwardly, weakly, a crimson ring forming around the man's midsection and spreading upward.

Yet another dart splashed into the pool within a hand's width of Nate's face. Breathing heavily, he reached the rock rim, his right arm aching terribly from the weight of the bag. He hooked his left elbow on the rim, bunched his shoulder muscles, and pulled himself out.

What he needed most was a respite to catch his breath, but Fate dictated otherwise. A pair of iron hands clamped on his neck from behind and he was bodily lifted into the air. In order to fight back he had to release the water bag, which fell under his feet, water pouring from the narrow neck.

Nate lashed backwards with his right elbow and felt it connect with what seemed like a solid slab of marble. He tried the same tactic with his left elbow, slanting it higher, and this time connected with the savage's cheek. Simultaneously he kicked to the rear, driving his foot up and in, knowing his life hung in the balance.

Gurgling in rage, the savage heaved Nate aside as if he was no more than a child's doll. Nate landed hard on his right side, pain lancing from his elbow to his shoulder. His arm tingled, going numb as he stood. He still held a useless pistol in his left arm, which he wielded as a club when the savage sprang.

Although shorter, the savage was much heavier, so much so that Nate lost his balance and fell, the Indian on top of him. He found himself looking into the darkest, beadiest, most animal-like eyes he had ever seen on another human being, so bestial they reminded him of the eyes of bears. And in those eyes gleamed the promise of his death.

Desperately Nate slammed the flintlock onto the man's jaw, but the savage was unaffected. Those thick fingers closed on his throat, shutting off his windpipe. In less than a minute he would lose consciousness if his neck wasn't crushed before then. Gritting his teeth, he managed to move his tingling right arm and grab his tomahawk. The savage's thumbs were gouging deep into his throat and he thought his flesh would be pried apart.

Nate wrenched the tomahawk free, swung it out to the side, then drove the wide razor edge into the Indian's torso below the left arm. With a pantherish screech, the savage let go and leaped upright, a hand pressed to the profusely bleeding wound above his ribs.

Twisting, Nate pressed his advantage, arcing the tomahawk in a tight half-circle that brought the blade down on top of the savage's foot. The toes were chopped clean off and a red geyser spurted from the stub.

The savage, howling in fury, lifted his foot and clasped it. Behind him the Indian with the wounded groin was trying to climb out of the pool.

Nate's foot flicked out and crunched into the knee of the savage in front of him, knocking the man backwards into the Indian struggling to clamber from the water. Both men plunged under the surface. In the clear at last, Nate slid the pistol under his belt, scooped up the water bag in his left hand, and ran for the cave.

Darts zipped from several directions. Big stones were hurled down at him from above. A lance came close to bringing his down.

A whirlwind of motion, Nate constantly zigzagged, never running in a straight line for more than a few feet at a time. He saw Flying Hawk jump over the barricade and begin shooting arrows at an incredible rate, covering him. His foot hit a rut and he tripped, almost falling but righting himself with a supreme effort at the last moment.

Then he was near the cave and sailing because he'd successfully thwarted death and bucked the odds. He saw Smoky Woman behind the barricade, smiling too because now they had enough water to get by for a while, more than enough to use to keep Cain's fever under control. But their joy was premature and short-lived.

He dashed past Flying Hawk, and tensed to leap over the barricade when something jarred his left hand. Assuming he had banged the water bag against the barricade, he went on over and dropped to his knees to catch his breath. Caked with sweat, he wiped a sleeve across his brow, then stuck the tomahawk under his belt and turned to the water bag.

Smoky Woman's gasp echoed his own.

A dart had struck the bag at the bottom, rupturing the old skin and creating a hole several inches in diameter. The water was pouring out, and already over half of the contents had spilled onto the dry earth.

Frantically Nate scooped the bag up and tried to stem the flow with his hand, to no avail. Rising, he ran to the chamber, to the pot, and emptied what was left into it. Barely an inch covered the bottom of the pot when the last drop splashed down.

Disheartened, Nate looked at Solomon Cain, and was surprised to see him awake and alert although coated with perspiration from the fever. Cain glanced from the water bag to the pot to Nate's face.

"You made it to the spring, I take it."

Nate wearily nodded.

"Thank you for tryin'," Cain said, and coughed. "You share that water amongst yourselves. There's no need to waste any of it on me."

"Don't talk foolishness."

"I'm no fool, King. I'm burnin' up inside. My wound is infected. There's poison in my system."

"You'll pull through."

"Like hell. I ain't goin' to make it and you know it."

A low cry heralded Smoky Woman's rush to Cain's side. "Not talk this way! You strong! You live!"

"I'd surely like to," Cain met her gaze. "But bein' as strong as an ox don't count for much when the Reaper

127

comes a-callin'. Even an ox dies sometimes."

Nate dropped the water bag and put a hand on Smoky Woman's shoulder. "Pay him no mind. It's the fever talking. We'll see to it that he gets out of here alive."

She knelt and touched Cain's face. "We need water. Much water."

"I'll try again as soon as I'm rested up," Nate proposed.

Cain tried to sit up but couldn't. "Now who's talkin' foolishness?" he rasped. "Those bastards out there ain't about to let you reach the pool a second time. They'll keep a real close guard on it, and they'll be ready for you if you try."

"I have no choice."

"Yes, you do. Come nightfall you have to get Smoky Woman out of here. Take that pigheaded brother of hers and light out for the mountains to the east. By mornin' you'll be in the clear."

"And what about you?"

Cain vented a bitter laugh. "I know my time has run its course. You just leave me here. I couldn't ride far anyway."

"We're not about to desert you," Nate declared, thinking that a day or so earlier he might have been differently inclined. "If we leave, you're leaving with us. And that's final."

"I'm surrounded by pigheads," Cain muttered.

Smoky Woman gently touched his lips and said sternly, "You be quiet! Rest until better."

Leaving them, Nate walked to the barricade and occupied himself with reloading both pistols while contemplating what to do. He had to admit that Cain was right. The savages would be clustered around the pool as thick as bees around a hive. He'd never make it there and back a second time. And since they couldn't very well stay in the cave and let themselves be starved into submission, they had to do just as Cain had proposed: cut out after dark.

They would ride light, taking only a parfleche or two filled with food. The rest of Cain's provisions—and the packs of gold—would have to be left behind.

He debated whether they should split up or stick together, and decided on the latter. There was strength in numbers, and if one of them went down the others would be right there to help. The next issue to decide was which direction to take. Going to the north was impossible because of the cliff, and riding westward, even though the land was flat and relatively open, would necessitate making too wide a loop through hostile territory in order to swing around and reach the mountain range to the east. If they went to the south they'd come on the dry wash, which he suspected harbored a few savages since it was an ideal spot to hide. So the only option left them was to ride like hell to the east, up and over the rise before the savages pierced then with lances and darts. Once they had the rise behind them, they could easily outdistance their pursuers.

Or so he hoped, anyway, as he finished reloading the flintlocks and wedged them under his belt. Retrieving the Hawken, he suddenly realized the Ute was staring pointedly at him. "You have a question?" he signed.

"I have an idea," the warrior clarified.

"Tell me."

Flying Hawk glanced at the bend, then moved closer to sign, "I say we give False Tongue to them. He is the one to blame for this, and he will not live long anyway. If we tie him to one of the horses and send the horse out, the strange ones who seek to count coup on us will go after him. While they are busy we can escape."

The cruel suggestion further impressed Nate with Flying Hawk's hatred of Cain. And while he could understand the Ute's feelings, he couldn't condone them. "Do you think your sister will stand by and do nothing while we send False Tongue to his death?"

"You can hold her while I do what is needed."

"No. I will not take sides in your dispute."

"Why do you care what happens to False Tongue? Look at all the trouble he had brought down on your head. You should want to see him dead as much as I do."

"I will not be a party to killing a man who can not defend himself."

Flying Hawk uttered an explosive "Wagh!" and turned away in disgust.

Nate didn't attempt to press the matter. He recognized doing so would be futile. Flying Hawk was too blinded by bigotry to ever listen to the moderating voice of reason, Only Cain's death would satisfy the Ute.

Nate went to the horses and gave Pegasus a rubdown. The gelding and the other two mounts stood with their heads hung low, hungry and thirsty and hot. Regrettably, there wasn't enough room for any of them to lie down. All three had relieved themselves in the passageway during the night and the smell was becoming worse by the hour.

Nate waited a sufficient length of time for Flying Hawk to cool down, then went over and broached the subject of leaving once night fell. The Ute made no comment until the very end.

"Who will Cain ride with? It will not be me."

"I have the fastest horse so I'll be the one," Nate volunteered, keenly aware of the disadvantage he would face when the time came for them to flee. He saw Flying Hawk smile. Why? Was the warrior inwardly gloating because he knew it would be a miracle if Nate and Cain got further than 30 yards from the cave?

Brooding, he sat down near the barricade and spent the next several hours racking his brain for another way out of their fix. He considered everything from sneaking out and trying to pick the savages off one by one to starting a huge fire at the cave entrance and escaping under cover of the smoke. Few of his ideas were practical. None were appealing. If they sneaked out the savages would probably pick them off instead. And thick smoke would blind them as well as the Indians, slowing them down during the precious span of seconds when they'd need all the speed their mounts could muster.

The golden sun climbed steadily upward, passed its zenith, and slid toward the western horizon. Outside nothing moved. The landscape gave off shimmering waves of heat that distorted objects in the distance.

Nate used an old trick that made a person salivate more than usual to partially ease his thirst; he stuck a pebble in his mouth. About two in the afternoon Flying Hawk asked him to stand watch for a while alone, and he agreed. The warrior promptly went back to the chamber. Shortly thereafter angry voices could be heard.

As Nate surveyed the ground outside he saw that the bodies of the Indians slain that morning had all vanished. Like the Apaches, these savages never left their dead behind, perhaps out of fear the bodies would be mutilated. Of course, they hadn't been able to get the ones in the cave. Yet.

The heat and the lack of activity combined to produce waves of drowsiness, which he fought off with repeated shakes of his head. To pass the time and to stay awake he sharpened his butcher knife and the tomahawk.

A while later Flying Hawk returned. His lips were thin slits, his eyes blazing with fury. "She will not listen to me!" he signed angrily.

Nate responded with, "If there is one important lesson I have learned from being married, it is that women have minds of their own. They do not like for men to tell them what to do. Most do not even like for men to make suggestions. So your sister is no exception. Women are more independent than most men give them credit for being."

"I am only concerned for her," Flying Hawk signed. "I do not want to see her spend the rest of her life in misery." He paused. "She belongs with my people, not with yours."

"She belongs wherever she will be happiest, and you have made it plain that your people will not take kindly to her having a child fathered by a white man."

"I have influence in our councils. I might be able to persuade our people to accept the child."

"And if you failed?"

"The Utes are many, with many villages. We would find one where they would allow my sister to live in peace, where they would let her child live as a Ute should."

Here was an unexpected development. Previously Flying Hawk had been unwilling to countenance the child's birth; now the warrior was willing to help his sister raise the child if she would stay with their people. There was hope for the man after all, Nate reflected wryly. "Smoky Woman does not want to do this?" he asked.

"No," Flying Hawk gestured sharply. "She still wants to live with False Tongue among your kind. All my words were wasted on her ears." He looked at Nate. "Would you talk to her?"

"It is not my place."

"Or is it that you do not agree with me? Do you believe she would be better off among your people than mine?"

"What I think does not count. She has made her decision and nothing I could say would change it."

Scowling, Flying Hawk leaned both arms on the top of the barricade, effectively ending their conversation.

The remainder of the afternoon passed in strained silence. Nate kept to himself and the warrior did the same. When, eventually, the shadows lengthened and the sun neared the horizon, Nate stirred and signed, "It is time to get ready."

He saddled Pegasus and brought the Palouse close to the barricade, then let the reins dangle. His parfleches were easy to locate and he strapped them on behind the saddle. The other horses were left bareback for the Utes.

Smoky Woman had Cain's head cradled on her lap and was wiping his face with a damp cloth when Nate entered. Mercifully Cain had passed out again.

"We'll be leaving soon," he announced.

"Him very weak."

"I know. We'll use some rope and tie him to me so he won't fall off."

"Tie him to me."

Nate touched her elbow. "I'm a mite bigger and stronger than you are. He's less likely to pull me off if he starts to fall."

Lambent pools of abiding affection were turned on him. "He pressed to my heart."

"I know."

"Take care of him."

"I will," Nate pledged sincerely.

Flying Hawk lent a reluctant hand at Nate's request in carrying the unconscious man from the chamber. They moved slowly to avoid jostling Cain, who mumbled the whole time, and set him down on his back next to Pegasus. Nate swung up, then inched forward as far as he could to make room for Cain.

While Smoky Woman helped to hold Solomon steady, Flying Hawk brought the rope over. With Nate helping, they quickly looped it several times around Cain's lower back and Nate's midsection, arranging the knot so it was just above Nate's buckle where he could get at it readily.

Smoky Woman mounted, Cain's pistol in her right hand, his rifle in her left, her eyes locked on the man she loved.

The warrior, ducking low, went to the end of the barricade and rolled the corpses aside to make an opening for the horses. Scooting back, he held his bow in his right hand and climbed onto the third animal.

Nate could feel the heavy weight of Cain's body pressing against him, compelling him to stiffen his back muscles to stay upright. It wasn't that Cain was heavy. Quite the contrary. But in Cain's current state he was just so much dead weight. Suddenly Nate was taken aback to feel Cain stir feebly.

"What the hell is goin' on? Why am I on a horse?"

"We're cutting out, Solomon," Nate said, twisting his head. "So shush until we're in the clear."

Cain blinked a few times, his forehead furrowed. "The gold, King? Are you bringing the gold?"

There was a despondent, pleading quality to Cain's tone that caused Nate to do something he rarely did. "Yes, we're taking it with us. Now don't talk and hold on tight."

A weak nod was Cain's reply.

Outside, twilight had claimed the wasteland. Nate held the reins loosely in his right hand, the Hawken tight in his left, and anxiously waited for the darkness to deepen. Solomon Cain passed out again and began breathing deeply. Pegasus fidgeted. So did the other horses. All three were eager to leave the cramped confines of the cave.

At last Nate judged the time to be ripe, and with a lash of the reins and a poke of his heels he rode Pegasus out into the ominous night.

Chapter
Eleven

The moment Nate was clear of the cave he reined to the left and galloped toward the rise, Smoky Woman and Flying Hawk right behind him. Twelve hoofs drummed in staccato rhythm, clattering on the rocky ground, making enough racket to alert every savage within a quarter of a mile. A harsh cry to the south was attended by a series of cries from the vicinity of the spring and a couple more from on top of the cliff.

Pegasus was a pied-colored streak, his head level with his flowing body, his mane flying. It was all Nate could do to stay in the saddle. Not because of the gelding. Solomon Cain was flapping wildly against him and swaying with every stride the Palouse took, threatening to topple them both. Too late Nate discovered the rope wasn't holding Cain as securely as he'd thought it would.

On he galloped anyway, knowing to slow down now was certain suicide. The rise loomed directly ahead. He swept up the slope, and had gotten a third of the way to the top when to his rear a horse whinnied in pain and there was a tremendous crash.

Now Nate did slow and glance back. He was horrified to see Smoky Woman's mount had gone down, a lance jutting from its heaving side. She had lost both guns in the tumble but was unhurt. Springing up, she lifted her arms at a yell from her brother. The next second Flying Hawk reached her and yanked her roughly up behind him. Then, using his bow as a quirt, the warrior started up the slope.

Darts were flying fast and thick. Lances cleaved the air. The enraged cries of the pursuing savages would have brought gooseflesh to a dead man.

Nate goaded Pegasus upward. The gelding had lost a lot of momentum and struggled to go faster. A whizzing dart clipped Nate's shoulder but didn't draw any blood. Another nicked the Palouse's ear and did.

"Go! Go!" Nate urged, slapping his legs against Pegasus's sides. All it would take was one lucky hit and any hope of escape would be shattered. He heard Cain groan and imagined the pain the man must be feeling, but there was nothing he could do about it until they were far, far away.

Suddenly Smoky Woman yelled something in Ute.

Looking back, Nate saw Flying Hawk hunched low over their mount and Smoky Woman tugging furiously at her brother's shoulder. He understood why when her hand appeared clutching a bloody dart. The warrior, his teeth clenched, straightened and kept on coming.

Just a little further! Nate told himself. Just a little further and they would be over the crest and safe from the deluge of darts and spears. Only 20 feet to go. Then 15. Then ten. He whooped for joy when Pegasus plunged down the other side, then caught himself and looked back at the Utes.

Brother and sister were hard on his heels.

Nate smiled broadly. They'd done it! A tingle of excitement at their deliverance coursed through him, only to be tempered by the sight of dark shapes appearing at the top of the rise. The savages were still after them and coming on fast!

Bending forward, Nate rode for his life and the life of the man strapped to his back. More darts reined down. Flying Hawk's horse neighed wildly but continued to race pell-mell across the sinister wasteland.

Soon the darts stopped seeking them. The shapes of the savages evaporated in the gloom.

Nate was exceptionally alert to the flow of the terrain. A misstep now could cost Pegasus or the other horse a broken leg. So he studied the land ahead with care. Thanks to a sliver of moon he could see well enough to avoid obstacles such as ruts, boulders, and crevices.

For 20 minutes they rode hard, until Nate was positive they were safe. Then he reined up in a spray of dust and waited for the Utes to catch up. During the flight they had fallen a dozen yards behind, and now, as they drew to a stop alongside him, their horse wheezed and stumbled.

Smoky Woman was off the animal in a lithe bound. Her brother, wincing, dismounted slowly and stood with a hand pressed to his wounded shoulder.

Nate was staring aghast at the horse. The poor animal had taken three darts, one in the neck and two in the side. Dark stains caused by copiously flowing blood marked its coat. Additional blood trickled from its flaring nostrils.

"How Cain?" Smoky Woman asked, stepping up and resting a hand on Solomon's thigh.

"Doing fine, near as I can tell," Nate said. He tugged at the stubborn knot, then impatiently whipped out his butcher knife and sliced the loops in half.

Cain promptly sagged, his chin touching his chest, and started to fall off. Instantly Smoky Woman braced him with her hands and said, "Help, please!"

Quickly sliding off, Nate jammed the knife into its sheath and took hold of Cain's waist to ease him from the saddle. Smoky Woman grasped Cain's slack legs. Together they carefully lowered him to the ground, onto his back, and she knelt to examine him closely, running her hands over his body as she probed for darts.

The wounded horse picked that moment to take a few steps, halt, and nicker pathetically. Staggering, it tottered to the left. Then its front knees buckled and it sank down, puffing like a steam engine.

Closer scrutiny showed Nate that the dart in the animal's neck was so firmly imbedded as to be impossible to get out by hand. It would have to be dug out with a knife. The other two, though, protruded enough to be firmly grasped, so with vigorous pulling he was able to pluck them loose. The horse whinnied in agony as the second was extracted, and a torrent of fresh blood pumped from the hole.

Nate cast the darts from him with an angry jerk. If they had the time and enough water and forage they might be able to nurse the wounded animal back to health. But of course they had none of those things. The poor horse was doomed and there was nothing he could do except put it out of its misery now rather than let it linger on for a few days in the most abominable torment. And he couldn't use a gun since the sound of a shot would carry for a mile or more in the rarified mountain air.

The hilt of the butcher knife molded to his palm as he stepped up to the horse's neck and felt for the telltale jugular groove. Draping his left arm over the neck, he squeezed to keep the neck still long enough for his right hand to slash open the jugular, then he jumped back before the crimson geyser that spurted forth could drench him.

Again the horse nickered, soft and low, and shook its head as if at buzzing flies. Its great breaths became more labored than ever. Slowly the head drooped.

Nate turned, unwilling to watch the animal die. He disliked having to dispatch it. His only consolation was that according to some old-timers he had talked to, bleeding to death was a painless way to go. There was little if any pain. It was more like the sensation of falling asleep, all drowsy and tingly and bizarrely pleasant.

Smoky Woman had her hand on Cain's forehead. "Him still much hot," she said.

"He'll be all right once we're in the mountains," Nate said, although inwardly he lacked complete conviction. First they must get Cain there, which promised to be a formidable task given there might be more savages around. And too, infections were difficult to eliminate under the best of circumstances; they still had many miles to travel across the inhospitable pocket of desolation, which would only make Cain's condition worse.

Nate glanced at Flying Hawk, who stood stoically nearby. "How are you?" he signed, as usual amplifying his motions so they would be easily understood in the dark.

The warrior grunted.

"Let me see," Nate signed, moving behind him. The dart, he saw, had penetrated several inches and left a finger-sized hole when it had been wrenched out. Thankfully, the wound had stopped bleeding, indicating the dart had not severed any large blood vessels.

Solomon Cain groaned and tossed as would someone having a bad dream.

"We have to press on," Nate said.

"Cain need rest," Smoky Woman objected.

"When we're safe. We haven't gone all that far yet, and for all we know our enemies can run long distances without tiring, just like the Apaches do. They might be closing in on us even as we speak. When we reach the mountains he can rest."

She thought for a moment, then rose and pointed at the gelding. "You go ahead. Take Cain."

Now it was Nate's turn to object. "I'm not leaving Flying Hawk and you here all alone," he declared.

"You go fast," she insisted. "We come later."

Should he or shouldn't he? Nate wondered. She had a valid point, namely that he could get Cain to safety, to that sheltered park where the grass was green and the water deliciously cold, well before dawn if he rode off right that minute. There Cain would get all the rest he needed. But Nate balked at the idea of deserting the two Utes, leaving them stranded, afoot, with Flying Hawk hurt. They would be unable to stand off the savages if they were found. Sighing, he said, "No. We'll stay together."

Simmering with frustration, Smoky Woman clenched her fists. "You go fast. Get Cain safe."

"No. We go together," Nate emphasized as he stooped and slid both hands under Cain's shoulders. A look and a nod at Flying Hawk was sufficient to bring the warrior over, and presently they had Cain in the saddle with his legs tied tight to the stirrups and additional rope securing him to the saddle horn.

Nate grasped the reins and assumed the lead, but he only took a single pace when the reins were torn from his grasp by Smoky Woman, who angrily motioned for him to keep walking. She intended to take care of Cain herself.

"As you wish," Nate said softly, going on. Her resentment upset him, yet not enough to make him change his mind. There were four lives at stake, not just one, and he had a responsibility to do his damnedest to insure all four of them survived. She would thank him, later, if they ran into trouble.

The minutes dragged past as if weighted with an anchor. A total and unnatural quiet pervaded their surroundings. Missing were the typical night sounds of yipping coyotes, howling wolves, hooting owls, and snarling panthers. Even the insects, if there were any, were silent.

Nate checked to their rear time and again. His warning about the savages being able to duplicate the feats of the Apaches was no idle chatter. Apaches were marvelous long-distance runners, able to cover 70 miles at a steady dogtrot. It was very possible the Diggers or Root Eaters, if such they were, could do the same.

Occasionally he tilted his head back to admire the magnificent celestial display overhead. Back in New York City, he had barely looked at the stars. Out here, among the mile-high Rockies, they resembled brilliant torches, flaring bright and proud in the sprawling firmament, countless in number, awesome in aspect. He never tired of viewing the nightly spectacle.

A faint scratching noise wafted on the breeze.

Pausing, Nate gazed to the northwest but saw nothing to arouse concern. Whether man or beast or freak of Nature had made the sound, he had no way of determining. Shrugging, he hiked on, staring at the inky silhouettes of the eastern range which seemed so very far away.

Flying Hawk joined his sister and the two conversed in soft whispers. The warrior, Nate noticed, held his right arm bent close to his body, evidence the shoulder wound was bothering him severely.

By Nate's reckoning an hour and a half had elapsed when they came to a ridge of caprock. At its base Smoky

Woman halted and cast a critical eye at him. "We stop little bit?" she asked.

Nate didn't see any harm in a few minutes of rest. "Yes."

With her brother's aid, Smoky Woman took Cain down and laid him on a flat stretch of solid rock. She borrowed her brother's knife to cut a strip from the hem of her buckskin dress, then moistened the strip with her spittle so she could cool Cain's face and neck.

Nate thought to open a parfleche and remove several pieces of jerked venison. He offered one to Flying Hawk, who accepted it with a nod, and to Smoky Woman, who vigorously shook her head. He extended his hand, saying, "You really should eat something. You need to keep up your strength." But to his consternation, she swatted his hand aside and shifted so her back was to him.

Deeply chagrined, Nate moved a couple of yards off and sat with his left shoulder propped against a boulder. So that was the thanks he got for trying to do the right thing! She didn't want to have anything to do with him.

He chewed absently, barely aware of the tangy taste that normally he liked so much. Gazing around, he realized Flying Hawk was staring at him. When he ventured a friendly smile, the Ute turned away. Puzzled, he scratched his chin and tried to make sense of the warrior's behavior. Were they both mad at him? Smoky Woman he could understand, but not her brother.

A few minutes later Nate stood and coughed to clear his throat. "We should be moving on," he proposed.

Without saying a word, Smoky Woman and Flying Hawk put Cain back on Pegasus. They tied him as before. Then Smoky Woman took the reins and moved out, staying close to the base of the ridge. Her brother fell into step behind her, leaving Nate to follow at his leisure.

Slanting the Hawken over his left shoulder, Nate did just that. He was almost sorry he hadn't taken Smoky Woman up on her request to ride off with Cain. It would serve them right, he reflected, if the savages caught up with them when he wasn't on hand to help in the fight.

Shortly thereafter Nate dimly heard an indistinct noise, this time to the south. Peering into the darkness proved unavailing. If there was something or someone out there, they were virtual ghosts.

He kept a close watch on their back trail from then on. If the savages were dogging them, the attack, when it came, would be swift and silent. He imagined getting a dart between the shoulder blades, and his skin prickled from head to toe.

Presently the wind picked up, gusting violently as it often did in the high country. There were no trees to rustle, no grass to bend, but it did howl among the benches and gorges, the bluffs and the canyons, moaning and wailing like a forlorn soul fated to endlessly wander the earth in search of eternal rest.

Nate hoped a storm wasn't approaching. Solomon Cain couldn't withstand a steady soaking; weakened as he was, Cain would come down with the chills, perhaps even contract pneumonia. Scanning the heavens confirmed the sky was cloudless, alleviating Nate's fears.

The encounter with the primitive Indians gave Nate cause to wonder how many other unknown tribes existed west of the Mississippi. The vast territory was essentially unexplored, so who could say what lurked in the depths of the verdant forests or in remote recesses like the wasteland he was now in? He'd heard tales of Indians living in fabulous cliff cities far to the southwest, and fantastic stories of Indians living on the northern Pacific Coast who hunted huge whales from flimsy craft. Previously he had been skeptical of any and all such reports, but the more he learned of the limitless land of mystery in which he had elected to dwell, the more he appreciated the truth of the age-old belief that there were more things in heaven and on earth than humankind dreamed of. And some of them were better left alone.

One day, though, Nate wanted to venture to the Pacific Ocean and perhaps explore regions of the continent seldom if ever visited by white men. Abiding within him was a perpetual curiosity about what might lie beyond the next horizon. He'd like to see those cliff cities and watch a boatload of Indians hunt one of the great whales. He'd like to penetrate to the heart of the many wonders waiting to be discovered by those bold enough to challenge the unknown.

When that day would come, he had no idea. For now he had a wife and son to think of. Providing for them was his first priority. He felt confident that at some point in the future an opportunity would arise to satisfy his craving to explore. Until then he would be patient.

His short sleep of the night before had done little to refresh him, and now the toll of the long day and the desperate flight brought fatigue to his limbs and drowsiness to his mind. Often his heavy eyelids tried to stay shut, and he would energetically shake his head and yawn each time as he fought to stay alert.

Solomon Cain commenced snoring, a low rumble like that of a hibernating bear.

Nate wished the man would stop. The snoring would drown out any slight noises that might herald an attack by the savages. He forced his sluggish faculties to razor sharpness and scoured the empty landscape on all sides. Not a hint of movement could be detected.

Then he got a surprise. He saw Smoky Woman hand the reins to her brother and come back to fall into step beside him.

"I sorry," she said softly in her heavily accented English.

"For what?" Nate responded without thinking.

"For treating you poorly."

"You had your reasons, I reckon."

"No excuse. You do what right by stay with us. Brother make that clear."

"He did?" Nate replied in mild amazement that the Ute had spoken up in his defense. "I figured he was mad at me too."

"Him not like whites, but him say you man of honor."

"Be sure and thank your brother for the compliment."

They strolled for a score of yards in taciturn introspection. Then Smoky Woman fixed her beautiful eyes on him.

"I love Cain."

"I know."

"You must understand. I never love man before, not like this. When Cain take me I much scared. But him nice. Him gentle. I think him pretty."

Nate listened attentively, mystified as to why she was baring her soul. She owed him no explanations. It was none of his business. Yet she went on talking, struggling to find the proper words, pausing between sentences to formulate her thoughts.

"Cain not like any man. He fire my heart, make me forget my people, my family. All I want was him."

True love, Nate mused, did have a way of jangling a person's brain so badly they couldn't think straight. Sweet memories of his first meeting with Winona reminded him of how he had been utterly swept away by her looks, her touch, even her scent. The mere sight of her had been enough to set his pulse to racing.

"Cain must not die. Our child have him for father."

Was it Nate's imagination, or did he read a certain tinge of anxiety in her tone? He could sympathize with her plight. If she lost Cain, she'd be on her own, raising a half-breed son or daughter in a world hostile to breeds, a taxing task that would make her old before her time.

Smoky Woman placed a hand on her stomach and smiled. "We be happy always. Child have much love. Grow to be good."

"Your child will be very fortunate," Nate declared. "Believe me, I want things to work out for you as much as you do yourself. And if you still want me to, I'll ride on ahead to the mountains with Cain once we're close enough and I'm convinced the other tribe isn't after us."

She impulsively gave his elbow a friendly squeeze. "Thank you, Grizzly Killer."

There was an odd lump in Nate's throat as he watched her return to her brother and take over leading the Palouse. Her love was so sincere, so pure. But what about Cain's love for her? Did Cain truly care for her, or had he pretended to care because he craved her companionship? If Nate was any judge, the only thing Solomon Cain cared about was the gold.

At last the lonesome wail of a distant wolf wavered on the crisp air.

Nate perked up and scanned the eastern range. They must be within a mile or so of the mountains! Then he had second thoughts. They'd not gone far enough yet. The wolf must be prowling the eastern perimeter of the wasteland and was trying to locate others of its kind.

Suddenly Smoky Woman and Flying Hawk halted. Pegasus whinnied and shied away, as if from a snake in his path.

In four bounds Nate learned the reason. They had unexpectedly come on a sheer drop-off of 50 or 60 feet, a slope impossible for the gelding to negotiate. "We'll have to go around," he advised, moving to the left along the rim.

The bottom was lost in the bleak gloom. It might well be a sepulchral pit, but he wouldn't know until he found a way down. He was encouraged by the fact the rim angled gradually lower.

A blast of wind struck him, flapping the whangs on his buckskins. It brought with it the weird cry of an unknown bird, the same bird he'd heard when he'd been after Smoky Woman's abductors. Only it wasn't a bird.

Stopping, Nate raised the Hawken and sought the source of the cry. A squat, pale form briefly materialized over a hundred feet off, then seemed to dissipate on the blustering breeze. Nate's stomach bound into knots as he hurried on, motioning for the others to do the same. Isolated on the rim as they were, with their backs to the drop-off, they were particularly vulnerable. They had to reach flat ground or find a spot to take shelter.

But the savages weren't about to let them. There was a sharp shout in an unfamiliar tongue, and a half-dozen shapes rose up and charged.

Chapter Twelve

Nate took speedy aim and fired, rushing his shot so much he was certain he missed. The intended target, and all the rest of the savages, promptly went to ground. "Keep going!" he urged the Utes, letting them take the lead so he could protect their flank and safeguard Pegasus.

A blurred object arced down from the inkwell sky, narrowly missing the gelding's neck and sailing out over the drop-off.

Drawing his right pistol, Nate searched in vain for an enemy to shoot. He berated himself for having stopped to rest earlier. Had they gone at a swifter pace, the primitives might not have overtaken them.

But such thoughts, he realized, were pointless. Survival was the issue. With that uppermost in mind, he took a gamble and wedged the pistol under his belt again so he could reload the rifle. Some of the powder spilled and he had a trying time inserting the ball and patch, yet when they came to the end of the incline the Hawken was loaded and cocked.

Smoky Woman cut eastward, walking faster. Flying Hawk stayed close to her, a shaft set to take wing.

Nate walked backward, his gaze roving over the rim they had just vacated. When several shifting forms appeared, he whipped the Hawken to his shoulder. Hesitation seized him. He'd already wasted one shot. Why waste another? Let the savages come nearer. Then he would show them why he had won a prime buffalo robe for his marksmanship at the Rendezvous the year before.

Huge boulders abruptly reared to the right and the left. On the one hand Nate was grateful for the cover. On the other he worried that the savages would take advantage of the situation by sneaking so close they couldn't miss. Logic told him the Indians would try to slay Pegasus first since killing the horse meant stranding their quarry.

The next moment Flying Hawk elevated his bow and let fly.

A short shriek testified to his accuracy.

Several darts served as retaliation. One smacked into the earth next to Smoky Woman. A second passed through the Palouse's swishing tail. The third flashed overhead.

A bold strategy occurred to Nate, and with a gesture at the warrior to go on, he darted behind a boulder they were passing and crouched with his back against the hard stone surface. The Utes and the gelding were soon dim figures in the night. Suddenly he heard the whispering tread of a stealthy stalker, and a heartbeat later a stout Indian stepped into view, a spear clutched in the man's brawny right hand. The Indian didn't see Nate, so intent was he on those he hunted.

Then the man halted, apparently aware one of the figures was missing.

Like a striking rattler, Nate pounced. Only he didn't use a gun. At the last instant he pulled his butcher knife and buried the keen blade in the savage's thick throat. The savage sprang rearward, his throat gushing red, and threw back his arm to hurl the spear. Belatedly, the shock of his wound staggered him and he shuffled weakly to the left, his spear arm waving.

Nate knew a dead man when he saw one. Whirling, he sprinted after his companions, sliding the damp knife into his sheath along the way. A harrowing reminder not to make rash judgments jolted him when the spear whizzed over his left shoulder. Twisting, he saw the savage collapse.

Increasing his speed, he soon came on Flying Hawk and Smoky Woman. The warrior had trained an arrow on him. Then those eagle eyes recognized who he was and the bow lowered fractionally. Side by side they followed Pegasus, covering a hundred yards before they were made aware of their blunder. One of them should have been in front of the gelding.

It was Smoky Woman's scream that caused them both to spin, and they both saw the muscular savage bearing down on her with a club held aloft. Nate sighted, but as quick as he was he wasn't quick enough, because Flying Hawk got off a shaft first, the arrow flying straight and true, the barbed point biting into the savage's chest above the heart.

Like a poled ox the savage toppled.

Flying Hawk dashed forward, leaving Nate to protect their rear alone. He anticipated another onslaught of darts and spears, but none was forthcoming. Every nerve vibrant, he glued his thumb to the hammer, his finger to the trigger. One of the Indians was bound to appear sooner or later and he would be ready.

Bewilderingly, time went by and no more savages appeared. Nate couldn't believe the band had given up so easily. They must be lurking out there somewhere, he figured, waiting their chance. So he didn't relax for an instant. But after a while his body grew tired of its own accord. There was just so much strenuous exertion and nervous excitement a human being could handle, and he had been through sheer hell ever since finding Cain strung up from that tree.

The seconds turned into minutes, the minutes, inexplicably, into an hour, then two hours, and three.

During all this time Nate's vigilance inevitably waned, his weariness waxed. Despite the danger, he longed to lie down and sleep. The lack of hostile action lulled him into suspecting he was wrong; the savages had decided to take their dead and leave. Or so logical reasoning led him to believe. His gut instincts were another story.

A graying of the eastern sky promised the imminent arrival of dawn.

The mountains were close but not close enough, two miles or better if Nate was any judge of distance, two more miles of arid desolation frequented by a blood-thirsty band of feral savages. If, he vowed, he made it out, he'd never, ever return unless it was at the head of an army.

A high gorge bisected by a dry wash blocked their route. On either hand skeletal ridges resembled imposing medieval ramparts. They could go around or they could go on through. Flying Hawk chose the shorter path.

Dwarfed into insignificance by the size of the gorge, Nate tried not to dwell on what would happen if the savages gained the high ground and proceeded to dislodge some of the gigantic boulders balanced precariously up above. A single rock slide would crush all four of them and Pegasus to boot.

Nerves taunt, Nate trudged on, his gaze never leaving the tops of the walls. Here at the bottom of the gorge the feeble rays of approaching daylight had not yet reached, and it was as if they were walking through a night-shrouded realm. He could see Flying Hawk, but not the Ute's features when the warrior turned his head from side to side.

Was it half an hour that went by? Forty-five minutes? Estimating time was difficult when there was no point of reference such as the sun or the positions of the stars to judge by, and the few stars visible from the depths of the gorge were too indistinct to be of any aid.

Shortly thereafter, when the end of the gorge showed as a pale patch of light blue up ahead, the unforeseen transpired. Solomon Cain abruptly awakened and tried to sit up in the saddle.

"What the hell!" he blurted out loudly, his words echoing off the walls. "Why am I tied down?"

In a flash Nate was there and touching a hand to Cain's cheek. "Quiet or we're all dead!"

"King?" Cain said, twisting his head with an effort. He blinked, then coughed. "What the devil is going on? Where are we? Everything is all fuzzy in my noggin."

"We're trying to reach the mountains but those savages are after us. I don't think they know where we are, but they will if we're not mighty careful."

"Sorry," Cain muttered, and grasped the rope securing him to the saddle horn. "Was this necessary?"

"It was if we wanted to get you out in one piece. Otherwise you would have fallen off hours ago and busted your head open," Nate said. "We sure as blazes couldn't tote you out on our backs."

"Well, cut me loose. I think my fever has broke and I feel a heap better now. I can walk."

"Stay up there a while longer," Nate suggested, afraid Cain would slow them down on foot. Every moment counted, and he felt a compelling urgency to reach the range quickly.

"No, damn it!" Cain snapped. "I'm sore as hell and my back is all cramped up. So cut me free, damn you! I want to stretch my legs a spell."

Disinclined to comply, Nate shook his head, and was about to explain why when Smoky Woman touched his arm.

"Please, Grizzly Killer."

Against Nate's better judgment, he gave in. He justified doing so by reasoning that he had no right to keep Cain trussed up if the man didn't care to be. And he certainly didn't want to become embroiled in a shouting match that might attract the savages.

"I'm waitin'!" Cain barked.

"All right," Nate growled, drawing his knife. "But if you can't keep up, back on Pegasus you go." Short strokes parted the rope strands, and Solomon Cain, with a grateful sigh, slid off the Palouse into Smoky Woman's waiting arms.

"We must hurry," Nate prompted.

"Hold your horses," Cain shot back, embracing Smoky Woman so tightly she could barely move. "And quit your worryin' about those naked bastards. They're no account anyways you lays your sight."

Strange words coming from a man those "no account" savages had almost killed, Nate reflected, but he held his tongue. He also thought it odd when Cain gave Smoky Woman a passionate kiss right there in front of him. For all their bluster and bravado, mountain men were uncommonly shy about sexual matters and preferred to do their romancing in the privacy of their lodges or cabins. Public displays of intense affection were rare.

At length Cain broke the kiss, clasped Smoky Woman's dainty hand in his, and walked slowly toward the end of the gorge. Neither of them bothered about the Palouse.

Nate grabbed the reins and fell into step behind them. Flying Hawk brought up the rear.

"You know, King," Cain said softly over his shoulder, "I reckon my partner and me never ought to have come here. This place is cursed through and through. Any fool could of seen that. But not us. We wanted that gold and . . ." He stopped, glanced at the gelding, then glared at Nate. "Damn you! You told me you were bringin' the gold!"

"Keep your voice down," Nate urged.

"Like hell I will," Cain barked, letting go of Smoky Woman, his face livid. "Simon and I worked like slaves to dig that yellow ore out and you went and left it all behind! How could you?"

"It was either you or the gold. My horse couldn't carry both."

"You could have brought *some*!" Cain virtually wailed. "This coon didn't go to all that trouble to leave empty-handed! I'm goin' back." So saying, he started to brush past Nate.

"No!" Smoky Woman exclaimed.

Nate gripped Cain's wrist and held on. "Now it's your turn to hold your horses. You're in no condition to travel all the way back to the cave, and even if you were you'd have the savages dogging you every step of the way. Be sensible, Solomon. Stay with us."

Cain tried to tear his arm loose. "I'm a free man and I can do as I damn well please without your say-so. That gold is rightfully mine and I don't intend to leave it there for any old hoss to discover and steal. So let go."

"Not until you give me your word you'll give up the notion of going back."

"Never," Cain said, again striving to free his wrist. Suddenly, without any forewarning, he blanched and buckled, sagging forward.

Fortunately Nate was right there to catch him and lower him to the ground. "You blamed fool," Nate said. "See my point? You're in no shape to go anywhere."

A fit of coughing prevented Cain from answering. Eyes closed, fist pressed to his lips, he hacked uncontrollably. Smoky Woman came and knelt beside him to affectionately stroke his brow.

Rising, Nate stepped back and draped an arm on Pegasus. In all his travels he had seldom met anyone as contrary as the jackass on the ground. Cain never seemed to learn. Anyone else, anyone with a shred of common sense, would know Nate had done the right thing and let it go at that. But not Solomon. Cain's lust for gold was a sickness which not even love could cure.

Impatient to be off, Nate tapped his fingers on the saddle horn and touched a sticky substance. Closer inspection revealed a few large drops of drying blood, not on the saddle horn itself but on the leather strap to his possibles bag which he often draped over the horn when riding, a habit his mentor, Shakespeare McNair, had been trying to break him of ever since they met. "Always keep your possibles on your person," Shakespeare had often said. "You never know when you'll be left afoot."

Most trappers crammed their possibles bag with their tobacco and pipe, thread and needle, flints and steel, maybe their bait box for beaver, and other odds and ends. But because Nate didn't smoke tobacco and carried his flint and steel in his ammo pouch, he felt no need to tote the extra weight along except when out working a trap line.

Solomon was sitting up now, his head bowed low, breathing deep. "I reckon I'm nowhere near fit yet," he said, rasping out the words. "You're right, King. Much as I hate the idea, my gold will have to stay where it is until I can come back for it. Just don't get any notions about taking it for yourself. I'd hunt you down to the ends of the earth if need be."

"Don't threaten me," Nate said. "Don't *ever* threaten me."

The edge to Nate's voice made Cain stiffen. "I didn't mean to get you riled," he mumbled, gingerly touching his shoulder.

Nate noticed a dark stain. "Are you bleeding again'?"

"Could be. My shoulder does feel a mite damp now and then."

Nate scanned the top of the gorge. For a minute there he had forgotten all about the savages, an oversight he dared not repeat if he valued his life. "We must keep going. I'll check the bandage later. Can you walk or would you rather ride?"

"Never let it be said that a little thing like a busted shoulder turned me puny," Cain responded. "I'll walk, with your permission, your highness."

"Suit yourself." Nate assumed the lead once again, the gelding at his elbow. Pink and orange harbingers of dawn painted the eastern sky in broad strokes, and a slender sliver of gold rimmed the skyline. The increasing light even penetrated to the bottom of the gorge. Of the well-nigh limitless number of stars visible an hour ago, now only several shone bright enough to stand out, and soon they would fade too.

Near the gorge mouth Nate slowed. Jumbled boulders on either hand afforded an ideal ambush spot. If somehow the savages had gotten ahead of them, a distinct possibility given the delay caused by Cain, here was where the Indians would strike.

He cocked the Hawken and treaded on silent soles, a useless precaution since there was no way of muffling Pegasus's hoofs. Or was there? He could cut his blanket into four pieces and wrap one piece around each hoof. Why hadn't he thought of it sooner? Sometimes he acted as if he had buffalo chips for brains!

By now he was too near the boulders to stop for any reason. Should savages be lurking there, they'd speedily drop him with their spears or darts. Hawken leveled, he padded toward a golden bowl of sunlight past the boulders.

His apprehension proved unfounded. Not only were there no savages in hiding at the gorge, but before him unfolded a flat tract of arid terrain that stretched clear to the base of the eastern mountains, a tract where they would be perfectly safe because no one could get anywhere near them without being seen. Should a lizard move out there, he'd know it. No matter which direction the savages came from, his rifle and the Ute's bow would keep them at bay.

Nate chuckled to himself and forged on. A stroke of good luck at last! he reflected. In two hours they'd be among the dense pines covering the lower slopes of the mountains. They'd be safe. He planned to make camp at the spring in the park and stay there for four or five days, long enough for Cain to recover sufficiently to be able to continue eastward. Perhaps he could persuade Flying Hawk to bring them some horses from the Ute village. If not, well, he'd stick with Smoky Woman and Cain until they were in safer territory.

He inhaled deeply, grateful to be alive. He'd outwitted the savages, bested them at their own game, and lived to tell the tale. And what a story he would have for Shakespeare and his other friends! Appropriately embellished, of course, to make it more exciting than the experience had been. If that was possible.

Pegasus perked up immensely at the sight of the mountains. The gelding sensed that water and food were his as soon as he reached the beckoning vegetation, so up came his head and his stride lengthened appreciably.

Nate glanced over his shoulder. Cain and Smoky Woman were strolling arm in arm, Cain remarkably recovered for someone who had been at death's door. Flying Hawk, while still vigilant, was not as tense as before. All of them realized the worst of their ordeal was over.

Crossing the flat took about as long as he'd calculated. Seldom had simple grass and spruce trees looked so appealing as they did when he reached the bottom of a green slope and paused to inhale the fragrant spicy scent of the pines. Pegasus promptly lowered his muzzle and cropped greedily at the grass.

"Not yet," Nate said. "Just a little further."

A survey of the range showed he was north of the ravine through which Flying Hawk and he had passed to reach the wasteland. Was that the sole way in and out or was there another? He put the question to Cain.

"It's the only one I know of," Solomon answered, and nodded at the mountain towering above them. "Simon and me searched this here range for twenty miles or better from north to south, but we never did find another pass through to the other side."

"Then the ravine it is," Nate said, turning southward and pulling a reluctant Pegasus after him. Once through the ravine they would be in the park, and only there would he feel completely safe.

Doubts crept in as he walked along. He was assuming the savages seldom penetrated deep into the range, but what if he was wrong? Perhaps they did only roam the fringes of the mountains, which would explain why no one was aware of their existence. But maybe, just maybe, they wandered farther afield than he gave them credit for. In which case even the park wouldn't be a safe haven.

Enmeshed in mulling over what to do, Nate paid scant attention to his surroundings except when he scoured

A SPECIAL OFFER FOR LEISURE WESTERN READERS ONLY!

Get FOUR FREE Western Novels

Travel to the Old West in all its glory and drama—without leaving your home!

Plus, you'll save between $3.00 and $6.00 every time you buy!

GET FOUR BOOKS TOTALLY *FREE*—A VALUE BETWEEN $16 AND $20

the land ahead for sign of the ravine. If he recalled correctly, it was situated snugly between a pair of peaks that effectively hid it until one was right on it.

Behind him Solomon Cain was talking. "You'll see, Smoky Woman. I ain't about to give up this easy. Once I'm well enough, I'll come back here and take out all the gold in that vein. The two of us will live in luxury for the rest of our lives."

"I no care for yellow rocks. I care for you."

"You're sweet. But if we're to live among white folks, we need the gold. You don't know how it is among my kind. Unless you have lots of money you're not considered worth much, and I'll be damned if I'm ever goin' to let any well-to-do folks look down their powdered noses at you."

"I be happy with just you," Smoky Woman stressed.

"Trust me. We need the gold."

"Is gold worth life?"

"I ain't about to die on you," Cain stated. "Not when I'm so close to havin' everything I've ever dreamed about, everything I could ever want. No, sirree."

Smoky Woman spoke so quietly Nate couldn't hear her words, but he did hear Cain's reply.

"Hell, no, woman. Don't be crazy. I ain't goin' to give up the gold for anything, not even you. If you love me you'll stick with me until this is all over and then the two of us will celebrate in St. Louis. Maybe we'll go on and do the same in New Orleans. The world will be ours." He paused and chuckled. "Why, we could even go to Paris, if we want. That's in Frenchy country."

"I see my people again?"

Nate could have counted to ten in the pregnant pause that greeted her query.

"Sure you will. I give you my word." Cain tittered. "And when you come back you'll have more foofaraw than all the women in your village put together. You'll be the talk of the tribe, the richest woman of them all."

"I just want you," Smoky Woman said plaintively.

Distracted by their conversation, Nate didn't recognize the opening to the ravine until he was directly abreast of it. Swinging around in surprise, he peered down its narrow length, jubilant at the thought that soon the wasteland would be a bitter memory and nothing more. Smiling, he beckoned the others and started into the ravine. Only now was he truly convinced they had eluded the savages. At long last they were really safe.

Suddenly a sharp cry of warning erupted from Flying Hawk's lips.

Spinning, Nate was horrified to see naked, hairy savages spilling from a wide crack he'd just passed in the left-hand wall, their intent signified by the feral gleams in their beady eyes and the lethal weapons poised in their brawny hands.

Chapter Thirteen

So swiftly did the savages strike that they would have been on Nate's party before anyone had a chance to react if not for Flying Hawk. The Ute's eagle eyes had registered motion in the crack a second before the ferocious savages spilled forth, giving him time to yell his warning and to snap his bow up. At such close range deliberate aiming was unnecessary. He simply trained his shaft on the chest of the foremost savage and released the string.

The lead savage managed two more steps with a shaft sticking from the center of his torso, then he collapsed soundlessly, falling prone and causing the two Indians behind him to stumble over his body. For a moment there was a logjam at the opening as the ones who had tripped regained their balance and those behind them slowed so they wouldn't collide.

In that precious interval Nate leaped to the left, nearer the crack, and jammed the Hawken to his shoulder.

161

He had to release the reins to shoot, and when he did Pegasus took off into the ravine, spurred by a screech from one of the fuming band.

Then, in the instant before Nate squeezed the trigger, time seemed to stand still. The thought flashed through his mind that he should have anticipated an ambush at the ravine since the ravine was the only way out of the wasteland on the east side. It wouldn't have taken a genius to figure out where they were headed and to send warriors on ahead to be waiting for them when they got there. The savages must have known all along. And now, like a rank greenhorn, Nate had walked right into their obvious trap.

The next moment Nate fired, sending a second savage into the hereafter. A third sprang at Smoky Woman, who stood temporarily paralyzed by shock. The savage's war club was poised to crush her skull, and would have done so the next moment if not for Cain, who leaped to her defense just as the club swooped down, putting himself between the Indian and her. Cain got an arm up in an effort to deflect the club, but in this he was only partially successful. The war club struck his forearm, glanced off, and smacked into the side of his head, dazing him. Before he could recover, the Indian swung again. This time the club caught him flush on the temple with a sickening thud.

Nate snatched a pistol out and took a hasty bead. The flintlock spat lead and smoke. Instantly the savage wielding the club sprouted a new eye.

Cain was on his knees, hands clasped to his head, blood pouring between his fingers. Smoky Woman, forgetting her own safety, leaned over at his side.

Another savage leaped toward her, this man armed with a spear. He would have impaled her if not for her brother, who streaked a glittering arrow into the man's soft throat.

Four enemies had been slain in the opening moments of the clash, yet more were spilling from the crack. Two more. Four. Five. And that was all, but it was more than enough.

Nate let the pistol he had just used fall from his fingers and grabbed at the other one, his hand closing on it just as a sneering savage charged and tried to smash his face in with a huge club. Hurling himself backwards saved him, but it also left him off balance, which the savage exploited by swinging at his midsection. The club grazed him, not doing much harm but acting much as would a shove by another person and sending him onto his backside in the dirt. His Hawken was jarred from his grip.

He began to scramble up and the club whistled at his skull. Throwing himself to the right, he rolled once. When he stopped, he held the flintlock. At the retort the savage's head whipped back, blood spurting from the man's mouth. Then the Indian staggered and fell.

Now the last of Nate's guns had been used, and as he was doing with increasing frequency of late, he relied on his tomahawk instead of his butcher knife. Jumping to his feet, he drew the tomahawk and spun. His heart, it felt like, leaped to his throat.

Two savages were grappling with Flying Hawk, the three men fighting tooth and nail. A third savage had Smoky Woman pinned and was trying to slit her throat. The last one was in the act of scalping Solomon Cain even though Cain was still alive, as demonstrated by his feeble resistance.

"No!" Nate roared. He was on the scalper before the Indian could rise, the tomahawk shearing the man's right eye in half and slicing off part of his face in the bargain.

Incensed, Nate spun again and attacked the savage on top of Smoky Woman. The savage saw him coming and shoved upright to meet his rush, but was unable to dodge the wicked swing that nearly took the Indian's head off.

Splattered with scores of red drops, Nate blinked and turned, intending to go to Flying Hawk's assistance. The pounding of feet gave him enough warning to brace himself, and then something struck him on his wounded shoulder and the world spun as he tottered rearward. Iron arms banded around his waist and he was borne to the ground. Knees gouged into his stomach.

Through a swirling haze he saw a grinning savage astride him, mouth curled in an expectant grin. He also saw the savage lift a war club. Urgently he tried to move his arms and legs, to buck the savage off, but his nerves refused to cooperate and send the proper signals from his brain to his limbs. All he did was twitch.

The savage, sensing his weakness, paused, perhaps to savor the moment. Then the club arced higher, bathed in the bright sunlight, and froze for a fraction of a second before beginning its downward plunge.

Nate stared eternity in the face and knew it. He gulped, strived to lift his arms. He saw a bestial light in his adversary's dark eyes. And then he saw something bulge out from between those eyes, a barbed point coated with crimson. The savage stiffened, gasped, and fell.

At last Nate felt he could move again, and he shoved the dead savage from him and rose. Not far off stood Flying Hawk, slowly lowering his bow. Closer were Smoky Woman and Cain, the latter flat on his back with a portion of his scalp hanging loose, the former in tears.

All of the savages were dead.

Or so they appeared as Nate surveyed the blood-soaked ground. Unwilling to leave anything to chance, he went from body to body, satisfying himself no spark of life remained in a single one. Then he joined the others in grim silence around Solomon Cain.

Suddenly Cain's eyes blinked open and his tongue touched his lips. "I reckon . . ." he said hoarsely, and stopped, grimacing in agony.

"Not talk," Smoky Woman chided, his hand cupped tenderly in hers.

Once more Cain's tongue moistened his lips. "Don't hardly matter, pretty one," he said. "I'm a gone beaver and I know it."

Nate almost replied, "No, you're not." But the side of Cain's head confirmed Cain's words. No man could live long with his brains oozing out. "Solomon, is there anything I can do for you?"

"Just do what you can for her," Cain said, his gaze flicking at the woman he loved.

"I will," Nate said, sounding as if he had a severe cold.

Flying Hawk added a string of words in Ute, then rested his hand on his sister's shoulder.

"Good," Cain said.

A nicker drew Nate's attention down the ravine where Pegasus was trotting back. When he next looked at Cain, Cain's eyes were closed. For a moment Nate thought the end at come, but he was premature.

"King?" Cain spoke in a strangled whisper.

"I'm here," Nate said.

"I have no kin to speak of, no one to mourn me when I'm gone. The gold is yours, all yours. Do what you want with it. I hope it brings you better luck than it brought me."

"I'm obliged," Nate responded, although he doubted he would ever be foolhardy enough to return to the cave. The savages were bound to keep an eye on it from now on. Perhaps—and here was a new thought that shocked him since it explained so much—perhaps the cave was a special place to the savages, a sacred site much as were the Paha Sapa hills to the Sioux and other areas to other tribes. If that was the case, any white man who set foot in the cave did so risking imminent death. All Indians were extremely protective of their sacred shrines, and every trapper who had lived with them for a while knew better than to violate a tribal sanctuary.

"You'll be rich," Cain was saying. "You can have anything you want."

Nate thought of his wife and son. "I already do."

"What?" Cain said. "You have gold already?"

"No," Nate said, and would have elaborated had not Cain erupted in a violent spasm of coughing and wheezing. The end was very near.

Smoky Woman threw herself on Cain's chest and unleased a torrent.

"I wish . . ." Cain cried, wild eyes fixed on the vast blue sky. "I wish . . ." But what he wished no one would ever know, for Solomon Cain's alloted time had run out. A gurgling whine escaped his lips. Then he went as rigid as a board, sucked in a great breath, and abruptly went totally limp.

Nate moved off to give Smoky Woman some privacy. Reclaiming his guns took a while, as did reloading them. When he led Pegasus over, she was standing in her brother's arms, but they self-consciously separated and took a step apart. "I'm sorry, Smoky Woman," he commented. "I truly am."

Too choked with emotion to speak, she merely nodded.

"We'll bury him, as is the custom with my people, and be on our way," Nate proposed. He nudged one of the savages with his toe. "There might be more of these Root Eaters or whatever they're called in the area, and we don't want to tangle with them again if we can help it."

"Where bury?" Smoky Woman asked.

The bottom of the ravine was hard, packed earth and rock. Without shovels and picks, digging a hole large enough to hold a man would take many hours. Maybe a full day. "How about near the spring yonder," Nate said, pointing toward the east opening.

Smoky Woman brightened slightly. "Yes. Please. That be nice."

They were a downcast lot as they trudged along, Nate with a hand on Cain to keep the corpse from sliding off Pegasus. The fight had added to his injuries and increased his fatigue, so when a patch of lush green grass appeared he barely checked a shout of unadulterated joy.

Before the burial each of them drank their full. Pegasus was still drinking when Nate located a suitable soft spot north of the spring and set to work with the tapered end of a stout branch. Flying Hawk watched him for a while, then joined in. Their corded muscles rippling, they excavated a suitable hole in less than an hour.

Nate stood on the lip and mopped sweat from his forehead. He could see a few thick worms wriggling at the bottom of the hole and he wished they had a buffalo robe or something else to wrap Cain in. But they didn't, so they would have to make do.

At a gesture from him, Flying Hawk grasped Cain's ankles. In unison they slowly lowered the body down on top of the worms. Nate began filling in the hole, working swiftly, oddly bothered by Cain's blank stare. Pausing, he reached down and closed Cain's eyelids.

Smoky Woman stood as if sculpted from marble the whole time. Her features inscrutable, she made no remarks whatsoever. Only when the final handful of dirt was cast down did she utter a soft, fluttering sigh.

"Do you care to say a few words?" Nate asked her.

"I not understand."

"Among my people it's customary to say a few nice things about those who have departed," Nate clarified. "It's our way of commending our souls to the spirit world."

"You say them."

"Me?" Nate blurted out, and repressed a frown. He was no minister. And while he must have read all of the Bible at one time or another, thanks to the influence of his mother and his required weekly church attendance, he wasn't exactly sure which words were appropriate for a funeral service. Not knowing what else to do, he recited the one passage in Scripture he knew by heart, the very first he had ever learned. "The Lord is my shepherd, I shall not want. He maketh me to lie down in green pastures; he leadeth me beside the still waters. He restoreth my soul: he leadeth me in the paths of righteousness for his name's sake. Yea, though I walk through the valley of the shadow of death, I will fear no evil; for thou art with me; thy rod and thy staff they comfort me." He stopped, unable to recall the rest. Then it came to him, haltingly. "Thou preparest a table before me in the presence of mine enemies: thou anointest my head with oil; my cup runneth over. Surely goodness and mercy shall follow me all the days of my life: and I will dwell in the house of the Lord for ever."

Smoky Woman stood with her head bowed in sorrow. Her brother had his arms folded across his chest, listening inquisitively.

"I reckon that's about it," Nate concluded. "Except maybe I should say that here was a man no better than most, no worse than many. I'm not fit to be his judge. But I was an accountant once, and I'd say his ledger came out on the plus side there at the end. For what it's worth."

Feeling uncomfortable, Nate donned his hat and walked to the spring. "I suppose we should rest up here a day or two, then go find your village," he commented without looking around. "That is, if you want to live with your people, Smoky Woman. I know how rough it's going to be rearing your child among your tribe. Maybe you don't want to. Whatever you decide, I'll help out the best I can. I gave my word to Solomon." He paused. "What do you want to do, anyway?"

There was no answer.

Nate turned, and was flabbergasted to see Smoky Woman and Flying Hawk hiking southward. "Wait!" he found his voice. "Where are you going?"

She glanced back. "My brother find village where we maybe live. Where we be happy." Her smile warmed the very air. "Good-bye, Grizzly Killer. We never forget you."

"But . . ." Nate began, and stopped, knowing his words would be wasted. For the longest while he just stood there, watching the two figures grow smaller and smaller bit by bit, until eventually they faded into the forest and were gone from his life forever.

Bright and early the next morning he turned the Palouse homeward, humming as he rode.

TENDERFOOT

To Judy, Joshua, and Shane.

Prologue

The five Gros Ventres were far from their home range. They had traveled high into the rugged, majestic mountains to the south of their customary haunts, and were strung out in single file as they crested a sloping ridge.

In the lead rode a tall warrior, who now drew rein to scour the verdant land below. Rolling Thunder was his name. He could boast of having counted over 20 coup, and many of his people were of the opinion that when their aged chief died he would be the successor. A born leader, he had led over a dozen successful war parties and never lost a man.

But today Rolling Thunder was not on a raid into enemy territory. His small band was after elk, which thrived in the high mountain valleys where abundant grass and pristine springs, lakes, and streams made the Rockies an animal paradise. So far the elk had been elusive, but he hoped to find some soon.

"Is it wise to keep going south?" a gruff voice asked

behind him. "We are close to Shoshone country."

Rolling Thunder twisted, regarded the speaker for a moment, then grinned. "Are you turning into an old woman, Little Dog? Are you afraid of the Shoshones?"

Before Little Dog could answer, the third warrior in line snorted in contempt and declared, "Only a fool would fear them! Shoshones are all cowards at heart. They run and hide at the sight of real warriors."

Rolling Thunder saw Little Dog's features cloud and spoke to forestall an argument. "I was joking, Loud Talker. All of us know how brave Little Dog is. Was he not the one who saved you from the Dakotas that time they shot your horse out from under you?"

Loud Talker frowned. He had spoken, as usual, without thinking, and as usual, he had upset one of his closest friends. "I did not mean to insult Little Dog," he said. "Yes, he did save me from the Dakotas that time. If not for him my hair would now be hanging in a Dakota lodge."

The last two men joined them. One, a husky warrior named Walking Bear, leaned forward and commented, "We are all brave. But we are few and the Shoshones are many. If a large war party should find us, we would be in for the fight of our lives."

"Good," said the last man, known simply as Bobcat. "We will give our people something to remember us by."

No one responded for several seconds. They all knew Bobcat was too bloodthirsty for his own good, but he was otherwise thoroughly dependable and the best man with a bow in their entire tribe. Bobcat had never lost an archery contest. No matter the distance, he always hit his targets dead center.

Little Dog cleared his throat. "I love a fight as much as any of you, but I see no reason why we should needlessly throw our lives away. If we are all slain, who will take word to our people? How will they learn our fate?" He gestured southward. "The Shoshones are not the cowards Loud Talker claims they are. He has not fought them, as I have done, or he would know they are as fierce as the Blackfeet when aroused."

No one disputed the point. Rolling Thunder noted the unease in some of their eyes and said quickly, "There is no cause for worry. We came here to hunt, not to make war. Our wives need meat to dry and put aside before the cold comes and the snow begins to fall." He straightened and stretched. "So we will avoid the Shoshones if at all possible, not because we are afraid of them but because our families are depending on us."

His words had the desired effect. The others smiled or voiced agreement and Little Dog visibly relaxed.

Pleased with himself, Rolling Thunder rode on. Since he was the organizer of the hunt, it was his responsibility to see that everything went smoothly. If they took to bickering among themselves, they would hunt poorly. They might fail to down a single elk. And under no circumstances would he return to the village empty-handed. Those few who resented his standing in the tribe would whisper behind his back, perhaps spread a rumor that his medicine was gone.

Rolling Thunder would let nothing tarnish his name. He took great pride in his accomplishments. At the age of 15 he had counted his first coup on a Nez Percé, and ever since he had steadily added to his prestige, until he was now widely respected and admired. The old chief came to him regularly for advice. Seats of honor were his at the council sessions. He owned more horses than anyone else, and the beauty of his wives made him the envy of every man. After working so hard to get where he was, he would do whatever was needed to maintain his standing.

Of equal importance in his decision to press on was

the fact he always kept his word. He had promised his wives he would bring them elk meat, and he would not let them down. To his way of thinking a man was no man at all if he could not provide for his loved ones, and he had a reputation for being an excellent provider.

In order to guarantee success, Rolling Thunder had brought his friends to this region where the elk were known to be more numerous than practically anywhere else. It mattered little to him that the Shoshones also hunted here. His wits and his strength had seen him through more dangers than he cared to remember, and he was completely confident he would prevail if he encountered them.

Once in the valley, Rolling Thunder stopped. "We must separate and search for sign. Little Dog and I will take the west side."

"Stay alert," Walking Bear advised, hefting his lance. He angled to the east, Bobcat and Loud Talker tagging along. "We will call out if we find anything."

The only sounds were the dull thud of hoofs and the noisy gurgling of a swift stream meandering along the valley floor. Rolling Thunder's keen dark eyes roved constantly over the ground. A skilled tracker, he sought evidence of a game trail. Where there was water, there was always wildlife. From past experience he knew that any elk in the vicinity would bed down in the dense timber above during the day and come down to drink toward sunset. Being creatures of habit, the elk would use the same route again and again, so if he could find the trail he could backtrack to where they were hiding.

The morning sun climbed higher and higher. They were halfway along the valley when Little Dog addressed him.

"Do you think any of the others suspect the true reason you insisted we come so far south?"

Rolling Thunder's iron will served him in good stead.

He continued riding, his face impassive, and remarked absently, "I do not know what you mean."

"You can fool them, my friend, but not me. We have been like brothers since childhood. I know your ways better than I know my own."

"You speak in riddles."

"Do I?" Little Dog said. "If so, it is a riddle you understand. And I am surprised you have not told them the truth. They are almost as close to you as I am."

"Speak with a straight tongue."

"Very well. Does White Buffalo know what you are up to?"

"Why should I tell him?" Rolling Thunder rejoined, the indignation in his tone obvious. "What is he to me? We are not even related." He was about to go on, to justify himself, when he saw where the grass ahead had been flattened and torn up by the passage of many heavy forms. And there in the bare earth were scores of large elk tracks. "Look!" he exclaimed, then trotted to them.

Rolling Thunder slid down off his war pony and sank to one knee to examine the prints. As his gaze roved along the game trail he suddenly stiffened, then lowered his face within inches of the earth.

"What have you found?" Little Dog asked.

"Fresh horse tracks," Rolling Thunder answered, touching his fingers to one of the depressions. There were two sets of hoofprints, those of a larger than normal animal that must be a big stallion and a much smaller set that might be those of a mare. Both had crossed the valley and gone up into the trees. "Someone else is hunting elk," he deduced, and rose.

"Shoshones, you think?"

"Perhaps," Rolling Thunder said, hiding his disappointment that neither of the animals were shod. Rising, he led his horse toward the stream, studying the tracks carefully as he went along, memorizing the individual characteristics of each animal.

"We will have to stay clear of them," Little Dog said.

"There are only two."

"But there may be many more."

"It will do no harm to follow them and see."

"But what—"

Rolling Thunder spun, anger clouding his expression. "Earlier I stood up for you, but now you give me cause to doubt my judgment. There is a fine line, old friend, between caution and cowardice. See that you do not cross that line or I will denounce you in front of the entire village."

Eyes flinty as steel, Little Dog closed his mouth.

Rolling Thunder spun, and walked on until he came to a spot by the water's edge where the two riders had dismounted and let their animals drink. The moccasin prints told him a large man was riding the stallion, but the rider of the mare was a mere child. If they were alone they would be easy to slay. Rolling Thunder tilted back his head and vented a series of piercing yips in a perfect imitation of a howling coyote.

From the other side of the valley came Walking Bear's prompt reply.

"Maybe we will count coup on this trip after all," Rolling Thunder declared.

Chapter One

"Did you hear something, Pa?"

Nathaniel King turned his amused gazed from an irate, chattering gray squirrel in a nearby pine and shifted in the saddle to stare at his young son. "No, Zach. What was it?"

"I don't rightly know, Pa. Something real faint." The boy had his head cocked and was listening intently. "It came from behind us, I figure."

Nate listened for several seconds, but heard only the temperamental squirrel and the northwesterly wind sighing through the tall trees. He was about to suggest that his inexperienced son had imagined hearing a sound when he saw the earnest look Zachary wore and realized the boy was doing exactly as Nate had often instructed him to do. "Always stay alert in the wilderness," he had repeatedly advised. "The man who stays alive is the man who is never taken by surprise. Use your senses, your eyes and ears and even your

11

nose, like you have never used them before. Use them like the wild beasts do. Learn from the animals, Zach. That's what the Indians have done since the beginning of time."

Nate smiled, pleased that Zach was trying so hard, and said, "If you hear it again, let me know."

"I sure will."

Cradling his heavy Hawken in the crook of his left elbow, Nate lifted the rope reins and clucked his pied gelding into motion. By nightfall or early tomorrow, he reflected, they would have their elk and he would teach Zach the proper way to remove the hide, butcher the carcass, and make jerky. In a week they would be back at the Shoshone village, where he would proudly boast of his son's prowess to all the other fathers.

He had to hand it to his wife. Winona had come up with the idea to take Zach off alone into the high country to hunt. The time had come, she'd asserted, for Zach to learn the all-important skills he would need to survive in the raw, untamed land her tribe called home. Already the boy was a skilled rider and could shoot a bow as well as his Shoshone playmates. But there was so much more Zach needed to know, and no one better qualified to teach him than his own father.

Which tickled Nate no end. He loved being a parent, loved being able to spend the precious time with Zach that his own father had been too busy to spend with him. He delighted in seeing the world through Zach's naive eyes, and in watching Zach slowly grow and mature. In a sense he was reliving his own childhood, and sometimes things that Zach said or did brought back forgotten memories of incidents from his own early years. As Zach discovered more and more of the world, it seemed that Nate rediscovered more and more of himself.

"Say, Pa?"

12

"Yes?" Nate idly responded as he surveyed the expanse of mountain above. The elk trail they had been following was winding ever higher, and unless he was mistaken he'd find them holed up in a belt of aspens less than a quarter of a mile away. Some of the leaves had begun to change, dotting the green background with patches of bright yellow.

"Why do some of the other boys keep calling me a breed?"

Involuntarily, Nate's grip tightened on the reins and his lips compressed into a thin line. He didn't turn because he was afraid his feelings would show. "Your mother is a Shoshone. I'm a white man. That makes you half-white, half-Indian," he explained. "A half-breed, some would say. Or a breed."

"The way they say it makes me want to punch them," Zach commented.

"It's not something a true friend would call you," Nate confirmed.

"Then I *will* punch them."

"Who has been calling you this?"

"Runs Fast, mostly, and a few that hang around with him."

"Runs Fast? Jumping Bull's boy?"

"Yep."

"How long has this been going on?"

"Oh, about ten sleeps, I reckon. Runs Fast has been picking on me every chance he gets lately. I don't know why. I've never done nothing to him."

"Why didn't you tell me sooner?"

There was a pause. "A man should always take care of his own problems. Isn't that what I heard you tell Uncle Shakespeare?"

Nate probed his memory for over half a minute before he recalled making such a statement, and he marveled that his son remembered the incident. It had been almost a year ago, during one of Shakespeare McNair's periodic visits to their cabin. McNair, his best friend and mentor, had been talking about a mutual acquaintance, a free trapper embroiled in a dispute with another man. Instead of confronting the offending party directly, the trapper had been trying to enlist the help of everyone he knew to side with him against his enemy. During the course of that conversation Nate had casually mentioned that any man worth his salt handled his own squabbles and didn't go around imposing on his friends.

"Isn't it?" Zach prompted.

"Yes, I do recollect saying something along those lines," Nate admitted. "But I was talking about grown men. It's perfectly all right for a boy your age to come to his folks when something like this happens."

"I'm not no whiner. I want to do what a man would do."

Nate looked over his shoulder and bestowed a kindly, knowing smile on his pride and joy. "You have a heap of growing to do, son, before you'll wear a man's britches. Don't rush things. These years are some of the best years of your life and you should enjoy them while they last."

"Why are these the best years?" the boy inquired.

"Because you don't have any responsibilities yet."

"I have my chores, don't I?" Zach said, sounding slightly offended. "I take care of the horses and chop wood and such."

"I'm not saying you don't do your fair share of the work," Nate assured him. "But it's a far cry from doing daily chores to having a wife and kids to keep fed and clothed and having a homestead to look after. Some responsibilities are bigger than others, and a wife and children are the biggest a man can have. He has to work real hard to give them the things he thinks they should have, and sometimes it can be almighty trying."

14

"Don't you like looking after Ma and me?"

Nate stopped until Zach came alongside him, and tenderly placed his hand on the boy's shoulder. "What a silly notion. Nothing in this whole wide world gives me greater pleasure than having to do for your ma and you. I never knew what genuine happiness was until I met Winona, and when you came along we were as happy as could be."

Zach pondered a bit. "If you like young'uns so much, how come I don't have any brothers or sisters?"

"The Lord knows we've tried, son," Nate said, inwardly amazed at the convoluted twists the boy's reasoning sometimes took. Nate was also a little bothered by the question. Had he somehow given Zach cause to doubt his love, or was the query merely prompted by idle curiosity?

"Running Wolf has three brothers and two sisters. He says that's too many, that they pick on each other all the time." Zach's brow creased. "If Ma does have babies, I hope she doesn't have five at once."

"I doubt she will," Nate said with a straight face.

"You never know, Pa. Beaver Tail's dog had a litter of six pups, and Tall Horse's dog had eight."

Nate made a mental note to have a long talk with his son about affairs between the sexes at the first opportunity. They'd already had a few discussions, but clearly he hadn't covered all he should.

The aspens were much nearer. Nate rested his Hawken across his thighs and scoured the wall of vegetation for sign of the elk. He saw nothing, and his mind began to drift. Instead of concentrating exclusively on the matter at hand, he found himself wondering why Jumping Bull's son had taken to giving Zach a hard time. He knew Jumping Bull, but not well. They were on speaking terms and would greet one another if they passed in the village, but Jumping Bull had never been overly friendly toward him. In fact, now that he thought about it, Jumping Bull had always been strangely aloof, even cold. Why?

Suddenly Nate spied a moving patch of brown among the slender trunks of the aspens. A moment later he made out the outline of a bull elk walking slowly westward. Quickly he snapped the rifle to his shoulder and touched his thumb to the hammer. He had to elevate the barrel to compensate for the slope. Fixing a bead on a spot behind the elk's powerful front shoulders, he began to cock the Hawken.

"Pa! Look!"

At the strident shout the elk whirled and vanished in the undergrowth so swiftly there was no chance for Nate to fire. One instant it was there, the next it was gone. Exasperated at his son's mistake, he swung around. "Zach, haven't I taught you better than to yell when you're closing in on game?"

The boy was pointing at the valley below.

Immediately Nate spotted them, three mounted Indians traversing the valley floor from east to west. They had just crossed the stream and were in plain sight in the tall grass. Sunlight glittered off a long lance one held. From so high up he couldn't tell to which tribe they belonged.

"Are they Shoshones, you think?" Zach asked.

"There are no hunting parties in the area I know of," Nate said.

"Maybe they're hostiles, Pa. Maybe they're Blackfeet."

"They only travel this far south to raid, and when they raid they like to go on foot," Nate pointed out. "I doubt they're Blackfeet." But they could, he thought to himself, be from one of a half-dozen tribes who were bitter enemies of the Shoshones. Warriors who would try to kill Zach and him on sight.

Zach was excited. "Should we hide and wait to see if they're after us?"

"No," Nate said calmly, hiding his blossoming worry. Where there were three, there might be more, *many* more, and here he was alone with his young son.

"They're awful close to the elk trail. Maybe they're just hunting elk like we are."

"They could be," Nate allowed, although he didn't believe that was the case. He scanned the expanse of craggy mountain beyond the fluttering tops of the trees while gnawing on his lower lip, his every instinct telling him to get the hell out of there, to get his son to safety. "Stick close," he cautioned, and angled higher.

Constantly winding right and left to avoid thickly clustered trunks, Nate slowly made his way through the aspen belt and into sparse pines above. The ground became rockier. Every now and then a stone would be dislodged by one of their horses and clatter downward. The air felt cooler, growing even more so as they approached a blanket of snow crowning the ragged summit.

A solitary hawk soared over the crest and swooped down above them, then banked and glided to a lower elevation.

"Was that a red hawk?" Zach asked.

"I didn't pay attention," Nate said, his eyes on a promising notch several hundred yards to their right toward which he was gingerly picking his way. He had to skirt several talus slopes where their horses might slip and fall. Always he tried to stay in cover in case the Indians below were scouring the mountain for them.

The notch was above the snow line, situated at the apex of a steep slope. Nate thought it prudent to climb down, and had Zach do likewise. The gelding and Zach's mare were as surefooted as mountain goats, but he dared not risk an accident. If one of their animals went lame

17

they would be hard pressed to elude pursuers. Taking the reins in his left hand, he worked his way upward, his knee-high moccasins finding scant purchase on the packed, slippery snow.

"This is the first time I've ever been up this high," Zach remarked breathlessly. "Everything looks so small down below. That stream looks like a string. And those Indians look like ants."

Indians? Nate twisted and held a palm over his eyes to shield them from the glare. Crossing an open tract between the valley floor and the trees on the lower slope were five warriors riding in single file, most with upturned faces. He could guess what they were doing: searching the mountain for Zach and him. "We'd better hurry," he suggested, increasing his pace.

Soon they were at the notch, which proved to be, as Nate has hoped, a narrow pass to the opposite side of the mountain. There were plenty of elk, deer, and big-horn sheep tracks, none made recently.

Nate passed through the gap quickly, anxious to learn if there would be a way down the far slope. He feared the pass would open out on a towering cliff or an impassable gorge, which would force them to either retrace their steps down to the valley or to try and swing in a wide loop around the climbing Indians and pray they weren't discovered.

The first sight Nate beheld when he emerged from the shadowy pass was a cliff, thankfully off to the left and not barring their way. To his right grew dense forest. Directly below, the alpine fastness inclined gradually for hundreds of feet into more aspens. Nate and Zach mounted, and made their way toward them.

Zach seemed to have sensed Nate's urgency. The boy made no further comments until they were near the bottom. Then, craning his neck to see the pass, he said, "There's no sign of them yet, Pa."

"They'll show. Count on it," Nate said. From the heights he had sought, in vain, for a stream they could ride in for a few miles to throw the Indians off. Now he cut to the right into evergreens that would shield them from scrutiny from on high. He rode faster, heedless of the occasional branch that snatched at his clothing. Zach stayed right behind him, guiding the mare as adeptly as a seasoned mountain man.

Nate lost track of the many minutes spent in flight. Never once did he leave the sanctuary of the forest. Always he shunned clearings or breaks in the trees where they might be visible from the heights.

At length, as they negotiated the base of a curving hill, Nate changed direction and galloped to the top where massive, jumbled boulders afforded concealment for their tired mounts. It was the work of a moment to clamber onto a flat boulder and to go prone with the Hawken in both hands.

"Did we lose them?" Zach asked, lying down at his elbow.

"We'll soon know."

From their vantage point they could see for miles along their back trail. In the distance, silhouetted against the azure sky, was the pass, now no more than a dark slit at the crest of the mountain. The lower portions were blocked from view by intervening peaks and hills.

More minutes dragged by. Zach fidgeted and kept glancing apprehensively at Nate. Presently he made bold to state, "Maybe they weren't after us, Pa. Maybe we went to all this trouble for nothing."

Nate lifted his right arm, his forefinger extended, and heard Zach's intake of breath when his son saw the five stick figures that had appeared out of the notch. "Whoever they are, they're persistent," he said.

"They sure are taking their sweet time. I bet if we try, we can shake them," Zach said.

"You up to a little hard riding?"

"Try me."

"Then let's show them what the King men are made of," Nate proposed, giving his son a reassuring grin. "By the time we're through they'll wish they'd never laid eyes on our tracks."

Zachary laughed, delighted at the challenge confronting them. "Lead the way. And don't fret none about Mary. She can keep up with Pegasus easy except on the flats."

Mary was the mare. Pegasus was the pied gelding given to Nate by the grateful Nez Percé after he helped them rout a raiding party of Blackfeet. Neither horse balked when they were goaded into a gallop, and they swept down the hill with their manes and tails flying.

In all Nate's wide flung travels he had never visited this particular region before, but he had heard enough about it from Shoshones who had to readily recognize prominent landmarks and to keep his bearings as he made to the east with the intent of locating a fork of the Stinking River that must, by his estimation, lie eight to ten miles off.

Since speed was crucial, Nate didn't bother sticking to the shelter of the restricting trees any more. He favored the open stretches where their animals fairly flew. In their wake were tracks a greenhorn could follow, which would enable their pursuers to gain ground but not enough ground, Nate prayed, to overtake the two of them before they came to the river.

Trying not to be too obvious, Nate checked on Zach time and again. His pride swelled as he saw how splendidly the boy rode. He'd given his son numerous riding lessons and frequently watched Zach riding with other Shoshone boys, but not until now had he realized how expertly the boy could handle a horse. Begrudgingly, he admitted to himself that Zach was a much better rider than he had been at the same age—indeed, a better rider than he had been until his fateful trip west from New York City to the untamed frontier during his 19th year.

Part of the explanation for his son's ability had to be the one month out of every twelve spent with the Shoshones. Zach had learned skills he never would have mastered back in the States, where boys his age were subjected to dull days filled with the drudgery of schoolwork, or else were forced by economic necessity to work from dawn to dusk in order to contribute to the family welfare.

Sometimes Nate envied Zach. He wished his own childhood had been similarly spent amidst the primeval glory of the Rocky Mountains among a forthright people who lived simply by design rather than circumstance. People who took each day as it came, without fear of what tomorrow might bring. People who had few needs and fewer wants and who would gladly give the last piece of pemmican they had to a hungry stranger. Such were the Shoshones.

Mile after mile fell behind them as Nate reflected on his active years in the mountains and on the various hardships he had endured, hardships made bearable by the love of the woman who had claimed his heart. He shuddered to think how his life might have turned out had he never met Winona. Perhaps he would have gone back to New York and settled down to the accounting career his father had planned for him, to a boring existence of muddling over thick books crammed with meaningless figures under the critical eye of a penny-pinching employer. He would rather have died.

It was strange, Nate mused, the unforeseen turns a person's life could take. The whims of Fate were as unpredictable as mountain weather, changing with fickle abandon. One day a man might be on top of the world, the next living in the gutter. Of course, that was back in the States. In the wilderness the extremes were more basic. One day a man might be alive, the next dead.

And Nate would not have it any other way. Living from hand to mouth, never knowing one day what the next would bring, had caused him to appreciate the pleasures life had to offer that much more. Oddly enough, the never-ending dangers he daily faced from savage enemies and brutal beasts alike only added to his lust for life. It was as if he was a knife blade and the wilderness the whetstone on which he was being slowly but inexorably honed.

A sheer gully suddenly loomed in Nate's path, shattering his reverie. The gelding cleared the gulf in a single leap. Shifting, he saw the mare do the same and his son's beaming smile of triumph. "Well done," Nate cried.

The land had become more and more level, which was a good sign. Nate reckoned they were close to the Stinking River, so named by a wandering frontiersman who had taken part in the famed Lewis and Clark expedition to the Pacific Ocean, a man by the name of John Colter, undoubtedly the first white man to ever set foot in that part of the country.

The name, though, didn't do the river justice. From all Nate had heard it was one of the finest in the mountains. Colter, it so happened, had come on the river at the one spot where a large tar spring fouled the water and the air alike. Consequently, the unflattering designation.

Shortly Nate spied a winding strip of deciduous trees a mile further on. They turned out to be cottonwoods, willows, and others, types requiring much more water than evergreens and which normally grew along the banks of waterways. He was certain they bordered the river he sought, and within five minutes his conclusion was borne out when he drew rein beside the sluggish waters of the Stinking River.

"We'll rest here for a spell," he announced.

"Is it safe to do that, Pa?" Zach inquired.

Nate nodded as he swung to the ground. "We have quite a lead on those Indians. They might not even know that we know they're after us, in which case they'll take their sweet time trailing us so as not to give themselves away. We can afford a short rest." He indicated Pegasus and Mary. "We have to stop for their sakes, anyway. If our horses give out, those Indians will catch us for sure. Never forget, son, that a man must always think of his horse first and himself second."

"Always?"

Again Nate nodded. "Think of how hard it would be for us to make it back to the village without our horses. It would take forever, and we'd be tempting prey for every grizzly we met. Even a panther might see fit to attack us. A man left stranded afoot in this country is like a fish out of water. He has to be on his toes every second if he wants to stay alive."

While the stallion and the mare drank greedily under Zach's watchful care, Nate walked a short distance downriver, then retraced his steps and went an equal distance upriver. He checked the depth, the speed of the current, and the general lay of the land in both directions.

By the time Nate hurried back, the horses were done drinking and Zach was giving them a rubdown using handfuls of grass. "Those Indians are in for a surprise when they get here," he mentioned.

"Are you fixing to ambush them?"

"No. The odds are too great. I can't risk something happening to me." Climbing on Pegasus, Nate entered the water and turned upriver, staying close to the bank where the water only came up to his ankles.

Zach imitated Nate's example and declared, "I get it, Pa. They won't be able to track us from here on out."

The river was flowing just fast enough to swirl away any mud raised by the hoofs of their animals. Although

23

cold, the water wasn't frigid enough to be uncomfortable. Nate hugged the side for over two hours, at last riding out onto a wide bench covered with gently waving grass.

"What now, Pa?"

"We let the horses graze, then go pick a spot to camp and turn in early so we get a good night's sleep. Tomorrow we're going after elk again."

"But what if those Indians are still after us?"

"I doubt they'll come this far, son. But even if they do, it won't be until sometime tomorrow. There's not enough daylight left for them to reach this spot before dark. If and when they do, we'll be long gone."

Zachary giggled. "I have to hand it to you, Pa. You sure outfoxed them. They'll never catch us now."

"That's the idea, son," Nate said, matching his son's grin, extremely pleased with himself and delighted at the impression he had made on Zach. Thanks to his cleverness, they were safe. Or were they? whispered a tiny voice at the back of his mind, a voice he ignored with a shake of his head. There was such a thing as being too cautious, and he wasn't about to become that. Tomorrow they would down an elk, and in a few days they would head home. It would be as simple as that.

Or would it? asked the tiny voice.

Chapter Two

"There is something strange about these tracks."

Rolling Thunder glanced up from the leg of succulent roast venison on which he had been chewing and stared at Bobcat, who was kneeling on the soft ground close to the river. The flickering light from their crackling fire revealed Bobcat's puzzled expression. "What is strange?" Rolling Thunder asked.

"See for yourself."

Standing, Rolling Thunder wiped his greasy left hand on his leggings and walked over. The footprints here were much clearer than those he had seen by the stream that morning, so clear he had been able to tell the style of stitching used in the construction of the moccasins. Since no two tribes in the entire Rockies made their moccasins exactly alike, from the stitching and the shapes of the soles he had confirmed that the pair they pursued were indeed Shoshones. "Now what bothers you about them?" he inquired.

"Take a look," Bobcat said, touching a finger to the toes of several tracks left by the man.

At first Rolling Thunder noticed nothing unusual. Then, abruptly, he realized what he had missed detecting before and his blood raced through his veins. "One of them is a white man!" he exclaimed.

The shout brought Little Dog, Loud Talker, and Walking Bear from the fire on the run.

"What is this about a white man?" Little Dog wanted to know.

It was Bobcat who answered, accenting his words by tapping one of the footprints. "The man's toes point outward. We all know what that means."

Little Dog crouched to study the tracks, thinking quickly. Yes, he did know that only white men walked thus; Indians always walked with their toes pointing inward. It was yet another example of the truth that whites always did everything backwards. But if Bobcat was right it did not bode well for their hunting trip. One look at the sparkling gleam in Rolling Thunder's dark eyes justified his concern, so he spoke before anyone else. "The toes do not point outward all the time."

"Then it is a white man who has lived among Indians and has practiced walking correctly but doesn't always do so," Bobcat said.

"Or it could be a Shoshone with a limp," Little Dog suggested. If he could convince the others, they might refuse to go along with the idea Rolling Thunder was bound to soon propose.

"There is no evidence of a limp," Bobcat stated. "I tell you it is a white man and a Shoshone boy."

"Or," Rolling Thunder said, "a white man and his half-breed son. I seem to remember hearing about a white dog who is living with the northern Shoshones."

"All of us heard the story," Walking Bear interjected. "Don't you remember? It was four winters ago when

26

we camped for a time with some Blackfeet. They told us about a white with powerful medicine who escaped from their clutches and in doing so killed one of their greatest warriors, White Bear." He paused. "They told us this white's name but it eludes me."

"Grizzly Killer," Loud Talker practically shouted. "They claim he has killed more of the giant bears than any man, Indian or white. They say he kills grizzlies as easily as other men kill flies."

Rolling Thunder smiled and gestured at the tracks with the leg bone. "Yes! I remember now! This must be him. The fierce Grizzly Killer." He said the last with marked contempt.

"We do not know that for certain," Little Dog said. "The Shoshones have other white friends. It could be any one of them."

"What does it really matter if it is Grizzly Killer or not? He is *white*," Rolling Thunder said.

"And that is all that is important," Little Dog said sarcastically.

Pivoting, Rolling Thunder swept them with his gaze. "Friends, what do we care about a few paltry elk when we have the chance to kill a hated white? Our wives can wait a while longer for the meat. Just think of the praise they will heap on us if one of us takes this man's scalp back."

Bobcat stood. "It would be quite an honor, especially if this is Grizzly Killer. We would have done what the Blackfeet could not do."

"We can prove we are the better warriors," Loud Talker said, and vented a bloodthirsty war whoop. "I say we go after these two. If the boy is worthy, I will take him into my lodge and raise him as my own."

"If he is the son of Grizzly Killer I would like to take him into my own lodge," Walking Bear objected. "He should grow up to be a strong warrior with potent medicine, a credit to the man who rears him."

"I say we kill them both," Bobcat said. "That way two of us can count coup."

Little Dog listened to the ensuing heated discussion in disgusted silence. His friends were letting their yearning for glory sweep aside their common sense. None of them, apparently, had noticed that this Grizzly Killer, or whoever the man might be, was leading them back toward the heart of Shoshone country. Their quarry was no fool. If they continued on, the danger of running into a large Shoshone war party grew with each hour. Little Dog feared they might even be tricked into riding straight into a trap.

Rolling Thunder had heard enough about what to do with the boy. Clearing his throat to get their attention, he adopted a solemn air and said, "We can decide the boy's fate when we have caught him. As for the man, it is only a question of which one of us gets to him first. But we must be very careful. We must be on our guard for the Shoshones at all times. I, for one, do not plan to have my hair adorn a Shoshone's lance."

"Why worry?" Bobcat said. "We will be in and out of their country before they know it."

"So you hope," Little Dog told him. Perturbed, he walked to their fire and cut off a large chunk of meat to eat. Squatting with his back to the river, he nibbled and considered whether to waste his breath objecting to their new quest. The others weren't about to change their minds just because he had an uneasy feeling about proceeding. They would say his nerves were on edge, or joke he was losing his courage as they had done previously.

"Why are you not being very sociable this evening?"

Little Dog involuntarily stiffened. He hadn't heard Rolling Thunder approach. For so big a man, Rolling Thunder could move like a ghost when he wanted to. "I was hungry," Little Dog responded.

"What is troubling you, old friend?"

"Not a thing."

"Do you have so little respect for me now that you lie to me? What have I done to deserve such treatment?"

Annoyed, Little Dog spat softly. "You know very well what you have done. Your heart's desire has come true and you are going to risk all our lives hunting this white eyes."

"If you knew what was in my heart, why did you come along?"

"Need you ask?" Little Dog said, and crammed a large bite of juicy meat into his mouth. He nearly started when Rolling Thunder's hand fell on his shoulder.

"I have always valued your friendship most of all, Little Dog, because you see me as I am and still you count me as your friend. I knew you would guess the truth, but I also knew I could count on you to go along with what I wanted to do."

Little Dog had to tuck the meat against a cheek to talk. He intentionally held his voice to just above a whisper. "The others are fools, but I am a bigger fool than all of them put together because I know what could happen and I am too timid to protest."

"You can go back if you want. No one would hold it against you."

"Perhaps not. But none of them would understand." Little Dog turned on his heels and regarded Rolling Thunder critically. "They are my friends too. What manner of friend would I be if I deserted them when they need me the most? No, I will stay. I will go along with your scheme, and I hope for your sake that everything works out and White Buffalo is put in his place."

"He will be. I am risking my life to make it so."

"You are placing all of our lives in peril," Little Dog corrected him. "I only pray it is worth it."

*   *   *

Not quite 12 miles distant, nestled in a hollow where the whipping wind couldn't extinguish their tiny fire, Nate and Zach hunched over the last of the fish they had caught at dusk. Except for a few essentials such as ammunition and black powder, they had not brought any supplies along with them, not even jerky to munch on along the way. They had been living off the land ever since leaving the village, all part of Nate's plan to give his son a true taste of life in the wild reaches of the uncompromising mountains. If they wanted full bellies they had to snare game, and so far they had not gone hungry a single day.

"What do you reckon Ma is doing right about now?" the boy wondered.

"Probably visiting her cousin, Willow Woman. I swear those two are like two peas in a pod. You can hardly pry them apart once they take to jawing."

Zach chuckled and tried to sound mature as he said, "You sure have them pegged, Pa. I reckon you know more about women than Uncle Shakespeare said you do."

"Oh? And what did dear Uncle Shakespeare have to say?"

"Do you remember that big fight Ma and you had once over me going along on a raid into Ute country?"

"Your mother didn't want you to go, and I thought it might be good for you since all you were going to do was tend the horses and lay low if we ran into Utes," Nate recalled. "So?"

"So I asked Uncle Shakespeare why Ma and you argue like that sometimes even though you love each other. He said it's only natural. He said men and women can't help rubbing each other the wrong way now and then 'cause they're so different. Then he used a lot of those funny words from that big book he carries around all the time."

"He quoted from the works of Shakespeare."

"Yep."

"When did he mention me?"

"When I asked what all those funny words had to do with Ma and you. He said you're still young so you don't rightly know much about women and it's not your fault if you get Ma riled now and then. He said your life is"— Zach thought for a few seconds—"a comedy of errors, whatever that is, and then he laughed so hard his face turned beet red."

"Remind me to pay your uncle a visit when we get back."

"Can we? I'd like that, Pa. He's a lot of fun to be around."

Nate spread out their blankets side by side, then strolled over to where their horses were tethered. Pegasus was grazing. The mare stood with her head bowed and her eyes closed. He patted the gelding, and scanned the adjacent forest while listening intently to the various night sounds around them. An owl posed its eternal question. A wolf wailed a lonesome lament far to the west. To the south, faint but unmistakable, arose the throaty snarl of a prowling panther, and Nate waited to see if it would be repeated so he might get some idea of which direction the panther was moving. But the big cat didn't cooperate.

After a while Nate walked toward the fire. He wasn't particularly worried about the panther since the solitary cats rarely attacked humans or went after livestock in the close proximity of humans. The horses should be safe. Even if the panther did venture near, he was confident the keen ears and nose of the gelding would detect its presence and that Pegasus would act up something awful, thereby awakening him.

The fire had burned low. Reddish-orange tongues of flame licked at the few pieces of wood not yet charred. Zach, exhausted from the many hours spent in the saddle, had already curled up and appeared to be sound asleep.

Nate gazed fondly at his son, feeling all warm inside. The boy tried so hard and did so well. Suddenly he saw a vague shape gliding out of the inky shadows toward Zach and he froze. The dancing firelight illuminated a low-slung creature on all fours. He glimpsed a hairy, triangular face framed by high, pointed ears and a long nose held close to the ground. For a second Nate thought it must be a wolf, and his right hand streaked to one of the two flintlocks wedged under his wide leather belt on either side of his metal buckle. As he took hasty aim the animal took another stride closer and was bathed in more firelight, allowing Nate to see that it wasn't a wolf after all.

Their visitor was a coyote.

Mystified, Nate held his fire. Coyotes were not noted for their ferocity, and this one gave no sign of being about to pounce. Rather, it seemed more curious than anything else as it slunk steadily closer to Zach. Nate could see its nose twitching as it tested the air, getting the boy's scent.

Abruptly, Zach shifted, rolling onto his back and uttering a low moan as he did. The coyote reacted as if shot, recoiling and wheeling to vanish in the brush with nary a sound.

Nate stuck the flintlock back under his belt, and returned to the blankets to take a seat next to his son. He scoured the shroud of darkness, but the coyote was long gone. Reflecting on its odd behavior, he thought of his wife and how, if she had been there, she would say the incident had been an omen. Like all Shoshones she was quite superstitious, reading meanings into everyday events that Nate tended to shrug off as simple happenstance. But it *was* strange, he conceded, that Zach, whose given Shoshone name was Stalking Coyote, should be visited by a wild coyote in the dead of night.

Shrugging, Nate positioned his Hawken next to his right side, and lay down on his back so he could gaze at the myriad of brilliant stars on high. Few spectacles inspired his soul like the celestial tapestry that nightly adorned the heavens. It was a time to lie quietly and think, to ponder what had happened during the day and plan for tomorrow.

He thought about the five Indians and hoped they had given up the chase. Many times in the past he had lost pursuers by taking to water as he had done today, so he was optimistic the five wouldn't pick up the trail again. Still, he would have to be vigilant for a while.

A twig snapped in the brush.

Nate smiled and held himself still. The coyote had come back, and he didn't want to do anything that would scare it off. He was interested to learn how close it would venture if he pretended to be asleep.

A second twig cracked.

Ever so slowly, Nate twisted his head, his eyes nearly shut, and waited for the animal to appear. An indistinct shape moved at the limits of his vision and he heard a loud crunch. For a coyote, the critter was uncommonly noisy. He had to suppress a laugh when it made yet another sound.

Gradually the indistinct shape solidified into a black mass, a huge black mass, an enormous lumbering bulk that strode fearlessly forward into the last of the light from the fire and grunted as if in surprise on finding two humans in its domain.

Nate's breath caught in his throat and his blood changed to ice. A shiver rippled down his spine. His right hand rested on the barrel of the Hawken, but he dared not try to use the rifle since he couldn't hope to put a ball into the monster standing in front of him before it ripped him apart with its giant claws. Even if, by some miracle, he did, it was rare that a single shot dispatched a full-grown grizzly.

The bear swung its ponderous head from side to side while sniffing loudly. Perhaps it smelled the lingering odor of the cooked fish, or perhaps another scent attracted it. Whatever, the grizzly stepped forward until its great head hung directly above the two figures on the ground.

Nate could feel its warm, fetid breath on his face and see the underside of its chin. From where he lay the bear resembled a living mountain of solid muscle. Within a foot of his face was a gigantic paw, the claws glistening dully. A drop of drool splattered on Nate's cheek but he ignored it.

Grunting, the bear nosed the man and the boy. The latter mumbled and fidgeted and the bear cocked its head, its cavernous mouth opening and closing. The scent of the morsel was tantalizing, but the grizzly had eaten half an hour ago and its stomach was full. Too, the bear had never seen anything like these two creatures, and it still remembered the bitter lesson it had learned at an early age when it tried to eat another creature it had never encountered before, a creature covered with long, sharp quills that had cut into its nose and mouth and had taken weeks to tear loose, causing no end of pain.

Nate saw the grizzly staring at Zach, and braced for the worst. His left hand inched to the tomahawk on his hip, and he started to ease the weapon free. He would undoubtedly be crushed to a pulp, but he was not about to lie there and let the monster devour his son. The wooden handle felt small against his palm, the weapon itself puny. Girding his courage, he tensed to leap erect and swing.

All of a sudden the bear backed up, spun, and shuffled off, plowing through the brush with all the finesse of a steam engine. The crashing and crackling grew progressively fainter until they were smothered by distance.

Nate sat bolt upright, his heart thumping in his chest. That, he told himself, had been too damn close for comfort! He looked at his peacefully slumbering son, and was so relieved that tears formed at the corners of his eyes. Then he quickly rose and gathered more fuel for the fire, bringing back a half-dozen loads of broken branches, enough to make a waist-high pile.

Not in the least sleepy, Nate fed wood to the few remaining flames until he had a roaring blaze going. From where he squatted he could see the horses, and he marveled that the grizzly had not caught their scent and that neither horse had whinnied in fright during its brief stay. Shaking his head in amazement, he verified that his two pistols, the tomahawk, and his butcher knife were all in place about his waist. The Hawken went across his lap. He sat up until near midnight, dreading that the grizzly might see fit to wander back, but the forest lay tranquil under a moonless sky.

Despite his best efforts, Nate's weary body succumbed to the inevitable. His eyes closed. He reclined on his side, the rifle in his hands, and decided to sleep a little while, just enough to refresh him. Then he'd build the fire up once more and keep watch over his son until daylight. That was all he needed. A few hours' rest.

The sharp neigh of a terrified horse slashed into Nate's consciousness like a hot knife through butter and he came instantly awake. He was upright and glancing every which way before he quite realized what had awakened him. The mare whinnied, providing an answer, and he heard both horses restlessly moving back and forth.

From the deep woods came a guttural growl.

For a second Nate believed the grizzly had returned and was about to attack their mounts; then the growl lengthened and grew louder, becoming a drawn-out, savage snarl such as only the largest of cats could utter. It was a panther, perhaps the same panther he had heard previously!

"Zach!" Nate said as he scooped up the Hawken. "Wake up, son. We have trouble on our hands."

The boy tossed and his eyelids fluttered.

"Wake up!" Nate urged, fearful the beast would spring before they reached their mounts. He prodded his son with his toe. "Come on!"

"Pa?" Zach said uncertainly, sitting up. He looked around in confusion. "What is it? What's the matter?"

"Panther," Nate explained. "Grab your gun and follow me."

Young Zach came to full alertness as the tension in his father's tone conveyed the danger confronting them. He grabbed the long rifle lying beside him, the first and only rifle he had ever owned, given to him by his parents just a few short weeks before the elk hunt began, and jumped to his feet.

"Stay close," Nate cautioned, treading warily toward Pegasus and Mary. Both animals stood stock-still, staring intently into the darkened woods to the north of where they were tied. He wondered why the cat had snarled the way it had since usually panthers were quiet when stalking prey, and he gave silent thanks that this cat was the exception rather than the rule. Had it approached noiselessly, by now one of their horses would be dead.

"Where is it, Pa?" Zach whispered, his small thumb on the cool metal hammer. He tried to keep his voice steady so his father wouldn't suspect how scared he felt. His mouth was dry, his palms damp.

"It could be anywhere," Nate responded. "Keep your eyes peeled."

Zach absently nodded, his mind whirling so that he couldn't think straight and didn't realize his father, being in front of him, couldn't see his head move. He scanned the line of trees on both sides, the dark, ominous trunks not more than ten feet off on either side, and remembered the many tales he had heard about how far panthers could leap. What if the cat charged his pa or him instead of the horses? It would be on them before they could get off a shot. The thought spawned terror that spread like wildfire throughout his body, causing an odd burning sensation on his skin and making his limbs tingle as if they were asleep.

Pegasus had raised his head to sniff the breeze. His front hoof stamped the ground hard twice and then he moved a yard to the left, his big eyes locked on the bole of a large tree in the forest directly across from him.

Nate could guess why. The Hawken cocked, he moved around the horses until he was between the gelding and the tree. "Get set, son," he said softly. "If it's going to attack, it won't wait long."

Zach, struck dumb by his terror, made no reply, and he saw his father glance at him. At the very same instant he saw something else: the panther, its claws extended, its razor teeth exposed, vaulting from concealment straight at them.

Chapter Three

To one who has never experienced raw, unbridled fear, the first time can be virtually paralyzing. There had been times in the past when young Zach had been afraid, but he had never, ever known such stark fright as that which seized him at the moment the panther sprang. He wanted to cry out, to warn his father, but his vocal chords had changed to stone. He wanted to raise the Kentucky rifle and fire, but his arms were frozen in place. All he could do was watch helplessly as the huge cat sailed gracefully through the air.

Nate was not taken completely unawares, however. He'd seen his son's eyes widen, and he pivoted toward the forest just as the panther slammed into him. By sheer chance he had the Hawken at chest height, so it was the rifle the cat's slashing forepaws struck instead of his body. Nate was spared from being ripped wide open. The impact, though, sent him stumbling backwards into Pegasus.

Hissing like a venomous serpent, the panther crouched and gathered its leg muscles to jump again.

At last Zach found his voice. Horrified by the mental image of the panther sinking its teeth into his father, a heartfelt *"No!"* burst from his thin lips.

Distracted, the big cat looked at him.

And it was then that Nate, having recovered his balance, hastily pointed the Hawken at the panther's head. His finger was tightening on the trigger when the courageous gelding, which was eager to close with the intruder, tried to get past him, jostling him roughly as it did and inadvertently jarring the barrel to one side. The Hawken thundered, but the ball missed by inches.

Swiftly Nate clawed at a flintlock, hoping against hope he would be able to fire before the cat pounced. The blast and the cloud of smoke had momentarily startled the panther into immobility, and he knew the spell wouldn't last long. It didn't. Just as the flintlock was clearing his belt, the cat snarled, whirled, and flashed into the undergrowth.

Nate extended his arm, but there was no target to hit. He listened, yet heard only the wind. Slowly he lowered the pistol as it dawned on him that the crisis was past. The panther had been scared off and wasn't about to bother them again.

"Is it gone, Pa?" Zach asked timidly.

"Yep." Nate studied the boy's ashen features and mustered a lopsided grin. "Gave you a bit of a fright, did it?"

Zach gulped and nodded.

"Happens to all of us at one time or another. It's nothing to be ashamed of."

"I'll bet you weren't afraid."

"There wasn't time for me to be scared. It all happened so fast."

Nate took a minute to reload the Hawken, then stroked each of the horses in turn, speaking softly to them to calm them down. Presently he headed for the fire, his son, head bowed, at his side. "Are you all right, Zach?"

"I'm fine, Pa," Zach lied, because his emotions were in seething turmoil. He felt so bad he wanted to crawl into a hole and die. The way he saw it, he had behaved like a coward. And in his estimation there was no worse fate in all the word than being yellow.

To Shoshone men, courage was everything, the most essential of manly traits. Some of Zach's earliest memories were of Shoshone warriors recounting the brave deeds they had done to earn the coups they had counted. Countless times he had listened in rapt fascination as Touch the Clouds, Spotted Bull, Drags the Rope, and others told of their daring exploits, and always he longed for the day when he would perform deeds to match or exceed theirs.

As if that wasn't unsettling enough, for years Zach had heard stories about his father, about the many grizzlies his pa had slain and the many foes his pa had killed in defense of the tribe. At least a half-dozen times various warriors had said that Grizzly Killer was one of the bravest men alive. More than once Zach had been told that he was a lucky boy to have such a stalwart father, and that when he grew up he must do his father proud by being equally as courageous.

And look at what had happened! Zach reflected sourly. He'd had a chance to show just how brave he was, and instead he had discovered that at heart he was a coward. He'd let his pa down and himself down. How could he ever hope to make his pa proud when he had no courage at all? His lower lip trembled as he held back the tears dampening the corners of his eyes, and he was glad his father couldn't see his face as he lay down on his side with his arms wrapped around the Kentucky rifle.

"You get some more sleep, son," Nate remarked. "I'll keep watch a spell."

"I'll try."

"Are you sure you're not feeling poorly? You sound as if you're coming down with a cold."

"I never felt better, Pa," Zach said, and then, under his breath, he repeated bitterly, "Never felt better."

The barking of a dog brought Winona out of her peaceful sleep. Snug and warm under a thick, soft buffalo robe, she rolled onto her back and stretched languidly while gazing up through the open smoke flap at the top of the lodge. A pink hue tinged the sky, signifying dawn was not far off.

Winona's instinctive reaction was to start to rise so she could prepare breakfast for her husband and son. Then, grinning at her forgetfulness, she sank down and tucked the robe up under her chin. Her beloved Nate and dearest Zach would not return for six or seven sleeps yet. She could sleep as long as she wanted. Why, she might even scandalize herself in the eyes of the other women and not get up until after sunrise. They would think she was becoming lazy.

The notion made her giggle.

Winona thought of her husband and son and wished them well. By now, according to the plans Nate had laid out for her before their departure, they should be well up in the mountains in an area where elk were as plentiful as chipmunks, having the time of their lives. She was glad she had talked her husband into doing it. Zach, in her opinion, was long overdue to learn those skills that would serve him in excellent stead as he grew to full manhood. He was already eight; by the same age most Shoshone boys were competent hunters and knew how to butcher a variety of game without wasting a shred of meat.

Voices sounded outside, those of women going to the nearby river for water. Somewhere a child laughed.

David Thompson

Throwing back the buffalo robe, Winona stood. Old habits were hard to break, and since she had been rising before daylight every day of her life, she felt uncomfortable doing otherwise. Life was meant for living, not for wasting. She wanted to attend to certain chores so she could visit her cousin, Willow Woman.

Shortly Winona emerged from the lodge, her lithe figure adorned in a beaded buckskin dress and moccasins. A large tin pan, 18 inches in diameter, was clutched in her bronzed left hand. The wind whipped her long raven hair as she strolled across the open space to the river and knelt.

"How is the wife of Grizzly Killer this day?"

Winona looked up into the smiling face of Rabbit Woman, who was short and unusually plump for a Shoshone, and who seldom spoke to Winona unless she had a sarcastic comment to make. The two had known each other since childhood but had never gotten along. "I am well. How is the wife of Knife in Hand?"

"Very tired," Rabbit Woman answered, squatting so she could dip the water bucket she held into the river. Made from a buffalo paunch, it had a leather strap for a handle that she clasped tightly as the bucket slowly filled. "My brother showed up at our lodge well before the sun came up and wanted my help in cutting up a buck he had shot."

"He should have cut it up himself," Winona said politely in sympathy while lowering the pan into the river.

"You know how Jumping Bull is," Rabbit Woman said. "He was in a hurry."

Winona had to use both hands to steady the pan, which became heavier by the moment. She listened with half an ear as her companion went on.

"It is sad that Jumping Bull has not found a new wife to take the place of Eagle Shawl. A man should not

42

live his life alone. And too, his son, Runs Fast, needs a mother."

"True," Winona said, being polite.

"Jumping Bull is a great warrior. He has twelve coup to his credit, and three of them were Blackfeet he killed with just his knife. Any woman would be proud to have him as her husband."

"I am sure he will find another wife," Winona said as she lifted the pan out.

"He has his eyes on someone who appeals to him, although what he sees in her I do not know. I have tried to talk him out of courting her, but he will not listen. Men can be so stubborn at times."

At this Winona grinned. "Men are stubborn *all* the time," she joked, and had started to leave when Rabbit Woman put a hand on her arm.

"I want you to know I argued against the idea until I was hoarse from talking, but he would not listen. When Jumping Bull sets his mind to something, nothing can change it. Many others will be angry at what he does, but that will not stop him. It would be better for all if the woman he wants moves into his lodge without causing trouble."

Mildly surprised that Rabbit Woman was confiding in her, Winona replied, "Jumping Bull is fortunate to have a sister who cares so much." She began to turn, but Rabbit Woman restrained her.

"I do care. I care with all my heart. He has always treated me kindly and helped me when I needed help. I can do no less for him, can I?"

"I suppose not," Winona said.

Opening her mouth as if to say more, Rabbit Woman evidently changed her mind, let go of Winona, and hurried off, walking so fast she spilled some of the water from her bucket. Soon she was lost among the lodges.

Winona ambled toward her own lodge. She was even more baffled, but she decided Rabbit Woman's problems were none of her affair. Behind her the golden crest of the sun peeked above the horizon. In the trees beyond the encampment birds were greeting the new day with their customary chorus. She passed several friends and exchanged pleasantries. To the south her uncle, Spotted Bull, stepped out into the sunlight and waved to her. All she could do, with her hands burdened by the pan, was smile back.

So preoccupied was Winona by the sights and sounds of the stirring village that she was only 15 feet from her lodge when she spotted something lying on the ground in front of the entrance. Eyes narrowing, she drew near enough to identify what it was and promptly halted, in shock, the full implication hitting her with the force of a physical blow. Now she understood why Rabbit Woman had sought her out. Now she knew why the woman had confided in her. A cold wind seemed to chill her to the marrow and she shuddered.

For there on a square piece of hide rested the haunch of a recently slain deer.

"We are wasting our time," Little Dog commented testily with a gesture at the river swirling past to his right. "There is no sign of where the two of them left the water. Why bother going on with this when our wives can use the elk meat we supposedly came after?"

Rolling Thunder, who rode a few yards ahead, snapped a look over his broad shoulder. "Are you saying I lied to you and the others?" he challenged.

Sighing, Little Dog gazed across the river at the opposite shore where Walking Bear, Bobcat, and Loud Talker were all scouring the ground for tracks their quarry might have left. They knew that the man and the child had gone up the river, but as yet they had been unable to find the spot where the pair took to the land again.

"I asked you a question," Rolling Thunder said, his voice low and hard.

Little Dog would rather have avoided the issue entirely, but since Rolling Thunder was so touchy about it, he reasoned that clearing the air would be best for all. "No," he said in resignation. "You did not deliberately lie to us. You truly intended to hunt elk." He paused. "Yet if that was all you planned to do, we would not have needed to travel so far from our own country. You insisted on traveling here to hunt. Why? Are the elk here fatter than they are in our own country? No. Are they easier to find? Perhaps. But in the back of your mind you have been hoping to find something else. You knew there are more white men in this region than elsewhere, and above all else you hope to count coup on one before we return to our people."

"And you hold this against me?"

"Not really, because I know why you do it. You want to be chief one day. The only other warrior who might dispute you is White Buffalo, who is just as brave as you are and has almost as many scalps hanging in his lodge as you do in yours." Little Dog spied a large trout out in the water and watched it swim lazily by. Oh, that he might be a fish and not have to contend with the ambitions of vain friends! "There is one big difference between the two of you, though. White Buffalo has the scalp of a white trapper; you do not. And so you want to add one to your collection so that he will not be able to stand up before our people and claim an honor that you do not have."

"*I* should be the next chief, not him," Rolling Thunder declared, striking his chest in his passion. "He sees himself as a mighty warrior, yet he is not half the man that I am."

"So you will do whatever is necessary to match his feats," Little Dog said rather sadly.

"Would you do otherwise if you were me?"

"I am not you so I cannot say."

In silence they rode on as the sun climbed steadily, warming the crisp mountain air. Rolling Thunder made no more mention of his true motive for venturing into Shoshone territory, but secretly he vowed that he was going to track the man and the boy down if it took an entire moon to do. Counting coup on a white man would increase his standing in the tribe to where no one, not even the redoubtable White Buffalo, could prevent him from assuming the mantle of leadership.

A sudden shout from the opposite bank drew Rolling Thunder's attention to Walking Bear, who was grinning and jabbing a finger to the northeast. Rolling Thunder looked. Then his mouth curled in elation.

Several miles away, spiraling skyward, was the pale gray smoke from a camp fire.

"I could sure use another piece of jerky, Pa."

Nate rummaged in the parfleche at his feet and handed over a strip of the dried, salted meat to his Zach. "This makes the sixth one. Sometimes I swear that you have a bottomless pit for a stomach."

Zach's face lit up, the first time all day, and he replied, "I take after you. Ma said so herself. And Uncle Shakespeare told me that you're the only man he knows who can eat a whole bull buffalo at one sitting."

"He should talk. Remind me to tell you about the time he drank the Yellowstone River dry."

"He did not," Zach said, and laughed.

"Just ask the Shoshones," Nate said, overjoyed that the boy was finally showing his customary spark. All morning Zach had been inexplicably moody and had never spoken unless addressed, which was so unusual that Nate, remembering the nasal twang in his son's voice the previous night, had twice checked his son's forehead to see if Zach had a fever and might be coming down with something.

Well shy of noon Nate had been inspired to call a halt to their ride so they could eat and he could down a few cups of hot coffee. So little sleep had he gotten after the panther attack that he needed the coffee to stay awake. Three hot cups had invigorated him, and he was ready to resume their hunt.

The fire had about died down anyway. A tendril of smoke wafted upward as Nate poked the embers with a stick, extinguishing the last tiny flame. "Always remember to put out your camp fires," he remarked for the boy's benefit. "A careless spark can start a raging fire which could burn for days, maybe weeks. And always build your fires small, like the Indians do, so there's less chance of an enemy spotting it."

"Anything else?" Zach asked, enthused to learn more. As with most children, his irrepressible spirit could not stay smothered forever. For the time being he had shut last night's cowardice from his mind.

"Yes," Nate said. "Have you noticed how I always arrange the branches for our fires?"

Zach nodded. "You put them down like the spokes in a wagon wheel instead of piling them on top of each other."

"It's the Indian way of making fires. The woods burns slower so you don't have to gather as much to last you. It also burns steadier, which makes it easier to keep the flames under control."

"So that's why they do it that way," Zach said thoughtfully.

"You've got to keep in mind," Nate elaborated as he discarded the tiny bit of coffee left in the pot, "the Indians have been living in the wild for a long time.

47

They're masters at woodcraft. It's safe to say they've forgotten more over the years than our own people will ever learn. They treat Nature with respect instead of contempt. Pay attention and learn all you can because you never know when what you learn will come in handy."

Shortly they were on the go again, Zach on Nate's left. "Pa, you lived a long time back in the States. Which is better, the white way of life or the Indian way of life?"

The question caught Nate off guard. He pondered a minute, not caring to say anything that would embitter his son toward the society of white men. His own decision along those lines had been made the day he took Winona as his wife, but he wanted Zach to one day make up his own mind. So he said, "They both have their merits."

"But which is the best?" the boy asked with the single-minded persistence of the very young.

"I suppose the answer depends on what a person wants out of life," Nate said. "If safety and security is what you're after, then the white man's life is best. East of the Mississippi you hardly ever have to worry about being set on by hostiles, and since they've killed off all the grizzlies and most of the wolves and panthers, you'd never have to fret about those either. Stores nowadays carry ready-made clothes, so you'd never have to bother with sewing your own buckskins together. And with all the restaurants and saloons and taverns and such, you'd hardly ever have to cook your own food. There'd always be somewhere you could eat if you had the price."

"The white way of life sure sounds easy."

"That it does, but the easy way isn't always the best way."

"How so?"

"Life was never meant to be easy, Zach. Take a good look around you sometime. See how every creature in the mountains has to struggle to survive." Nate indicated a circling eagle to the south. "Wild animals have to work hard if they want to live. They spend their days hunting or foraging or seeking water, and the whole time they have to be on the lookout for their enemies because if they let down their guard for just a short while, they could wind up dead. But does all this hardship make them sickly? On the contrary. Most of them are as sleek and healthy as they could be."

Zach was listening attentively.

"The only animals that have it easy are those that have all their needs taken care of by man. Take cows and pigs, for instance. They have it about the easiest of any animals anywhere. All they do is stand around and eat all day, growing fatter and lazier as they get older and older. The same holds true for men and women. If we have it too easy, we grow fat and lazy just like cows and pigs."

"I see," Zach said. He regarded his father with frank admiration. "Tarnation, Pa. You sure know a lot. I bet you're the smartest man around."

"Not quite," Nate said, and chuckled.

Half a mile was covered before Zach broached another question that showed how deeply he had been thinking about his father's words. "I'd rather be a mountain lion than a cow any day. Why do folks wants things so easy?"

"Because they're afraid to take risks, I imagine. They don't want anything to do with something that might upset the orderly lives they like to live." Nate arched his spine to relieve a kink. "Most of them work at dull jobs where they do the same thing day after day, month after month, year after year, and earn just enough money to get by. But they put up with the drudgery because they can fill their bellies three times a day and wear new clothes now and then and have a roof over their heads."

"And they're happy living like that?"

"That's the strange part, son. Most of them say they're not all that happy, but they won't lift a finger to change things."

A few more yards fell behind them.

"If you don't mind, Pa, I figure I'd like to live in the mountains the rest of my life. City living doesn't sound like something I'd be interested in."

"It's your choice," Nate said, realizing he had done exactly what he hadn't wanted to do and inadvertently influenced his son's thinking. He shifted, and was about to point out some good aspects of white culture when to their rear there arose a succession of crackling and crunching sounds as something crashed through the brush directly toward them.

Chapter Four

Winona saw a shadow fall across the open flap of the lodge, and glanced down at the butcher knife lying partially concealed under a folded blanket at her side. The hilt was within easy reach. Girding herself, she looked at the entrance and the husky man squatting there, keeping her features composed. "This is an honor, Jumping Bull," she said pleasantly.

The warrior, attired in his finest buckskins, his hair braided and adorned with several feathers, scowled and rested a hand on the deer haunch. "You did not touch this."

"It is not mine," Winona said, devoting herself to the pair of Zach's leggings she was mending.

"I left it for you."

"I know."

"Then you should have claimed it."

Pausing in the act of using her buffalo-bone sewing

awl, Winona met his gaze. "My husband provides for me. There was no need for you to take it on yourself to share your kill with us."

Jumping Bull poked his head inside and started to ease his wide shoulders and chest through the opening. Almost as an afterthought, he asked, "May I enter?"

"No."

The man stopped, but made no move to back up. "I need to talk to you," he declared.

"You may talk to me from outside. My ears work quite well and I will hear everything you say."

"This is foolish," Jumping Bull said gruffly, lifting a foot inside and beginning to straighten.

"No!" Winona's voice rang out so loudly that she was heard 20 yards away.

Again Jumping Bull stopped, his expression becoming one of baffled annoyance. A look behind him showed a number of men, women, and children who were studying him curiously. Since to enter a lodge uninvited was a serious breach of tribal etiquette, he sank back on his heels just beyond the flap. "You are being most inconsiderate," he chided. "All I want is to tell you what is on my mind."

"Of what interest are your thoughts to me?" Winona countered disdainfully.

"They will be, once you know them," Jumping Bull predicted. "I have decided the time is ripe for me to take another wife, and I have chosen you."

A merry laugh tinkled from Winona's throat. "You are forgetting that I already have a husband."

"A white man is no fit husband for a beautiful woman like you. You are a full-blooded Shoshone. You should have a full-blooded Shoshone as a mate."

Bristling at the insult against Nate, Winona hid her feelings and commented, "I am quite content to be the woman of Grizzly Killer. He is a great warrior who cares for his family very much. No man could make me happier."

"I could," Jumping Bull asserted. "And I have decided you will come live with me this very day. So pack your things and we will go."

Winona set down the awl, her right hand drifting to the smooth hilt of the butcher knife. "It seems to me that you are making a lot of decisions concerning others without first consulting them. I have no desire to live with you, Jumping Bull. I love Grizzly Killer."

"You will forget him in time. Come." He beckoned her.

"No."

"I can easily drag you out if you continue to be so stubborn. Remember, you have no father or brothers to defend you. And the dog you call a husband is gone."

"I will be certain to tell him you said that," Winona said, maintaining her calm demeanor with difficulty. She refused to let him know how rattled she was by the dreadful conflict that was brewing. "And as for protectors, you should remember that my uncle, Spotted Bull, is close by, and that he has regarded me as he does his own daughter since the deaths of my parents."

"Spotted Bull will mind his own business," Jumping Bull said. "He will see that this is between the white dog and me."

"Can you be sure of that?" Winona asked. "And what about his son, Touch the Clouds, who is not only my cousin but one of the best friends my husband has? Will he stand by and do nothing while you mistreat me?" She detected a hint of indecision in the man's dark eyes, and knew that mentioning the name of the most renowned of all Shoshone warriors had had the desired effect.

Touch the Clouds was aptly named. He was a giant standing almost seven feet high and endowed with a massive physique to match his towering height, and his prowess in warfare was legendary among his people.

Winona went on. "And do not forget my husband's many other friends. Drags the Rope, Lone Wolf, He Who Rides Standing—none of them will like my being bothered while he is away."

"They have no right to interfere," Jumping Bull said petulantly. "This is my affair, not theirs." He shifted his weight from one heel to the other, and immersed in thought, did not say anything for quite a while.

Waiting in tense expectation, Winona barely breathed. She could hardly believe this was happening to her, that her happy existence was being threatened by someone she had rarely spoken to in years. They had been friendly during their childhood, but that had been over 20 years ago and she had been friends with all the boys in the village, not just him.

Jumping Bull cleared his throat. "I want you and I mean to have you. No one will stand in my way." He picked up the haunch. "For now, think on my words and settle in your mind that you are going to be my wife whether you like the idea or not."

"Never!" Winona declared, her eyes flashing. "I would rather . . ." She then fell silent because the object of her wrath had risen and departed.

Suddenly Winona began trembling uncontrollably. Doubling over, she clutched her stomach and uttered a series of low, pathetic groans. Acute misery tore at her soul. Clenching her fists, she craned her neck back and gazed out the opening at the top of the lodge. *Oh my Nate!* her mind cried. *Where are you?*

Rolling Thunder held a hand aloft as he reined up, and the other four also halted. The scent of smoke was strong in his nostrils, and he could hear an unusual thumping sound. They were close to the fire, he knew, so he slid off his war-horse, tied it to a bush, and motioned for the rest to follow him.

Hefting the slender lance in his left hand, Rolling Thunder glided through the undergrowth until he spotted a meadow ahead. There was movement at the far end, so he dropped into a crouch and snaked forward until he had an unobstructed view. His face fairly gleamed with bloodlust when he discovered the source of the fire.

A bearded white man had made camp beside a small spring and was busily chopping wood with an ax. Several packs lay on the ground by the fire, as did a bundle of beaver pelts. To a tree behind him were secured two mules and a horse. Leaning against the tree was a rifle.

Rolling Thunder glanced at his companions and used sign language to convey his directions. Walking Bear and Loud Talker he sent to the left, Bobcat and Little Dog to the right. As they moved away he sank to his hands and knees, then onto his belly, and crawled into the open, moving through the high grass as would a slinking wolf.

When a mere 15 feet from the unsuspecting trapper, Rolling Thunder released his spear and lowered his right hand to his knife. Killing a foe in personal combat rated as a braver act than killing one from a distance, so rather than hurl the lance he intended to get in close and dispatch the man with the keen blade that glinted in the bright sunlight.

Rolling Thunder edged nearer, his eyes exclusively on the white man. The others would hold back, giving him the honor of making the kill. He gripped the knife firmly and closed to within ten feet.

Abruptly, the trapper stopped chopping and looked up sharply, his blue eyes roving over the meadow and the ring of pines. By the anxious glances he shot in all directions it was apparent that he sensed danger but had nothing solid on which to base his apprehension. He lowered the ax, stared at the horse and mules to see if they were agitated, and when he saw them standing placidly, chuckled and resumed chopping.

Coiling his legs under him, Rolling Thunder waited until the man had finished splitting the thick piece of wood and was bending over to pick it up. Then, like a shot, Rolling Thunder charged, his knife held on high for a killing stroke.

The trapper, on hearing onrushing footsteps, whirled. There was no time for him to grab the flintlock under his belt. Clasping the ax at opposite ends, he swept it up and blocked the powerful swing of Rolling Thunder's arm. Backing away to give himself room to maneuver, he reversed his grip and drove the ax head at the Gros Ventre's face.

By the merest fraction Rolling Thunder ducked under the swing and felt a breath of air fan his cheeks. He lunged, striving to bury his knife in the trapper's chest, but the man was quicker, flinging himself to one side and dropping a hand to the flintlock.

Rolling Thunder knew he must not let the trapper draw that gun. Cutting loose with a feral war whoop, he leaped, his arms outstretched, and collided with the man just as the flintlock was yanked free. Together they toppled, Rolling Thunder on top, his legs preventing the man from raising the pistol.

The trapper's eyes showed fear as Rolling Thunder lifted the knife, shrieked with joy, and buried the blade into the man's throat. Gurgling and wheezing, spurting blood on the two of them and the grass, the trapper bucked, vainly trying to toss the Gros Ventre off. Tenaciously, Rolling Thunder clamped his thighs harder and held onto the knife. He could feel the man's movements growing weaker and weaker. A single word escaped the trapper's blood-flecked lips.

"God—!"

Suddenly it was over. The trapper went limp, his eyes blank. Rolling Thunder jerked out the dripping knife and pushed erect. Whooping deliriously, he jumped up and down over and over.

From the trees came his friends. Loud Talker reached the trapper first and struck the body with his tomahawk. "I claim second coup!" he shouted.

"The bastard is dead," Bobcat said. "You cannot claim coup on a dead man."

"I thought I saw him move," Loud Talker objected.

"You wished you saw him move," was Bobcat's retort.

Loud Talker turned to Rolling Thunder. "Was he dead? Do I count coup?"

Rolling Thunder stopped jumping and faced them. He found it hard to think, so furiously was his blood pounding in his veins. Gradually the words sank in, and he looked down at the trapper. According to custom, up to four men could count coup on the same enemy in the heat of battle. The highest coup always went to the warrior who struck an enemy while the enemy was alive, severely wounding him. Second coup would go to another warrior who might then strike the weakened foe. Third coup went to yet a different warrior if he dispatched the wounded adversary, while fourth coup could be claimed by yet another if he did the scalping.

"Do I?" Loud Talker repeated eagerly.

"Yes," Rolling Thunder said, and saw Little Dog frown and turn away. "There was a breath of life left in him when you hit him. The coup counts. I will vouch for you."

"I would have sworn he was dead," Bobcat said, adding instantly, "but you should know better than I, so I will accept your judgment."

Walking Bear was staring enviously at the trapper's

long black hair. He tapped his knife. "Do you want the scalp or may I have it?"

Indecision made Rolling Thunder hesitate. He wanted the scalp badly so that he could gloat to White Buffalo and prove to the rest of the tribe that he could do anything White Buffalo did. But clearly this wasn't the white man they had been after; this wasn't the one who had a boy along, who might or might not be Grizzly Killer. And how much better it would be if he could claim the famous Grizzly Killer's scalp! But if he insisted on having this one, the others would have every right to demand that they be given the chance to count first coup on Grizzly Killer. What should he do? he asked himself. Take a chance on adding Grizzly Killer's hair to his collection and let Walking Bear have this scalp? Or take this one and possibly have to pass up Grizzly Killer's?

As he stood there hesitating, Rolling Thunder noticed Little Dog look at him and smile. Somehow, he knew what his friend was thinking, that he wasn't generous enough to pass up any white man's scalp, no matter how much benefit he might later derive from doing so. Galled, he impulsively stated, "The scalp is yours, Walking Bear."

Turning, Rolling Thunder walked to the tree and claimed the rifle for his own. He also claimed the horse and one of the packs. The rest divided up the spoils as they saw fit. Both Loud Talker and Walking Bear thanked him repeatedly, and to each he was properly humble. He made no mention of the elation he felt at having the two of them in his debt. They were so grateful they would go along with whatever he wanted—and shortly he spoke out. "I would like to try one more time to find the trail of the man and the boy."

"Why go to the bother?" Little Dog said. "They are many miles from here by now."

"I want to try."

"You've killed a white man. What more do you need?"

Rolling Thunder made no reply, but the tinge of sadness that touched his face combined with the air of slightly hurt feelings he so cleverly projected had the result he hoped.

Loud Talker promptly came to his defense. "I do not understand why you object to going after them, Little Dog," he declared indignantly. "What harm can it do?" He bobbed his head at Rolling Thunder. "Thanks to him we will be the talk of the village when we return. Why not do as he wants and maybe count more coup?"

"I agree," Walking Bear threw in. "Going back with elk meat is one thing, going back with scalps and many coup to boast of is another. So I say we go after these other two."

Bobcat interjected his predictable opinion. "I would rather kill enemies than elk anytime. Count me in."

Recognizing a lost cause when he saw one, Little Dog walked off. "I will get our horses," he offered so he could be alone with his thoughts. He heard harsh laughter and wondered if he was the source of their humor.

A smoldering anger filled his breast at the way Rolling Thunder was manipulating them. The others were too blinded by bloodlust to see it, but he could. He was of half a mind to desert them and go back alone. Yet he couldn't bring himself to abandon them to their own stupidity no matter what the personal consequences might be. The true mark of genuine friendship, he had long maintained, was that friends stuck together through good times and bad, through periods of peace and happiness and interludes of danger and death. So what sort of person would it make him if he went back without them?

Little Dog went around a tree, still pondering. Since

his was the sole voice of reason, it was his responsibility to see that the others didn't put themselves in an unnecessarily perilous situation. He would serve as their guardian spirit for the duration of the hunt, and if in his estimation they wanted to take any pointless risks, he would advise them accordingly. Should they heed him, fine. If not, then at least he would have done all that was required of a true friend.

In due course they were on their way to the river. Rolling Thunder was confident they'd find the trail again if they continued searching both shores. Peeved that Little Dog was still questioning his judgment, Rolling Thunder studiously avoided talking to him until they were both again moving along the bank, their eyes studying the soft earth for telltale spoor.

"Call out if you see anything," he said.

"Do you think I would not?" Little Dog responded.

"I can no longer tell what you will do," Rolling Thunder said gravely. "There was a time when you were the most dependable man I know, but now you are like an old woman whose mind no longer works right. If you persist in disputing every idea I have, I doubt I will take you along the next time I lead a raiding party."

"Whatever you feel is best," Little Dog said coldly, and resolved right then and there to sever his ties with Rolling Thunder once they were among their own kind again. It would serve Rolling Thunder right if he went on a raid with White Buffalo instead, thereby making public his dissatisfaction and showing everyone else which warrior he felt was better suited to be their next chief.

Considerable time had elapsed when Rolling Thunder passed a dense thicket that grew right down to the water's edge. He had been forced to enter the river to swing around it, and as he angled to the shore he happened to glance back. Instantly he wheeled his war-horse and cut loose with piercing whoops in elation. Imprinted in the soil were the familiar tracks he sought. Jumping down, he examined the impressions, grinning at the craftiness of their quarry.

If it was Grizzly Killer, the man knew all the tricks. Plunging into the thicket when he had left the water was a smart move since the tangle of vegetation hid most of the hoofprints.

"But not all of them," Rolling Thunder said softly to himself, and remounted. Walking Bear, Bobcat, and Loud Talker were fording to his side. He waited for them, pointed out the trail, then assumed the lead.

Little Dog brought up the rear. Secretly he had hoped they wouldn't find the tracks again so they could get on with the business of hunting elk. Now, knowing Rolling Thunder as he did, he was certain they would push on until nightfall and resume the pursuit at first light, stopping only for short periods, and then only because their horses needed occasional rest.

Once again, Little Dog noted, the trail was taking them deeper into Shoshone territory, although in a roundabout manner. He speculated that the man they were after must think he had lost them. Soon they came to where the pair had camped.

Rolling Thunder jumped down to press his palm to the charred embers. He was on one knee when the brush to their left rustled loudly and out stepped a squat, stocky animal that bristled at the sight of them and voiced a challenging snarl.

None of them moved. None of them spoke. They did not want to do a thing that would provoke the newcomer into attacking, since despite its relatively small stature the wolverine was one of the most feared creatures in the mountains. It was only three feet long and less than two feet high, but what it lacked in size it more than compensated for by possessing a tenacious, savage disposition unmatched by any other beast or man.

This one was a female, her color a mix of black and brown, her long claws visible as she unexpectedly turned to one side to go around the party. Exhibiting an odd shuffling gait, she took her time, her baleful gaze fixed on them the whole time.

Rolling Thunder was tempted to use his lance. A wolverine pelt was a rare trophy, even more prized than that of a grizzly. But being the only one dismounted, he would be the object of her unstoppable wrath should he hurl his lance into her but fail to drop her on the spot. Prudence made him hold still until she darted into the undergrowth and continued on her undisturbed way.

Just like that the incident, so fraught with the potential for violence, was over. In itself it was not remarkable, since many such incidents occurred in the lifetime of the Gros Ventres. But it gave one of them an opening he tried to exploit.

"That was a bad omen," Little Dog said. "We should turn back."

"It would have been a bad omen had the animal attacked," Rolling Thunder disagreed, rising. "That it did not is proof that our medicine is strong and that soon Grizzly Killer and the young one will be our captives."

Loud Talker grunted assent. "Yes, friend! Our medicine is strong! No one can stand up to us, not Grizzly Killer, not even the entire Shoshone nation. Let us hurry, and maybe by tonight one of us will be the proud owner of a new scalp."

Presently five warriors rode on, but only four of them were smiling in anticipation.

Chapter Five

Nate King raised his Hawken and trained the barrel on the large four-legged shape that had materialized behind them among the pines. Before he could take deliberate aim, however, the thing was on them. Or rather, going around them. Father and son sat in amused amazement as a ten-point blacktail buck dashed like lightning past their horses and into trees a dozen feet away.

Zachary broke into relieved laughter. "Tarnation, Pa! What caused that critter to act up so?"

"Something must have spooked him a ways back," Nate said. "Sometimes deer will run for miles when they're scared."

"Too bad we didn't shoot it," Zach said. "I'd like some roast venison. Wouldn't you?"

"Perhaps tonight," Nate said, and resumed their interrupted journey. To the southwest reared a large mountain sprinkled with patches of white at the summit—lingering vestiges of last year's snows that had not melted over the summer, and probably wouldn't melt before the first snow of the new winter season struck the Rockies. Some of the mountains were so high that snow stayed on their peaks the year around. They made their way toward this lofty monarch, always mindful to check their back trail now and again for signs of the five Indians.

On the bottom slope they came on a small, oval pond created by runoff from higher up. At one end grew cattails in profusion. Nate indicated the clusters of long, rigid stalks, swordlike leaves, and brown seed heads, then said, "You'll never go hungry with those around."

"Why, Pa?" the boy asked.

"Because there isn't a plant in all creation that fills a man's belly so many ways like a cattail," Nate said, and launched into detail. "In early spring you can peel and eat the stalks. Raw or boiled, they're delicious. In late spring you can cut off the green heads, husk them, and throw them in a pot to boil until they're tender. In early summer the heads are ripe enough to eat raw. Then, from the end of summer on through until the next spring, you can eat the horn-shaped sprouts that grow down at their base."

Zach was duly impressed. "Where did you learn all that?"

"From your mother and other Shoshones," Nate said. "And that's not all. If you mash a cattail flower up, you can use it as a salve for burns and cuts. Never forget too that the leaves give off a sticky juice that kills pain."

"I'll be!" Zach exclaimed, eyeing the growth at the border of the pond with new appreciation. "I could have used some the time I had a toothache."

Nate nodded, and moving Pegasus closer to the cattails, he reached out and tapped a brown head. "These make great tinder for starting a fire." Bending down, he touched a stalk. "And these, in a pinch, make do as an arrow shaft."

"Is there anything a cattail *isn't* good for?" Zach joked.

Once in the pines Nate carried on with his lesson, instructing his son in how to tell the different types of pines apart. All of them, he stressed, had parts a man could eat; the bark itself would keep someone alive indefinitely, a tasty tea could be concocted from a handful of needles if the needles were chopped up into tiny bits and boiled for about five minutes first, and the seeds were as edible for people as they were for squirrels.

Zach paid careful attention. He knew that the skills he was learning now might make the difference between life and death at some later time in his life. Fresh in his fertile mind were the many times he had encountered the dead: free trappers who had succumbed to hunger or hostiles or the elements, warriors slain in warfare or while out hunting, women who had died during enemy raids or who had been torn apart by fierce beasts. Having seen so much death, he was the more determined not to add his own life to the Grim Reaper's toll. The wilderness was no place for greenhorns, as his Uncle Shakespeare had so often said, so Zach wanted to learn all he could. One day, he vowed, he'd be as competent a mountain man as Shakespeare or his father.

So engrossed did Nate become in enlightening his son about the varied bounties lying all around them that he was surprised, on gazing beyond Zach, to discover they had traveled over a mile up the side of the mountain. Facing front, he rode from the trees into a grassy belt separating the pines from the higher aspens, and as he did a tremendous gust of chill air rushed out of the north and fanned him from head to toe.

Startled, Nate stared to the north, and was disturbed to see a few slate-gray clouds floating over the crest of an adjoining peak. If he didn't know better, he told himself, he'd swear there might be snow on the way. But it was too early in the year for a snowstorm. The worst he could expect was a dusting, which worried him not at all. It would not be hard to locate or construct adequate shelter in which the two of them could wait out any cold snap.

So upward they rode, Nate on the constant lookout for elk or sign of elk. In the aspens he slowed and searched diligently, thinking some had possibly bedded down there for the day. Yet it was not until the aspens were a hundred yards below them, when they were riding along the base of a serrated line of huge boulders situated close to the patches of snow at the summit, that Nate finally spied what he had journeyed so far to find.

Three elk stood on a barren spine that split the aspens as a cleaver would meat. One was a bull, the others cows, and all three had their attention riveted on something or other down at the bottom of the mountain. They had not, as yet, heard the horses.

Stopping, Nate beamed at his son and pointed. Zach nodded excitedly. The range, Nate estimated, was close to three hundred yards. To be certain of bringing one down he must get closer, and with that end in mind he dismounted, used sign language to direct Zach to do the same, and led the boy into a ravine that would bring them out very near the unsuspecting elk.

Halfway along, Nate tied both horses to high bushes. His Hawken clutched in two hands, he crept lower and lower until he caught sight of the three animals. They were still staring downward. Motioning for Zach to stay close to him, he worked his way from cover to cover and reached a boulder 70 yards away and 20 yards below the elk.

Quietly resting the Hawken barrel on a boulder, Nate cocked the piece and took a bead on the bull, aiming at a spot just behind its front shoulder. A properly placed ball would either kill it outright or pierce its lungs and so weaken it that the animal would not be able to flee very far. He was all set to squeeze the trigger when an idea occurred to him that brought a gleam to his eyes. "You do it, son," he whispered.

"Me, Pa?" Zach was dubious. "I ain't never shot an animal that big before."

"Then it's time you learned."

"But what if I miss?"

"Every man does, one time or another. Now hurry before they walk off."

Gulping, dismayed at the responsibility suddenly thrust on him, Zach reluctantly stepped to the boulder and rested the tip of the Kentucky's barrel on the upper edge. He had to lift onto the balls of his feet to see clearly the length of the gun. Wedging the stock tight against his shoulder as his father had taught him to do, he sighted on the bull. Then he hesitated. Butterflies swarmed in his stomach and his arms felt unaccountably weak.

"Relax," Nate whispered. "Remember to cock the hammer, and don't touch the trigger until you're ready to fire." He reached out. "I have complete faith in you."

Zach felt his father's hand squeeze his shoulder in encouragement and his nervousness drained from him, to be replaced by a budding confidence in his own ability. His father never lied. If his father trusted him to make the shot and believed he was capable of making it count, then he must be able to do it.

Curling his small thumb around the hammer, Zach pulled back until there was an audible click. He aimed down the barrel, taking his time, wanting to be sure, to make his pa proud of him. The bull took a step, so he slid the barrel a fraction along the boulder to compensate.

Zach recalled everything his father had ever taught him about shooting a rifle. "Hold the barrel steady.

Match up the sights in a straight line to the target. Right before you're about to shoot, hold your breath. Never jerk the trigger. Squeeze it gently."

A booming retort rolled out across the slope and echoed off nearby mountains. All three elk broke into a run, but the bull staggered, took several faltering strides, and collapsed in a whirl of limbs and antlers. Never slowing, the two cows fled into the aspens.

"You did it!" Nate cried happily, and clapped the boy on the back. "I knew you could."

Zach gaped at the prone bull, then at the smoke curling upward from the rifle muzzle. "I did, didn't I? I really and truly did."

"Come on," Nate urged, dashing around the boulder. "The bull might still be alive. You never want to let an animal suffer any more than is necessary."

They chugged up to where the elk lay in a spreading pool of blood. More blood seeped from its nostrils and trickled from the corners of its mouth. The bull's eyes were locked wide and lifeless, its tongue hanging out. No more shots were needed.

"You did right fine," Nate complimented Zach again. "Perforated its lungs. I couldn't have done any better myself."

"My first elk," Zach said, in awe of his accomplishment. Close up, the bull was immense, over five feet high at the shoulders and nearly ten feet long. It had a dark brown mane of sorts under its throat and its legs were much darker than the body. The rump patch and the tail were yellowish-brown. "How much do you reckon this critter weighs, Pa?" he inquired.

"This one?" Nate made some mental calculations. "I'd figure eight hundred pounds or better."

"Eight hundred!" Zach exclaimed. "Why, that's enough meat to last us ten years."

"Not the way you eat."

"How will we get it back to the village? We can't pack out that much on our horses."

"We'll rig up a travois, just like the one we use to haul the lodge back and forth to our cabin when we visit the Shoshones."

"You think of everything."

Nate smiled and patted his son on the head. "In the wilderness a man has to. One slip, one little mistake, can cost you your life." He motioned at the ravine. "Now why don't you fetch the horses and I'll start the butchering?"

"Right away," Zach said, whirling. But he had covered only ten feet when his father called his name. Puzzled, he halted and looked back. "Sir?"

"Aren't you forgetting something?"

"What?"

"That Kentucky of yours won't do you much good if you run into a grizzly or a panther."

"Why . . . ?" Zach began, and abruptly knew what his father was getting at. Grinning sheepishly, he set the stock on the ground and grasped his powder horn. "Always reload as soon as you shoot," he said, repeating his father's previous instruction. "Only an idiot goes traipsing off into the woods with an unloaded gun."

"You're learning," Nate said proudly.

The remainder of the afternoon was a busy one. They rolled the bull onto its back, then removed the hide. The first step entailed slitting the elk open down the back of each hind leg and across the middle of its belly to its chin. Slits were also made down the inside of the front legs, from the knee joint to the belly cut. Next the hide was peeled from the body. They had to cut ligaments and muscles which held it to the carcass, and Nate taught Zach how to always keep the edge of the knife slanted toward the carcass and away from the hide to keep from cutting it.

Nate had planned to rig up a travois and take the carcass down into the trees where they would dry strips of meat over a low fire, but the weather dictated differently. Within an hour after Zach had shot the bull the temperature had dropped some 30 degrees and kept on dropping. The azure sky was transformed into a gray slate with low, ominous clouds stretching from horizon to horizon. They could see their breath when they breathed, and the tips of their fingers were becoming numb with cold.

Zach stuck his hands under his arms and hopped up and down. "I'm about froze, Pa. Is it going to snow?"

"Looks that way," Nate said, casting an apprehensive glance at the threatening heavens. He'd lived through enough winters in the Rockies to know the makings of a first-rate storm when he saw one. Every indication was there: the plummeting temperature, the northerly wind, the moisture-laden clouds. But he kept telling himself that there wouldn't be much snowfall because it was too early in the year.

Just as they finished cutting off the hide and set to the messy work of butchering the meat, the first flakes fell. A few initially, great, flowery flakes that resembled flower petals floating through the air. They landed here, there, and all around the father and son, growing in number with surprising swiftness until within the short span of several minutes the air swarmed as with a multitude of silent white bees.

Nate stopped carving and glanced skyward. Flakes plastered his face, getting into his eyes. He wiped the back of his sleeve across them and straightened. Already the snow was so thick that he could barely distinguish the horses, standing not quite ten feet off. The wind picked up, blowing against his back so strongly it sent the whangs on his buckskins to flapping crazily.

"Pa," Zach commented, "I think we're in for a blizzard."

"It won't be that bad," Nate assured him, although he didn't feel quite as confident as he sounded. Suddenly an eerie howling erupted from on high, caused by the wind shrieking past the high peaks and jagged pinnacles. Mary, the mare, frightened by the din, whinnied in fright. As if to accent her fear, the snow increased.

"What'll we do, Pa?" Zach asked nervously.

Nate was debating their options. The meat would keep for days if the temperature stayed low enough. Already the carcass had started to freeze, rendering the butchering job extremely difficult and making it next to impossible to complete the chore in under an hour to an hour and a half. By then they would be half-frozen themselves and the horses would be suffering terribly. Shelter was their first priority; a fire their second.

Which way should they go? Nate wondered. He gazed down the mountain, but could see no further than a few yards. Finding somewhere down below to take cover in the driving storm would be next to impossible. Fortunately, he knew of one place, a spot they'd passed earlier, higher up. Squaring his shoulders, he jammed his knife into its beaded sheath, rolled up the hide, picked up the Hawken, and stepped to Zach's side. "We're going up to those boulders near the summit. Whatever you do, don't stray off."

"I understand."

Nate took his son's left hand and hurried toward the horses. To his consternation, he couldn't see either one. The swirling snow formed an impenetrable white shroud. Pausing, he focused on where he thought they should be, and walked on until he nearly bumped into Pegasus. Then he quickly gave Zach a boost onto the mare.

After tying the hide on behind the saddle, Nate climbed into the stirrups, and was set to start off when a chilling thought prompted him to reach into a parfleche hanging just in back of his right leg and take out a length of rawhide rope he always toted. One end of the rope he tied to his saddle, the other to Zach's saddle. "This way," he explained as he made the knots fast, "we won't get separated."

"You might not ever find me again if we did," Zach said, grinning. He was cold to the bone, but not overly worried since his father appeared to be taking the advent of the storm so calmly. Positive his pa would take care of him, he tucked his chin in and listened to the howling wind.

Nate took the lead and gingerly picked his way down the slope toward the ravine, relying on his finely honed sense of direction since the whipping snow obscured every landmark. Once, years ago, when he was still a greenhorn, he would have been hopelessly lost had he been caught in a driving snowstorm. Now, thanks to the countless miles he'd spent crisscrossing the mountains in search of beaver, he'd developed an innate sense for telling which way was which, almost as if an internal compass guided him. Many Indians shared the same knack.

Several times over the years, in inclement weather, he'd been compelled to rely on his instincts when there had been no other means of determining the right direction to proceed, but never had he been caught in anything so elementally fierce as the raging storm that enveloped them. It had gotten so bad he could barely see his hand in front of his face, so he relied on other factors such as the slant of his horse to confirm when they came to the bottom of the spine and were on level ground again. Turning to the right, he carefully picked his way, watchful for boulders and other obstacles that were often no more than indistinct dark shapes against the background of the falling snow. By exercising unflagging attention he was able to avoid them.

Advancing at a snail's pace was the only way to be safe, but Nate chafed at the delay. He wanted to get his son under cover rapidly, and he knew just the spot. As they'd been riding along the base of the huge boulders a couple of hours ago, they'd passed a wide crack in the ground between two of the monoliths. Covered by a dome of earth, the opening would be an excellent shelter in which to wait out Nature's fury.

First, though, Nate had to find it. An eternity dragged by as he picked his path up the ravine. Once Pegasus, despite his best efforts, blundered into a boulder, but was not seriously hurt. Eventually, when his teeth were close to chattering and his body felt like it was covered with gooseflesh, Nate became sure they had emerged from the ravine, and guessed the boulders lay ahead and to his left.

Nate bore onward toward his goal. An inch of snow covered the ground, and he tried not to think of what would happen should the gelding slip and fall. He and Zach would both go down. He dreaded the idea of one of them sustaining a broken neck or some other horrible injury, and redoubled his concentration so as not to invite a mishap.

Another eternity went by. Nate began to think he'd made a mistake after all, and that somehow he had missed the long row of rocky sentinels. Then, looming black and stark in front of him, one of them appeared. Instantly another problem presented itself. He had no way of knowing if he was north of the cleft or south of it. If he picked the wrong direction, they might never find it, and vermin would be gnawing at their bones come the spring.

Briefly Nate hesitated. Mary had halted next to Pegasus, and one look at his freezing son, hunched low against the biting wind, covered thick with snow, was enough to goad him into action. Forming a silent prayer for deliverance, he turned southward and hugged the base of the boulders.

Here the wind was not quite as strong, the snow not quite as heavy. Still, his range of vision was restricted to ten feet straight ahead. The gelding walked briskly, as eager as he was to get out of the storm. And shortly, as welcome a sight as an oasis to a wandering soul in a blistering desert, the cleft materialized on his right.

Nate drew rein and slid to the ground, his legs stiff, his body devoid of all warmth. The opening was wider than he had remembered, twice the width of a horse. Poking his head in, he found the interior to be as spacious as his single-room cabin and close to eight feet high.

Delighted, Nate lost no time in leading both horses within. Mary balked, and had to be persuaded with a cuff and a sharp tug before she would enter. In a single step he reached Zach, and tenderly lifted the boy to the dirt floor. "Let me help you," he said as he did.

"I'm about plumb frozen," Zach mustered manfully, and smiled. "The next time we go elk hunting, can we do it in the summer?"

Nate's laugh was longer and louder than it needed to be, but his son apparently didn't notice. Gazing about, Nate was overjoyed to find that someone—Indians, most likely—had sheltered here once before. Near a back corner lay the charred remains of a fire, and beside it were a dozen or so branches that had been gathered but not used. In addition, a number of weeds had taken root near the entrance, and although they were now brown and withered, they were dry and would burn readily.

Working swiftly, Nate pulled out handfuls of the weeds and hurried to the corner. Making a circular bed of the weeds, he properly arranged some of the branches on top, using the limbs sparingly, acutely aware the limited supply might have to last them quite a while.

Tenderfoot

From his possibles bag he took his flint and steel and tinderbox. Bending down, he prepared a small bed of punk, which consisted of dry, decayed maple wood he had collected over the summer. Next he proceeded to strike the steel against the flint to cause showers of sparks to fall on the tinder. Once he saw it catch, he carefully fanned the infant flames with his breath, nursing them to life.

"You're doing it, Pa!" Zach cried at his side.

The tinder caught, the flames grew, and Nate added bits of dry weed, feeding the hungry fire. Presently one of the branches also burst into flames, and soon light and spreading warmth filled the cleft.

"I never saw a fire look so good," Zach said.

"Me neither," Nate agreed, and cast a glance filled with misgivings at the opening. Outside, the wind continued to wail, the snow continued to fall. The full magnitude of their predicament hit him, and he realized with a start that his son had been right. This was no ordinary snowstorm. It was a full-fledged blizzard.

Chapter Six

The giant pounded his chest with a brawny fist and angrily declared, "There is an easy solution to the problem. I will challenge Jumping Bull, and when we fight I will cut out his heart and feed it to my dogs."

A period of silence ensued as everyone in the lodge exchanged glances. Winona looked at their host, her uncle Spotted Bull, who had called together their immediate relatives and closest friends so the grave situation facing them could be discussed at length and a course of action decided upon. A venerable warrior who had lived over 50 winters, Spotted Bull was not one to let raw emotion eclipse his seasoned wisdom.

"It is all well and good to talk of killing the fool, my son," he now said, resting his hand on the shoulder of the giant. "Many of us would like to do the same. But we must be discreet. This affair must be handled delicately."

Touch the Clouds snorted. "Was Jumping Bull discreet when he brazenly demanded that Winona leave Grizzly Killer and go live with him? Was he discreet when he went out and told everyone what he had done and bragged of how he would humiliate Grizzly Killer if Grizzly Killer objected?" He paused, then answered his own question. "No, he was not! He has not only insulted Grizzly Killer and Winona, he has also insulted all of us who call them our friends. I say let me kill him and be done with it."

Winona scanned the faces of those present, gauging their feelings. Beside her sat Willow Woman, her cousin, whose worry was evident. On her other side was Spotted Bull's wife, Morning Dove, her features grave. And the majority of the men were equally somber. Besides Spotted Bull and Touch the Clouds, there were Lame Elk, one of the oldest men in the tribe, and younger warriors: Drags the Rope, He Who Rides Standing, Paints His Ears Red, and others.

It was Lame Elk who spoke next, and everyone gave him their attention. "It is rare that one man tries to take the wife of another," he mentioned. "In all the time I have lived, I have only seen this happen once before, and that was when Raven Wing tried to take Nape of the Neck's woman. There was much blood shed, and in the end the woman wanted nothing to do with either of them and went to live with someone else."

"I will never leave Grizzly Killer," Winona boldly stated. Normally at such councils the men did all the talking. A woman never volunteered anything unless specifically asked to do so. But she could not sit there and say nothing when her entire future was at stake.

"We all know that," Lame Elk said, bestowing a smile on her. "Not one of us here doubts your love for him or his love for you. But your love is not the issue. The

77

issue is what we must do about Jumping Bull's unwanted advances."

"Grizzly Killer will be back soon," remarked Drags the Rope, who had been Nate's friend longer than any of the others, "and then none of us will have to do a thing. He will put Jumping Bull in his place."

"Until then we must protect Winona," Spotted Bull said. "Jumping Bull might become impatient and try to drag her off against her will. He has a violent temper. We all know how he used to beat his first wife."

"Maybe he will change his mind and nothing will come of this," Paints His Ears Red, the youngest warrior present, remarked.

"Jumping Bull is not one to turn back from something he has started," Spotted Bull said.

Lame Elk leaned forward. "There is more involved here than his interest in Winona, which might be genuine, although I have my doubts."

"What do you mean?" Touch the Clouds interjected.

"Has it not struck any of you as strange that Jumping Bull has shown no interest in Winona before?" Lame Elk said. "And if he wants a new wife so badly, why pick a woman who has pledged herself to someone else? There are many unmarried women who would be happy to share his lodge."

"So?" Touch the Clouds prompted.

"Think about it," said Lame Elk. "How many times have you heard Jumping Bull say that it is a mistake to be friendly with the whites? How many times has he spoken in councils and urged our people to fight the whites and drive them from our land?"

"Many times," said Spotted Bull.

"He hates all whites with a blinding hatred," Lame Elk said. "And he is not alone. There are a few others who share his sentiments. They have never treated Grizzly Killer as one of us and never will. Some of them have gone so far as to say in council that we should turn our backs on him and not allow him to live with us now and again as we do."

No one said anything for a while. Winona, along with the rest, was deep in thought, contemplating the implications of the old warrior's statements. Fresh in her mind were Jumping Bull's words: "A white man is no fit husband for a beautiful woman like you."

Spotted Bull voiced the thoughts they all shared. "So the real reason behind Jumping Bull's despicable conduct is that he wants to provoke Grizzly Killer into a fight and kill him."

"Such would be my guess," Lame Elk said. "He may truly desire Winona, but he is using his desire to justify his hatred. He hopes that when Grizzly Killer returns and learns that he has been courting Winona, Grizzly Killer will go after him. Which Grizzly Killer will. Then Jumping Bull can kill him and claim he had to do it in self-defense."

"The bastard!" Touch the Clouds said. "We should report this to the Yellow Noses."

The suggestion sparked hope in Winona's breast. Like many another tribe, the Shoshones boasted certain special societies for both men and women, among them the Yellow Noses, an elite group including only the bravest of warriors. Among their many functions was the policing of the village and the maintaining of order when the Shoshones were on the march. If disputes arose, the Yellow Noses settled them, and their decisions were final. Any warrior who opposed them was liable to be beaten, perhaps have his weapons confiscated or broken, or have his lodge cut to pieces. They had the authority to tell Jumping Bull to leave Nate and her alone, which would end the whole matter. But the next moment Winona's hope was dashed by Lame Elk.

"No, we cannot go to the Yellow Noses. I will tell you why." His craggy features were downcast. "The Yellow Noses can only act when tribal rules have been broken, such as when a man goes off and hunts alone even though the word has been given that we will make a surround. And this is as it should be, for a man who does that might scare off all the game and leave the rest of the village hungry." He sighed and gazed sadly at Winona. "But there is no rule against one man taking another's wife if he can convince the woman to go with him. So long as he does not assault her husband, he does nothing wrong."

"So you are saying we must sit back and do nothing?" Touch the Clouds inquired in disgust.

"Our people have always been free to do as they want so long as they do not harm others," Lame Elk said. "This is as it should be."

"So we do *nothing*?" Touch the Clouds said harshly.

"I am afraid so," Lame Elk said. "Unless Jumping Bull harms Winona, we are powerless. Grizzly Killer must deal with this himself when he gets back."

Touch the Clouds looked at Spotted Bull. "And you, Father? What do you say?"

"I am sorry. I must agree with Lame Elk."

Winona averted her face so none could see the sorrow and disappointment reflected in her eyes. Accustomed as she was to handling her problems herself, it had been hard for her to confide in her cousin, Willow Woman, and even harder to agree to a council after Willow Woman had gone and informed her father, Spotted Bull.

"Do not fear, Winona," Spotted Bull now said. "We will make it known that Jumping Bull must answer to us if he lays a hand on you before your husband returns. He will not dare bother you."

Tenderfoot

* * *

Twilight covered the village as, a short while later, Winona made her slow way toward her lodge, her heart heavy at the outcome of the meeting. Despite the sympathy and the promises her relatives and friends had voiced, she knew that she was on her own. It had been foolish, she reflected, to expect them to resolve the situation for her. They had their own lives to live. A grown woman had no business running to others when trouble presented itself. What would Nate think of her behavior?

Ironically, it was on his behalf that Winona had swallowed her pride and done the unthinkable. She knew her husband's temperament, knew he would tear into Jumping Bull the moment he heard what had transpired. Neither of them would give any quarter; one or the other would die. And while she had complete confidence in Nate's prowess, she had heard about too many outstanding fighters who had been killed by unworthy adversaries not to worry about him. All it would take was a single misstep or a fleeting instant of distraction and Nate might be slain.

Suddenly her pondering came to an end. A shadow had detached itself from between two nearby lodges and fallen into step at her elbow. "I would walk with you," Jumping Bull said.

"Go walk off a cliff," Winona responded bitterly, slanting to the left so their arms would not brush together.

"I have important words to say."

"Tell them to a tree."

"You will listen," Jumping Bull declared, and seized hold of her wrist.

Red rage transformed Winona into a furious she-wolf. She whirled, yanking her wrist free, and snarled spitefully, "Don't touch me! Don't *ever* touch me."

81

Something in her tone made Jumping Bull take a step backward. He saw her hatred, saw her fingers clenched like claws, and for a moment he believed she was about to spring on him. Instinctively he went to raise an arm to strike her across the face and put her in her place. Then, awakening to the gravity of the error he was about to commit, he let the arm drop. She was not his *yet*.

"If you ever lay a hand on me again I will not wait for my husband to slay you," she said. "I will do it myself."

"Calm down so we can talk without arguing," Jumping Bull coaxed.

"Do not waste your breath," Winona responded. Pivoting, she stalked off. She was so mad she trembled. Her right hand touched the knife on her hip and she closed her fingers on the hilt.

"Very well," Jumping Bull said. "If you do not want to hear how bloodshed can be avoided, do as you please."

Winona stopped, her curiosity contending with her loathing of the vile animal who presumed to try and steal her affections from the man she loved. Reluctantly, suspecting she was somehow playing into Jumping Bull's hands, she turned. "Explain."

"I thought you might like to have the white dog's life spared and I have a way it can be done."

"Try talking with a straight tongue for once."

The corners of the husky warrior's mouth curved upward. "If you will agree to come with me, right this moment, I will let your husband live."

"What game is this you are playing?" Winona snapped. "You already know how I feel. But since you seem to have your ears plugged with wax, I will tell you again so there will be no mistake." Lightning danced in her eyes. "I will never, ever live with you. I would rather open my wrists first. And from now until my husband comes back, I will keep a loaded pistol at my side. If you dare bother me again, I will use it."

Rolling Thunder's features clouded. Everyone in the village knew her white bastard of a husband had taught her how to use the weapons of the whites, and it was said she could hit a mark 20 yards away dead center ten times out of ten. He moved toward her, his muscular arms tensing. "Then I shall see to it that you never reach your pistol. I will take you with me now."

"Try!" Winona cried, the single word a ringing challenge.

"Yes," spoke a deep voice from the darkness. "Why not try, Jumping Bull, and see what happens next?"

In a blur, Jumping Bull spun, his right hand dropping to the tomahawk at his waist, a malevolent scowl twisting his countenance. "You!" he blurted.

"Yes, me," Touch the Clouds declared as he strolled forward to stand next to Winona. So huge was he that next to him she seemed a little girl by comparison. "I heard the words you spoke."

"What of them?" Jumping Bull snapped, prudently easing his hand from the tomahawk. He was no fool. The weapon would make no difference at all in a clash between them; he stood absolutely no chance against the giant. With his own eyes he had once witnessed a fight between Touch the Clouds and three Sioux in which the giant had slain them without working up a sweat. Another time he had seen Touch the Clouds, armed with just a war club, slay a panther half the size of a bear. Only someone with a death wish would confront the giant alone.

"You can thank your guardian spirit that my father has made me give my word that I will not kill you before Grizzly Killer returns," Touch the Clouds stated sternly, "or you would now be lying in a puddle of your own blood."

Jumping Bull glanced toward Spotted Bull's lodge. "Your father made you make such a promise?" he asked in scarcely concealed delight.

"Regrettably, yes." Touch the Clouds rested a hand on Winona's shoulder. "But if you persist in molesting this dear woman, who is like a sister to me, I will be strongly tempted to do something I have never done before. I just might break my promise and gut you like the cur you are."

A hot retort was on Jumping Bull's lips, but he held his temper in check. This development, he reflected, was too good to be believed. His main worry had been that friends of King's would interfere with his plan, and of them all Touch the Clouds was the one to fear the most. But not any more.

It was obvious the giant was restraining himself with an effort. His enormous fists clenched and unclenched as he said, "My father and others are of the opinion that this is a matter strictly between Grizzly Killer and you. Against my better judgment, I have gone along with them." His voice lowered. "But heed my words, Jumping Bull. I will not stand by and let you have your way with Winona. She is Grizzly Killer's woman, not yours, and knowing her as I do, I know she will be his until the day he dies."

"Which may not be far off," Jumping Bull could not resist saying. Drawing himself to his full height, he gestured at Winona and said, "But let us not argue over a matter that does not, as your wise father has decided, concern you. I would honor Winona by taking her into my lodge. For the time being, her misguided loyalty to someone who does not deserve her love has clouded her thinking. I am confident, though, she will come around to my way of thinking eventually. And when she does, and she is my wife, I hope the two of us can be friends."

Winona had listened to all she was going to. Turning to Touch the Clouds, she asked, "Would you do me the favor of walking me to my lodge?"

"Gladly," the giant rumbled.

Side by side they moved off. Behind them a mocking laugh came on the chill breeze.

A shiver rippled down Winona's spine, but whether from the cold or her reaction to Jumping Bull's arrogance, she could not say. Then she realized she could see her breath, and pausing, she gazed to the northwest. A vast bank of ugly gray clouds were roiling their frenzied way toward the valley in which the encampment lay.

"We are in for some snow," Touch the Clouds noted absently.

Winona was thinking of her husband and her son. What if they had been caught in a storm? She reminded herself that Nate's woodcraft was the equal of any Shoshone's, that he knew how to survive in the very worst weather. Still, as she well knew, there were always many things that could go wrong. A flickering wave of anxiety washed over her and she pressed a hand to her bosom.

Touch the Clouds, misunderstanding, remarked, "You need not fear Jumping Bull for now. He will not do anything until after Grizzly Killer comes back."

"I hope not," Winona said, continuing toward her lodge.

"If you want, I will keep watch over you until then."

"Think of the talk!" Winona replied, trying to be lighthearted. "Every gossip in the village would wear out her tongue telling about it. And I do not think your wife would like that very much."

"My wife knows I would never dishonor her," the giant said rather defensively.

"As do I," Winona acknowledged, touching his arm. "We have been friends since childhood, and I know there is nothing you would not do for me. But I cannot allow you to put yourself in such a position."

"I do not mind."

"No, Touch the Clouds. My husband would think less of me as a woman if he were to hear that I needed you to fight my battles in his absence. Grizzly Killer is my defender, and if anyone is to put Jumping Bull in his place, it is he."

"Very well. But I will still be around if you need me." Touch the Clouds glanced over his shoulder, insuring they had not been followed. "And I swear that if Jumping Bull lays a hand on you, I will send him on to meet his ancestors."

Her lodge reared before them. Winona stood next to the flap and smiled. "Thank you for escorting me. When Grizzly Killer hears of your concern, he will be very grateful."

"I wish there were more I could do," the giant said. "In my heart I feel that my father and Lame Elk are wrong, but my head says I must do as they want."

"You are the best of friends," Winona assured him. Stooping, she swung the flap wide and entered. The interior was dimly lit by the glowing coals of her fire, which she promptly stoked. The last of her meager supply of limbs had to be used to rekindle the flames, and she knew she would need more long before morning. With snow on the way, the night promised to be extremely cold.

Donning a buffalo-hide robe, Winona walked outside and headed for the bank of the river where cottonwoods grew in profusion. There she moved among the trunks, collecting downed limbs as she went.

Ahead of the oncoming storm raced brisk northerly winds that rustled the brown leaves overhead and bent the more slender trees. Occasionally the wind howled as if alive. In the village horses were neighing, dogs barking, children yelling. The noise was such that Winona could not hear her own footsteps, let alone anyone else's.

The search carried her near the swirling water. As she bent over to pick up a slender branch, her gaze drifted toward the lodges and she saw something or someone move in the undergrowth between her and the village. Freezing, she stared at the vague shape and wondered if it was a person or an animal.

A possible answer occurred to her, causing a gasp to escape her lips. Jumping Bull might have seen her leave her lodge, then followed her! And in her haste to gather wood she had left her pistol behind! Slowly she lowered her knees to the ground and set the branches quietly down. Should Jumping Bull attack, she wanted her hands free to defend herself.

Winona reached under her heavy robe and drew her knife. The shape was moving again, advancing toward the river, and would pass within ten feet of her position, on her left. She could not make out many details, but she saw enough to convince her it definitely was a man and not a beast.

Crouching low, Winona clasped the knife close to her chest. She must make the first strike count. A skilled warrior like Jumping Bull would not give her a second chance, so she must go for his throat or his heart. Her own heart was thudding wildly, and to her dismay her hands started to shake. Gritting her teeth, she steeled her will to the deed she must do.

Suddenly the figure changed course, moving directly toward her.

Winona waited for him to step from the bushes, and then, with a low cry of defiance, she sprang.

Chapter Seven

Rolling Thunder, greatest of Gros Ventres warriors and next in line—in his own mind if not in the minds of all his people—to be the next war chief of the tribe, was in the foulest of moods, as foul as the raging blizzard that had unexpectedly stranded the members of his hunting party deep in Shoshone territory. He stood in the midst of wildly waving aspens and mentally cursed the spirits for placing him in such damnable straits.

His anger was fueled by the knowledge that they had been very close to the man and the boy when the snowstorm hit. He'd pushed the others hard prior to the change in the weather, so hard they had gained a lot of ground on the unsuspecting pair. In his opinion the two would have been in his clutches before the sun set.

And now? Rolling Thunder glared skyward and wished he was a medicine man that he might use his power to make the snow stop. If it kept falling at the current rate, by morning there would be five feet or more covering the mountain. High, high above, the wind shrieked past the peaks, the siren scream matching his disposition perfectly.

The sound of wood being chopped fell on Rolling Thunder's ears, and he turned back to the crude but serviceable conical forts his companions were constructing. There were three such shelters, much like those frequently used by the Blackfeet and their allies. Since they had been caught in the aspens and unable to find a convenient cave or other sanctuary, they were making do as resourcefully as they knew how.

In the middle of the forts blazed a fire protected on two sides by lean-tos. When one of the warriors grew cold, as one often did, he would warm himself by the fire for a while, and then resume chopping and aligning the slender saplings used in the building of their forts. Right now it was Little Dog's turn to rest, and as Rolling Thunder squatted across from him, he glanced up.

"Do not say a word," Rolling Thunder warned.

"I was not planning to."

"No? You do not have to. I know what you are thinking. You blame me for this. If I had not insisted on trailing the man and the boy, we would be on our way back to our own country instead of huddled here in these trees. The storm might have missed us."

"No harm has been done. We can go home when the storm ends."

"Which should make you very happy," Rolling Thunder spat. "You never wanted us to come this far." He pulled his robe tighter around his broad shoulders, and when he spoke next his tone had softened. "Perhaps I should have listened to you, old friend. I do not relish the thought of being stranded here for several sleeps."

"Maybe it will be less."

Rolling Thunder made a sound reminiscent of a bull buffalo about to charge. "Listen to that wind! Look at how heavy the snow falls! This is a blizzard, and we will be lucky if we are not snowed in for an entire moon."

"What does a delay matter? You have your new horse and rifle to take back, and you can tell everyone of the coup you counted on a white man. I would say the hunting trip has been the success you hoped it would be."

"It would have been more of a success if we had caught Grizzly Killer."

"If it is him we were after."

"It is," Rolling Thunder declared.

"How do you know?"

"I feel it deep inside."

Little Dog, saying nothing, selected a broken branch from the pile at his side and fed it to the leaping flames. While he dared not admit to it, he was profoundly thankful the blizzard had obliterated every last trace of the tracks they had been dogging, forcing them to abandon the chase. Further incursions into Shoshone territory would be pointless. Thanks to the snow, they all stood to reach their village with their scalps intact. Had he been alone he would have laughed with relief.

"Why are you smiling?"

Taken aback, Little Dog cupped his hands to his mouth and breathed on his fingers to warm them. He was stalling so he could come up with a suitable answer. "I was thinking of my wife and how happy I will be to see her again."

"You always have been too sentimental," Rolling Thunder said. "I have three wives, and I would rather be out here than stuck in a smoky lodge with any one of them. Their unending chatter is enough to give any man a headache, and their constant nagging makes me want to throw them all off a cliff."

"Why insult them so when you know you love them?"

"Do I?"

There was such heartfelt sincerity in the question that Little Dog looked around sharply. He had long held the opinion that the only person Rolling Thunder truly loved was Rolling Thunder. Tactfully, he had never voiced his belief. And he was quite shocked to have his friend practically admit as much.

"Sometimes I wonder," Rolling Thunder said.

"We all have times where we wish our wives would be eaten by wolves," Little Dog commented. "They probably feel the same way about us."

"Do you really think so?" Rolling Thunder said, his brow creased. "Possibly the wives of other men do, but mine are too content and grateful at having me for their husband to ever speak or think ill of me."

"What man truly knows what goes on in a woman's mind?" Little Dog said.

At that juncture Walking Bear joined them and held his hands out to the fire. "If you two are done warming your bottoms, there is still work to be done. One of the forts is not yet complete."

Little Dog, sighing in resignation since he knew how much Rolling Thunder despised doing menial work, put his palms on the frigid ground and began to push upright. But Rolling Thunder restrained him by pressing on his shoulder.

"You rest, my friend. I will help finish."

"I must do my share of the work," Little Dog protested.

"You have already done more than your share and I have not."

Mystified, Little Dog watched Rolling Thunder walk off. How, he wondered, could someone be so selfish and rude one moment and so considerate and polite the next? Rolling Thunder was a bundle of contradictions, as complicated a man to get to know as Little Dog had ever encountered. There were instances when he wanted to embrace him in friendship; at others he wanted to wring Rolling Thunder's neck.

Life was so strange sometimes.

"Let that old blizzard go on forever!" Zach declared contentedly, shifting his feet so they were closer to the fire, so close his moccasins were in danger of bursting into flames. "We're snug and warm in here."

"For now," Nate agreed, gazing anxiously at the constantly shifting white shroud blanketing the landscape outside of their refuge. "If the snow goes on forever, I'm afraid we'll never dig ourselves out."

"It won't," Zach said, laughing. "I wasn't serious, Pa."

Nate touched his son's knees. "Pull your feet back a bit or you'll be going barefoot when we leave."

The boy complied, and bit off a large piece of jerky.

"Go easy there. We don't know how long our supply of food has to last us."

"Sorry," Zach said, and replaced the portion he had not touched in the beaded parfleche on the earthen floor to his left. He was embarrassed that he had been making a pig of himself, and figured it would be best to talk about something else. "How long do you reckon the wood will hold out?"

"A few more hours yet."

"Then what will we do?" Zach asked, thinking of the bitter cold he'd experienced before his father got the fire going. He'd been as close to being frozen stiff as he ever wanted to be, and he dreaded having to go through the ordeal again.

"I'll go down to the trees and fetch more," Nate said.

"In this?" Zach saw puffs of snow blown into the cleft by the squalling wind. Fleeting panic assailed him as he imagined the sheer horror of being left alone should calamity befall his pa. "How will you find your way back?"

"Simple, son," Nate said, pointing at their piled supplies in the corner. "I'll tie one end of my rope in here, to my saddle, and the other end around my waist, then go down the slope, feeling my ways along, until I find fallen branches or a tree I can chop limbs off of."

"But what if the rope isn't long enough?"

"We have two blankets I can cut into strips to add to it if need be."

"But what if the rope or strips break or become untied?"

Their eyes met. Nate gave his son a light tap on the point of his chin and stated, "It has to be done. There's no way around it. We won't last a day without a fire."

"I wish the snow would stop."

"A minute ago you didn't much care if it snows forever."

"I changed my mind."

Smiling, Nate leaned his back against the wall. The warmth and security made him drowsy and he wearily closed his eyes, wishing he could sleep the clock around. Sleep, however, was a luxury he could ill afford until the weather broke and the cold abated. One of them had to keep the fire going at all times, and Zach was hardly old enough to be entrusted with so important a responsibility.

"Pa!"

Nate's eyes shot open and he straightened, his right hand gripping a pistol. His son was staring at the entrance, but a glance showed Nate only thick snow. "What's the matter?"

"I saw something."

"What?"

"I'm not sure, Pa. An animal of some kind. It poked its head in, spotted us, and backed right out again."

Had Zach imagined seeing something? Nate couldn't help but ask himself as he rose and moved cautiously to the opening. The boy was wound as tight as a fiddle, and Nate knew how a bad case of nerves could play havoc with a person's mind. He'd checked the cleft floor shortly after starting the fire, and except for a few chipmunk tracks had found no evidence of previous inhabitants. Peering out proved pointless; visibility was now restricted to a foot or two, at best. A blast of wind lashed snow in his face, driving him inside.

"See anything?"

"No."

"I saw something, Pa. I really did."

Nate studied the ground bordering the opening, which was covered by three inches of snow, but there were no prints. The wind might have wiped them out, if there had been any there to begin with. He walked back to the fire. "I might as well fetch that wood now as wait until later. The storm doesn't look like it will let up before Christmas."

Zachary stood and visibly composed his features. "Right this minute, you mean?"

"No sense in letting grass grow under us," Nate quipped, yet the boy's somber mood was unaffected. Taking the rawhide rope, he carried his saddle to within a foot of the opening and looped the end of the rope around it.

"What about cutting up our blankets?" Zach asked.

"Only as a last resort," Nate said. He yanked on the rope, testing the knot. "Keep your piece charged and your eyes peeled while I'm gone."

"Shoot sharp's the word," Zach said, stepping to the saddle.

Nodding, Nate made fast the rawhide to his waist,

checked his pistols to verify they were still snug under his belt, and slowly edged outward.

"If you need me, Pa, tug on the rope."

"I will," Nate replied, amused at the notion of Zach coming to his rescue should he find himself in trouble. One so tender in years quite understandably lacked a mature appreciation of the severe dangers that might befall any wanderer in the wilderness at any time.

A tremendous gust of wind punctuated Nate's reverie by nearly bowling him over as he moved into the open. Whirling flakes flitted all around him, and he was encased from head to toe in a fine layer of white. Seizing the rope firmly in his left hand, he tucked his chin low and barreled his way down the slope, battling the wind every foot of the way. His body was buffeted mercilessly; at times he felt as if he was being hammered by invisible fists.

And the cold! Now that Nate was away from the warming influence of the fire, the cold sliced into him like a knife made of ice. In seconds he was freezing, his teeth chattering. He might as well have been naked for all the good his buckskins and buffalo robe were doing him.

Somewhere below was the wood they needed. Hunching forward, Nate dug in his feet and made slow but determined progress. Several times he slipped, but each time his grip on the rope enabled him to stay erect. Twice his moccasins banged against rocks. His right ankle started throbbing.

When Nate guessed he had covered 20 feet, he crouched and felt the ground in front of him with his right hand, seeking the precious wood they needed to survive. His frantic fingers found stones by the bushel, rocks by the score, and a few boulders here and there. He also found weeds and a patch of grass. Yet no branches, not so much as a solitary twig.

His fingers were rapidly numbing. Intense pangs racked his lungs. Suddenly his beaver hat began to slip from his head and he pulled it down tight. In doing so he lost his hold on the rope, and as he swung his arm to grab it his left heel went out from under him. Unable to keep his balance, he fell hard.

For a moment Nate lay there, annoyed at his clumsiness. A snowflake landed in his open mouth, alighting on the very tip of his tongue. Instantly it melted and he swallowed the drop of water. There were so many flakes filling the air that another immediately flew between his lips and he swallowed again. "We won't want for water," he said aloud, and chuckled, envisioning how he must look lying there like some simpleton.

Slowly Nate rose, gathering in the rope as he did. "You're not beating us, storm," he declared, then shouted into the raging elements, "You're not beating us!"

Pressing on, Nate searched faster. Visibility had dropped to less than six inches. His arms and legs were so cold they hardly had any feeling left in them. His toes were either numb or missing. The norther was the culprit. High winds invariably intensified cold temperatures.

Desperation tinged his movements now. They needed wood, and he refused to go back to the cleft until he found some. Swinging right and left, he tried to make sense of the objects his fingers touched. A moment later his right hand brushed against something long and hard. Pausing, he examined it carefully and recognized the smooth texture of bark. His prize was a downed tree limb!

Quickly, Nate seized it under his right arm and stood. As he turned a dark blur moved through the snow. He caught a brief glimpse of something on four legs, and knew his son had indeed seen an animal. But what kind?

Nate warily headed for the cleft. Whatever the thing was, it must have followed him down. Would it attack? Or was it as cold and disoriented by the blizzard as he was? His palm curled around a flintlock.

He must have traveled ten feet when the dark blur reappeared a yard in front of him. So swiftly did the creature move that again its identity eluded him, but he did see enough to roughly gauge its size, which was not half as high as his knees and not more than two feet long. A measure of relief fortified him and on he went. Perhaps it was a raccoon or a bobcat, even a rabbit, he speculated. Although why any wild animal would be so close to him was puzzling.

Slowly Nate took in the rope as he ascended. Judging by the weight, the limb under his arm must be a big one, and would be a welcome addition to their dwindling pile. But a single limb, no matter how large, was insufficient for their needs. He would have to make another foray, possibly many more. The thought sparked a shudder.

An interminable interval went by, and Nate swore he had been plodding through the ever-deepening snow for hours when a glimmer of pale light outlined the cleft entrance. Coated liberally with snow, he staggered inside and nearly collapsed with relief.

"Pa!" Zach shouted, coming off the saddle in a rush. "Let me help you."

Ordinarily Nate would have told his son that he could handle the job himself. In his exhausted state he did not argue, but rather helped Zach lower the limb to the floor. Then, shuffling awkwardly, he lumbered to the fire and sank down.

"Are you all right?" Zach inquired anxiously.

"Never felt better," Nate tried to answer, and was shocked by the croaking noises that issued from his throat instead of words.

"Pa?" Zach said, swinging around so he could kneel next to Nate's legs. "What's the matter with you? Why can't you talk?" He placed his hand against his father's cheek. "Tarnation! You're frozen!"

"No," Nate rasped. He had to swallow several times and massage his throat before his vocal cords would work correctly. "I'm fine, son. And I saw your animal."

"You did? What kind is it?"

"I couldn't tell, but it's nothing to worry about." Nate inched nearer the fire, savoring the pleasant tingling in his arms and legs. As an experiment he tapped a finger on his nose but felt no sensation.

"Is there anything I can do?"

"Maybe drag that limb over here and see if you can chop it down to size," Nate requested. The tingling was spreading, growing painful. Grunting, he reclined on his left side, his face to the flames, unwilling to move a muscle until either he thawed completely out or spring came, whichever happened first. He heard Zach begin chopping, a rhythmic thunk-thunk-thunk that lulled him to the verge of sleep. In his nostrils was the spicy scent of burning wood.

With a start, Nate opened his eyes. He knew he had dozed off, and wondered how long he had slept. The fire seemed the same, but Zach's chopping had ceased. Tensing, he rose up on an elbow and glanced over his shoulder to see if the chore had been done. What he saw caused him to scramble awkwardly to his knees and clutch both flintlocks.

"Shhhh, Pa," Zach whispered. "Don't spook it."

"It" was a young wolf, no more than a pup, standing just within the opening with head held low and its thin lips pulled up over its tiny fangs. It glared from Zach to Nate and back again, doing its best to appear as fierce as it could but failing miserably. Size alone did not belie its savagery; the soaked, haggard condition of its fur and its gaunt body did. Its thin legs trembled so hard, the pup shook from nose to tail.

"I was chopping and looked up and there it was," Zach revealed. "It must want in out of the cold real bad."

"Now we have fresh meat," Nate said, easing his left pistol out. Wolf meat wasn't regarded as exceptionally tasty, but as hungry as he was he'd eat it raw.

"No!" Zach yelled, and the pup instantly backed away and twisted, about to flee out into the blizzard. So weak was it that it tripped over its own feet and stumbled against the side of the entrance. "Don't shoot, Pa. Please."

"Why not?" Nate wanted to know.

"I want to keep it."

"You what?"

"Raise it as a pet, just like we did with Samson."

"Samson was a dog," Nate noted, recalling the huge black mongrel that had lived with them for so many years it had been part of the family. All too vividly he remembered Samson's death at the hands of murderous Apaches down near Santa Fe.

"So?"

"So this is a *wolf,*" Nate stressed, his finger on the trigger. The pup had stopped and was framed in the opening, as easy a target as he could wish for. One shot, right between the eyes, would . . .

"Drags the Rope raised a wolf once for a couple of years," Zach said. "He said it made a fine pet."

"He did?"

"Yep. Please, let me try to make friends with it."

"Of all the harebrained notions," Nate muttered, wavering between the rumblings of his empty stomach and the silent yet eloquent appeal in his son's eyes. "Just because Drags the Rope took one in doesn't mean this one will take to being domesticated. A wolf is about as wild a creature as walks God's green earth. It has a mind of its own."

"Please, Pa."

"The darn thing will likely try to bite you if you get too close."

"Please."

Nate resisted the impulse to give in. He had their lives to think of. Should the blizzard last for more than three or four days, they'd face the grim specter of starvation. If he had to choose between sacrificing a wretched pup or his son, the outcome was a foregone conclusion.

The wolf made bold to come a few feet nearer, drawn by the heat of the fire. A pitiable whine passed its lips.

"What do you say?" Zach prompted.

Against Nate's better judgment, he slowly lowered the flintlock and shook his head at his own stupidity. "Go ahead," he said wearily, taking solace in two facts. One, they weren't starving yet. And two, if they kept the pup around they could always eat it later.

Chapter Eight

Even as Winona leaped at the shadowy figure, he straightened to his full height, and as her knife streaked at his chest she realized there was only one person in the entire tribe who was so huge. Too late, she attempted to angle her blow away from him, but the blade was so close that the best she could hope to do was bury it in his shoulder. Fortunately, his reflexes were as astounding as his stature, and the keen tip was an inch from his flesh when his enormous hand seized her wrist, checking the swing effortlessly.

"It is I, Winona," Touch the Clouds said. "Not him."

She sagged against him then, overcome by the dreadful mistake so narrowly avoided. Her previous statement that he was like a brother to her was no idle declaration. Since childhood they had been the best of friends, and before Nate came into her life it had been Touch the Clouds who served as her protector as well as his sister's. "I am so sorry," she mumbled.

"I saw you come this way and thought I should make certain he did not bother you," the giant explained, wisely not aggravating her misery by referring to her attack.

"I needed wood."

Touch the Clouds saw the pile. "Let me," he said. Disengaging himself, he walked over and retrieved the limbs. In his arms they looked like twigs.

All the way back to the lodge Winona said nothing, so preoccupied was she. Head bowed, she wrestled with the guilt that assailed her. To think she had almost killed one of her closest friends! She had long prided herself on her ability to deal with any crisis that might arise, and she was devastated by her failure.

At the lodge Touch the Clouds deposited the limbs and stepped back, his dark eyes studying her intently. "Perhaps it would be best if you spent the night with my wife and me."

"I will be fine," Winona said softly, finding the courage to look him in the eyes at last.

"If not us, then with Willow Woman and her husband."

"I do not want to impose on your sister either."

"Neither of us would be bothered. Rather we would be honored that you allow us to look out for you."

"Am I a grown woman or a child?" Winona said petulantly, and in so doing defined the core of her problem. Would she dishonor her family and her husband by falling to pieces, or would she persevere and prove herself worthy of the famous Grizzly Killer? "Please go. I am in no danger."

Like a wraith, Touch the Clouds disappeared in the night, and Winona took her wood inside. Three steps in she abruptly stopped and stared at a neatly folded buffalo robe lying near her fading fire. It hadn't been there when she left, and she knew immediately it wasn't hers.

Going forward, she set down the wood and picked up the robe.

Her hands told her this was a new one, the hide in excellent condition. Her mind did not need deductive insight to know who had placed the robe there in her absence. Striding to the opening, she shoved the flap aside, tossed the robe out, and shouted, "When I need a new robe I will ask my *husband* to kill a buffalo for me."

Securing the flap, Winona fed branches to the fire and sank down beside it. She thought of Nate and Zach and wondered where they might be. How she wished they were with her now! But since they weren't, and probably would not show up for some time, she must deal with the situation as she saw fit.

What could she do that she hadn't already done? Winona wondered. She had made her feelings emphatically clear to Jumping Bull, yet he persisted in courting her. So she must continue to ignore him and hope he would not become more aggressive. If he did, she must deal with him accordingly.

The reminder moved her to the wall, where she took a polished pistol from a parfleche and methodically loaded the gun as Nate had instructed her. She had balked when he first proposed teaching her, and was glad he had refused to take no for an answer. In a clash between a man and a woman, where size and strength were decided masculine advantages, a gun equalized things. Jumping Bull would think twice before trying to force his will on her if he knew he risked getting a lead ball in the gut.

Winona tied a rawhide cord around her slim waist and wedged the flintlock under it so it would always be handy. Jumping Bull was devious; whatever he tried, he would do it when she least expected, so she must be ready at all times. Moving to another parfleche, she removed several pemmican cakes and took a seat facing the entrance. As she bit into one she heard a faint snap from outside, possibly made by someone stepping on a twig.

Intuition filled her with foreboding. It might be anyone passing by, but somehow she knew that was not the case. Jumping Bull was out there, keeping an eye on her lodge. Why? Did he intend to sneak in and take her to his lodge against her will? Would he be so reckless? Yes, she realized. He just might.

The pemmican lost its taste, and Winona set the cakes aside to eat later. Rising, she tiptoed to the flap and made doubly sure it was fastened. A strong man might easily break in, but in so doing he would make enough noise to arouse her from slumber. Or such was her hope.

Winona spread out her robe by the fire, put the pistol and the knife within easy reach, and lay on her side, her head cradled on her hands. I must be strong! she told herself. I must not give in to fear or indecision!

She gazed forlornly into the writhing flames, thinking how lonely the lodge was without her loved ones. Memories of the first time she had ever laid eyes on Nate, when he saved her from marauding Blackfeet, stirred her heart. He had charged out of nowhere, putting his life in peril for total strangers, and from the moment she saw him, she was his. She could not explain how it happened; she only knew it had. An indefinable yearning had drawn her to him with irresistible force, and that first night of their acquaintance she had gone walking with him under his robe. Her brazenness, in retrospect, amazed her. Had her grandmother been alive, she would have been reprimanded severely. "Only a woman of loose morals," her grandmother had often intoned, "allows a man to touch her before they are joined together as man and wife." She had sincerely believed those words, yet when the test came, love had prevailed.

Love. What a mystery it was! When her daughter was of age—and she fervently hoped the baby due in eight moons would be a girl—she must remember to be patient with her and to understand that love made people commit acts they would not otherwise contemplate. She must also point out that when two people were meant to be together, no force in the world could keep them apart.

Gradually Winona's eyelids drooped, and the last sound she heard was the howling of the wind as it raged among the lodges with renewed vigor. A storm must be coming, she thought. Then sleep claimed her.

"Isn't he cute, Pa?"

"Wonderful."

"It tickles when he licks my hand."

"I suppose it does."

"Is anything wrong?"

"I'm tired of being cooped up in here. A whole day has passed and it's still snowing."

"But not quite as hard."

"Hard enough to keep us penned in."

"Would you like to play with Blaze for a spell? It might cheer you up."

"Maybe later."

The second morning after the blizzard struck Nate awakened to a peculiar sensation on his face and he lay still, trying to figure out why his cheeks and chin felt wet. The reason was forthcoming seconds later when a moist tongue pressed against his jaw and left a path of cool drool clear up to his forehead. Opening his eyes, he found himself nose to nose with the pup. From nearby came a youthful giggle.

"You're downright hilarious, son," Nate said, sitting up. Without warning, the pup launched itself into his lap and nipped playfully at his shirt. "Now get this critter off me."

"Blaze likes you, Pa," Zach said, taking the skinny wolf in his arms. "After all the jerky you've fed him, you're his friend for life."

"I was trying to put some flesh on his bones in case we needed to . . ." Nate said testily, and suddenly fell silent, aware of a drastic change outside. "The wind has stopped!" he declared. Shoving erect, he dashed to the opening and gazed in breathless awe on a sweeping white vista extending for as far as the eye could see. Snow four to five feet deep covered everything. Not a single blade of grass or weed was visible. Trees laden heavily with clumps of clinging snow were bent under the oppressive weight. Rocks, boulders, logs—they all were buried. It was as if a heavenly artist had painted the landscape white with a single sweep of a celestial brush.

"Isn't it glorious, Pa!" Zach breathed at Nate's elbow.

"Yep." Nate ventured outside, inhaling the fresh, frigid, invigorating air, and craned his neck to scan the sky to the west and the north. A few fluffy white clouds floated sluggishly on the currents. "The storm is finally over," he said thankfully.

"Does this mean we head home right away?"

Nate glanced at the spine, where the elk carcass lay blanketed by thick snow. More than anything he wanted to be on his way to the village, but leaving now would make a mockery of Zach's hunt and leave hundreds of pounds of prime meat to spoil or be devoured by scavengers. "We'll stick to our original plan and butcher the elk first."

"Do Blaze and me get to help cut up the elk?" Zach inquired hopefully.

"Blaze?" Nate said, looking down. The pup stood next to Zach's leg, its tiny black nose twitching as, with tilted head, it tried to catch scents from below. Nate had to admit he'd been surprised at how readily the scrawny beast had taken to the boy. That first night, when Zach had slowly approached with outstretched hand, Nate had expected the wolf to either flee or tear into Zach with all the innate ferocity of its kind. Instead, to his amazement, the pup had sniffed, whined, sniffed some more, and then tentatively licked Zach's fingers.

Now, at Nate's mention of the name that Zach had used so many times the pup already associated the name with itself, the wolf looked up at Nate, its white throat patch bright in the morning sun.

"You'd better keep the pup here," Nate advised. "This snow is so deep it'll drown in the stuff."

"Awww, he'll be lonely all by himself," Zach said, running his fingers over the pup's back.

"You can't carry him and your rifle both," Nate admonished. He saw his son frown, and resting a hand on Zach's arm, he said, not unkindly, "There comes a time when every boy has to accept not being a boy anymore, a time when he has to take on bigger responsibilities than he ever had before." Nate paused. "You're at the age now where I'm going to expect more out of you, and I know you won't let me down. When it's time to work, you have to put your nose to the grindstone and forget about playing and wolf pups and nonsense like that. Do you savvy?"

"I savvy, Pa," Zach responded halfheartedly.

Squinting down at the approximate spot where the elk was hidden, Nate said, "Tell you what I'll do. I'll ride on down there and dig out the carcass so the sun can get at it and thaw the meat a bit. Then the two of us will do the butchering later on."

Zach was not dense. He knew his father had made the suggestion so he would have a little more time to spend with Blaze. "Thanks, Pa. That would be fine."

Saddling Pegasus took but a minute. Nate sat loosely astride the gelding as it moved downward, ready to hurl himself to either side should the horse slip and fall. The brilliance of the snow made him squint. He noticed the surface was as smooth as glass and unmarred as yet by animal prints. His own tracks, those he had made on his half-dozen excursions in search of wood, had long since filled in. So had the big holes he'd made when digging down to locate grass and other forage for the horses.

Nate skirted the ravine this time due to the many large boulders dotting the bottom of it, obstacles he would be unable to see and which might injure Pegasus if the gelding collided with one. Riding a bit further north, he then swung around and rode up the slope of the spine. The going was rough, the snow in places up above the tops of Pegasus's legs.

Both of them were breathing heavily when Nate reined up and slid off. The snow came to his waist. Straining, he plowed to where the elk should be and began scooping with his left forearm. In due course he realized he had picked the wrong spot. Moving a few feet to the right, he tried again.

On the third attempt Nate uncovered a frozen rear leg. Encouraged, he dug until he had exposed the rear half of the kill, then stopped to rest for a minute. Strenuous exertions at extremely high altitudes were exceptionally tiring, and he didn't care to wear himself out so soon, not with the butchering to do.

Nate glanced at the cleft but saw no sign of his son. A survey of the valley showed nothing was moving about. For once, total tranquility reigned in the Rockies, a fleeting interlude he took advantage of. Industriously he dug, and didn't stop until the entire carcass had been uncovered.

Caked with sweat, Nate sat down on the elk and mopped his brow with his sleeve. There was still no sign of Zach. Since he had no desire to ride back up to fetch the boy when Zach was perfectly capable of saddling the mare and following the trail he had broken, Nate cupped a hand to his mouth and bellowed, "Zachary! Do you hear me?"

The words echoed off the high peak far above. Somewhere a bird squawked, as if in reply.

"Zach!" Nate shouted. "Do you hear me?"

Once again the cry bounced off the snow-encrusted summit and seemed to roll out across the valley below.

"He must be playing with that mangy pup," Nate complained under his breath, and rising, he impetuously drew one of his pistols. He had to get Zach's attention, and what better way than with a gunshot? Pointing the barrel into the air, he cocked the hammer, waited a second to see if Zach might yet appear, and when the boy didn't step from the cleft, squeezed the trigger.

For the third time a sharp sound echoed off the top of the mountain.

Nate lowered the flintlock and smiled on seeing Zach dash outside, the wolf on the boy's heels. Beckoning with his free hand, he called up, "Saddle Mary and head on down. We have a heap of work to do."

Before Zach could acknowledge the yell, a tremendous rumbling erupted, coming from the upper reaches of the rocky heights. Nate glanced up and felt a chill pierce his soul. In his annoyed state he had carelessly overlooked a very real, imminent danger, and now he was about to pay the price for his rash folly.

The blizzard had dumped three times as much heavy snow on the higher reaches of the mountain as on the lower slopes. In spots drifts 20 feet high had been sculpted by the whipping winds, and many of these massive drifts were perched precariously over steep inclines. All it would take to send them hurtling down the mountainside with the unstoppable force and deceptive speed of a steam engine were a few sudden, loud noises, as anyone familiar with the high country knew.

Nate knew this. He was fully aware of the risk of an avalanche after a heavy snow, especially above the tree line. But his anger had prompted him to act impulsively, and here, before his anxious eyes, he saw a great crack appear in a vast bank of snow hundreds of feet above. The crack widened rapidly. Resembling distant thunder, the rumbling increased in volume until the ground itself appeared to shake, and a moment later tons of snow tumbled violently downward in a showery spray of white.

"Take cover in the cleft!" Nate screamed at Zach, hoping the din of the onrushing snow wouldn't drown him out. Whirling, he retrieved the Hawken and raced for Pegasus, his legs churning, the elk carcass completely forgotten.

The avalanche was growing quickly in size and ferocity. Much as a snowball grows when rolled down a hill, the avalanche was sweeping up more and more snow and thereby adding to its monumental proportions with every passing foot. Stretching for over a hundred yards end to end, rearing 30 feet in the air, the roiling sheet of choking death cascaded over enormous boulders and dwarf trees and propelled both along with it.

Nate reached Pegasus and vaulted into the saddle. Reining around, he put his heels to the gelding's flanks, making for the cleft. He could see Zach gawking upward. "Get inside!" he screamed. "Inside, where it's safe!"

Zach, apparently, couldn't hear him. Spellbound, the boy watched the awe-inspiring spectacle as crucial seconds ticked by. Then, when the leading edge of the avalanche was less than 50 feet above the cleft, Zach must have seen the peril he was in because he cast a terrified glance at Nate, spun, and ran for the opening.

A heartbeat later a swirling wall of snow engulfed Zach and the cleft.

"I tell you that I heard a shot," Bobcat had insisted a minute earlier, and without waiting for his companions, who had been laughing uproariously at a crude joke told by Walking Bear, he had started up through the aspens.

"I heard nothing," Loud Talker said.

"Bobcat's ears are sharper than ours," Walking Bear commented. "Perhaps he did hear something."

Little Dog, in the act of getting his horse ready to leave, gazed at the swiftly moving figure of their friend and sighed. He had not heard anything either, and he doubted very much that Bobcat had. The last thing he wanted was another delay when they were finally about to start for their own country, so he said, "Let us ride out. He will catch up soon."

"No," Rolling Thunder declared. "We must stay together." Lance in hand, he strode upward. Walking Bear and Loud Talker trailed him.

"Wait for me," Little Dog said with no enthusiasm whatsoever. All he wanted to do was go home. Dejected, he followed them, certain Bobcat had heard a limb break under the weight of snow, nothing more. He laughed lightly, bitterly. Except for the killing of the trapper, the whole trip had been a waste of time and energy. But he was the only one who saw it that way. The others, as they'd made clear during their discussions while the blizzard raged, saw their trip into Shoshone country as a great success. Sometimes, he reflected, his friends were utter fools. He swore to himself that this would be the last time he went anywhere with them, although in his heart he knew he didn't mean it.

Suddenly there was an excited shout.

Breaking into a run, or as much of a run as he could manage in the deep snow, Little Dog soon caught up with his companions, all of whom were standing at the edge of the aspens and staring at something much higher up on the mountain.

"It is a white man!" Bobcat exclaimed.

"You are sure?" Rolling Thunder asked doubtfully, taking a step forward.

Then Little Dog spotted the distant figure, but he too could not determine if the rider was white or Indian. Above the rider streaked an avalanche, and to Little Dog's astonishment he realized the rider was heading straight for it. "What is he doing?"

"Committing suicide," Loud Talker said.

"Look!" Bobcat declared. "Now he is fleeing."

In silent fascination they observed the tableau unfold. Being over half a mile to the south of the snowslide, they were well out of harm's way.

"White or not, he will never make it," Rolling Thunder said.

Little Dog had to agree. The avalanche was almost on the rider. Whoever the man was, he was doomed.

"Noooooo!" Nate wailed at the instant his son and the cleft were swallowed by the deluge of snow and debris. Shocked by the horror he had witnessed, he rode in a daze for ten more yards, until his brain awoke to the personal peril he was in from the white maelstrom. The avalanche would soon be on him!

Jerking on the reins, Nate urged Pegasus downward. The gelding floundered, caught itself, and barreled through a drift. Impeded by the clinging snow and the treacherously slippery ground under its driving hoofs, the horse could do no better than a lurching run, try as it might.

Nate looked back, saw the avalanche gaining. Grimly he rode on in the vain hope that if he got low enough the avalanche might bowl him over but would leave him otherwise unscathed. In his ears was a hissing roar, as if a gigantic serpent pursued him. The air vibrated to the beat of invisible hands.

Occasionally Nate had given thought to his own death. Often he had speculated that he would probably be killed by hostiles, or fall to the slashing claws of a great grizzly. Never once had he considered an avalanche as the possible cause of his death, and now, as he girded himself to meet his Maker, he wished it *had* been Indians or a bear that did him in. The end would likely have been swift, in the heat of combat, infinitely preferable to being smothered alive or having every bone in his body broken and lying helplessly paralyzed until starvation or the cold claimed him.

Something slammed into the middle of Nate's back, causing him to fling his arms out, and he was nearly unhorsed. Regaining control of the reins, he hunched low, twisted, and beheld a mammoth rippling wave of snow lapping at the gelding's flying hooves. The sky was blotted out by the curling crest. A heartbeat elapsed. Two. Then, with a muted growl, the avalanche swooped down upon him and enclosed him in its icy grasp. He went sailing head over heels and heard a terrified squeal from Pegasus. On and on and on he flew, flipping like an ungainly acrobat, his limbs flailing wildly, losing his beaver hat and his Hawken. His powder horn, ammo pouch, and possibles bag battered him ceaselessly. He had no idea which way was up, which way was down. He didn't know right from left, or north from south, east from west. Sheathed in the roiling snow, he was totally helpless, his strength as inconsequential before the might of the avalanche as would be that of a gnat trapped in a tornado. Vaguely he was conscious of traveling a great distance. Always he plummeted downward.

Of a sudden, Nate struck a hard object. Stunned, he tried to lift his head to see what it had been, but he slammed into something else. His vision swam. His consciousness faded. Dimly he glimpsed a glimmer of sunlight, or thought he did, and felt himself sliding over a smooth surface, or believed he was. At long, long last he coasted to a stop. Blood was on his tongue. He blinked, attempted to rise, and was sucked into a void more frightening than that of the avalanche. Then all went black.

Chapter Nine

"Your husband and son are both dead!"

Winona stiffened at the belligerent declaration behind her, and slowly lowered the shirt she had been stitching to her lap. Adopting a mocking smile, she faced the lodge entrance and responded casually, "My husband is hard to die, as the white men say. He will be home soon enough, Jumping Bull, and you will have your chance to settle with him. Although"—and she paused deliberately—"were I you, I would pack up my belongings and go live in Canada for the rest of my life."

"Why would I want to live there?" he baited her.

"Living there is better than dying here."

Jumping Bull bristled. "You think your weakling of a husband can slay me? With my own two hands I have strangled a Blackfoot!"

"How many of the mighty humped bears have you killed?" Winona retorted, and hid her delight at the flush that infused the warrior's cheeks. She had no means of preventing him from paying her a dozen visits a day, so she had decided to make each of his visits a poignant lesson in humiliation.

"Mock me while you can, woman," Jumping Bull snapped. "But we both know the high mountains were hit by a blizzard. Our hunters have told us as much. Can your cherished Grizzly Killer kill storms as well?"

Fear blossomed in the depths of Winona's soul. Touch the Clouds had informed her of the reports of heavy snow to the northwest, and she knew Nate had not packed any supplies with him because he had intended to live off the land. She shuddered, thinking of the dire consequences if he and Zach had been caught unawares, and prayed the blizzard had missed them.

"I thought not," Jumping Bull said, noticing, and smiled triumphantly. He crossed his legs, making himself comfortable as was his custom. "We have much to talk over."

"In the next life."

Ignoring her sarcasm, Jumping Bull asked, "Why have Willow Woman and her friends been spreading rumors about me?"

"They have?" Winona said in genuine surprise. It was common knowledge her situation was the talk of the camp, but this was the first she had heard of her friends contributing to the general gossip.

"You know they have. My sister, Rabbit Woman, overheard them saying I had no right to cause so much dissension among our people and that the Yellow Noses should run me off for the good of all."

They should! Winona wanted to say, but didn't. The village was undergoing the worst upheaval in her memory. Men and women were taking sides, with the majority expressing their support for Nate and her, while a small but vocal minority were doing their best to convince everyone else Jumping Bull was in the right. Several heated arguments had occurred, and a pair of warriors, former best friends, had come close to blows. All this among a people who prided themselves on their ability to live together peacefully.

"And they are not the only ones," Jumping Bull was saying. "I do not like what Touch the Clouds, Drags the Rope, and their friends have been doing."

"Which is?"

"They have been trying to decide who should take in my son after your husband returns."

A merry laugh came from Winona's lips. The only reason anyone would adopt Runs Fast would be if Jumping Bull died. Touch the Clouds and the others, by going around broaching the subject when they knew what they said would get back to Jumping Bull, were discreetly putting pressure on Jumping Bull to desist before he wound up dead at Nate's hands.

"I do not find it humorous," he said.

"You would be wise to heed their warning. Or do you want your son to lose his father as he has already lost his mother?" Winona shook her head. "Your hatred has clouded your judgment."

"Do you think less of me because I despise the whites?"

"I do not understand why you hate them so. They have never harmed us. The trappers are our friends."

"Friends!" Jumping Bull exploded. "Are they being friendly when they trap all the beaver from our streams? Are they being friendly when they kill our game? Are they being friendly when they take our women as their wives and then desert the women once they have all the pelts they want?"

"Grizzly Killer will never desert me," Winona said defensively.

"Now whose judgment is clouded? Is your Nate any

different from the rest? Is he more loyal than they? More decent?"

"Yes."

"Waugh!" Jumping Bull said, and spat on the ground. "You are being deceived and you are too foolish to see it." Bending forward, he eyed her craftily. "Answer a question for me."

"Why should I?"

"Prove me wrong. I know your Grizzly Killer has sold many furs at the rendezvous. Tell me that he does not hoard the money he receives."

"He has taught me the value of saving for our future needs. What of it?"

"Heed my words. When he has saved enough, he will take his money and leave you. The whites value their bits of paper and little pieces of metal more than they do life itself."

Winona stared at him in disbelief. "How is it," she inquired, "that one who has lived so many winters, who has married and raised a young son, can be so ignorant of life? I feel sorry for you, Jumping Bear."

The warrior recoiled as if slapped. "I do not want your pity, woman. I want your love. And I *will* have it once I prove to you that I am the better warrior."

"If you kill him, I will hate you forever."

"For a while you will hate me, but in time you will come to see I was right all along. We will grow old together."

Once again their conversation had come full circle, and once again Winona's loathing had been kindled to a fever pitch. She glanced down at her pistol, partially hidden by a fold of her buckskin dress, and felt, stronger than ever, the temptation to pick it up and end her woes by shooting Jumping Bull in the head. But she could not bring herself to do it. She had killed enemies before, yet always when her life or the lives of her loved ones had been at stake. And since Jumping Bull was not threatening her physically right at that moment, she could no more slay him than she could slit the throat of a newborn.

Disappointed in her lack of resolve, Winona looked at the entrance, about to tell Jumping Bull to leave. He had saved her the trouble by having already left. But she knew he would be back.

He always came back.

"I see a hand!" Bobcat yelled, and goaded his perspiring mount across the shimmering slope to where several pale fingers jutted from the cold snow. Leaping down, sinking to his knees, he scrambled to the slack fingers and energetically set to work digging out the person to whom they were attached. In seconds he had the entire hand exposed. "Help me!" he urged. "We do not want him to die before we test his manhood."

"You are wasting your time," Walking Bear said as he reined up. "No one could have survived that avalanche. The man is already dead."

Bobcat continued to dig anyway, spurred by the promise of the thrills he stood to experience if the white man was alive and could be tortured. Of all life's pleasures, Bobcat enjoyed inflicting pain and killing the most. And above all else he enjoyed inflicting pain on and killing white men, the arrogant intruders who presumed to treat the land as if it was their very own, and who had formed alliances with long-standing enemies of the Gros Ventres, such as the Shoshones.

In a flurry of snow Rolling Thunder arrived on the scene and leaped down beside Bobcat. "Let me help you," he said, scooping both of his brawny hands in to the wrists. With a powerful flip of his fingers he excavated a large hole.

"Did either of you see what happened to his horse?" Walking Bear asked. "I want it for my own." Shifting, he studied the swath left by the avalanche, consisting of a jumbled mass of snow and boulders and shattered tree limbs. About 40 yards off, Little Dog and Loud Talker were examining something partially buried in the snow. "I wonder if they found it," he said to himself, and rode toward them.

Rolling Thunder watched him leave, then resumed digging at a frenzied pace. He cared nothing for the stupid horse. It was the man he wanted, a man he hoped was white so he could make up for the blunder he had committed in giving the trapper's hair to Walking Bear. Soon he had dug down to the elbow. Then the hair. Working in concert with Bobcat, he brushed the snow away from the man's head, revealing the face.

"He is white!" Bobcat cried

Touching his fingers to the man's neck, Rolling Thunder found a pulse. "And he is alive."

Shoulder to shoulder, they burrowed downward until the man's chest was clear of the snow. Then each one took an arm, gripped firmly, and heaved. Slowly, laboriously, they pulled the man out, then set him down on his back.

"I hope he is not broken up inside," Bobcat remarked, kneeling to give their captive a thorough going-over. He lifted a limp arm, then a leg, and let both drop.

"Why do you care if the white bastard is hurt?" Rolling Thunder inquired.

"Because I want him to live long enough for me to show him what true pain really is," Bobcat said. "I saw him first, so I will decide what to do with him." He tapped a knot the size of a duck egg on the man's forehead. "I see many bruises, cuts, and scrapes, but his bones do not appear to be broken and he breathes steady."

Rolling Thunder draped a hand on the hilt of his knife. "I want his hair."

"Find your own white dog," Bobcat responded, plucking a pistol caked with snow from under the man's wide belt. "This one is mine."

"I want his hair," Rolling Thunder repeated softly.

Bobcat glanced up, his smile disappearing, his features hardening. "His scalp is mine. I have every right to it. Who saw him first? Who was the first to reach him? His hair will hang in my lodge."

"I want it."

Indignation brought Bobcat to his feet, his right hand closing on his tomahawk. Anyone who led a war party or a hunting party was entitled to express his wishes freely, but the leader was not allowed to dictate to those who accompanied him. "Why should I give such a prize to you? You have done nothing to earn it."

"I know. And I do not dispute that. But if you allow me to claim it, you will have my deepest gratitude."

"I would rather have the scalp."

"Think about this," Rolling Thunder said. He was determined to have his way so he could ride proudly into their village waving the hair from the end of his lance, effectively putting an end to any hope White Buffalo had of challenging him to be the new chief. "Is it not true that one day soon our chief will die and I will become the most important man among our people?"

"Yes. What difference does it make?"

"Would it not be to your benefit to be on friendly terms with me when I have the power to grant you anything you might want? Horses, guns, the woman of your choice—as a chief I can use my influence to help you obtain everything you have ever desired."

Gradually the anger seeped from Bobcat's dark eyes and he relaxed his grasp on the tomahawk. It would be nice, he reflected, to have such influence, especially when the time came to divide the spoils of future raids. And too, there was a certain woman he liked whose father refused to let him enter their lodge simply because he didn't own as many horses as some of her other suitors. As chief, Rolling Thunder could perhaps persuade the reluctant father that letting Bobcat court the daughter was in the best interests of everyone concerned.

"Well?" Rolling Thunder prompted, sensing victory.

"You can have the scalp," Bobcat declared. He glanced quickly at the others, who were approaching but still 30 feet off, then stepped close to Rolling Thunder and said, "But if you do not honor your words, I will consider you an enemy."

A caustic retort was on Rolling Thunder's tongue, a retort he never uttered. To do so would antagonize Bobcat, who in turn would deny him the scalp. Far better, he reasoned, to overlook the affront for now. After he became chief would be the time to pay Bobcat back. "I always speak with a straight tongue to you. I will honor my words."

"See that you do."

Further conversation was interrupted by the coming of their three companions.

"How is the man?" Little Dog asked, staring at the prone form.

"He survived," Bobcat answered.

"His horse did not. Its neck is broken. We tried moving the body to get at the saddle, but the horse is too heavy."

"I would not want a white man's saddle anyway," Loud Talker said. "They are too soft and uncomfortable." He chuckled. "Do you remember the time White Buffalo killed the trapper and brought back the trapper's saddle? We all were allowed to try it. I thought I was riding on a pile of hides!"

Little Dog nudged the man with the toe of his moccasin. "What do you plan to do with him?"

"I will build a fire and we will test his courage," Bobcat replied.

"Out here in the open?" Little Dog said.

"In the aspens then."

"And delay our return to our village?" Little Dog bobbed his chin northward. "I think it would be wiser to take him with us and do as you want after we have stopped for the night. Remember, we are still in Shoshone country."

"I do not fear them," Bobcat stated.

"Who does?" said Rolling Thunder. "But I agree with Little Dog. We have far to travel and we should go now while the day is young. Tie this white snake on the horse I took from the trapper and we can be off."

"As you wish," Bobcat said docilely, and moved to their mounts.

It was a totally mystified Little Dog who stood aside while the prisoner was bound and gagged and thrown over the back of the animal. Perplexed by Bobcat's highly unusual conduct, he tried to think of a reason. Ordinarily, Bobcat gave in to no man, not even Rolling Thunder, yet here Bobcat had behaved as meekly as a little puppy.

Moments later they were all on their horses and riding, single file, down the slope of the mountain to the less perilous valley floor. Turning northward, they spent the rest of the morning contending with deep drifts and blowing snow. By midday they had covered a bare four miles.

"At this turtle's pace it will take us a full moon to reach our people," Walking Bear groused when they halted to give their mounts a rest.

Rolling Thunder pursed his lips. "The day is growing warm. Tomorrow will probably be warmer. In three sleeps much of the snow will have melted, and before the eighth sleep comes we will be home."

"Home," Little Dog said reverently.

The temperature did climb, but little of the snow had melted by twilight. For hours their horses struggled to make headway. On several occasions where the snow was too deep and the animals floundered, they all dismounted and pulled each horse to firmer footing again. They were a weary band when they made their night camp in a clearing by a stream.

Walking Bear and Loud Talker went into the woods after game while Rolling Thunder and Bobcat attended to the animals. Little Dog collected wood and soon had a fire crackling. As he arranged the branches to his satisfaction, he heard a low groan and turned to see the white man open his eyes and blink.

"You would have spared yourself much misery if you had died," Little Dog commented, and could tell by the other's expression that the man did not comprehend his tongue. The trapper studied him most carefully, and Little Dog was impressed to note a complete absence of fear. Leaning over, he yanked the gag out.

The man spoke in a strange, musical language.

"I cannot talk like a bird," Little Dog said. "And I do not know Shoshone." An idea goaded him into gesturing in sign language. "My name is Little Dog. I am Gros Ventre. Do you understand?"

Again the man spoke and motioned with his bound wrists.

"Yes, I think you do," Little Dog said. Moving to the trapper's side, he lifted the man's arms so he could get at the knots under the wrists.

"Stop!"

Pausing, Little Dog pivoted as Bobcat hastened up. "He knows sign language," said Little Dog. "We can question him if his hands are untied."

"I did not bring him with us so we could *talk* to him," Bobcat said. "There is nothing he might say that would interest me." Leering, he suddenly kicked the trapper in the stomach, doubling the man over in anguish. "All I want is to hear him scream when I gouge out his eyes and cut off his ears."

Although disappointed, Little Dog left and devoted himself to building the fire higher. He was curious to learn about the white way of life and to hear what had brought this trapper so far from the white world into the land of the Shoshones. Unlike his friends, he had long suspected that the whites were much like his own people in many respects and that if the two sides could sit down and discuss their differences, a peace might be worked out. The Gros Ventres, though, did not make peace with their enemies. They exterminated them.

Bobcat walked off again, and out of the corner of his eye Little Dog saw the trapper surreptitiously appraise each of them. He liked that. Some captives, knowing the fate awaiting them, would have yelled or pleaded, but not this one. This man used his brain; he was taking their measure and perhaps trying to think of a means of escaping. Sadly for someone so brave, there was none.

Presently Loud Talker and Walking Bear showed up bearing a rabbit. Rolling Thunder and Bobcat came and sat by the fire. Little Dog listened as they joked and recounted battles they had been in and told about wild beasts they had slain. He bided his time until Walking Bear glanced at the captive and asked whether anyone had tried to communicate with him.

"I did," Little Dog answered. "He knows sign language. But Bobcat does not want his hands freed."

"Why not?" Walking Bear asked. "It will be amusing to let him spew his lies, and we have nothing else to do."

"We will soon be very busy," Bobcat said, glaring at the trapper. "He dies when we are done eating, and all of you can have a hand in it."

"Why rush?" Walking Bear inquired. "Our journey back is a long one." He scratched his chin, pondering. "If I had caught a white man, I would rather take him back to the village for all the people to see. No one has ever done that before. Think of the songs the women would sing of my prowess!"

"I would do the same," Loud Talker mentioned.

The ensuing silence was broken by Rolling Thunder. "Some might say it is bad medicine to bring a white man into our village. Better that he die before we reach our land." He stared across the fire at the object of their disagreement. "But like Walking Bear I am interested in learning what this dog will tell us."

"Then so be it," Bobcat abruptly declared. He crouched by the captive and worked long and hard at the tight knots before they parted. Eyeing the trapper with contempt, he backed up and remarked, "Now make fools of yourselves."

All of them were surprised when Rolling Thunder shot upright, stalked around to the white man, and leaned close to the man's face. "How are you known?" he signed with sharp gestures.

The trapper never batted an eye. "I am called Grizzly Killer," he answered in flawless sign language.

Rolling Thunder took a quick step back, as if he had been punched, then raised his face to the heavens and smiled at the sparkling stars. His prayers had been answered! He clenched his fists and shook them in exultation.

Little Dog and the rest exchanged glances. Of them all, Little Dog was the only one who correctly guessed why Rolling Thunder was acting so oddly. He shifted his gaze to the white man, admiring the man's composure. The stories that whites were all craven cowards were clearly not true.

Grizzly Killer scanned them and fastened on Little Dog. "What happened to my horse?" he inquired.

"It was killed," Little Dog said, and added, "I could see that it was a fine animal."

"The Nez Percé gave it to me," Grizzly Killer signed, his mouth curling downward. "I will miss it."

Bobcat laughed. His fingers and arms flew. "You will not be alive along enough to miss it, bastard! I, Bobcat, am going to cut out your heart and piss on it."

"How many will hold me down when you do?" Grizzly Killer retorted.

In a flash Bobcat was up and at the captive, his knife streaking from its sheath and spearing at the white man's throat. Twisting, Grizzly Killer evaded the thrust, caught Bobcat's wrist, and jerked, sending Bobcat sailing over him to sprawl in an undignified heap in the snow. Grizzly Killer shoved to his knees, his movements slowed by his bound ankles, and turned awkwardly to face Bobcat. As he did, Rolling Thunder stepped in close and swung the butt end of his lance, striking Grizzly Killer on the temple. Soundlessly, the white man crumpled, and the next instant Bobcat was poised above him with the gleaming knife held aloft for a fatal stab.

Chapter Ten

As young Zachary King turned and saw the terrifying vision of the avalanche sweeping down the steep mountain slope toward him, a wave of fear bathed his body from head to toe and he stood rooted in fright to the spot outside of the cleft. He knew he should move, should dash through the opening before the snow struck him, but he could not seem to make his limbs obey his mind. Dimly he heard his father shouting. Closer and closer came the gigantic, turbulent mass, until with a sinking feeling in his gut he knew the avalanche would engulf him in another few seconds. That was when the pup whined.

"Blaze!" Zach cried, roused from his shock. Horrified at the thought of the wolf being killed, he was galvanized into action. He cast a glance at his father far below, then moved to grab the pup by the scruff of its neck, but it darted into the opening on its own. He promptly followed.

Tenderfoot

No sooner did Zach gain the shelter of the cleft than he was roughly hurled from his feet by an invisible hand that slammed into him from behind. Flying forward, he hit the floor hard and slid to a stop. A peculiar hissing arose. Zach put his hands flat, pushed up, and turned.

Once again terror seized him. Snow was streaming in the entrance and spilling out over the dirt floor, fanning to the right and the left. Frantically Zach backed up. He was afraid the snow would fill the whole interior and smother him.

The wolf stayed at his side. Legs spread, hair bristling, it snarled at the seething spray as if trying to frighten the snow into stopping.

Zach gulped and wished his father was there. His father! "Pa!" he cried, feeling new fear, but not for himself this time. His father had been out in the open, exposed and helpless to avoid the avalanche. What would happen when . . . ?

Shaking his head, Zach refused to give the matter any consideration. "Pa will be all right," he said softly. "He *has* to be." His own problem was more important at the moment. Already several inches of snow covered the ground near the opening.

Unexpectedly, the spray ended, the hissing ceased. A muted, rapidly fading roar showed the avalanche had passed and was rolling on down the mountain.

"Pa!" Zach yelled, running to the entrance. He attacked the snow with his hands, digging furiously, but soon realized the snow was too tightly packed to be easily dug aside. Stepping back, he glanced up at the top of the opening. There appeared to be less snow higher up, so girding his legs he started up the short incline, digging in his moccasins to gain extra purchase.

At the bottom of the pile the wolf uttered a tentative whimper.

"Don't fret, boy," Zach said. "I ain't about to leave

you. But if I don't get us dug out, we'll never see the light of day again."

He reached the apex of the crack and began scooping out handfuls, the snow cold on his palms and fingers. Outside all was now as quiet as a tomb, and the silence made him shiver. "Please let him be all right, Lord," he said. "Please, please, please."

Zach had a lump in his throat as he continued digging. Part of his apprehension was for his father; part was for his own welfare. If anything had happened to his pa—and simply framing the words in his mind was so painful he cringed—what would then happen to him? How would he survive on his own? He glanced over his shoulder at the mare, standing calmly in the back corner, munching on grass his father had brought the day before, as unconcerned as if she was in a stable somewhere. "Stupid horse," he muttered.

For how long Zach dug, he could not say. He made a deep hole in the snow, but still saw no hint of daylight. His fingers became numb, compelling him to halt for a while. Dejected, he carefully climbed down and went to the fire. Blaze followed him.

"We're in for it now, little fellow," Zach said, fighting back tears. He held his hands close to the low flames, barely noticing the warmth. "If I don't find my pa, I don't think I can ever make my way home again."

Blaze lay down with his pointed chin resting on his small paws, and regarded the boy with an expression that could only be described as one of tender affection.

"But I'll bet you Pa made it to safety," Zach went on, bobbing his head. "Yep! I'll bet he did. There isn't nothing my pa can't do."

An ember popped in the fire.

"I never expected anything like this to happen," Zach said, so worked up he was unable to keep from speaking. "I mean, I know bad things can happen in the mountains.

Pa is always telling me to stay alert, to always be on the lookout for hostiles and grizzlies and such. He says the wilderness is no place for greenhorns. A man has to know the ways of the animals and the Indians and, most of all, the ways of Nature, if he's to live to a ripe old age like Uncle Shakespeare has done." He paused, suddenly all choked up. "But I'm not no man, Blaze"

Zach lowered his head and stifled a sob of despair. How could he ever hope to measure up to his pa's expectations? Twice now he had been so scared he had nearly leaked in his britches, first when the panther had attacked, and then minutes ago when the avalanche had swarmed toward him. He must be yellow. Why else had he been so darned afraid?

Morosely, Zach stared into the lowering flames and lamented his sorry lot in life. To be born a coward to a man like Grizzly Killer! He'd always taken immense pride in his father's accomplishments, and he'd looked forward to the day when he would prove his worth as a man, when he too would prove he was a brave Shoshone warrior. But cowards were not permitted to go on raids. Cowards were assigned to the ranks of the women and forced to do the same work the women did. They were the laughingstocks of the tribe, shunned by any man who had ever counted coup.

"Oh, Lord," Zach said, almost sorry the avalanche had *not* killed him.

Blaze touched his damp nose to the boy's hand.

"Not now," Zach said. He took a deep breath and felt a slight dizziness. Pressing a hand to his brow, he waited for the spell to pass, then laughed. "Look at me! I'm so scared I'm about to pass out."

Mary whinnied softly.

Zach idly gazed at her and saw her head drooping. "Now what's the matter with you, stupid?" he asked. He flexed his fingers, ascertained they were warm enough for him to go back to digging, and stood. But he managed only a single stride before he halted and swayed as a second bout of dizziness made everything spin. "Oh!" he exclaimed, reaching out for support that wasn't there. He tottered, nearly fell. Seconds elapsed and the dizziness went away, leaving him shaken and experiencing a queasy sensation in his stomach.

"What the dickens is the matter with me?" Zach asked. He glanced at Mary, whose sides were heaving, then at the fire, at the flames that had been reduced to the size of his little finger. "What's happening?" he wondered aloud.

Suddenly Zach remembered! His pa had once given him a lesson on the basics of getting a fire going. "Flames are just like you and me," his father had said. "They need air or they'll smother and die."

Comprehension sent a chill down Zach's spine. There was little air left in the cleft, and unless he dug them out quickly they would all perish. Swiftly he sprang to the mound and clawed his way upward. More dizziness gnawed at his mind, but he steeled his will against it. If he collapsed, he was dead.

Fingers and hands a blur, Zach dug and dug and dug, heedless of where he threw the snow. The wolf tried to stand close to the incline, but was driven back by the rain of clumps. Mary, leaning against the wall, watched the boy.

At length Zach had a small tunnel excavated, yet still there was no glimmer of bright light beyond the snow in front of him. Frustrated, he sank his right hand in to the wrist and tried to pull more snow back. But there was even less air in the tunnel, and the next moment he found himself on his face, gasping loudly, his mind totally awhirl.

"No!" Zach cried. He must not give in when so much was at stake! There was more than his own life to think of; there was Blaze, Mary, and most of all his pa. "Get up, you weakling!" he chided himself, and used a word his parents frowned on. "Damn you, you good-for-nothing!"

Somewhere Zach found a slender shred of strength. Rising on his hands and knees, he thrust both hands into the snow, bunched his shoulders, and wrenched. He expected the snow in front to give way. Instead, without warning, the whole roof caved down on top of him, knocking him flat.

In a panic, Zach screamed and clawed at the clammy coffin embracing him. He kicked wildly. His arms pumped. His heart beat like a drum in his ears. In a frenzied fit he got to his knees and tried to back up, to get out of the tunnel before more snow crashed down on him. A brilliant shaft of light struck him in the eyes and he instinctively raised a hand to block the glare as he scrambled rearward.

The significance of the light brought Zach up short. Slowly, he lowered his arm and sat up, amazed to see blue sky above, a white slope below, and bent aspens laden heavy with snow further down. "I did it!" he blurted out. Ecstatic, he took deep breaths and stumbled to his feet. "I did it!"

Then Zach remembered his father. He anxiously surveyed the slope but saw nothing moving. *"Pa!"* he shouted. "Where are you?"

There was no answering cry.

Fearing the worst, Zach moved away from the hole. His left leg bumped something and he bent his head to discover Blaze at his feet. "So you followed me out, did you?" he said, glancing back. The cave-in had created a tunnel over three feet high and two feet wide. Plenty of air would reach Mary.

Zach hiked lower. He spotted a large, dark object protruding from the snow lower down and off to the north. "Please, no," he prayed, and broke into a run, the snow able to bear his weight where it would have crumpled under the heavy tread of an adult.

The wolf trotted alongside him.

They were yet 15 yards away when Zach recognized the body as being that of a horse, and from the pied markings on the hindquarters he knew which horse. "Pegasus!" he called forlornly, and ran faster, so fast he collapsed out of breath next to the dead steed and clasped his arms to his stomach. "Pa liked you," he said softly.

A scan of the slope showed only a sea of snow. After a while Zach rose and swept his gaze over the lower portions of the mountain, but there was only more of the same. Moving in a circle, he looked and looked and grew more despondent with each passing minute. His pa, he figured, must have been buried alive. Then he glanced at the snow at his feet.

It took a few seconds for the tracks to register as such; they were so deep the impressions left by the hoofs at the bottom of the holes were difficult to discern. Startled, Zach turned and saw many more fresh horse prints and marks where the animals had slid now and then. He saw where a group of riders had emerged from the aspens, some going directly to Pegasus, the others to a point about 40 yards away.

"What's over yonder?" Zach mused aloud, and ran to see. There he found a hole, a lot more tracks, and a trail leading to the north. Hope flared as he reconstructed what had happened. "There's seven or eight of them, Blaze. Indians too,'cause their horses aren't shod. They must have dug my pa out and taken him with them, and they wouldn't have gone to all that trouble unless he was still alive." Thrilled to his core, he jumped into the air and laughed merrily. "My pa is alive!"

A moment later Zach had sobered. "But what do I

do now?" he wondered. "Since they're heading north, they can't be Shoshones. There ain't no friendly tribes up that way." He paced back and forth, a hand on his chin. "The first thing I have to do is get me a branch and dig Mary out. Then we're going after Pa, Blaze, and if those Indians have hurt him, I aim to make them pay."

He tramped toward the nearest aspens, the wolf padding as always at his side. Halfway there, struck by a devastating thought, he stopped and stared timidly in the direction the abductors of his father had taken. Here he was, a mere sprout of a boy, about to pit himself against a half-dozen skilled enemy warriors. He must be touched in the head to believe he had a realistic chance of saving his pa.

"I'm only a boy," Zach whispered into the wind. "I can't do the impossible." Dejected, he stared up at the cleft, and remembered he had left his rifle inside by the fire. "See?" he addressed the wolf. "I don't even have brains enough to keep my rifle with me at all times like Pa said."

Mechanically Zach moved on, the weight of the world bearing down on his shoulders. There were certain limits to what he could do, he realized. Rescuing his pa was a job for a grown man. He considered trying to find the Shoshone village and alerting Touch the Clouds and the others so they could chase the hostile band, but he knew that by the time he reached the village—if he did—the band would be long gone, the trail long cold.

"No," Zach said, "if Pa's to be saved, then someone has to go after him now. And I'm the only one who can do it. Me. Zach King."

Then Zach thought of his other name, the Indian name bestowed on him by his folks shortly after his birth. "Me. Stalking Coyote," he said dolefully to the pup. Although he had never admitted as much to his parents, he'd never been especially fond of that name since he'd always rated coyotes as rather low in the animal kingdom. Grizzlies and panthers were far more formidable, wolves far more regal, foxes far more intelligent. The only traits coyotes possessed worth admiring were a certain dogged persistence in the pursuit of prey and crafty dispositions. The tricksters, some called them, for the way they often outsmarted badgers and other predators; if a coyote came on a badger in the act of trying to dig a rodent out of its burrow, the coyote would then find the rodent's escape hole and wait patiently there for the noisy digging of the badger to drive the rodent right out into its mouth.

Zach grinned at the recollection. "Now if only I was that tricky," he declared, and lines furrowed his brow as he recalled how once, after he'd won a game he and some of the Shoshone children had been playing, one of the boys had come up to him and complimented him by saying he was the trickiest boy in the whole tribe. "Maybe I am," he now commented.

But trickiness wasn't everything. Only someone with a vast store of wilderness skills could hope to save his pa. The notion made him stop. Hadn't he learned all about survival from warriors who were masters at doing so? He'd made it a point to learn all he could, prompted by advice his Uncle Shakespeare had given him years ago during a talk about Zach's wish to become a great warrior: "You will be one day, Zachary. You've got a sharp mind, as sharp as your pa's, and you can see what he's made of himself. The secret to getting on in life is to always listen and learn from your betters, then go out and apply what they've taught you. And the more you practice at it, the better you'll get, until one day you'll wake up a growed man, a respected warrior of the tribe, and a credit to your family."

So maybe, Zach reflected, he already had the knowledge he needed; he just had to go out and apply it.

With renewed confidence he hurried lower. Among the aspens—where in spots the snow had drifted deep, and in other spots only inches of snow covered the ground—he found a suitable branch. This he toted to the cleft, and once there he had to sit and rest.

"I'm going to make my pa proud," Zach announced to Blaze. "I'm going after him, and I'll fetch him back if it's the last thing I ever do."

Once Zach was refreshed from his climb, he turned to the tunnel and set to work enlarging it, using the branch as a lever to pry large chunks of snow loose. Gravity would then take over, tumbling the snow down the slope. In this fashion he cleared an opening large enough for a man to walk through in not quite half an hour.

Fatigued from his labors, Zach went inside, fed the last of the grass to Mary, and rekindled the fire. Warmth filled the cleft and brought renewed life to his chilled body. Relishing the comfort, he sat with his arms draped around his bent knees and his chin on his wrists. His eyelids became leaden. Twice he started and sat up, only to slump wearily down again.

The next thing Zach knew, he opened his eyes and realized to his horror that he'd fallen asleep. Upset that he could be so careless when his father's life was at stake, when every precious moment counted, he leaped to his feet and applied himself to the snow blocking the opening.

When, eventually, Zach stopped, his shoulders were throbbing and his arms ached, but he had excavated a gaping cavity of which he could be rightfully proud. There was no time to savor his feat, however. Tossing the branch down, he saddled the mare and led her out into the bright sunlight.

Blaze tagged along, sitting when Zach stopped. The boy thoughtfully regarded the wolf, then remarked, "If I leave you here, you might not live out the week. You're too little to get by on your own. But you're also too little to keep up with Mary, so I reckon there's only one thing I can do."

Turning, Zach opened the pair of parfleches hanging on the mare behind the saddle. He removed extra leggins and a spare buckskin shirt from the one on the near side and crammed them into the one on the far side. A few other items were also transferred into the second pouch; then it was closed.

"How are you going to take to this?" Zach wondered as he gently lifted the wolf and nestled it in the first parfleche. He had left just enough room for the pup's head to stick out, and it showed no display of fear as he climbed up and took the reins in his left hand. The Kentucky rifle was in his right.

"Well, here we go," Zach said, clucking the mare into motion. He repeatedly checked the wolf to see if it would thrash around or try to jump out. Thankfully, Blaze did neither, so Zach concentrated on his riding, avoiding steeper sections of the slope where Mary might fall. Presently he was moving northward as rapidly as the mare dared safely go.

Zach was immensely pleased with what he had done so far. He figured he was five to six hours behind the band of hostiles, which made overtaking them before nightfall unlikely. The next day should be different. Since they had no idea they were being chased and would consequently take their time, he should come on them before the second night fell.

The golden sun arced higher in the tranquil blue vault of sky. Zach was hungry, but refused to stop to eat. He was thirsty, but when he came on a thin ribbon of water meandering from west to east, he let the mare and the wolf drink heartily, and only took a few sips of the freezing cold water himself. "Never drink too much when you're out in the wild," his father had counseled.

"Doing so can give you a bellyache or make you outright sick, and a sick man alone is easy pickings for unfriendly Indians and beasts alike."

Zach remembered other lessons as well. He avoided looking directly at the sun to measure the passage of time, which could harm his eyes, and instead gauged how long he had been in the saddle by the lengths of the shadows. He also squinted constantly in order to reduce the glare and spare him from being struck by snow blindness. When he began to sweat, he didn't open his shirt or remove his hat, which would have brought on an attack of the chills after the cold mountain air turned his sweat to ice. Quite a few greenhorn trappers had been found frozen solid, victims of their ignorance of the deadly combination of cold wind and perspiration. A man grew so cold so fast, there was no time to even build a fire.

Zach also scanned for hawks and eagles to the north. Often, when birds of prey spotted something below them that aroused their curiosity, they would glide in tight circles above it until their interest was satisfied. If he should see one doing that now, it might be studying the Indians who had taken his father. None of those he saw, though, circled.

By late afternoon Zach was on the lookout for a spot to stop. He didn't much like the prospect of having to dig down through the snow to find grass for the mare, yet he recognized that if she died, he would too. Whatever was required to keep her alive, he must do.

Fickle fate smiled on the boy. He crested a low hill, wound down into a narrow valley which had been sheltered from the brunt of the blizzard, and turned from the trail into a quiet corner where he found a spring and a tract of ground that had received just a light dusting. With the sun perched above the jagged peaks to the west, he opted to halt.

Everything was done exactly as his pa had taught him. First he attended to Mary, removing his saddle and watering her. He was tempted to let her roam free so she could eat where she chose, but so many times had he heard his father or one of the other mountain men remark that "it's better to count ribs than tracks," that he tied her securely so she would be right there when he wanted her in the morning.

Zach built his fire Indian-style, and warmed himself a short while before taking his rifle and going after game. The hostiles were so far ahead he need not fear the shot being heard. Blaze at his heels, he trudged toward a snow-shrouded meadow where he hoped to find wildlife. So hungry was he that he'd settle for a bird, if such should be all he found.

Suddenly Zach heard a crackling in the brush off to the right and he swung around, leveling the Kentucky, hoping it was a deer or a rabbit. His mouth watered in anticipation that changed to utter terror when, an instant later, into the open lumbered a monster grizzly.

Chapter Eleven

Zachary King went pale and took a step backward, on the verge of fleeing. His pa had told him about the grizzly that visited their camp in the dead of night, and he suspected this was the same bear since grizzlies were known to range over a wide area in their ceaseless quest for food. The deep snow meant nothing to the great brute covered with thick hair and fat put on for the lean winter months ahead.

As Zach started to turn, he paused, recalling yet another tidbit of information gleaned from his father. "Never run from a bear, son. That's what its prey usually does, so when it sees something running away the bear naturally goes after it. Stand your ground, or back away slowly. And don't take your eyes off it. There are some folks who claim bears are afraid of the face of man, that they won't attack you if you stare them down. I don't put much stock in such tales, but it's plain good sense not to turn your back to something that wants to eat you."

So Zach now faced the mighty bruin, his thumb on the rifle hammer. He preferred to go down fighting rather than being taken from behind like an errant coward.

About 20 yards off, the grizzly had halted and was regarding the boy intently. Raising its huge head, the bear sniffed the breeze, trying to detect his scent.

Zach realized the wind was blowing from him to the grizzly, which should be to his advantage. Often bears fled at the smell of man, and since this one had left him unmolested the night of its visit, it might do so again. Yet to his dismay, the monster grunted and moved toward him, its enormous muscles rippling under its fur.

Quickly Zach sighted. He would have time for one shot, then flee to the closest tree and climb like a squirrel to the safety of the highest branches. Grizzlies were too heavy to climb, but they were exceptionally tall, this one looking to be about eight feet when fully erect, with a reach of another three feet, not counting the long claws. Meaning somehow he had to climb over 11 feet in the two or three seconds it would take the bear to reach the tree.

Zach touched his forefinger to the trigger and tensed his finger to squeeze. Unexpectedly, an eerie howl erupted at his very feet, the wavering, ear-piercing wail of a wolf, so startlingly loud that Zach jumped. He glanced down, hissed, "Shush, Blaze!" then glanced at the grizzly.

On hearing the howl the bear had abruptly stopped. Now it backed off to one side, venting an angry growl.

Blaze howled louder, as if crying for his mother.

With a disgusted toss of its head, the grizzly whirled and ran into the brush, vanishing in seconds.

Just like that the encounter was over.

A reaction set in, causing Zach to tremble as he lowered the hammer. Blaze still howled, and he didn't object.

The foolish wolf had inadvertently saved both of their hides. After an anxious minute spent scouring their vicinity to be certain the grizzly was gone, he knelt, grinned, and embraced Blaze with his right arm, holding the now silent animal so tight he swore he could feel the frantic beating of its little heart.

"You did good, boy," Zach said, and was licked on the cheek in return. "I'm right glad you're with me. I don't know how I'd hold up if you weren't."

Rising, Zach pointed due west. "That's the way the bear went." He turned to the east. "So we'll go this way. No need to invite trouble, as Pa always says."

The near-tragic incident made Zach feel oddly lighthearted. He'd met the scourge of the Rockies and lived to tell of it! His confidence was further fortified, and there was a slight swagger in his stride as he hunted, a swagger that became more pronounced after he stumbled on and shot a rabbit.

Countless times had Zach eaten rabbit, yet this one tasted better than any he'd ever known. He lingered over every morsel, chewing with gusto while reviewing the deeds of the day. Ultimately, he decided his fears had been groundless, that if he applied himself, and most of all if he used his head, he would be able to meet the wilderness on its own terms and come out the winner. Or, as he phrased it to Blaze, "Living off the land ain't so tough if you have half a brain."

His elation carried him through an untroubled sleep, and on through the next morning until he found where the Indians had made their first camp. There, as he walked about familiarizing himself with the tracks as his father had taught him to do, he saw something which made his heart skip a beat and his breath rasp in his throat.

It was a small frozen puddle of blood.

*   *   *

Nate King wanted to kill.

He sat astride the horse to which he had been tied, blood trickling from the left corner of his mouth and seeping from his nose, his chin split open, nasty bruises discoloring most of his face, and glared at the Gros Ventre who was leading his mount. Bobcat, they called him, and Nate wanted nothing so much as the opportunity to clamp his brawny hands on Bobcat's throat and squeeze until the son of a bitch turned purple.

But weakness pervaded his body, reminding Nate that he couldn't throttle a rabbit, let along a healthy warrior. He shifted position to relieve an annoying cramp in his right thigh, and winced as sharp pains lanced through his chest. Several of his ribs must be broken, or at the very least fractured. His stomach ached constantly from having been without food since his capture. And his lips were parched and puffy, only partly because his captors wouldn't let him have a drink; the puffiness had been caused by all the blows to the face he had received.

Four of the five Gros Ventres had used every stop to beat mercilessly on him, taking turns punching and kicking and slapping him until they tired of the sport. Of the four, Bobcat was the worst. The warrior became like a madman, striking Nate repeatedly until Nate collapsed from the ordeal. Then Bobcat would throw snow on Nate's face to revive him and begin the torment all over again. It was Bobcat who, the night before, had kicked and kicked until Nate thought his ribs were about to cave in.

Yet Nate was powerless to prevent the Gros Ventres from having their way. His hands were always kept tied behind his back, and whenever they stopped for any length of time his ankles were also securely bound.

While on the move, Bobcat always held fast to the rope used to guide Nate's horse.

Nate gingerly touched the tip of his tongue to his lower lip, and grimaced at the pang that shot along his jaw. He would be lucky if he was ever able to talk again! The thought made him snort lightly at his unwarranted optimism. Being able to talk was the least of his worries. Of more immediate concern was living out the day.

The Gros Ventres had made no secret of the fact they were going to kill him, and they had also let him know they intended to take their time doing so. Bobcat, in particular, liked to brag of the tortures he would inflict on Nate over the next several days. Apparently, they wanted him dead for some reason before they reached their village, but they were going to keep him alive until a day or two before they got there so they could have more fun with him.

Nate wished he had his weapons. He longed for a fighting chance. That was all he asked. But he might as well wish for a fortune in gold because there was no denying the inevitable. He was going to die, and he knew it.

The certainty had been difficult to accept the first day, when Nate had instinctively balked at the notion of being killed in the prime of his manhood. He had seen enough of the wild to know that all forms of life tenaciously cling to their existence, as evidenced by the fierce struggle a rabbit would put up against a panther, or the efforts of a lowly frog to escape the clutches of a snake that was swallowing it alive. To the very last that frog would thrash and kick in a futile attempt to avoid its doom. And humankind, in this respect, was no different from the animals.

Nate wanted to live. Lord, how he wanted to live! He wanted to see his wife again and help her live through the sorrow of Zach's death. He wanted to be there when their second child was born, and his keenest regret was for poor Winona, who had finally been blessed with new life within her after years of longing for an addition to their family. Now she would have to raise the child alone, or perhaps she would marry one of the Shoshone warriors.

The likelihood didn't disturb Nate as much as he would have expected. Men and women were not meant to go through life alone, and he'd rather she found someone else than spend the remainder of her days mourning him and withering into old age.

Oh, Winona! Nate cried in his mind, and bowed his head in sorrow. He wearily closed his eyes, started to sway, and jerked his eyes open again. If he dozed off he might fall, as had happened once before, and the Gros Ventres would let him hang until they made their next stop, as they had done the last time. For hours he had bounced and flounced upside down over the rough terrain, his body occasionally battered by the hoofs of the horse.

Damn their hides all to hell! Nate thought, and glanced back at the others. Directly behind him was the leader of the band, Rolling Thunder, an arrogant brave who always smirked whenever he caught Nate's eye, like now. Nate gazed past Rolling Thunder at the next man, the quiet one known as Little Dog, the only one of the bunch who did not derive enjoyment from inflicting pain on him. Little Dog had not beaten him once. Why not? he wondered. He'd noticed Rolling Thunder had been treating Little Dog with cool reserve, and guessed the two were at odds over something, but he had no idea what it might be.

Nate waited for Little Dog to look his way so he could smile at him, but the warrior was preoccupied and had his attention idly fixed on the ground. A desperate man will clutch at any straw, and Nate's straw was a feeble hope that Little Dog would take pity on him and perhaps set him free late at night so he could sneak off. He knew the hope was ridiculous, yet he entertained it nonetheless.

Facing front, Nate surveyed the landscape ahead. They were coming down out of the mountains onto a wide plain that stretched to the northern horizon, a new region which Nate had never visited before. There was no snow here. Grazing far out were scattered clusters of buffalo and antelope.

As they rode from the forest into the high grass, Nate spotted a coyote to the west. Intense misery racked him and he almost blacked out. In his mind's eye he saw again his young son standing before the cleft as the monstrous avalanche bore down on the boy. The moment was branded indelibly in his memory, and he relived the horror of it countless times each hour.

Such an innocent idea—to take Zach off on his first elk hunt—had resulted in such heartbreaking tragedy! Had Nate been alone he would have buried his head in his arms and sobbed until his tears ran dry. Zach had been his pride and joy, his precious firstborn, the living legacy he had expected to leave on the Earth after he went on to meet his Maker, the precocious promise that the King name would persist through future generations and live to see whatever glorious destiny awaited the human race. Or so Nate had imagined in his flights of fancy.

Now dark and somber depression cloaked Nate's soul and made him exceedingly bitter. He'd been a reckless fool to take Zach off alone, and the boy had paid the ultimate price for his foolishness. Staring skyward, he thought, "Can you ever forgive me, son?" and moisture made his eyes glisten. Overcome by remorse, he sank his chin to his chest, and paid no attention as the Gros Ventres rode on across the plain.

*   *   *

The incident Winona had feared would occur took place when her guard was down.

For two sleeps Jumping Bull had not bothered her, had not shown up once at her lodge to taunt her, had not offered her unwanted presents. For two days she had enjoyed peace and quiet, and she had about convinced herself that Jumping Bull had seen the error of his ways and decided to stop courting her in order to avoid bloodshed. Or so she hoped.

Then came the third day. Most of the men were gone from the village, off hunting buffalo. Winona had seen them depart early that morning, and among them had been Jumping Bull, Touch the Clouds, and Drags the Rope. Touch the Clouds had smiled and nodded at her, but Jumping Bull, oddly enough, had completely ignored her.

About midday Winona decided to check the snares she maintained in the forest to the northeast of the village. With Nate gone, she had to rely on her own resources in order to obtain fresh meat, and since she refused to impose on her relatives or friends, she resorted to the snares. Her mother had taught her how to make them and how to find rabbit runs and other small game trails when she was still a youngster, and over the years she had perfected her technique to where she now supplied almost as much meat as Nate did.

Taking her knife, an empty parfleche, and a lance that had belonged to her father, Winona strolled through the quiet encampment and into the cool shade of the forest. She should have checked the snares every day, but she had been loath to venture far from the village for fear of what Jumping Bull might do.

Winona didn't fear for herself; she was afraid for Nate and the consequences to her family if she was molested. As things now stood, since Jumping Bull had not laid a

148

hand on her, the dilemma might be resolved without violence. But if Jumping Bull did touch her, Nate's wrath would be uncontrollable; he'd slay Jumping Bull, and in doing so would antagonize a sizable minority of her people. There would be ill will between Jumping Bull's relatives and hers. Some of Jumping Bull's friends might even seek vengeance on Nate. The whole village would be in an uproar for many moons with everyone taking sides, and if at all possible she wanted to avoid such a nightmare.

The day was pleasant, the air cool. Winona ran a hand through her long tresses and hummed as she walked. This was the first moment of true relaxation she had enjoyed in some time and she was in no rush to get back.

The first snare contained a rabbit. Winona hefted the animal a few times, judging how rigid the body had become, which in turn told her exactly how long it had been dead—in this case for at least one sleep. A few hours of boiling and she'd have a stew fit for a chief.

Loosening the cord around the rabbit's neck, Winona stuffed the rabbit into the parfleche and reset the hook snare. To do so she had to bend the sapling she had initially used down nearly to the ground, then lightly wedge the end of the sapling under the hooked branch she had previously pounded deep into the earth. The hook held the sapling in place until an unwary animal came along and stuck its head into the cord snare, which was attached to the sapling. The animal's struggles would then pull the sapling free of the hook and the slender tree would snap upright, sometimes breaking the animal's neck as it did. If not, the animal died from slow strangulation.

Winona patted the parfleche, picked up her lance, and moved on to the second snare. This one employed a cord greased thick with animal fat as bait on the stick that served as the lever for the sapling. A loop was positioned inches from the greased cord so that the only way an animal could get at the grease was by sticking its head through the loop. Once it did, it triggered the stick and up whipped the sapling. Here she found a raccoon, its body still warm, which she stuffed into the parfleche on top of the rabbit.

After resetting the snare, Winona ambled off toward the third and last trap, situated at the base of a hill half a mile from the village. She daydreamed as she walked, thinking of the husband and son she loved so much and envisioning how happy she would be when they came back. She couldn't wait to hear about how Stalking Coyote shot his elk. She was positive he had, since Nate was an expert hunter and would guide the boy right to one.

Presently Winona came within sight of the third snare. She could tell from a distance that it had not been sprung, but she went close to make sure. Standing in a grassy clearing, she bent down and peered through the undergrowth until she distinguished the outline of the cord and the trigger. Both were untouched. Nodding, she began to rise when she heard rushing footsteps to her rear, and the next instant iron arms seized her from behind and she was lifted bodily into the air, then thrown down hard.

Winona hit on her left side. Stunned, she felt the lance being ripped from her grasp, the pistol being yanked from under her belt. Then a laugh that was more like a growl fell on her ears and gooseflesh erupted all over her body. Getting to one knee, she glanced up and snapped, "Jumping Bull!"

The warrior grinned triumphantly, turned, and hurled her weapons into a nearby thicket. "You won't be needing these," he commented.

"I thought you went hunting," Winona said, rising slowly, careful to keep her right hand on the hilt of her knife. She had to stall, to keep him talking until she recovered. Then she would do what she had to, what she had already made up her mind she would do if this ever happened. It would be better if Jumping Bull's friends and family were incensed at *her*, not Nate. After all, they would hardly dare seek vengeance on a woman who had merely defended her honor.

Jumping Bull laughed and put his hands on his hips. A knife and a tomahawk adorned his waist and a quiver full of arrows rested on his back. Over his left shoulder was slung his bow. "I wanted you to think I had left with the others, when in truth I turned back once we reached the plain and circled around to where I could watch your lodge." His eyes roved over her from head to toe. "I've been watching and waiting for a long time, and now my patience has been rewarded."

"I do not see why you are so pleased with yourself," Winona said, backing up a stride so she would have room to swing her arm. "The men of our village will be furious with you once they hear you attacked me."

"You will never tell them."

"Why not?"

"Because I know women," Jumping Bull said. "I know the games you play with men, and how you say one thing when you really mean another."

"You think you know me?" Winona said coldly.

Jumping Bull lowered his arms and chuckled. "Once I have made you mine, you will not dare let anyone know what happened. You will pretend you are ashamed when really you are pleased that a man of your own people has taken you under his wing."

"And how will you make me yours?"

"How else?" Jumping Bull leered, and came toward her.

In a flash Winona's knife was out, the blade pointing at his stomach. "I will give you this one warning. Do not think to lay a hand on me or you will never live to see your son grow to manhood."

Jumping Bull hesitated and stared at the gleaming blade. "You will not stab me," he declared. "In your heart you want me as much as I want you."

"I would sooner mate with a skunk."

"We shall see," Jumping Bull said confidently. Suddenly he lunged, grabbing at her wrist, but she was quicker, the knife licking out and slicing across his left palm. Drawing back, he held his hand up and blurted out, "You have drawn blood!"

"And I intend to draw a lot more unless you give me your word that you will leave me alone and not cause trouble for my husband when he comes back," Winona said, her legs coiled to spring or dodge depending on his next move. She was giving him this one final chance out of a innate reluctance to take the life of one of her own people. Since childhood she had been raised to regard the killing of another Shoshone as the supreme taboo, and she would violate it only as a last resort.

"How dare you!" Jumping Bull roared, and raising his other hand, he advanced to strike her. Again the knife flicked toward him, forcing him to pull away or be slashed open.

"What is wrong?" Winona taunted. "Is the great Jumping Bull afraid of one woman? What about all the coup you have counted? Were they on children?"

The warrior's face flushed bright scarlet. In his rage he sputtered, choking on the words he wanted to scream at her. Then, uttering a bestial snarl, he sprang.

Winona was prepared. She shifted and drove the point of the blade at his stomach. Jumping Bull jerked aside but the knife nicked him, tearing his buckskin shirt and pricking his flesh. Further incensed, he aimed a fist at her head, which missed when Winona skipped away. She circled again, crouching low, the flinty narrowing of her eyes showing that she was going for the kill. All her inhibitions had been stripped away in the heat of the moment. To preserve her family she was going to slay him or die in the attempt.

Jumping Bull, glowering fiercely, started to close with her, but the look on her face drew him up short. His glower vanished, to be replaced by astonishment. "You want to kill me!" he exclaimed.

"Yes!" Winona practically shouted, waving the knife. "So attack me! Come on! Do it! I want you dead so you will never bother me or my loved ones again."

A twisted smirk was Jumping Bull's reaction. "So that is it. You do this to save your man from my lance." He laughed harshly. "A nice attempt, woman, but I am no fool. I will not attack you." So saying, he calmly folded his arms across his chest and jutted his chin into the air. "But if you want to kill me, go ahead. I will not resist."

Winona swung her knife on high and advanced to strike, yet at the very moment she should have plunged the blade into her tormentor, she froze, chilled by the realization of the deed she was about to commit: outright murder.

"What is wrong?" Jumping Bull mocked her, using the same tone she had when mocking him. "Where is your courage? Can it be you will not kill someone who is defenseless?"

In desperation Winona took another half step and elevated the knife higher. For an instant their eyes locked, and to her horror she felt her resolve fading, her limbs weakening. But she must do it! she told herself. She must! She must!

The question was: Could she?

Chapter Twelve

Zach King was out of breath by the time he crawled to the top of the low hill, not from the exertion required but from the tingling excitement that rippled through his entire body, excitement so overwhelmingly intense he feared he might pass out. He paused, took a breath, and licked his lips, then glanced over his shoulder at the base of the hill where Mary and the pup stood. Over the past several days he had taught the little wolf to stay, and most of the time it obeyed reasonably well. Now, more than ever, it must do as he wanted, since any noise made might forewarn their enemies.

Holding the rifle close to his chest, Zach resumed his ascent. At the top a bush afforded enough shelter for him to rise to his knees. Carefully parting the thin branches, he gazed at the meadow below and nearly cried out in his consternation.

There were four Indians in sight, two of whom were busy gathering wood, a large pile of which already had been collected and placed on a spot between two adjacent cottonwoods. The other two were engaged in the act of tying his pa to those same trees, only they were tying him upside down so that his head hung a few feet above the growing stack of branches.

Zach's excitement gave way to unbridled fear. He knew enough of Indian ways to know they were going to burn his pa alive, a grisly form of torture made worse by the great suffering the victim endured since the flames were not permitted to engulf the unfortunate at once, but instead would burn slowly and thereby heighten the anguish.

From Zach's perch he could tell his pa was bad off. Blood caked his father's face and there were many welts and bruises. Worse, his pa hung limply, making no attempt to resist as the pair of warriors lashed him tight to the trees with stout cords. Tears welled up in Zach's eyes and he fought them back. His pa would soon die unless he did something.

But what? Zach wondered. He stood no chance against four grown men who would not think twice about slaying him on sight. Suddenly Zach stiffened, the thought forgotten. During the days spent on the trail he had figured out there were five warriors in the band, no difficult feat since two of the animals, evidently the two mules he saw tethered with the horses near the camp, had left shallower hoofprints, indicating those two had not borne the weight of riders. So his guess had proven right, but *where was the fifth warrior?*

Zach scanned the meadow and the surrounding forest. The last one must be in the woods somewhere, he figured, and he dared not make his move until the man reappeared. He didn't want to be taken by surprise at a crucial moment.

From the style of the shirts, leggins, and moccasins the Indians wore, Zach knew they weren't Blackfeet as he'd initially suspected. From the direction they were taking to go home, they might be Bloods, Piegans, or even Gros Ventres. It mattered little, since all of them had vowed to drive the whites from the mountains.

The pile of wood was growing apace. Soon the fire would be started. The warriors were talking and laughing as they worked. Every so often one of them, a lean, hawkish man, would walk up to their prisoner and strike him in a fit of sheer savagery.

Zach watched and went all cold inside. The time had come. His pa might already be close to death, so he dared not wait until the fifth Indian came back. Easing back from the bush, he angled to the left, working his way down the hill until he was in a thicket. From there he glided toward the camp, placing his feet down slowly and with his toes pointed inward as he had been taught so he made no noise. He stepped over twigs, avoided brush that might snag his clothes.

Soon Zach was close to where the horses and mules were tied. Beyond was the camp fire, and beyond that the pair of saplings from which his pa hung. He was close enough now to see a rivulet of blood flowing from his pa's mouth. For the first time in his young life, Zach experienced an unquenchable impulse to kill.

Flattening, Zach inched toward the animals. They were facing the fire so they wouldn't know he was there until he was right among them. Hopefully, they wouldn't whinny in alarm. He came up behind a mule, rose cautiously into a crouch, and patted the mule lightly on the flank as he stepped to the rope and drew his knife. Next to him a horse shifted and turned its head to eye him quizzically. Perhaps the fact he was a child allayed any fears the animal harbored, because it shortly looked away and ignored him.

Zach moved down the line, cutting each horse loose, keeping his eyes on the Indians in case one should face his way. None of them, though, were paying the least bit of attention to the animals; they were all too busy preparing the fire. At the end of the rope Zach ducked low and went around the last horse into tall grass.

Once under cover, Zach moved swiftly around behind the animals and past them into the sheltering forest. Rising on the shaded side of a towering pine, he cast about for a suitable stone, picked it up, and began to chuck it. Then his nerve faltered. What if something went wrong? he thought, and he actually trembled. The same old nagging objection presented itself, the thought that he was just a boy about to fight skilled warriors and he didn't stand a prayer.

Then Zach stared at his pa, the man he so dearly loved, the man who would do anything for him, who had saved his life more times than he cared to count. Could he do less in return? Gripping the stone firmly, he checked once to be sure the fifth warrior had not shown up yet, picked the nearest mule as the best target, and hurled the stone with all his might while at the selfsame instant he vented a screech like those he had heard panthers make.

Braying wildly, the mule executed a vertical leap, its back bent, its legs as stiff as boards. As it came down it crashed into the other mule, which in turn was knocked against a horse, and a moment later every last animal was in fearful flight across the meadow, the fleet horses in the lead.

Zach was also moving. He remembered what his pa had once said about fighting against superior odds: "Never stay in one place too long, son, or they'll pin you down and kill you at their convenience. Keep on the go and you can keep them off guard." So, bent at the waist, he dashed northward until he was about even with the cottonwoods but still 15 yards from them.

A large log offered Zach a place to hide. On his hands and knees, he lifted his head to see what the Indians were doing. Two of them were in hot pursuit of the animals, but the other two were advancing with weapons at the ready toward the spot where he had just been. By their tread and their attitude they were apparently uncertain as to the cause of the screech.

Zach waited until the two were out of sight before taking the next bold step. Without hesitation, he slid over the log and sprinted toward his unconscious father. He stayed low, watching the pair across the meadow enter the trees after the horses and mules. In moments he was at the pile of limbs. Crouching, he reached up and tenderly touched his father's severely bruised cheek. "Pa? It's me, Zach."

There was no response.

"Pa?" Zach persisted urgently, inadvertently raising his voice. "Can you hear me? You have to wake up?" He shook his father's shoulder. "Please, Pa!"

A few seconds went by. Nate's eyelids fluttered, and he became dimly aware of being upside down and in the most exquisite pain he had ever known. He also glimpsed his son, as if through a dense fog. "Zach?" he mumbled. "Is that you, son?"

"Yep," Zach answered, his throat so constricted he could barely talk. "We have to get you out of here, Pa. Those men will be back in a bit. Do you understand?"

"Do what you have to," Nate mumbled.

"Get set for a fall," Zach cautioned, applying his knife to the cords. "You're too heavy for me to hold up." He cut rapidly, the razor edge parting loop after loop. First he did the wrists. Then, resting the Kentucky rifle on the stacked branches, he quickly shimmied up the left-hand cottonwood until he was high enough to sever the cord binding his father's ankle. The instant he did, his father dropped, banging against the right-hand tree, still held fast by the cord around the other ankle.

In the forest someone began shouting.

Zach's scalp prickled as he scrambled down, stepped to the other tree, and worked his way up to where he could get at the last cords. Feverishly, he sawed through them, and tried to grab hold of his father's leg to keep his pa from falling too hard. In this he only partially succeeded.

The shock of hitting the ground revived Nate again. He found himself on his back, staring up into a tree where his son clung to the slim trunk. "This isn't the time to be playing around," he chided, and tried to stand but couldn't. His legs were like mush, his mind not much better.

Zach let go and dropped. "Let me help, Pa," he said, looping an arm around his father's waist. The strain was tremendous and his knees nearly buckled, but somehow he got his father upright. "Hold steady now," he advised, and released his hold long enough to grab the rifle. "All right. Here we go."

To Nate they seemed to be walking in slow motion, even slower than his brain was working. He had difficulty recalling where he was or what was happening. Gradually, the more he moved, the more his circulation was restored, the more of his capture and subsequent torture he relived in his mind. He spied a log ahead. Abruptly, with startling vividness, he realized the grave risk his son was taking and his heart swelled with pride. "Where are the Gros Ventres?" he asked softly.

"Two of them are after their horses," Zach whispered. "Two more are in the trees yonder. I don't rightly know where the fifth one got to."

"You shouldn't have done this. You could be killed."

"If you don't go home, I don't go home."

"Zach—"

"Don't talk now, Pa. They might hear you."

Nate was too weak to protest. He did his best to walk under his own power, but his long-unused legs refused to cooperate. Gritting his teeth against the pain, he turned and checked the meadow and the line of trees to his left. "No Gros Ventres yet," he mumbled.

Zach prudently skirted the log, knowing his father was incapable of climbing over it. He breathed a hair easier when they were under cover, but he never slackened his pace. The Gros Ventres would return to the cottonwoods at any moment, and when they found their captive gone they would fly into a rage. If they were competent trackers, and most warriors were to some degree, they'd immediately give chase.

Suddenly Zach remembered the telltale spoor he must have left between the pine tree and the log. He'd tried to walk lightly, but everyone, no matter how good they were, made tiny smudges or bent grass or weeds as they went by. It surprised him that the two Gros Ventres who had gone into the forest hadn't found his trail yet.

The train of thought prompted Zach to look back, and it was well he did, for stealthily closing in were the warriors in question, the tall one in the lead grinning as if he was playing some grand game. The pair were less than ten feet away; they could have slain Zach and his father at any time. That they hadn't told Zach they wanted him and his pa alive.

"They're on us!" Zach shouted, slipping his left arm free and spinning. He brought the rifle up as he completed the turn. The tall warrior, still grinning, leaped, his arms outstretched, making no attempt to employ his lance. For a heartbeat Zach felt fear tug at his innards, and then he had the hammer pulled back and his finger was squeezing the trigger even though he didn't have the stock braced against his shoulder as he should.

Tenderfoot

The Kentucky boomed. A cloud of smoke enveloped the warrior's face. Zach was knocked backwards. He stumbled, and fell to one knee. Reversing his grip on the rifle, he held it like a club, ready to rain blows on the tall Gros Ventre. But there was no need. The warrior lay on his stomach, his head cocked to one side, his eyes locked wide in amazement, a gaping hole in the middle of his forehead.

Through the smoke rushed the second warrior, his features contorted in hatred. It was Bobcat, and his fury at having witnessed Rolling Thunder's death was boundless. Whatever their differences, they had been friends, had hunted and fought together for many years. Now he would avenge the loss. He blocked the awkward swing of the heavy rifle, grasped the barrel, and wrenched the gun loose. "Puny mosquito!" he rasped, throwing the gun down. "I will peel your skin off piece by piece!"

Zach didn't understand a word of the Gros Ventre tongue, but the meaning was clear. Drawing his knife, he slashed at the warrior's leg and missed. In trying to dart to one side, he misjudged his enemy's speed, and had his knife arm seized in an unbreakable grasp. He tried to pull loose, but was jerked off his feet and dangled in the air like a helpless minnow. His knife was torn from him and allowed to fall.

"You are brave, child," Bobcat declared. He glanced at Nate, who had collapsed and was doubled over. "If you were not white I would take you into my lodge and raise you as my own." Scowling, he shook Zach violently. "But you *are* white. You are an insect to be ground underfoot."

Zach had his teeth clenched to keep them from crunching together as he was shaken. He struggled uselessly to tear his arm free, then kicked at the warrior's groin. Much to his surprise, his foot connected, the Gros Ventre gurgled and turned scarlet, and he was unceremoniously dumped onto the ground.

"You die, boy!" Bobcat screamed, a hand over his privates. "Sing your death song!" Hissing, he drew his knife and pounced.

Lying flat on his back, Zach was helpless. He brought up his hands to try to ward off the blade and cast his final-ever glance at his father, but his father wasn't there. The next second he heard a thud and a grunt, and he looked up in bewilderment to behold a knife hilt jutting from the side of the warrior's neck. Then, over the Gros Ventre's shoulder, he saw his pa.

So intent had Bobcat been on the young one, he hadn't seen Grizzly Killer pick up the boy's discarded knife and rise. The first intimation he had of danger was the searing pain of the blade's penetration. He reached up, touched the hilt, realized what had occurred, and ignoring the pain, whirled to plunge his own knife into Grizzly Killer. Unexpectedly, his ankles were seized by slender arms. His momentum brought him down, and as he fell Grizzly Killer moved aside.

Bobcat saw the boy holding onto his legs and tried to kick the gnat off. He opened his mouth to vent his fury, but all that came out was blood. In a burst of temper, he seized the hilt of the knife in his neck, ripped it out, and leaned forward to plant both blades in the boy's back. He never completed the act. His head abruptly swam, his arms became leaden. He sagged, keeled over on his side, and felt his body convulsing. Stop it! he wanted to scream. I have whites to kill! Through a crimson haze he saw the boy stand, saw the father appear beside him. Vainly he endeavored to lunge at them, but a black veil enfolded him in its ebony clutches.

"He's dead, son," Nate said softly, leaning on Zach's shoulder for support. "Now get me out of here before the others show up."

Zach nodded mechanically, watching the growing puddle form under the slain Gros Ventre.

"Now," Nate reiterated.

As if awakening from a deep sleep, Zach stirred to life and nodded. He reclaimed his knife, shoved it in its sheath, then gave the other knife to his father, who also took the lance and tomahawk belonging to the tall warrior. Zach scooped up his rifle.

"This way, Pa. We have to go south now."

They hurried as best they were able, managing no better than a rapid walk, the boy lending a hand when the father's exhaustion gained the upper hand. Zach expected to see the remaining warriors come racing through the brush at any moment, and he wanted to stop so he could reload the rifle. Every delay, however, increased the odds of being overtaken. They must press on and hope they reached the mare before the Gros Ventres showed.

In a short while the hill reared before them, and Zach led his father to the left along its base. They bypassed the thicket since Zach wasn't sure his father could make it through, and as they stepped into the open a hair-raising shriek pierced the air.

Loud Talker was the one who uttered it as he took several long strides and swooped down from the slope above them like an oversized bird of prey. His powerful body rammed into Grizzly Killer's chest, clipping the boy in the bargain, and all three of them went down in a whirl of arms and legs and weapons.

The first on his feet, Loud Talker dove at Grizzly Killer. He rated the father as the deadlier foe, the one to be dispatched first. In so doing, he neglected to take into account the compelling power of the love of a child for its parent. His right hand was on Grizzly Killer's throat, his left sweeping the tomahawk high for a lethal stroke, when excruciating, burning pain exploded in his lower back and spiked the length of his spine.

Loud Talker pivoted on his left heel, or tried to, but was thwarted when his legs went numb. Stupefied, he spied the boy a few feet off holding a dripping knife. "You!" he blurted, whipping the tomahawk back to throw it. Again was he frustrated when his arms also went numb. Then his neck. And his face. The boy speared the knife at his chest, but all Loud Talker could do was gape in dumb disbelief. He felt nothing, no pain, no blood on his skin, absolutely nothing until an icy mist gushed from within the core of his being and bore him into an abysmal chasm.

Breathlessly, Zach leaped clear as the warrior toppled. He dashed to his rising father and wordlessly offered his body as a living crutch. Together they hastened toward Mary, visible through the trees.

Suddenly the fourth Gros Ventre was upon them. Walking Bear had been sprinting over the top of the hill when Loud Talker was struck low, and with his lips set in a grim line he bore down on the shuffling white and the slight breed. Slaughter was in his heart, fire in his glare, a lance poised in his right hand. He knew they heard him, saw them swing around, and threw his lance.

Had it not been for the tomahawk Nate held in his left hand, his life would have ended right then and there. The lance struck the flat head of the tomahawk, smashing the weapon against his chest and stunning him. But the head deflected the tip of the lance enough to send it sailing over his shoulder.

Walking Bear never broke stride. In a trice he was on the boy, a corded arm clubbing him to the ground before the knife could be employed. Like a striking snake his hand lashed out, closing on the boy's throat. Gleefully, Walking Bear hoisted the squirming Zach into the air and squeezed.

Tenderfoot

At that juncture a new element was added to the fray, a flash of fur and teeth that clamped onto Walking Bear's right leg, razor teeth buried to the bone.

Agony coursed up Walking Bear's thigh and he looked down, dumfounded to discover a feral wolf pup trying to chew his limb completely through. Instinctively he snapped his leg, yet the wolf proved persistent, clinging to him like glue. Infuriated, he flung the boy to the earth and grabbed for the wolf, never seeing the weaving specter that drove the glittering point of a lance clean through his skull.

Zach shoved to his feet as his father fell. "Pa!" he exclaimed, at Nate's side in two bounds. "Pa?"

The effort had nearly depleted Nate's meager reservoir of strength. He smiled wanly and rose onto his elbows. "I can make it to the mare," he said. "But I'll need a hand."

"Anything."

Nate bunched his shoulders, started to rise. A bundle of sinew and hair materialized under his face and commenced licking him energetically. "Call this brute off," he joked. "I don't care to be eaten alive."

Clasping the pup under one arm, his other about his father, Zach steered them toward Mary. Repeatedly he scanned the hill and glanced over his shoulder. There was still the fifth warrior to deal with, the one who had been missing earlier. The man was bound to have heard the noise. So where was he?

The mare shied as they approached, frightened by the tangy scent of moist blood. She bobbed her head, the reins flying, and pranced a dozen yards from the hill.

"Remind me to shoot her when we get back," Nate muttered, slumping to his knees. "You fetch her, son. I couldn't catch a turtle."

Zach dutifully complied, setting Blaze down so he could grab the reins when Mary let him get close enough.

Anxious minutes were spent chasing her before she finally did, and he was tempted to cuff her until he recalled his father saying that any man who mistreated an animal was an animal himself. Yanking hard to let her know who was boss, he led her back.

If ever a man appeared to have a foot at death's door, it was Nate. His breath was ragged, his chest heaving. Blanching, he fanned his stamina, and managed to stand and grip the saddle. Without his son's assistance he wouldn't have been able to mount, and once astride Mary he had to hold on with both hands for fear of falling.

Zach climbed up in front of his father, adjusted the rifle on his hips, and remarked, "Hold on to me, Pa. I'll get you home. I promise."

Blaze yipped, Mary snorted, and they were off, heading south, making for the mountains. Zach constantly shifted to check to their rear.

"What's wrong?" Nate asked.

"The fifth warrior, Pa. Where did he go?"

"Hunting, I think."

"He must have gone far."

"Far enough. Be thankful he didn't make it back. We never would have gotten out of there."

A solitary figure standing on the south slope of the hill amidst a cluster of trees slowly lowered the bow he had taken from Bobcat's corpse and relaxed his fingers. The arrow he had ready to fly slipped from the string. He stared at Loud Talker, then at Walking Bear, and out at the retreating riders and their frisky friend. "I knew," he said softly.

Turning, the figure wended his lonely way up and over the hill, and paused to somberly regard the pile of branches between the cottonwoods. "I knew," he repeated. "Why wouldn't he listen?"

Slinging the bow over his shoulder, he hiked to the bottom of the hill and made one more pertinent comment: "It is for the best. White Buffalo will make a better chief than *he* ever could have been."

Epilogue

The women were out gathering roots to the northwest of the village when one of them saw the horse and called out. Since they never knew when enemies might conduct a raid, they were tensed to flee until Winona recognized the two people on the weary mare. Throwing her basket aside, she sped to meet them with joy on her face.

"Grizzly Killer! Stalking Coyote!" she cried, tears filling her eyes. So happy was she to see them safe and alive that she gave no thought to them both being on Mary. They alighted and came to her, arms flung wide.

Winona was nearly bowled over. Elated, she hugged them and smothered their cheeks with wet kisses. "I missed you!" she declared. "What took you so long?"

Neither of them uttered a word.

Drawing back, Winona noted their moist eyes. She also got a good look at her husband's face and recoiled, aghast. "What happened to you? Who did this?" Her gaze strayed to Mary. "And where is Pegasus?"

"Dead," Nate said simply.

"Gros Ventres," Zach added.

Intuition told Winona the extent of their ordeal, and she wisely refrained from badgering them with questions. They would, she knew, tell her later, when they were comfortably settled in the lodge. "Come. You must be hungry. I have rabbit stew simmering."

"Can Blaze have some too?" Zach asked, reverting to English since there was no word in Shoshone that corresponded to the name he had bestowed on the pup.

"Who?"

Zachary pointed toward the mare. The wolf lay close to Mary's front hoofs, chin on its paws, its tongue lolling. "Pa said it's all right for me to keep him."

"He did?" Winona said, recalling how Nate had vowed to never have another such pet after the death of their devoted dog. "Then I guess I have no objections so long as it stays outside as the rest of the dogs in the village do."

Nate coughed and said rather sheepishly, "It can sleep inside if it wants."

"Oh."

Keenly aware of her penetrating stare, Nate changed the subject by pointing at a tall tree to the west in which a large platform had been constructed high in the branches. "Did someone die while we were gone?"

"Yes," Winona said, walking to the horse and taking the reins. "I will bring Mary. You two can go on ahead and help yourself to the stew."

"Who was it, Ma?" Zach inquired. "Anyone we were close to?"

"No."

"Who then?"

David Thompson

The answer was a full five seconds in coming, and when it did her voice was level, composed. The faintest of smiles touched the corners of her mouth as she responded, "Jumping Bull."

WILDERNESS
VENGEANCE TRAIL
DEATH HUNT

**The epic struggle for survival in
America's untamed West.**

Vengeance Trail. When Nate and his mentor, Shakespeare McNair, make enemies of two Flathead Indians, their survival skills are tested as never before.
And in the same action-packed volume....
Death Hunt. Upon the birth of their first child, Nathaniel King and his wife are overjoyed. But their delight turns to terror when Nate accompanies the men of Winona's tribe on a deadly buffalo hunt. If King doesn't return, his family is sure to perish.

___4297-5 $4.99 US/$5.99 CAN

Dorchester Publishing Co., Inc.
P.O. Box 6640
Wayne, PA 19087-8640

Please add $1.75 for shipping and handling for the first book and $.50 for each book thereafter. NY, NYC, and PA residents, please add appropriate sales tax. No cash, stamps, or C.O.D.s. All orders shipped within 6 weeks via postal service book rate. Canadian orders require $2.00 extra postage and must be paid in U.S. dollars through a U.S. banking facility.

Name_____
Address_____
City_____ State_____ Zip_____
I have enclosed $_____ in payment for the checked book(s).
Payment <u>must</u> accompany all orders. ❏ Please send a free catalog.

WILDERNESS DOUBLE EDITION

SAVE $$$!

Savage Rendezvous by David Thompson. In 1828, the Rocky Mountains are an immense, unsettled region through which few white men dare travel. Only courageous mountain men like Nathaniel King are willing to risk the unknown dangers for the freedom the wilderness offers. But while attending a rendezvous of trappers and fur traders, King's freedom is threatened when he is accused of murdering several men for their money. With the help of his friend Shakespeare McNair, Nate has to prove his innocence. For he has not cast off the fetters of society to spend the rest of his life behind bars.

And in the same action-packed volume...

Blood Fury by David Thompson. On a hunting trip, young Nathaniel King stumbles onto a disgraced Crow Indian. Attempting to regain his honor, Sitting Bear places himself and his family in great peril, for a war party of hostile Utes threatens to kill them all. When the savages wound Sitting Bear and kidnap his wife and daughter, Nathaniel has to rescue them or watch them perish. But despite his skill in tricking unfriendly Indians, King may have met an enemy he cannot outsmart.

__4208-8 $4.99 US/$5.99 CAN

Dorchester Publishing Co., Inc.
P.O. Box 6640
Wayne, PA 19087-8640

Please add $1.75 for shipping and handling for the first book and $.50 for each book thereafter. NY, NYC, and PA residents, please add appropriate sales tax. No cash, stamps, or C.O.D.s. All orders shipped within 6 weeks via postal service book rate. Canadian orders require $2.00 extra postage and must be paid in U.S. dollars through a U.S. banking facility.

Name_____
Address_____
City_____ State_____ Zip_____
I have enclosed $_____ in payment for the checked book(s).
Payment <u>must</u> accompany all orders. ☐ Please send a free catalog.

CHEYENNE

DOUBLE EDITION
JUDD COLE

One man's heroic search for a world he can call his own.

Arrow Keeper. A Cheyenne raised among pioneers, Matthew Hanchon has never known anything but distrust. The settlers brand him a savage, and when Matthew realizes that his adopted parents will suffer for his sake, he flees into the wilderness—where he'll need a warrior's courage if he hopes to survive.

And in the same volume...

Death Chant. When Matthew returns to the Cheyenne, he doesn't find the acceptance he seeks. The Cheyenne can't fully trust any who were raised in the ways of the white man. Forced to prove his loyalty, Matthew faces the greatest challenge he has ever known.

___4280-0 $4.99 US/$5.99 CAN

Dorchester Publishing Co., Inc.
P.O. Box 6640
Wayne, PA 19087-8640

Please add $1.75 for shipping and handling for the first book and $.50 for each book thereafter. NY, NYC, and PA residents, please add appropriate sales tax. No cash, stamps, or C.O.D.s. All orders shipped within 6 weeks via postal service book rate. Canadian orders require $2.00 extra postage and must be paid in U.S. dollars through a U.S. banking facility.

Name_____

Address_____

City_____State_____Zip_____

I have enclosed $_____ in payment for the checked book(s).

Payment <u>must</u> accompany all orders. ☐ Please send a free catalog.

DOUBLE EDITION
They left him for dead, he'll see them in hell!
Jake McMasters

Hangman's Knot. Taggart is strung up and left out to die by a posse headed by the richest man in the territory. Choking and kicking, he is seconds away from death when he is cut down by a ragtag band of Apaches, not much better off than himself. Before long, the white desperado and the desperate Apaches have formed an unholy alliance that will turn the Arizona desert red with blood.

And in the same action-packed volume....

Warpath. Twelve S.O.B.s left him swinging from a rope, as good as dead. But it isn't Taggart's time to die. Together with his desperate renegade warriors he will hunt the yellowbellies down. One by one, he'll make them wish they'd never drawn a breath. One by one he'll leave their guts and bones scorching under the brutal desert sun.

_4185-5 $4.99 US/$5.99 CAN

Dorchester Publishing Co., Inc.
P.O. Box 6640
Wayne, PA 19087-8640

Please add $1.75 for shipping and handling for the first book and $.50 for each book thereafter. NY, NYC, and PA residents, please add appropriate sales tax. No cash, stamps, or C.O.D.s. All orders shipped within 6 weeks via postal service book rate. Canadian orders require $2.00 extra postage and must be paid in U.S. dollars through a U.S. banking facility.

Name_____
Address_____
City_____State_____Zip_____
I have enclosed $_____ in payment for the checked book(s).
Payment <u>must</u> accompany all orders. ☐ Please send a free catalog.

Jake McMasters

**Follow the action-packed adventures of
Clay Taggart, as he fights for revenge against
settlers, soldiers, and savages.**

#7: *Blood Bounty*. The settlers believe Clay Taggart is a
ruthless desperado with neither conscience nor soul. But
Taggart is just an innocent man who has a price on his head.
With a motley band of Apaches, he roams the vast Southwest,
waiting for the day he can clear his name—or his luck runs
out and his scalp is traded for gold.

__3790-4 $3.99 US/$4.99 CAN

#8: *The Trackers*. In the blazing Arizona desert, a wanted
man can end up as food for the buzzards. But since Clay
Taggart doesn't live like a coward, he and his band of
renegade Indians spend many a day feeding ruthless
bushwhackers to the wolves. Then a bloodthirsty trio comes
after the White Apache and his gang. But try as they might
to run Taggart to the ground, he will never let anyone kill
him like a dog.

__3830-7 $3.99 US/$4.99 CAN

Dorchester Publishing Co., Inc.
P.O. Box 6640
Wayne, PA 19087-8640

Please add $1.75 for shipping and handling for the first book and
$.50 for each book thereafter. NY, NYC, and PA residents,
please add appropriate sales tax. No cash, stamps, or C.O.D.s. All
orders shipped within 6 weeks via postal service book rate.
Canadian orders require $2.00 extra postage and must be paid in
U.S. dollars through a U.S. banking facility.

Name_____
Address_____
City_____ State_____ Zip_____
I have enclosed $_____ in payment for the checked book(s).
Payment <u>must</u> accompany all orders. ☐ Please send a free catalog.

 **Jake McMasters**

Follow the action-packed adventures of Clay Taggart, as he fights for revenge against soldiers, settlers, and savages.

#9: Desert Fury. From the canyons of the Arizona Territory to the deserts of Mexico, Clay Taggart and a motley crew of Apaches blaze a trail of death and vengeance. But for every bounty hunter they shoot down, another is riding hell for leather to collect the prize on their heads. And when the territorial governor offers Taggart a chance to clear his name, the deadliest tracker in the West sets his sights on the White Apache—and prepares to blast him to hell.

__3871-4 $3.99 US/$4.99 CAN

#10: Hanged! Although Clay Taggart has been strung up and left to rot under the burning desert sun, he isn't about to play dead. After a desperate band of Indians rescues Taggart, he heads into the Arizona wilderness and plots his revenge. One by one, Taggart hunts down his enemies, and with the help of renegade Apaches, he acts as judge, jury, and executioner. But when Taggart sets his sights on a corrupt marshal, he finds that the long arm of the law might just have more muscle than he expects.

__3899-4 $3.99 US/$4.99 CAN

Dorchester Publishing Co., Inc.
P.O. Box 6640
Wayne, PA 19087-8640

Please add $1.75 for shipping and handling for the first book and $.50 for each book thereafter. NY, NYC, and PA residents, please add appropriate sales tax. No cash, stamps, or C.O.D.s. All orders shipped within 6 weeks via postal service book rate. Canadian orders require $2.00 extra postage and must be paid in U.S. dollars through a U.S. banking facility.

Name_____
Address_____
City_____ State_____ Zip_____
I have enclosed $_____ in payment for the checked book(s).
Payment <u>must</u> accompany all orders. ☐ Please send a free catalog.